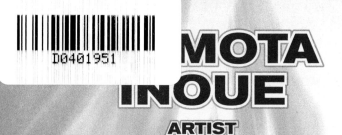

MOTA INOUE

ARTIST

MOMOTA ♀Lv.1
HP
Ink
A weak Momota has appeared!

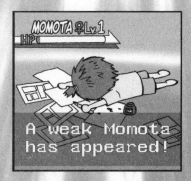

Victini is a Pokémon who shares its power with those in need. Isn't that wonderful? Please, Victini, share your power with me. My deadline is looming!!

Born on June 19, 1985, in Saitama Prefecture, Momota Inoue received the 58th Shogakukan Rookie Comic Grand Prize for the Children's Division in 2006 for *Red Enza*.

POKÉMON THE MOVIE: WHITE—VICTINI AND ZEKROM
VIZ Kids Edition

Story and Art by MOMOTA INOUE

© 2012 Pokémon.
© 1997-2011 PIKACHU PROJECT. TM, ®, and character names are trademarks of Nintendo.
© 2011 Momota INOUE/Shogakukan
All rights reserved.
Original Japanese edition "VICTINI TO KUROKI EIYU ZEKROM" published by SHOGAKUKAN Inc.

Translation/Adrienne Beck
Touch-up & Lettering/Vanessa Satone
Design/Kam Li
Editor/Hope Donovan

Printed in the U.S.A.

Published by VIZ Media, LLC
P.O. Box 77010
San Francisco, CA 94107

10 9 8 7 6 5 4 3 2 1
First printing, March 2012

Pokémon

POKÉMON THE MOVIE WHITE
VICTINI AND ZEKROM

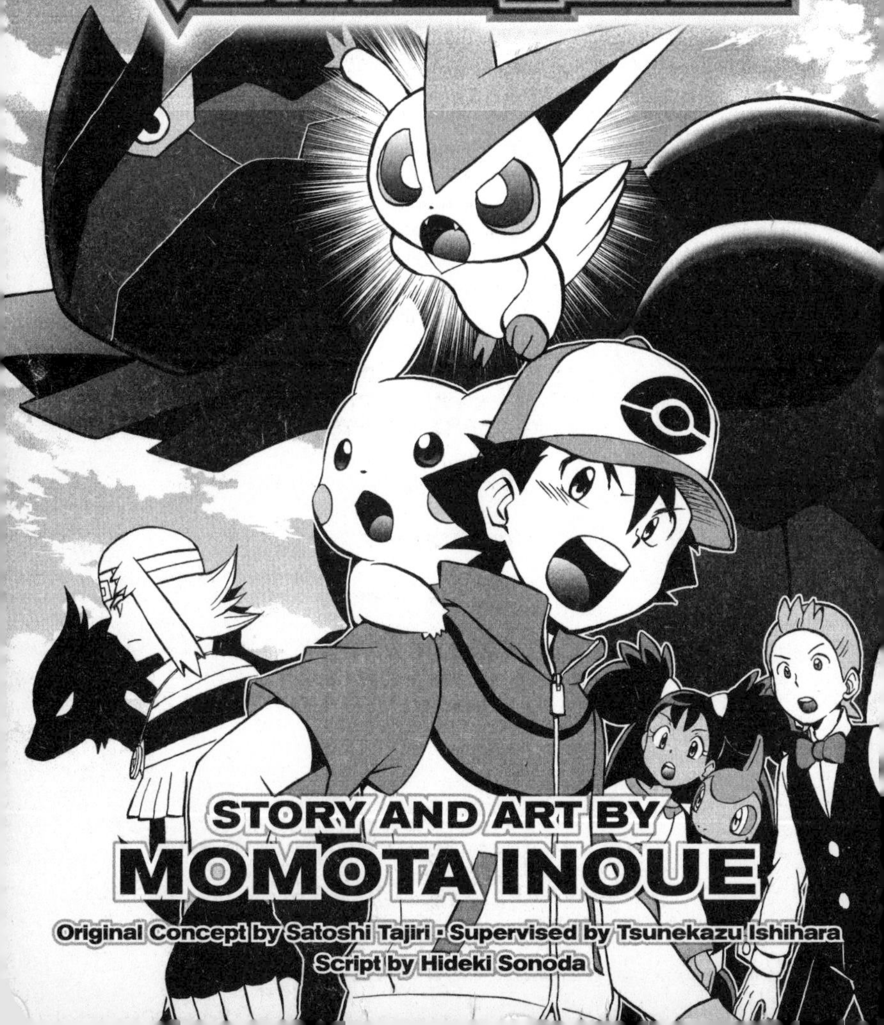

STORY AND ART BY

MOMOTA INOUE

Original Concept by Satoshi Tajiri · Supervised by Tsunekazu Ishihara

Script by Hideki Sonoda

Main Characters & Pokémon

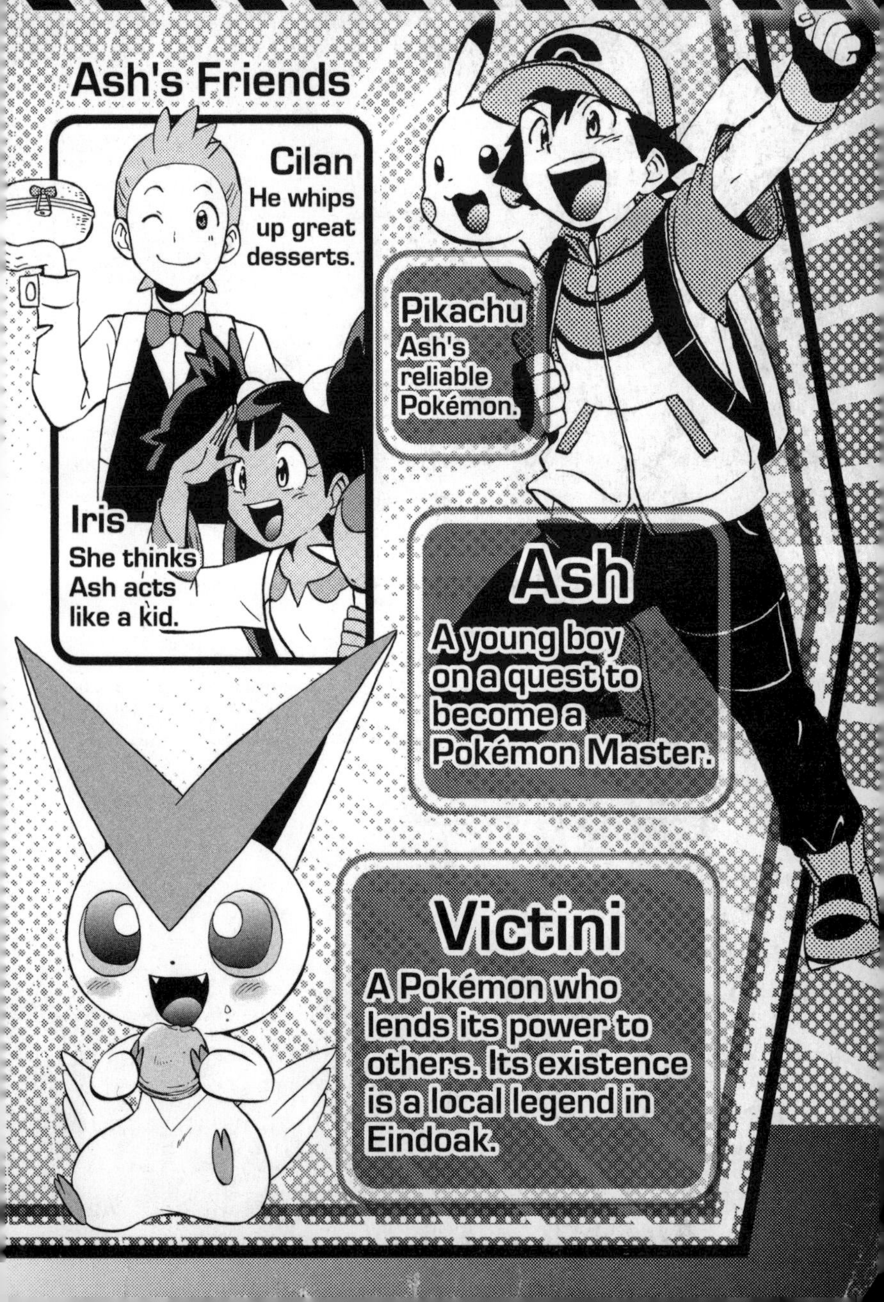
Ash's Friends
Cilan
He whips up great desserts.
Iris
She thinks Ash acts like a kid.
Pikachu
Ash's reliable Pokémon.
Ash
A young boy on a quest to become a Pokémon Master.
Victini
A Pokémon who lends its power to others. Its existence is a local legend in Eindoak.

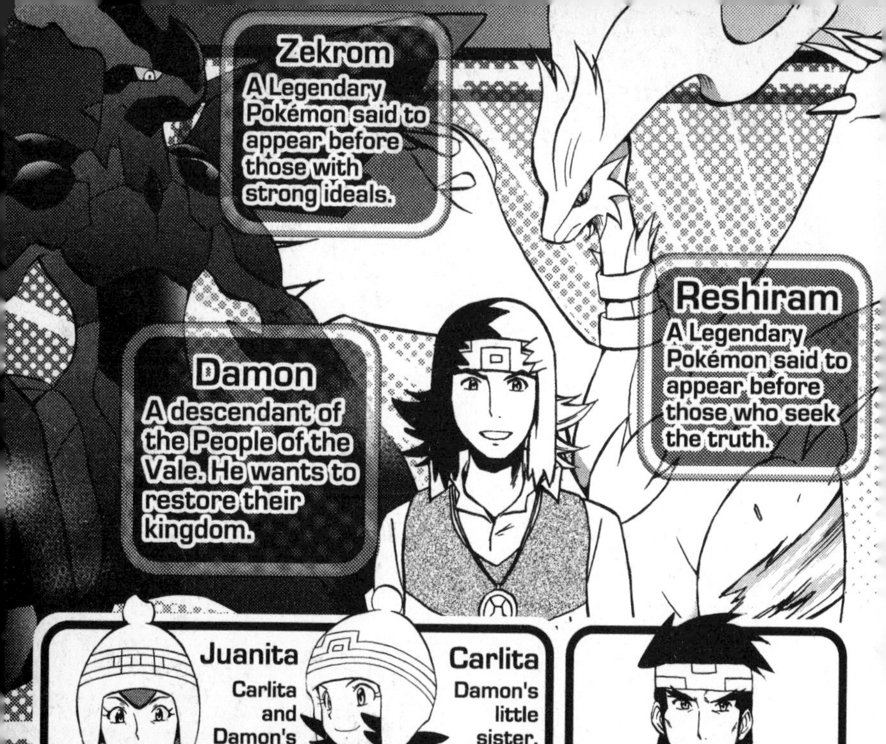
Zekrom
A Legendary Pokémon said to appear before those with strong ideals.
Reshiram
A Legendary Pokémon said to appear before those who seek the truth.
Damon
A descendant of the People of the Vale. He wants to restore their kingdom.
Ravine
A wandering descendant of the People of the Vale.
Carlita
Damon's little sister. She lives in Eindoak.
Juanita
Carlita and Damon's mother. She knows a lot about Victini.
Team Rocket
Jesse
James
Meowth
Mannes
Mayor of Eindoak.

Table of Contents

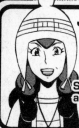

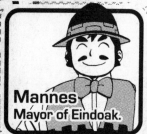

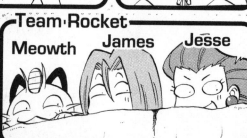

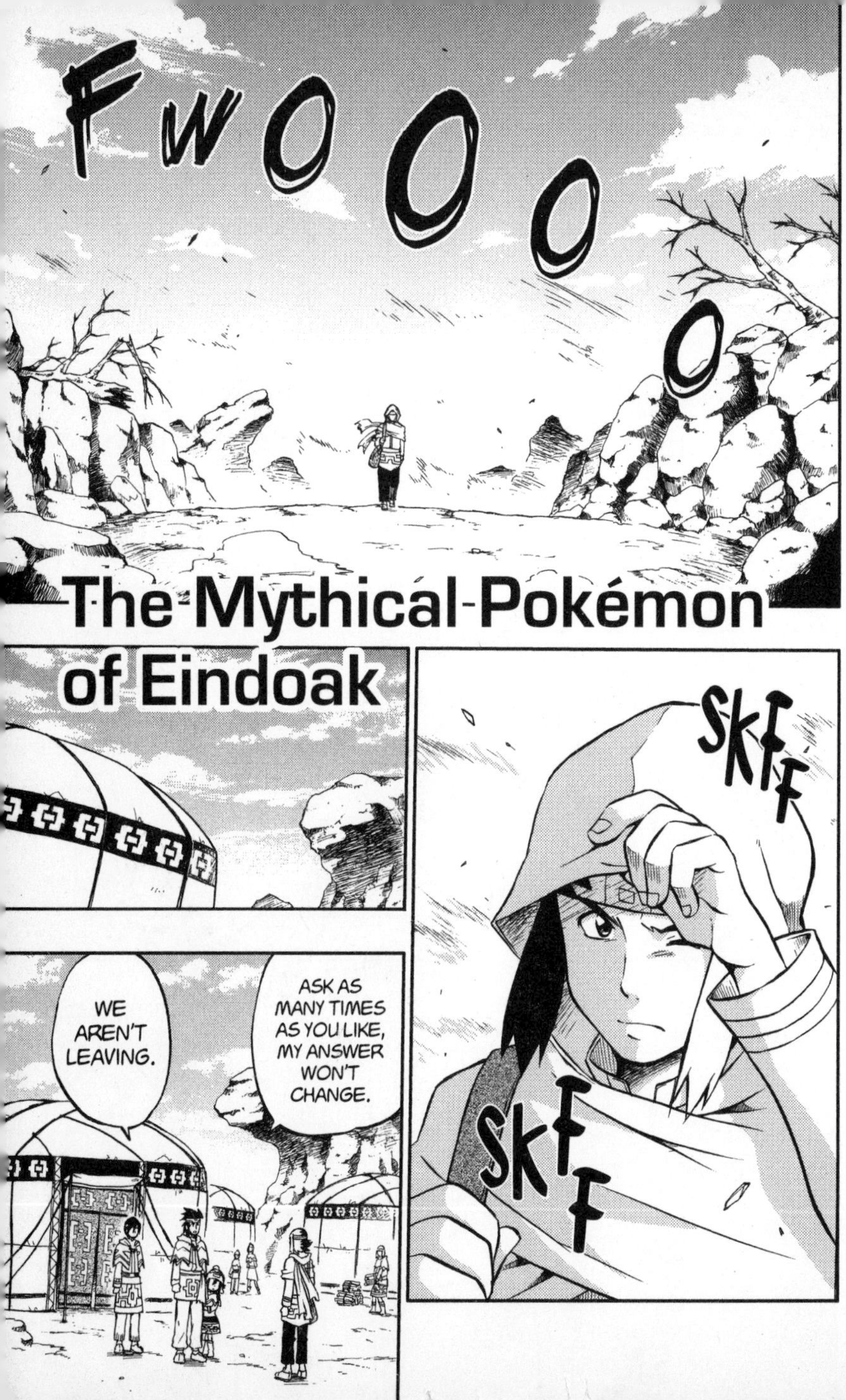
FWOOOOO
The Mythical Pokémon of Eindoak
SKFF
SKFF
ASK AS MANY TIMES AS YOU LIKE, MY ANSWER WON'T CHANGE.
WE AREN'T LEAVING.

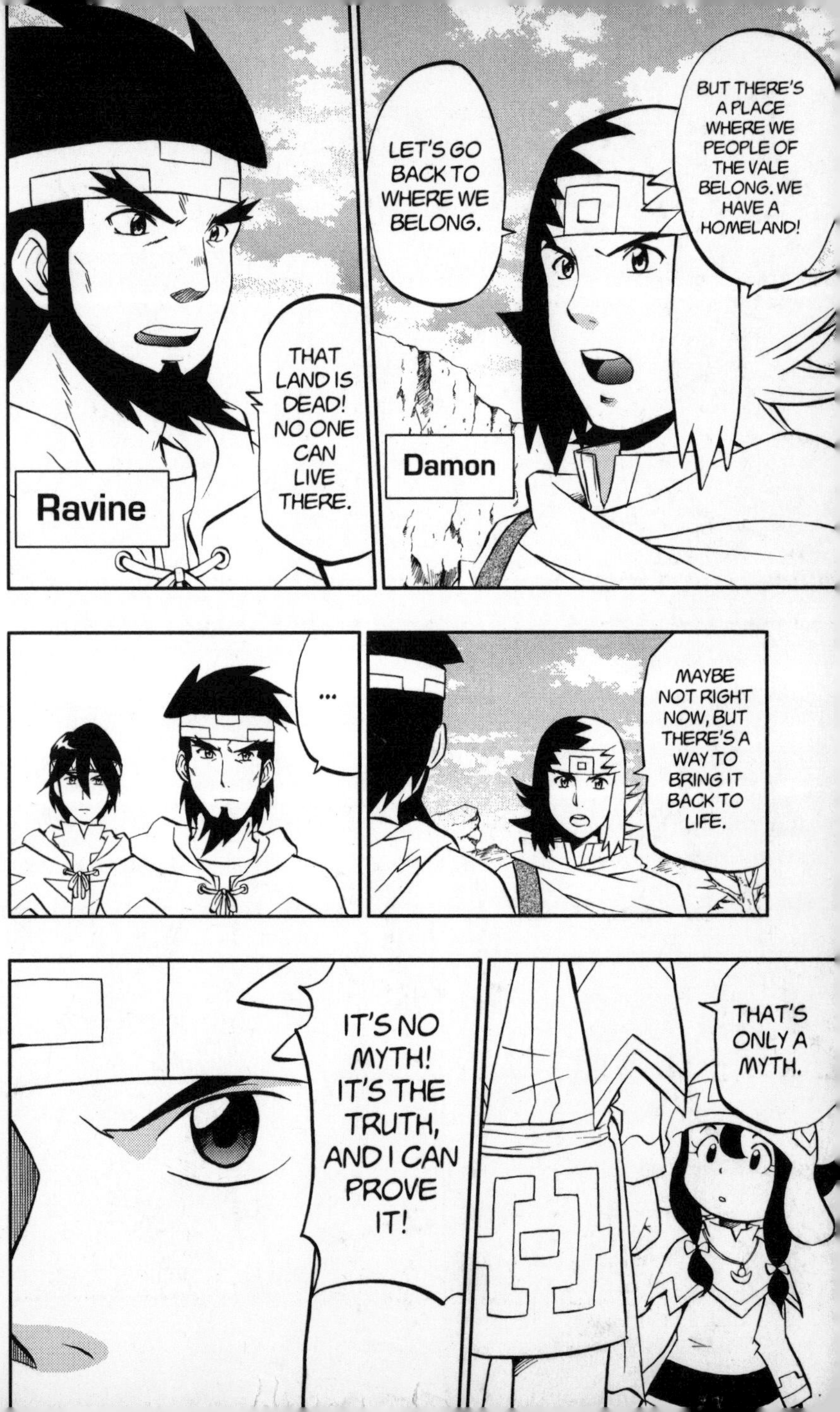
BUT THERE'S A PLACE WHERE WE PEOPLE OF THE VALE BELONG. WE HAVE A HOMELAND!
LET'S GO BACK TO WHERE WE BELONG.
Damon
THAT LAND IS DEAD! NO ONE CAN LIVE THERE.
Ravine
MAYBE NOT RIGHT NOW, BUT THERE'S A WAY TO BRING IT BACK TO LIFE.
...
THAT'S ONLY A MYTH.
IT'S NO MYTH! IT'S THE TRUTH, AND I CAN PROVE IT!

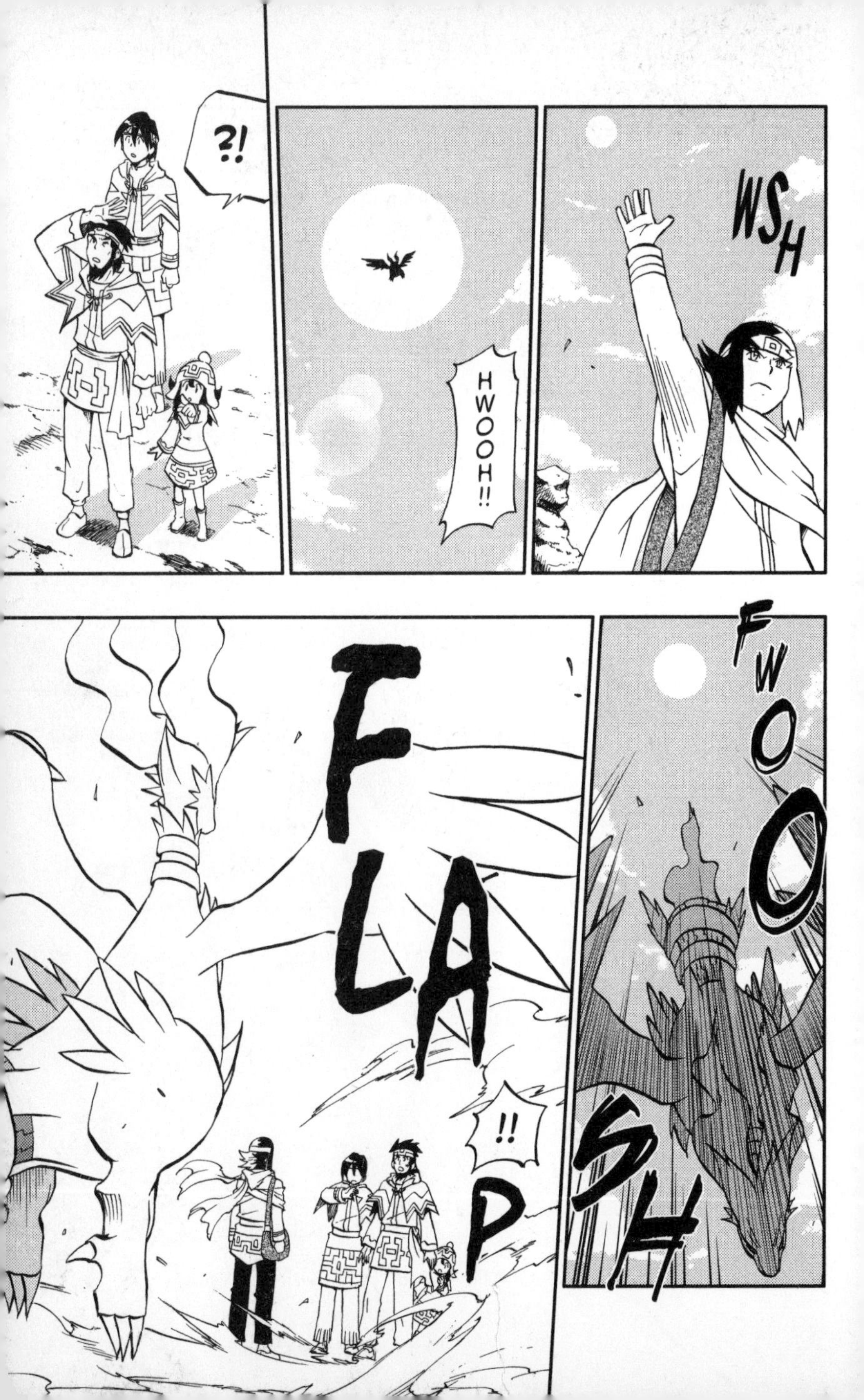
WSH
HWOOOH!!
?!
FWOOOSH
FLAP
!!

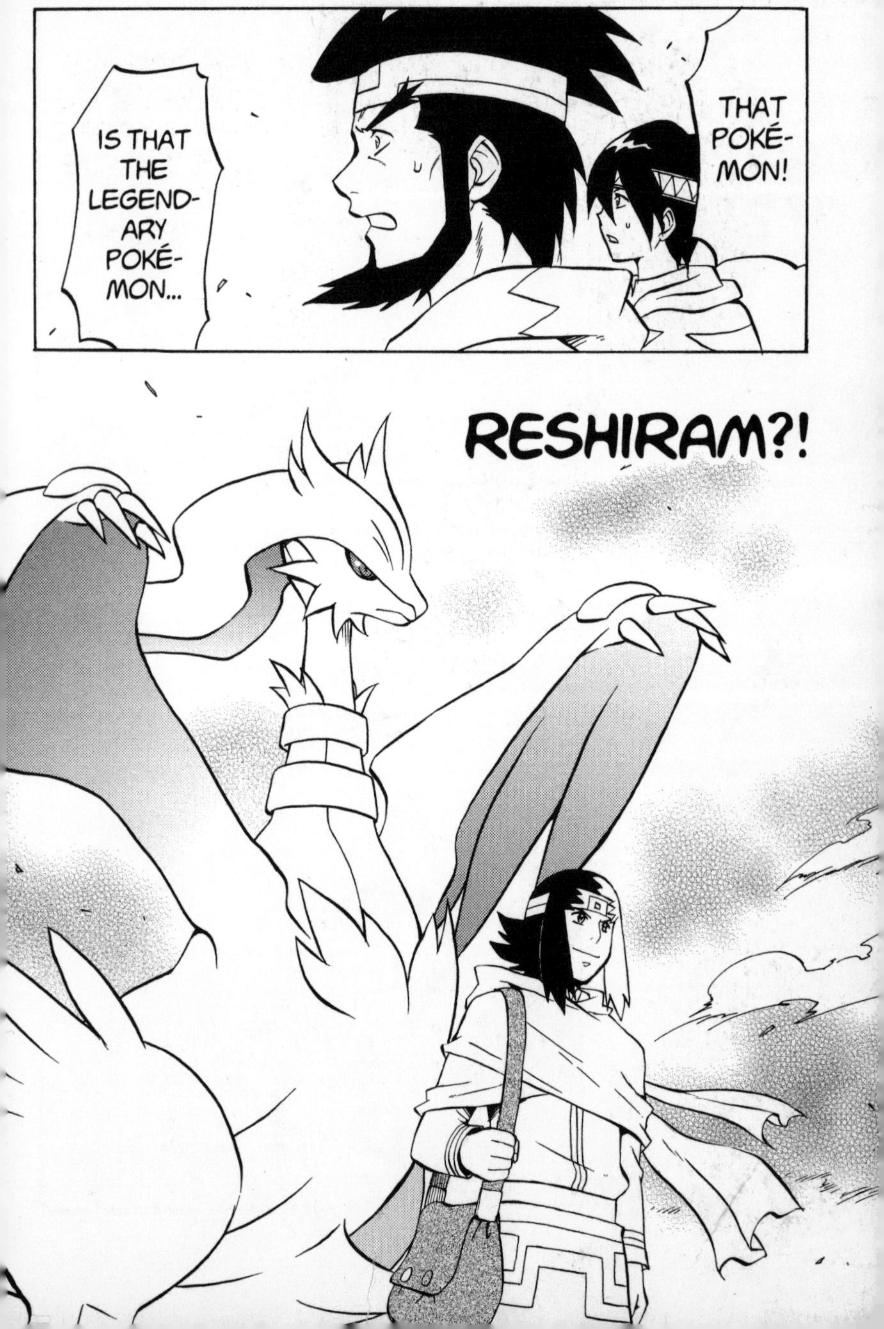
THAT POKÉ-MON!
IS THAT THE LEGENDARY POKÉMON...
RESHIRAM?!

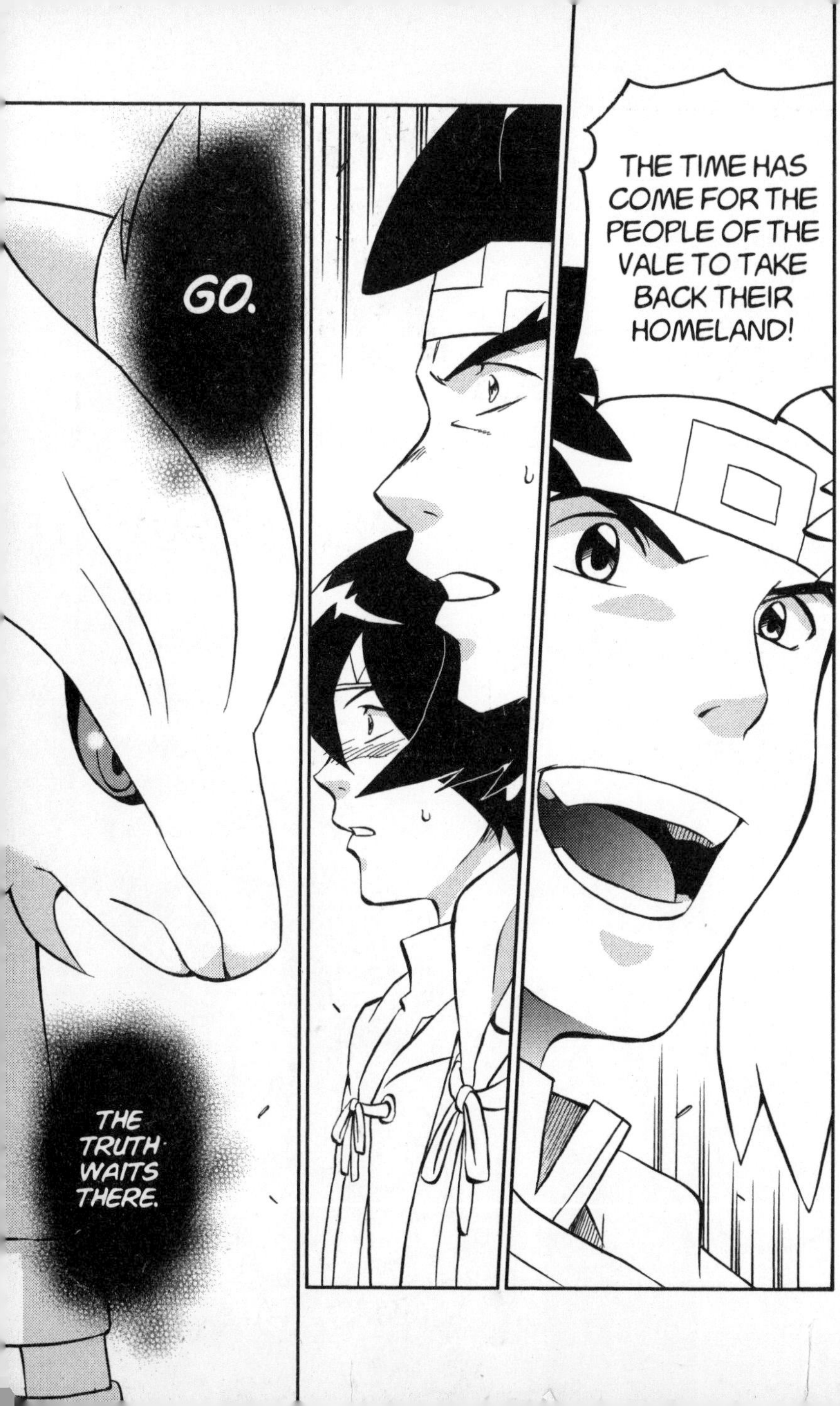
THE TIME HAS COME FOR THE PEOPLE OF THE VALE TO TAKE BACK THEIR HOMELAND!
GO.
THE TRUTH WAITS THERE.

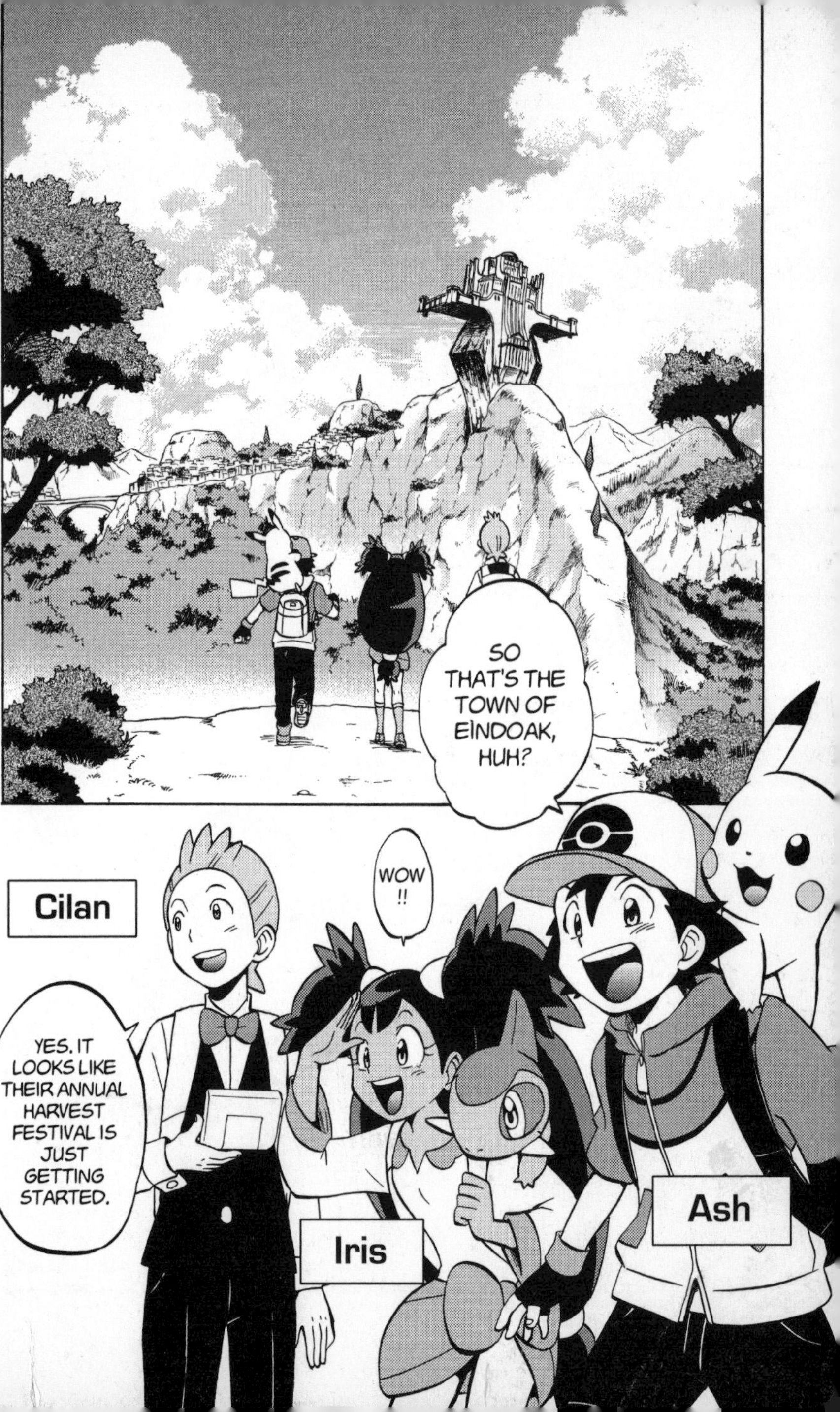
SO THAT'S THE TOWN OF EINDOAK, HUH?
WOW !!
Ash
Iris
Cilan
YES. IT LOOKS LIKE THEIR ANNUAL HARVEST FESTIVAL IS JUST GETTING STARTED.

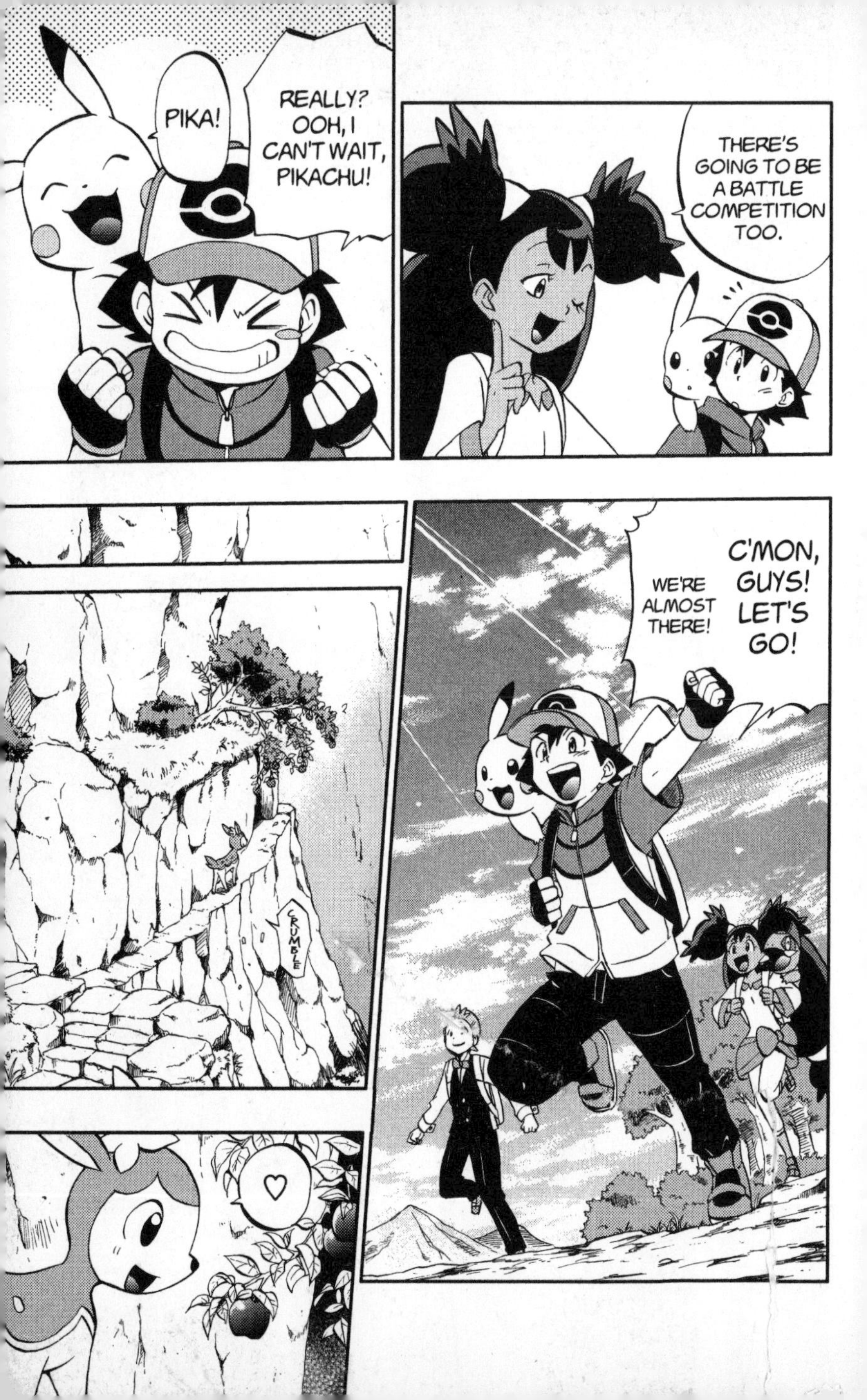
THERE'S GOING TO BE A BATTLE COMPETITION TOO.
REALLY? OOH, I CAN'T WAIT, PIKACHU!
PIKA!
C'MON, GUYS! LET'S GO!
WE'RE ALMOST THERE!
CRUMBLE
♡

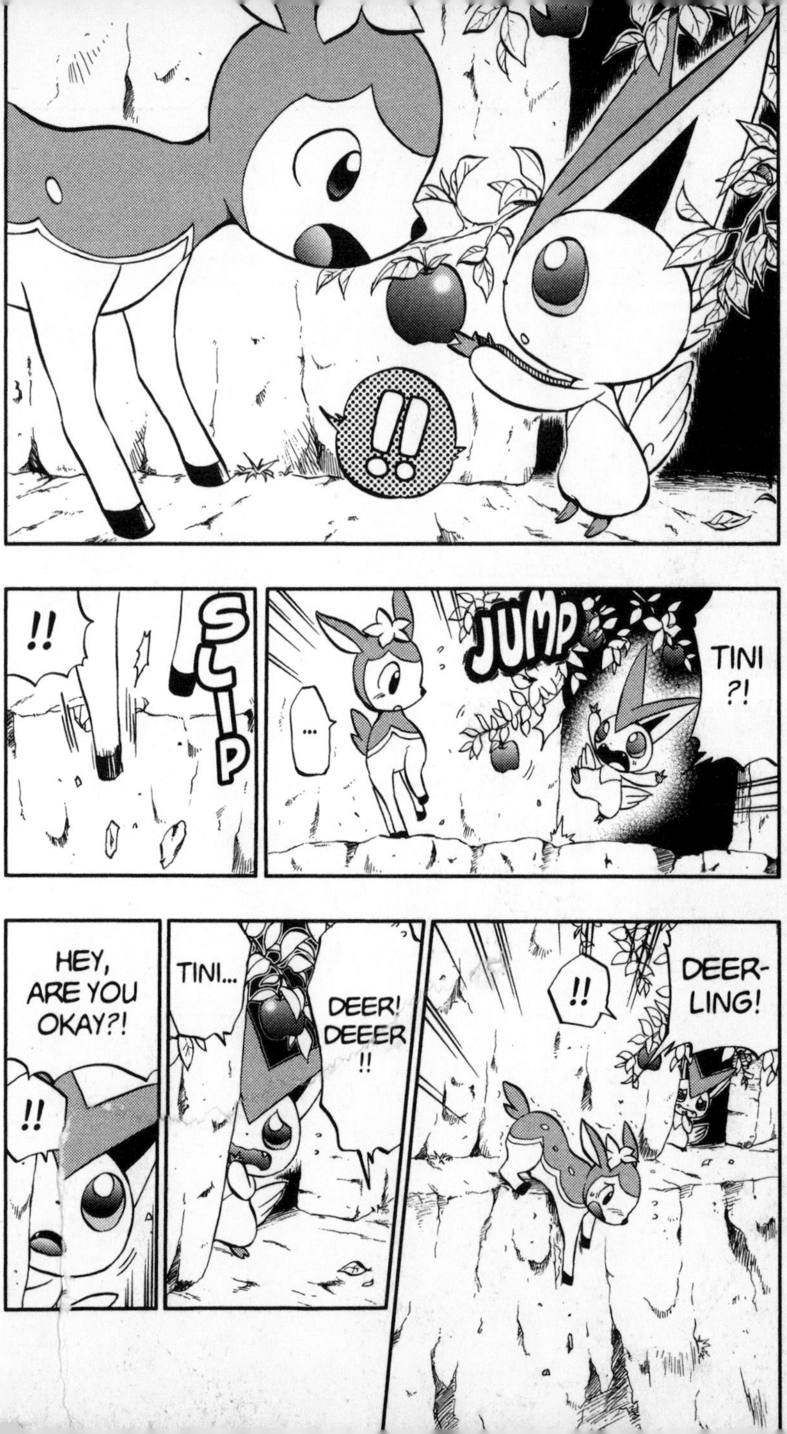
!!
TINI ?!
JUMP
...
SLIP
!!
DEER-LING!
!!
DEER! DEEER !!
TINI...
HEY, ARE YOU OKAY?!
!!

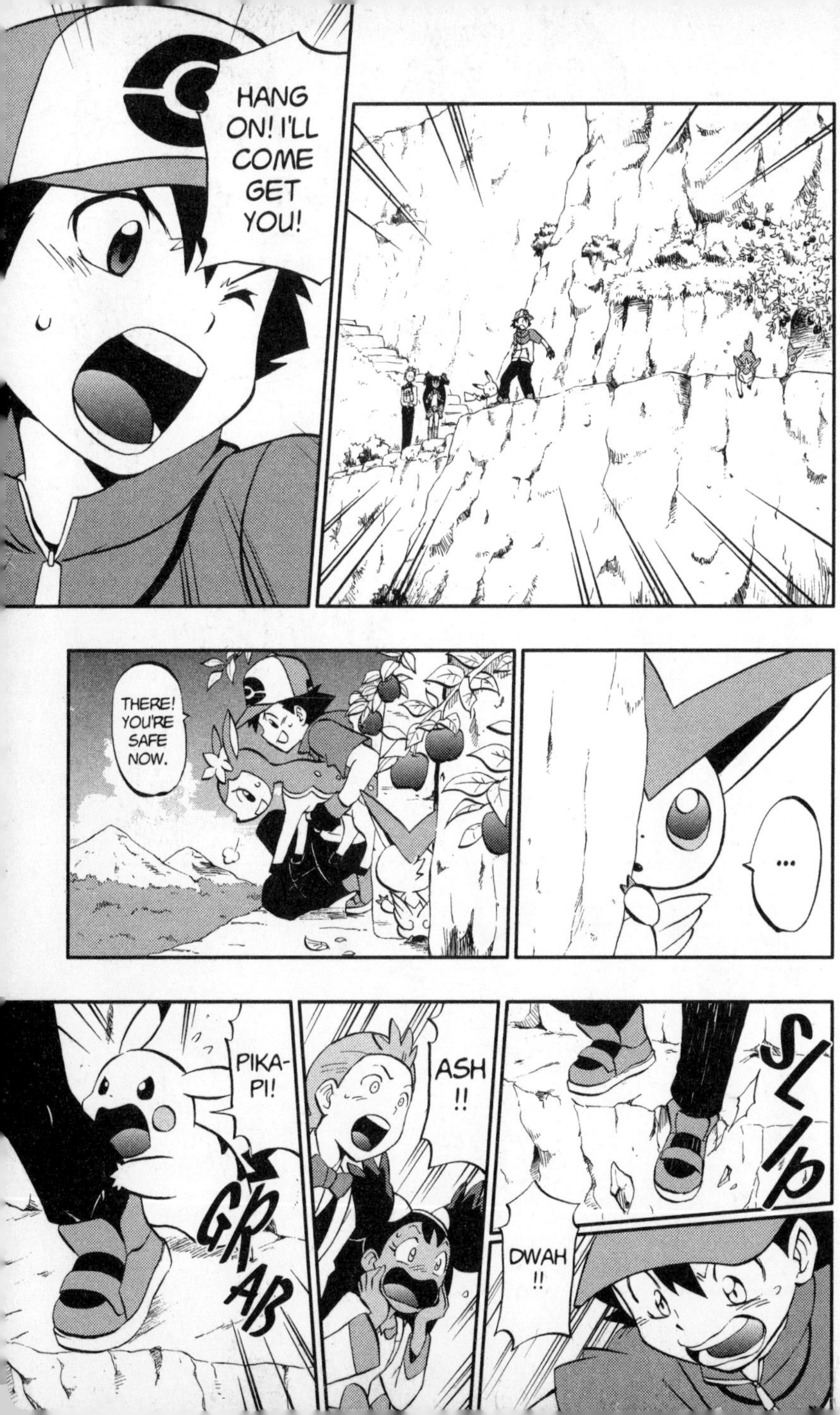
HANG ON! I'LL COME GET YOU!
...
THERE! YOU'RE SAFE NOW.
SLIP
DWAH !!
ASH !!
PIKA-PI!
GRAB

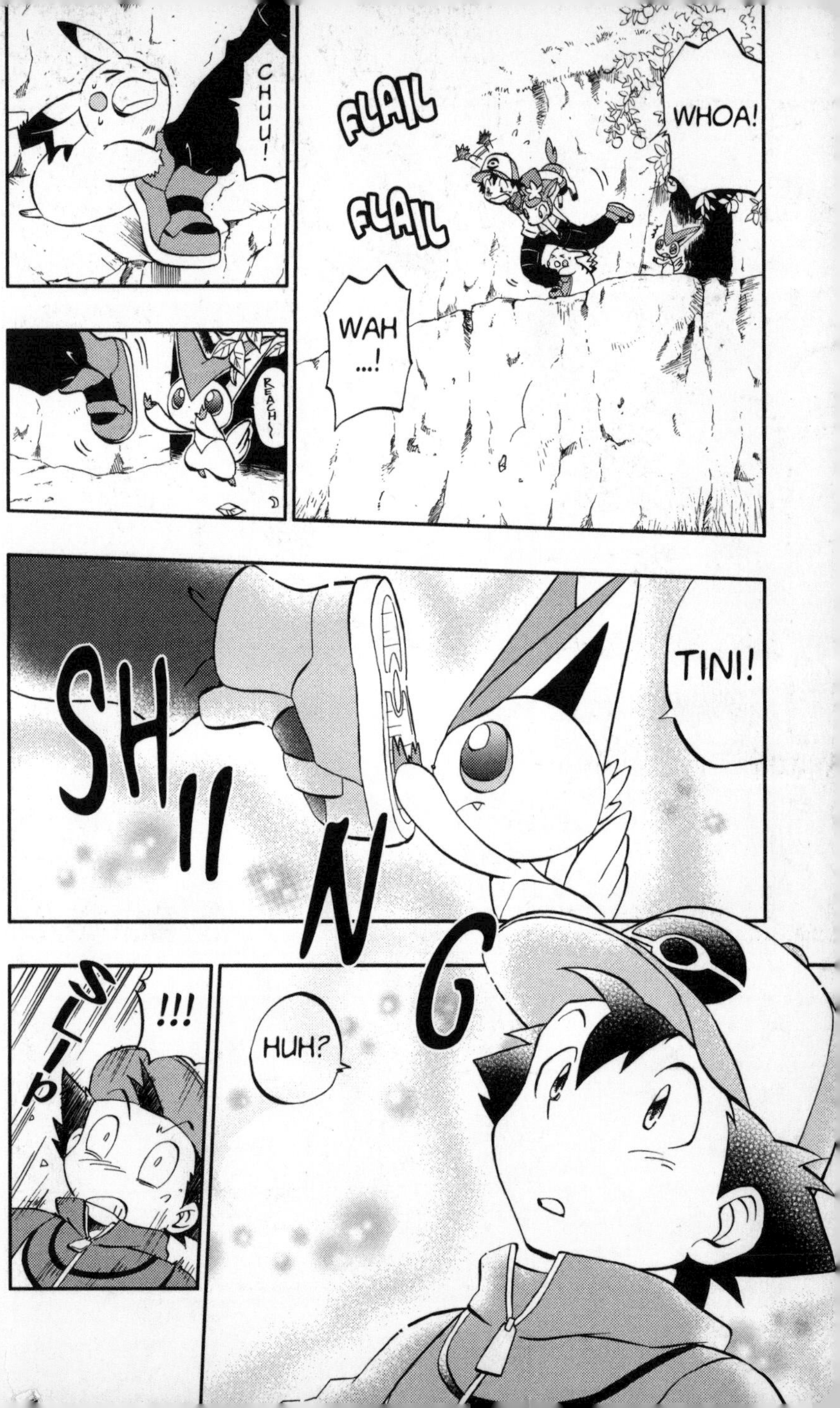
WHOA!
FLAIL
FLAIL
WAH ...!
CHUU!
REACH~
TINI!
SHIING
HUH?
!!!
SLIP

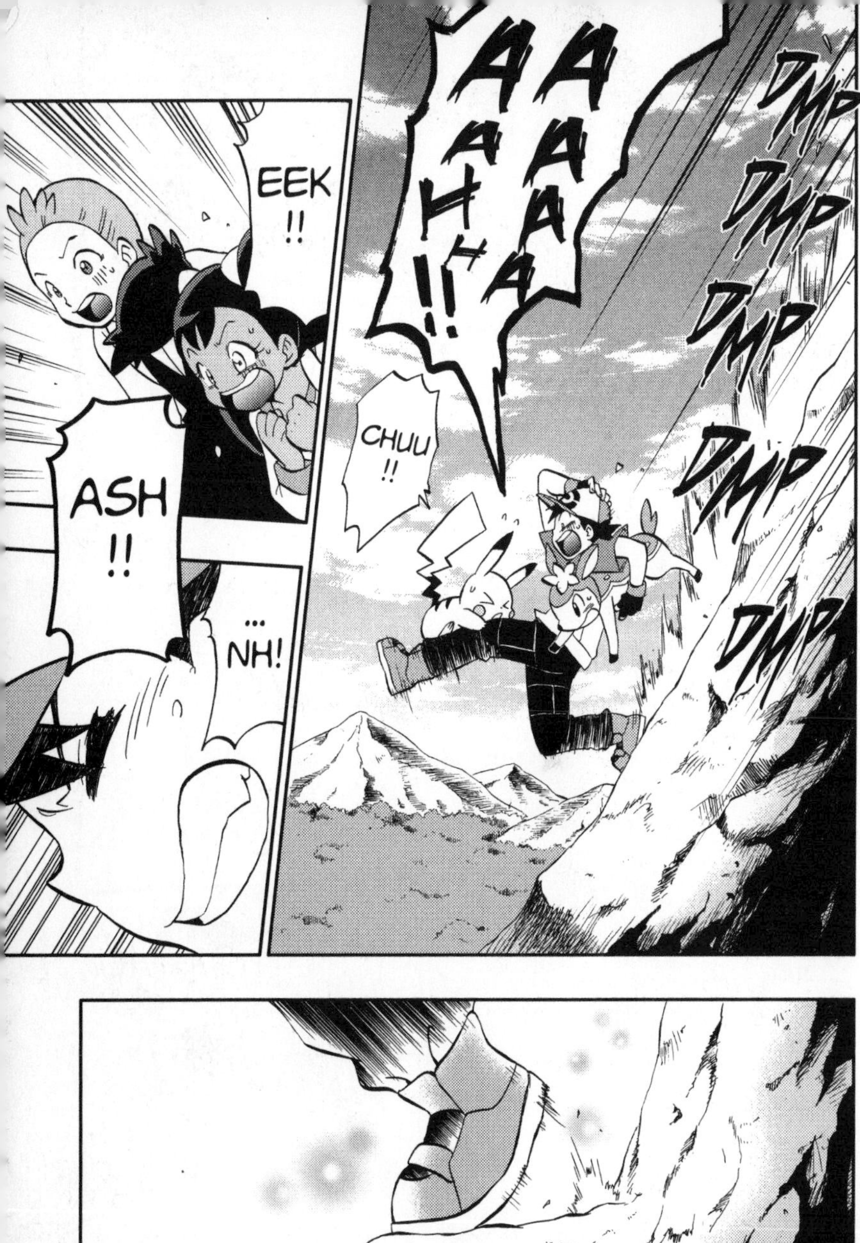
AAAAAAHAHA!!
DMP DMP DMP DMP DMP
CHUU!!
EEK!!
ASH!!
...NH!

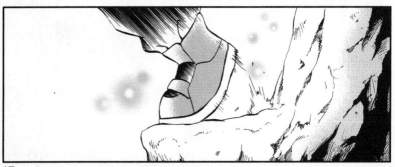

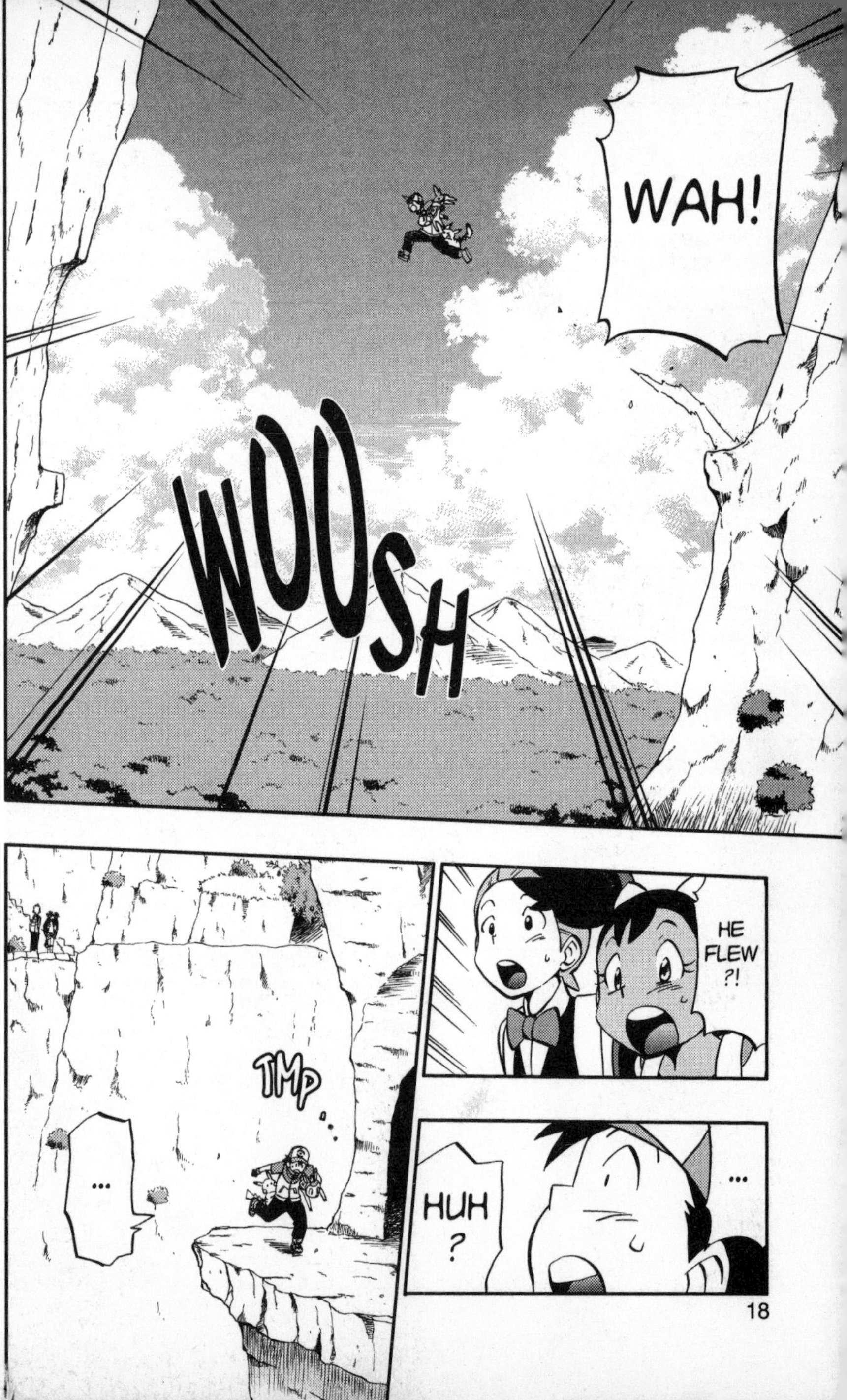
WAH!
WOOSH
HE FLEW ?!
...
HUH ?
TMP
...

READ THIS WAY

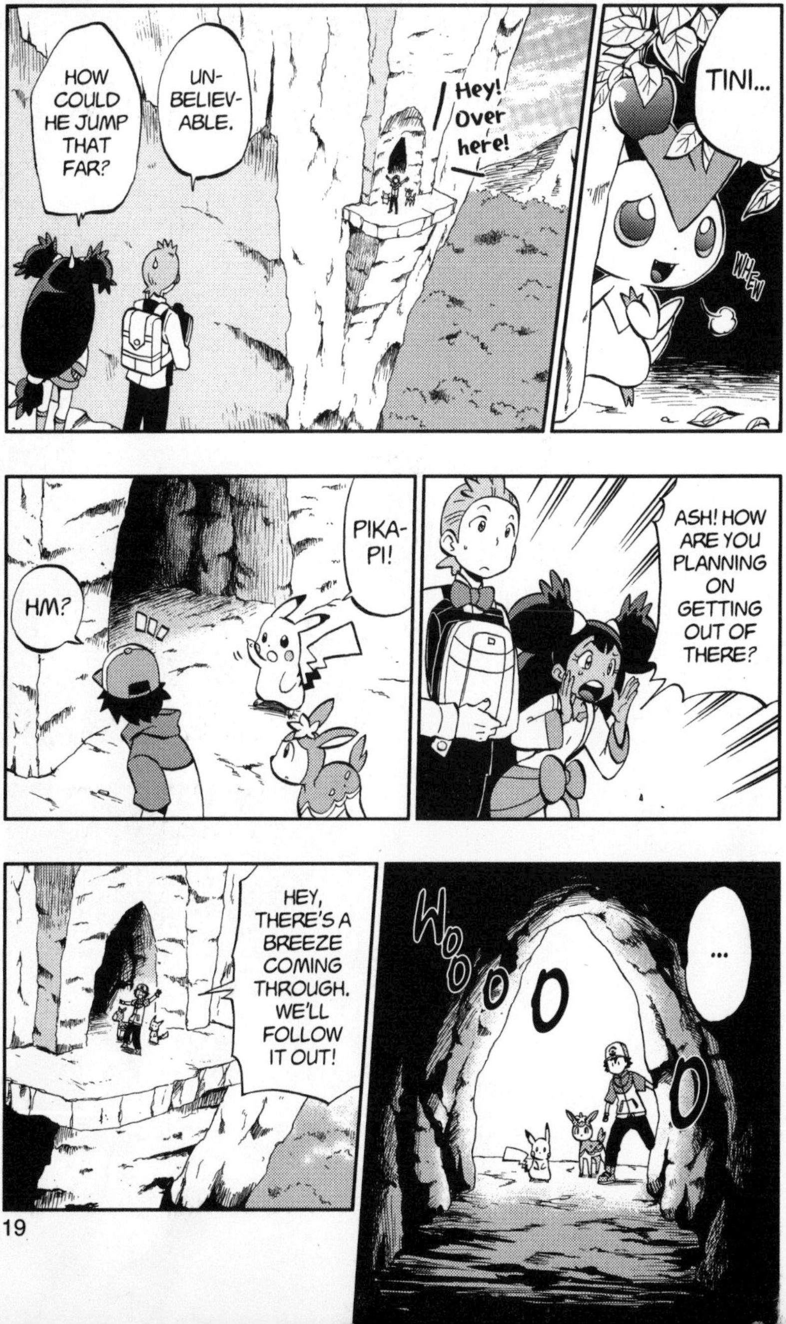

TINI...
WHEW
Hey! Over here!
UN-BELIEV-ABLE.
HOW COULD HE JUMP THAT FAR?
ASH! HOW ARE YOU PLANNING ON GETTING OUT OF THERE?
PIKA-PI!
HM?
WOOOOO
...
HEY, THERE'S A BREEZE COMING THROUGH. WE'LL FOLLOW IT OUT!

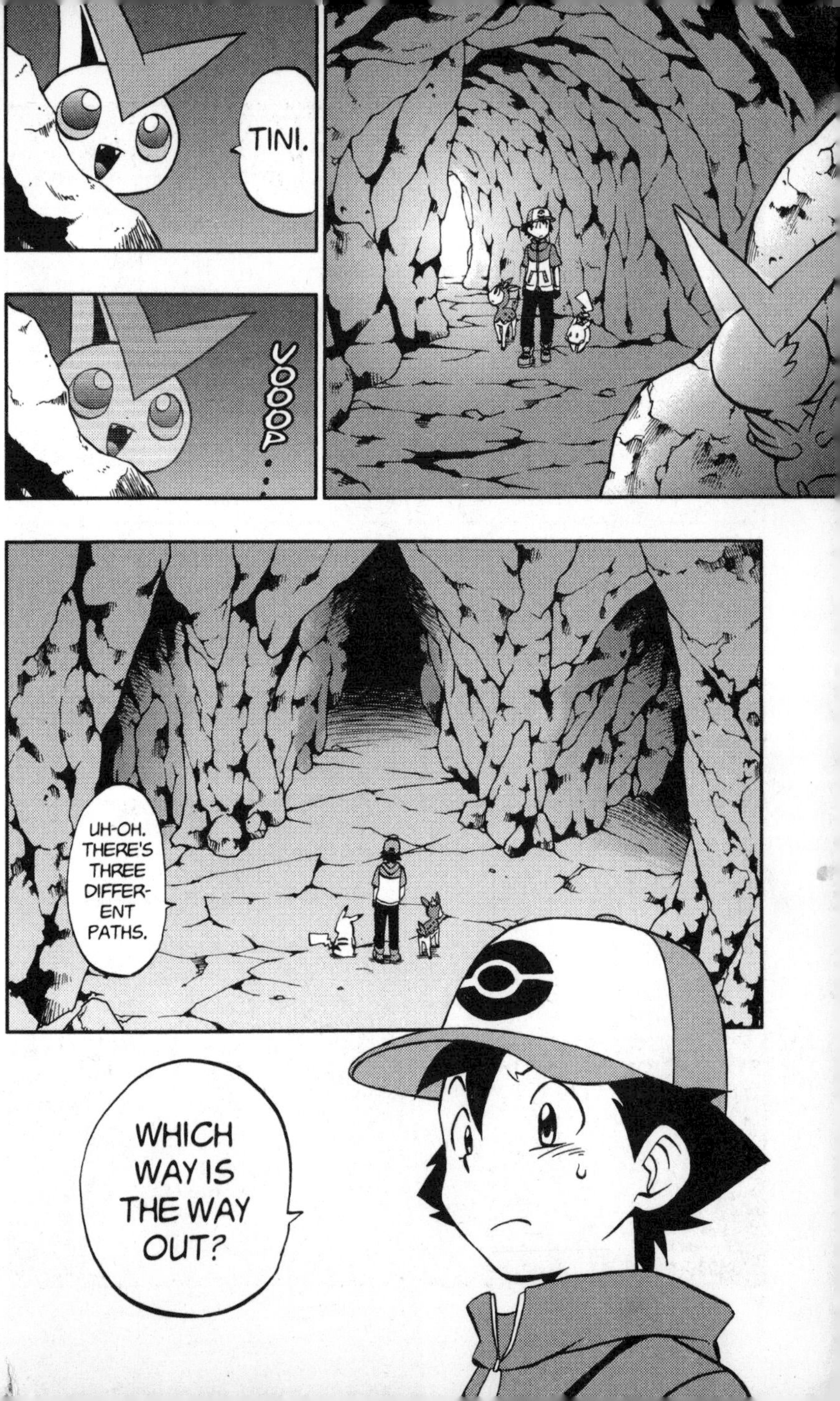
TINI.
VOOOP...
UH-OH. THERE'S THREE DIFFERENT PATHS.
WHICH WAY IS THE WAY OUT?

READ THIS WAY

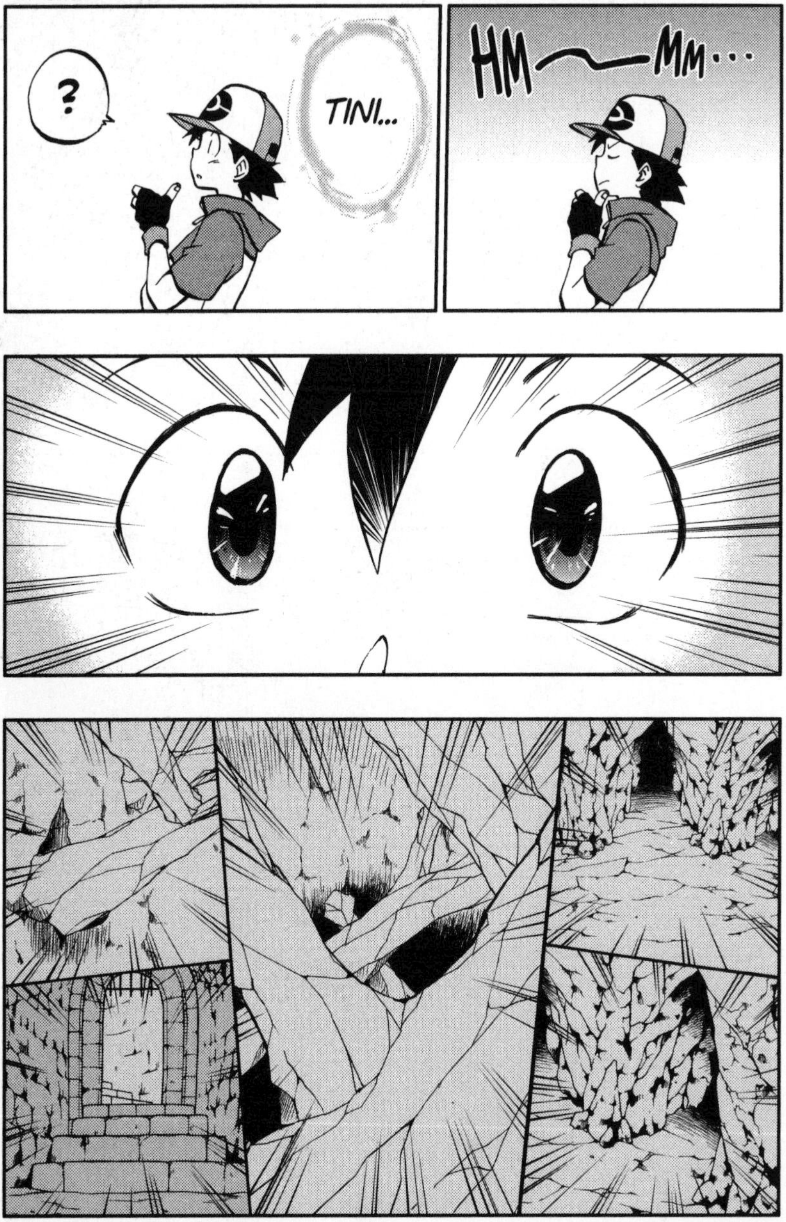
HM~~MM...
TINI...
?

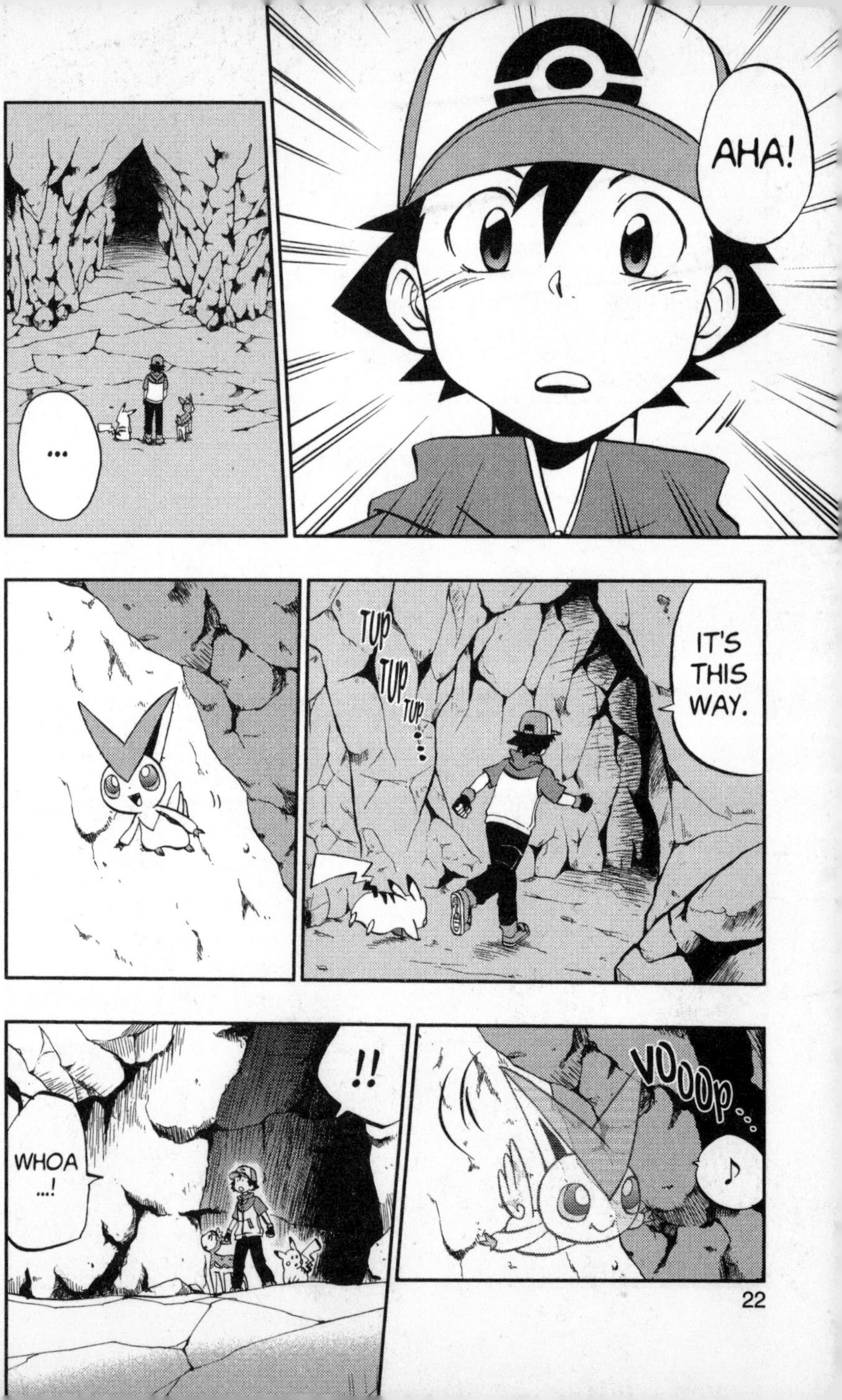
AHA!
...
IT'S THIS WAY.
TUP TUP TUP
VOOOp...
♪
!!
WHOA ...!

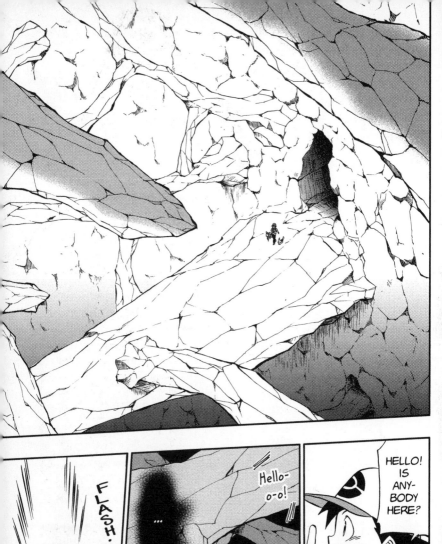

FLASH...

Hello-o-o!

...

HELLO! IS ANY-BODY HERE?

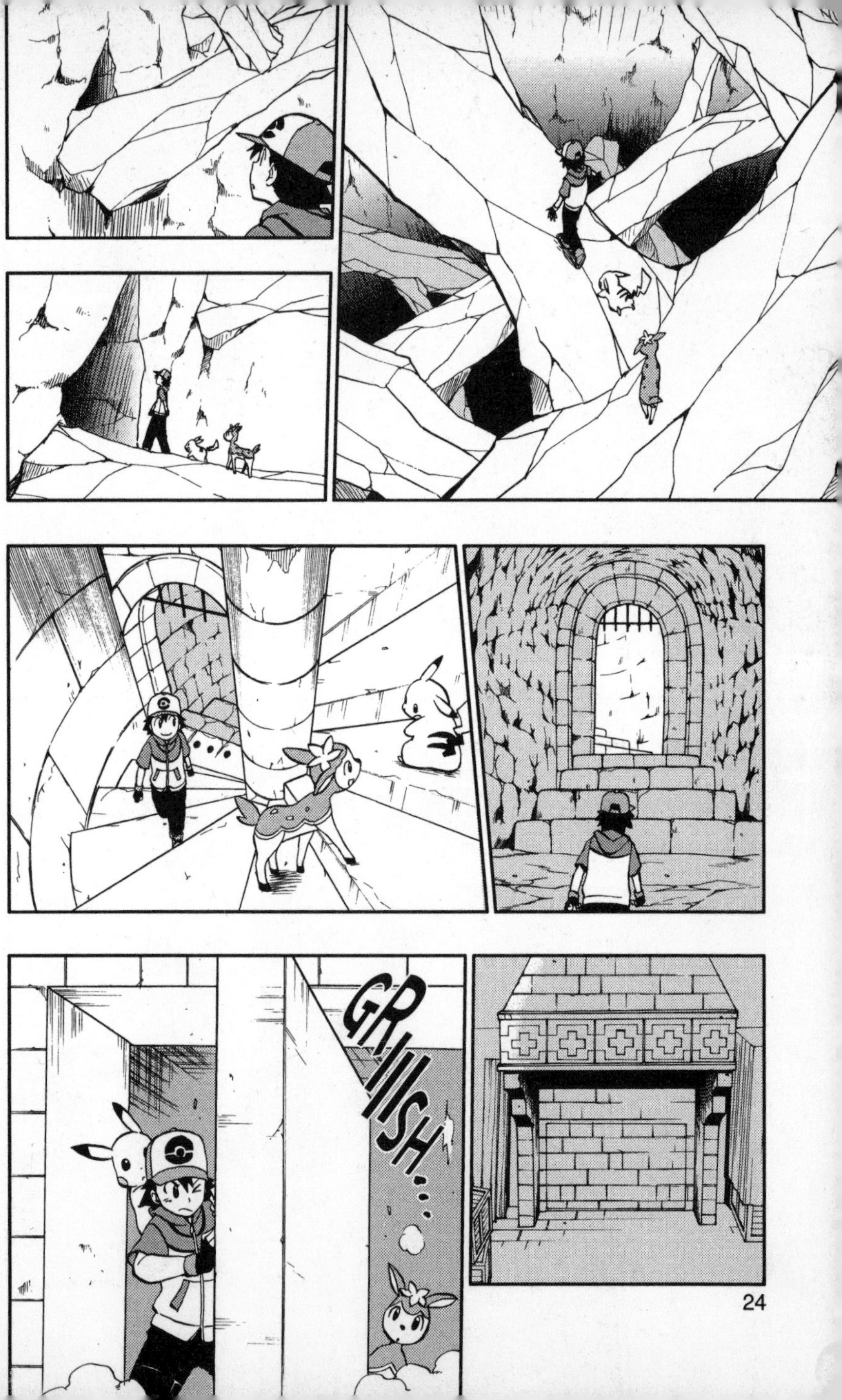
...
GRIIISH...

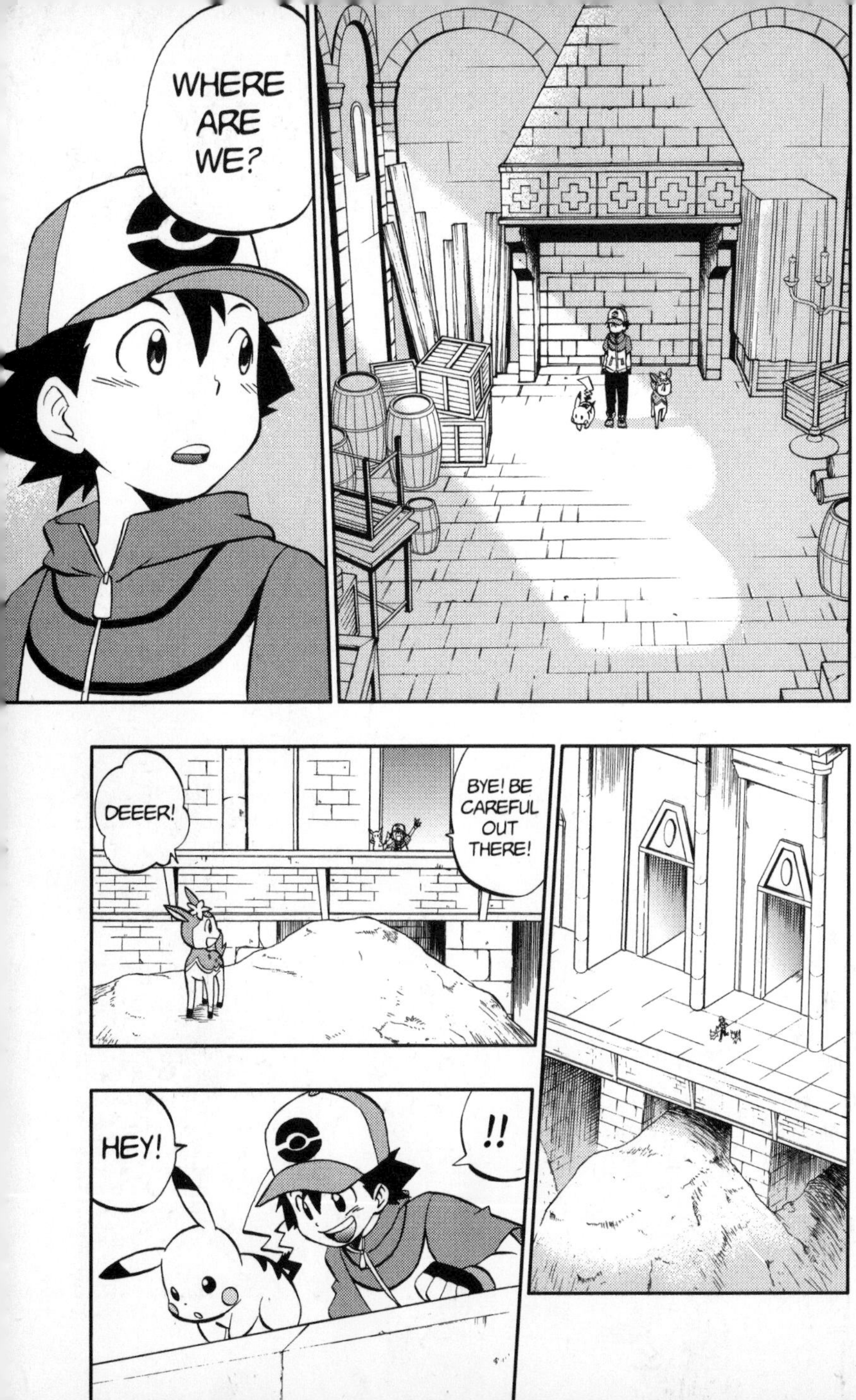
WHERE ARE WE?
BYE! BE CAREFUL OUT THERE!
DEEER!
!!
HEY!

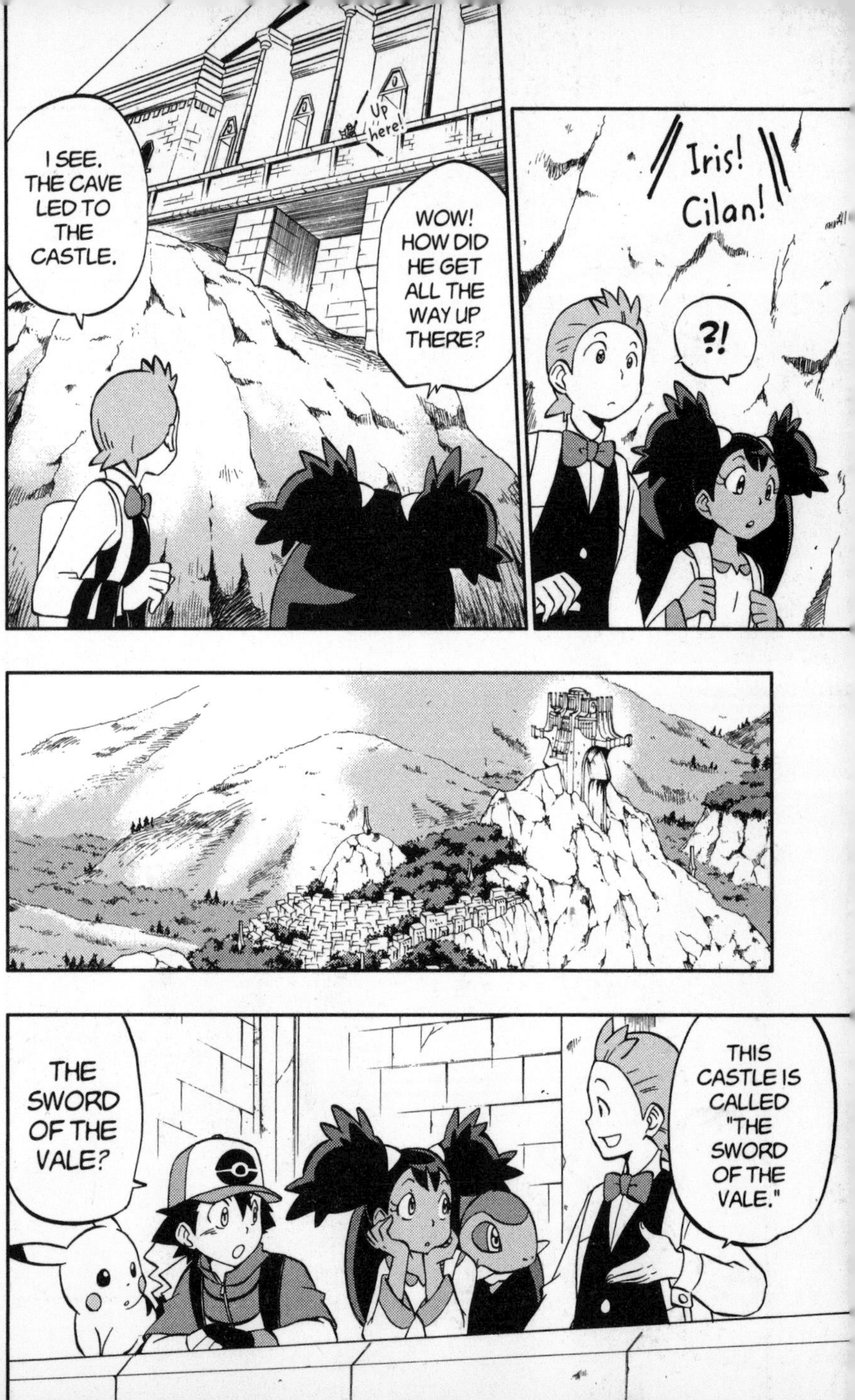
Iris! Cilan!
?!
Up here!
WOW! HOW DID HE GET ALL THE WAY UP THERE?
I SEE. THE CAVE LED TO THE CASTLE.
THIS CASTLE IS CALLED "THE SWORD OF THE VALE."
THE SWORD OF THE VALE?

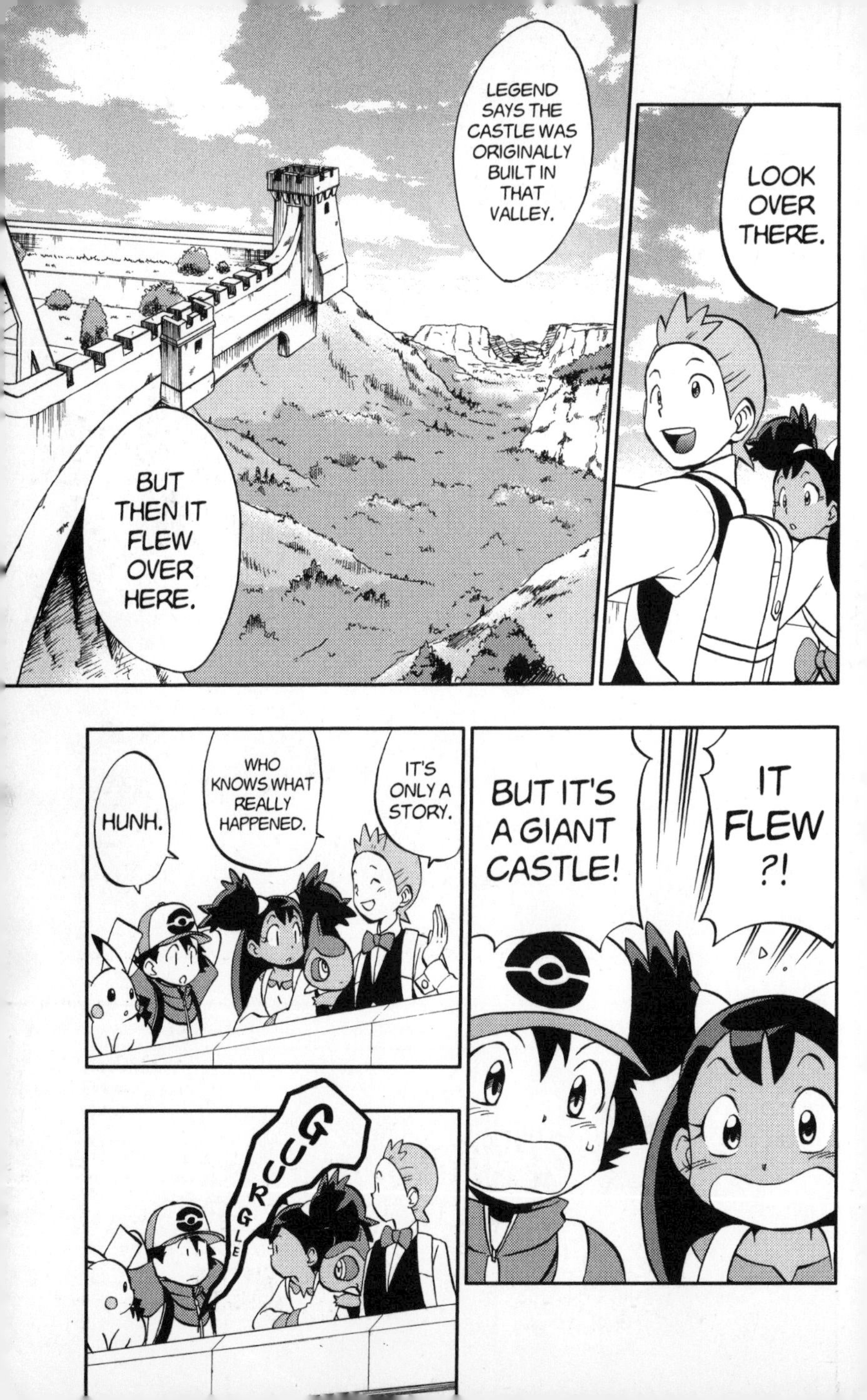
LOOK OVER THERE.
LEGEND SAYS THE CASTLE WAS ORIGINALLY BUILT IN THAT VALLEY.
BUT THEN IT FLEW OVER HERE.
IT FLEW ?!
BUT IT'S A GIANT CASTLE!
IT'S ONLY A STORY.
WHO KNOWS WHAT REALLY HAPPENED.
HUNH.
GUURGLE

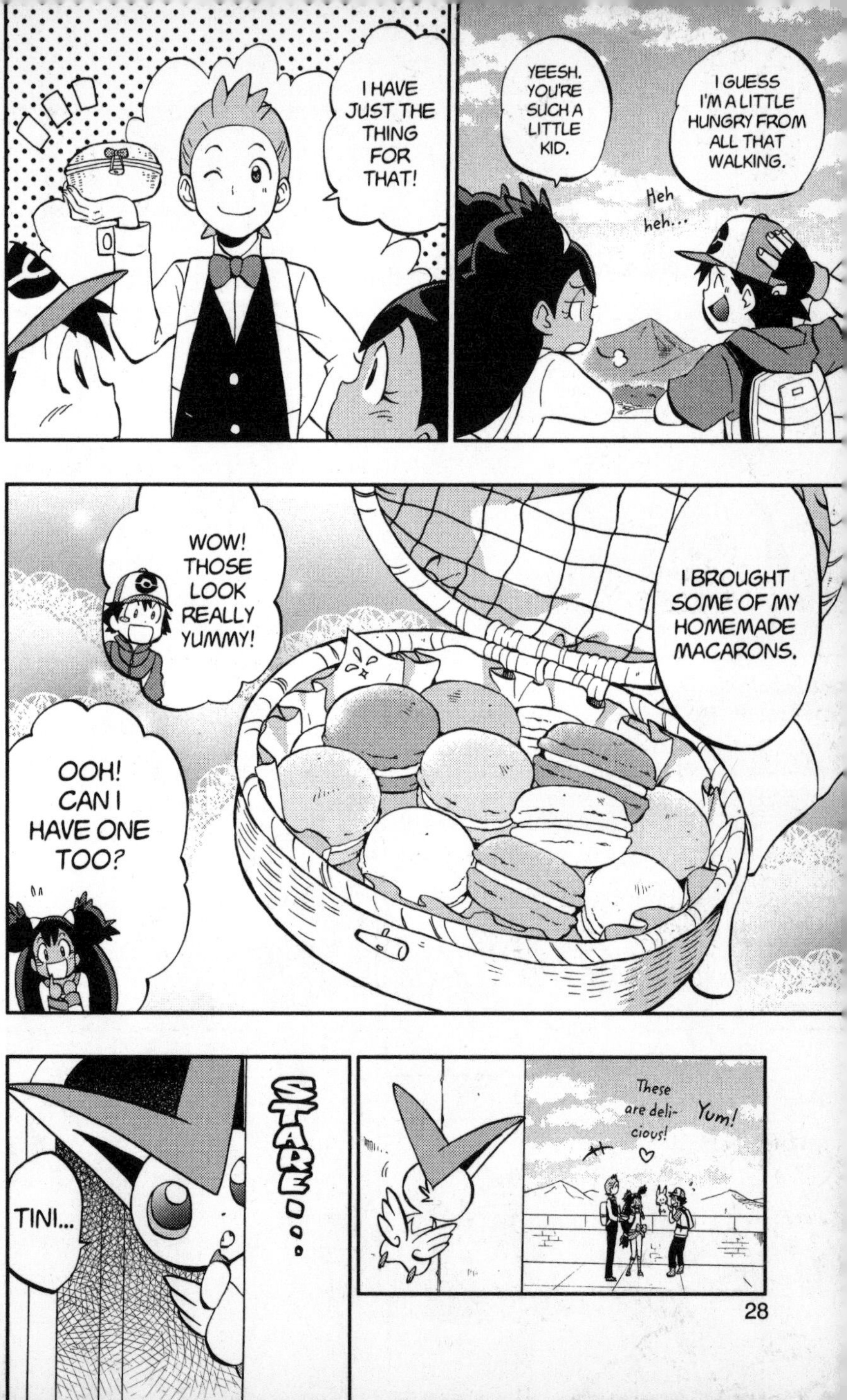
I GUESS I'M A LITTLE HUNGRY FROM ALL THAT WALKING.
Heh heh...
YEESH. YOU'RE SUCH A LITTLE KID.
I HAVE JUST THE THING FOR THAT!
I BROUGHT SOME OF MY HOMEMADE MACARONS.
WOW! THOSE LOOK REALLY YUMMY!
OOH! CAN I HAVE ONE TOO?
Yum!
These are deli-cious!
STARE...
TINI...

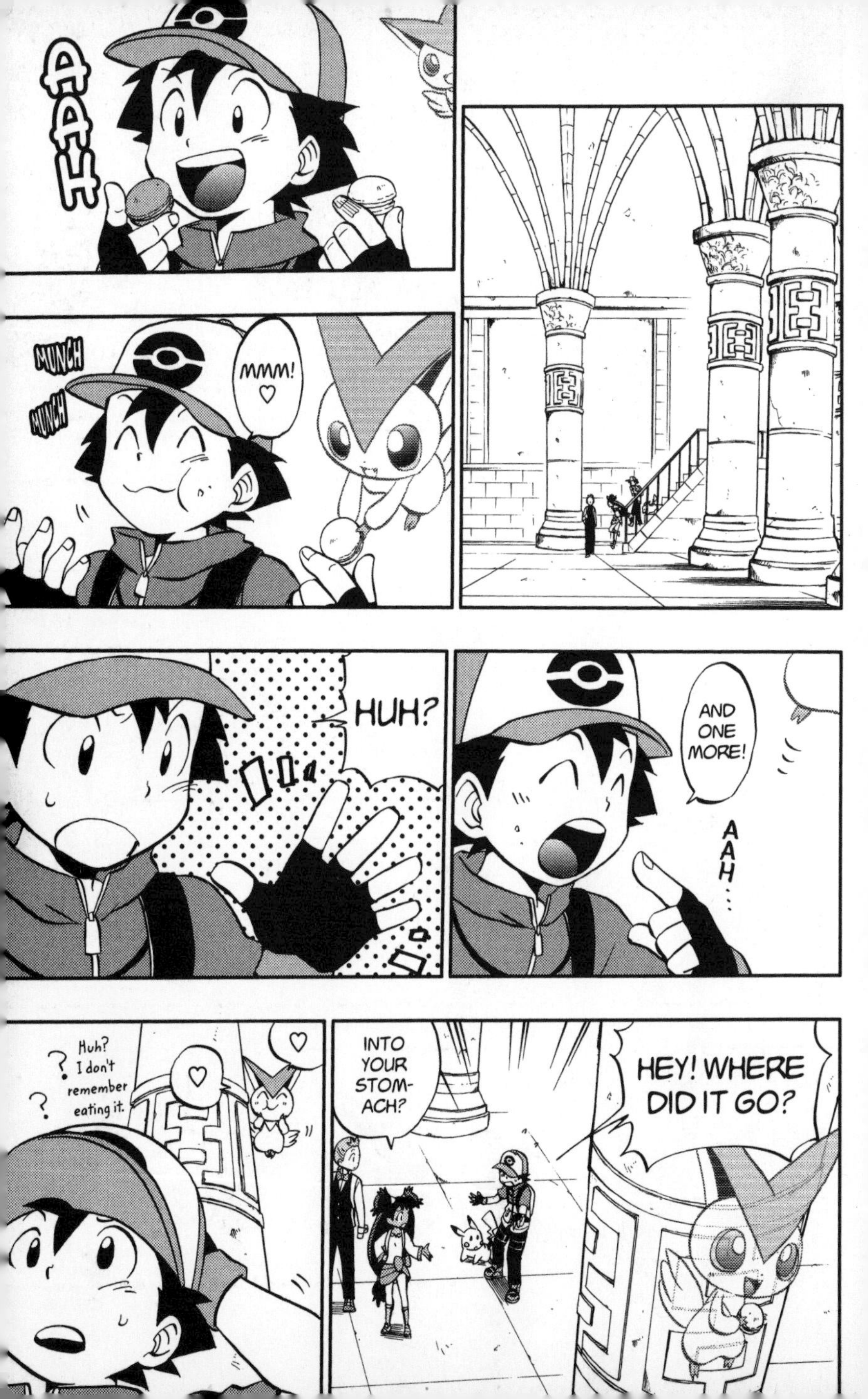
AAH
MUNCH
MUNCH
MMM! ♡
AND ONE MORE!
AAH...
HUH?
HEY! WHERE DID IT GO?
INTO YOUR STOM-ACH?
♡
♡
Huh? I don't remember eating it.

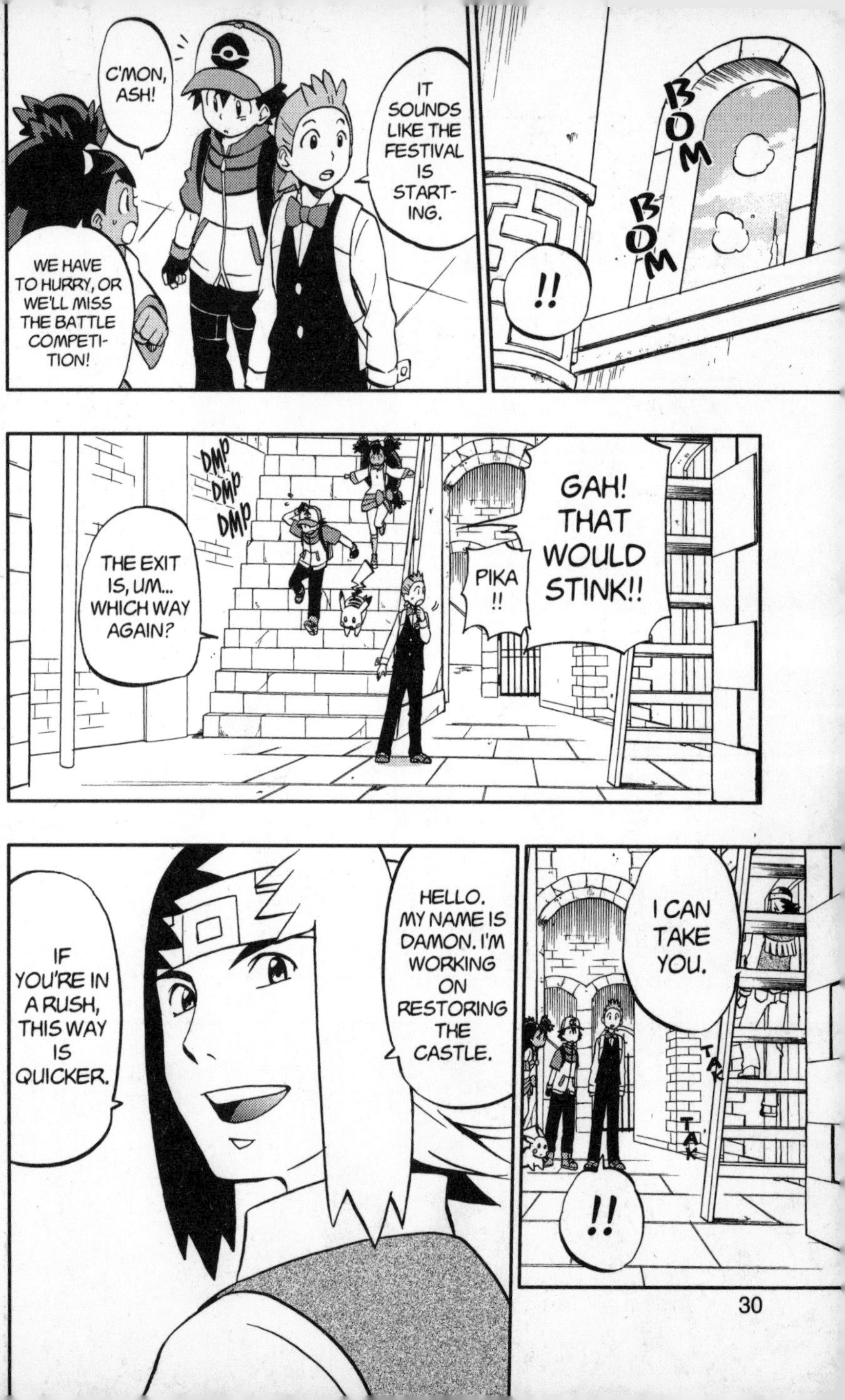
BOM
BOM
!!
IT SOUNDS LIKE THE FESTIVAL IS STARTING.
C'MON, ASH!
WE HAVE TO HURRY, OR WE'LL MISS THE BATTLE COMPETITION!
GAH! THAT WOULD STINK!!
PIKA !!
DMP DMP DMP
THE EXIT IS, UM... WHICH WAY AGAIN?
I CAN TAKE YOU.
TAK TAK
!!
HELLO. MY NAME IS DAMON. I'M WORKING ON RESTORING THE CASTLE.
IF YOU'RE IN A RUSH, THIS WAY IS QUICKER.

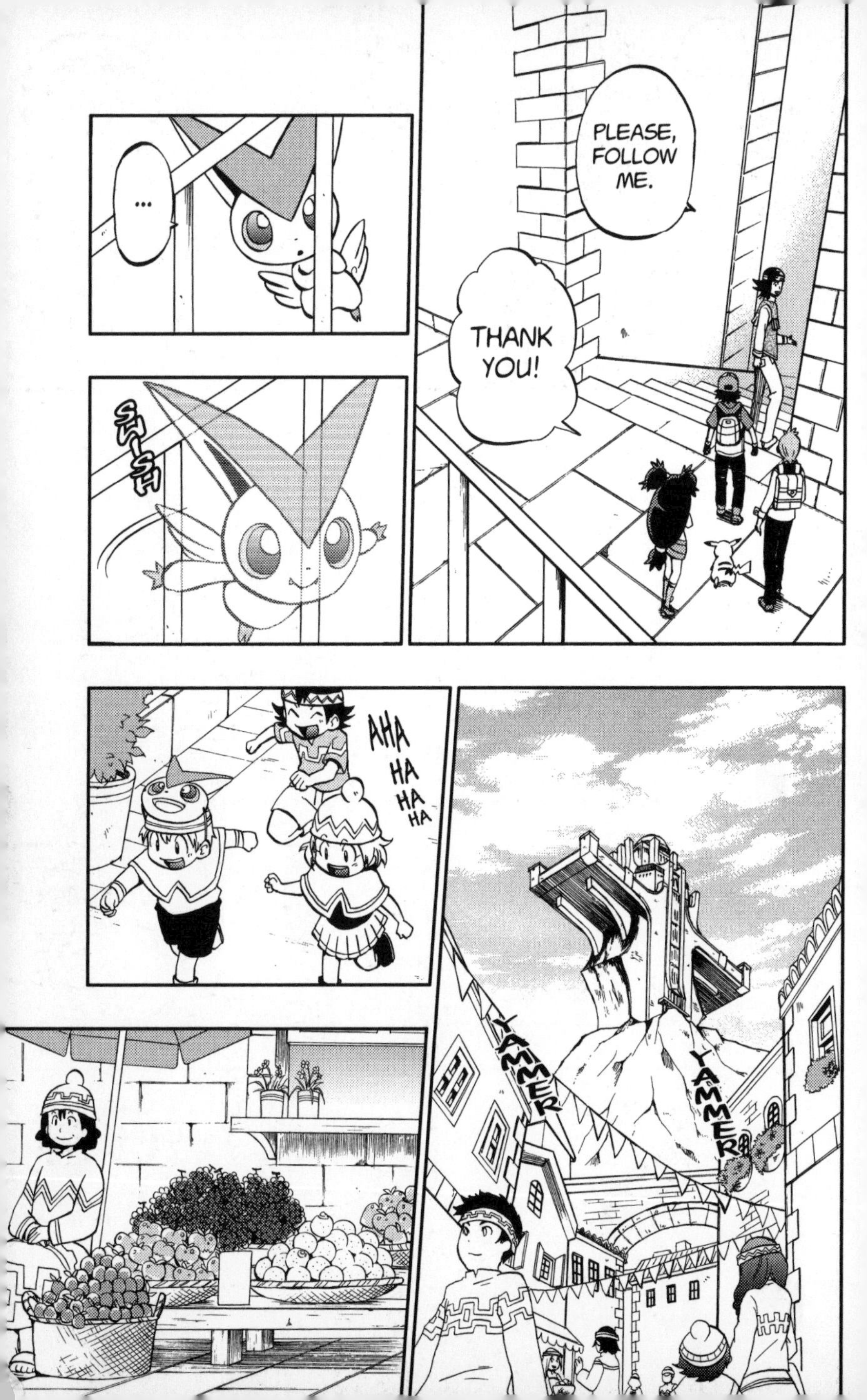
PLEASE, FOLLOW ME.
THANK YOU!
...
SHISH
YAMMER
YAMMER
AHA HA HA HA

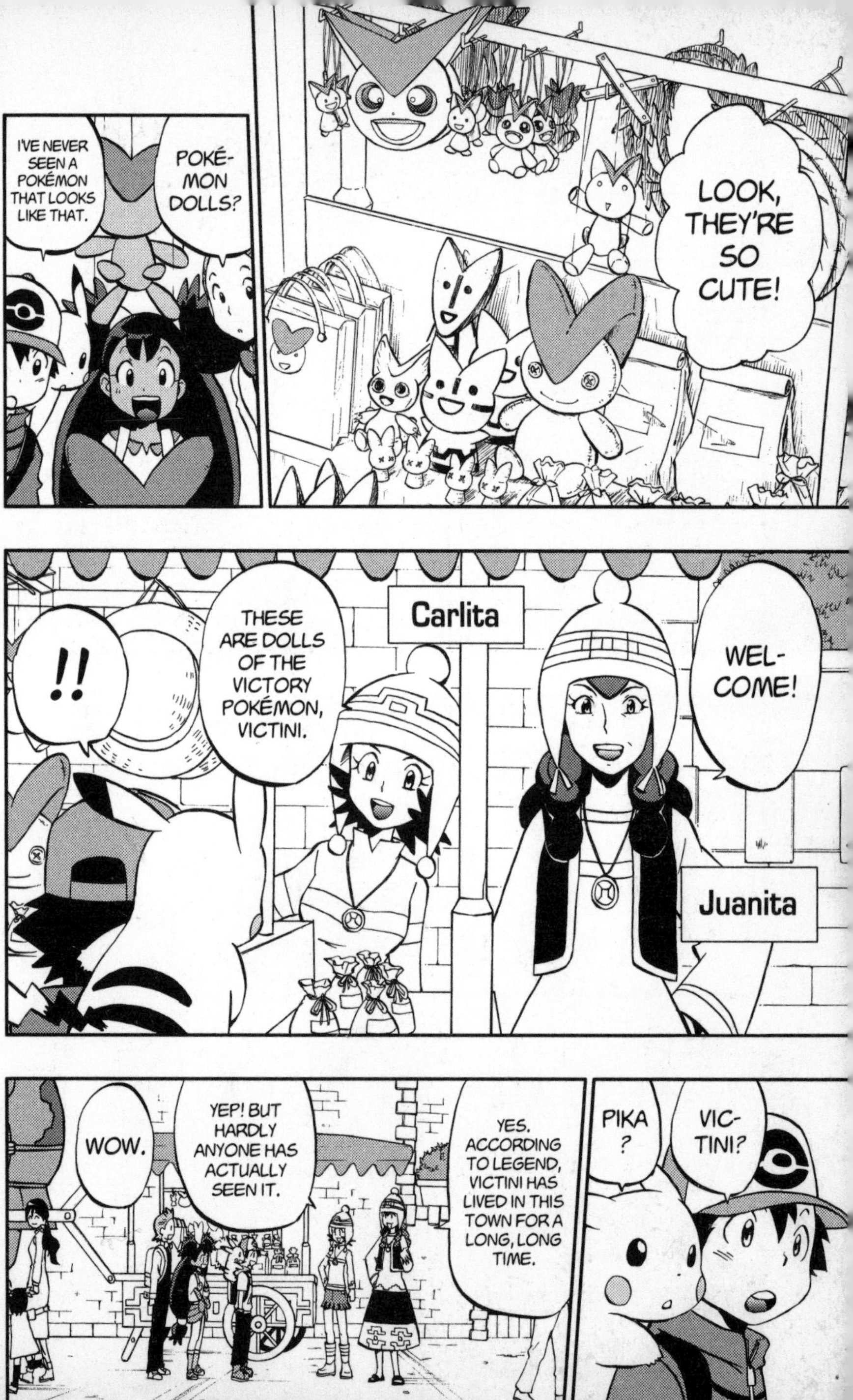
LOOK, THEY'RE SO CUTE!
POKÉ-MON DOLLS?
I'VE NEVER SEEN A POKÉMON THAT LOOKS LIKE THAT.
WEL-COME!
Juanita
Carlita
THESE ARE DOLLS OF THE VICTORY POKÉMON, VICTINI.
!!
VIC-TINI?
PIKA?
YES. ACCORDING TO LEGEND, VICTINI HAS LIVED IN THIS TOWN FOR A LONG, LONG TIME.
YEP! BUT HARDLY ANYONE HAS ACTUALLY SEEN IT.
WOW.

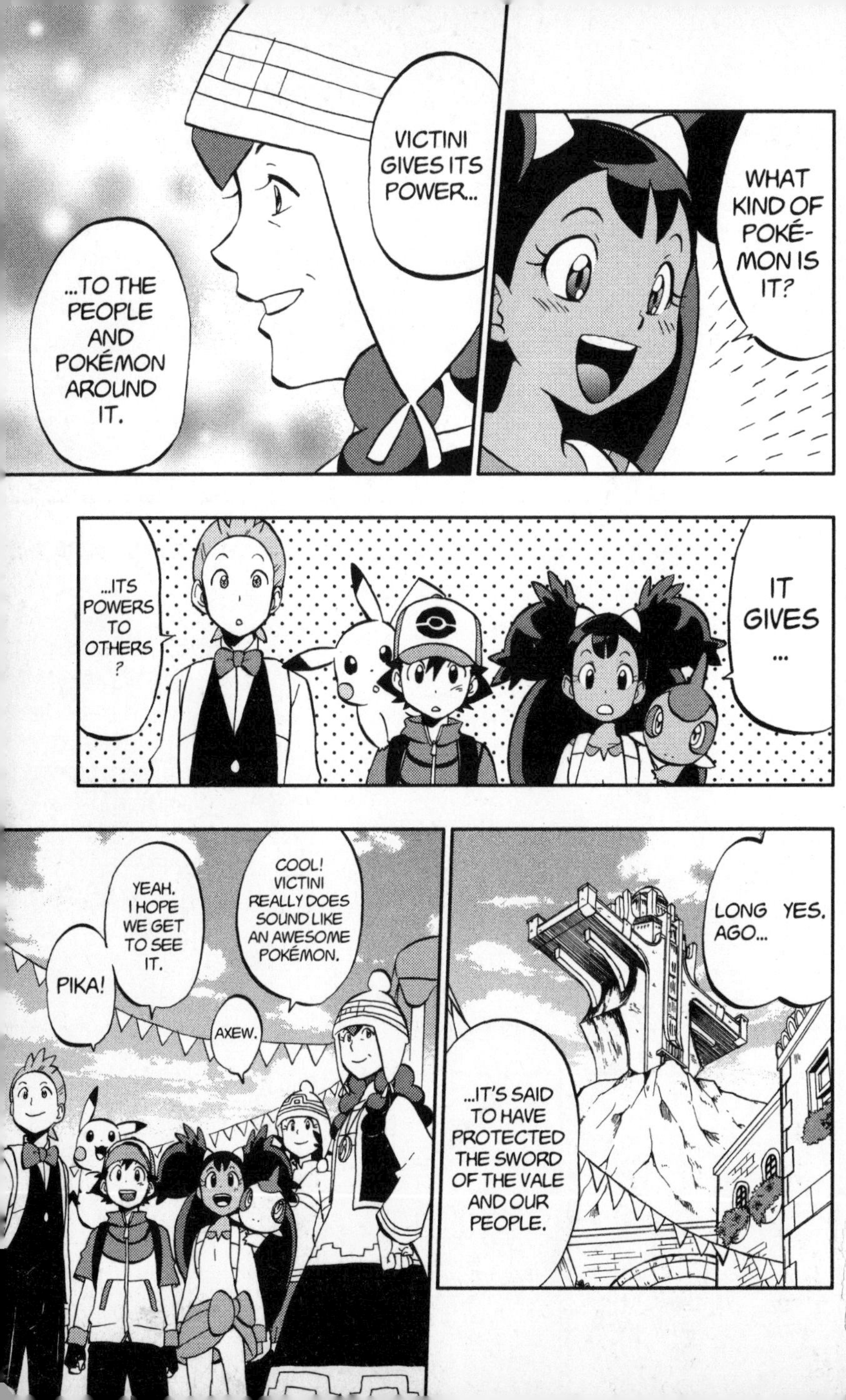
WHAT KIND OF POKÉMON IS IT?
VICTINI GIVES ITS POWER...
...TO THE PEOPLE AND POKÉMON AROUND IT.
IT GIVES ...
...ITS POWERS TO OTHERS ?
YES.
LONG AGO...
...IT'S SAID TO HAVE PROTECTED THE SWORD OF THE VALE AND OUR PEOPLE.
COOL! VICTINI REALLY DOES SOUND LIKE AN AWESOME POKÉMON.
YEAH. I HOPE WE GET TO SEE IT.
PIKA!
AXEW.

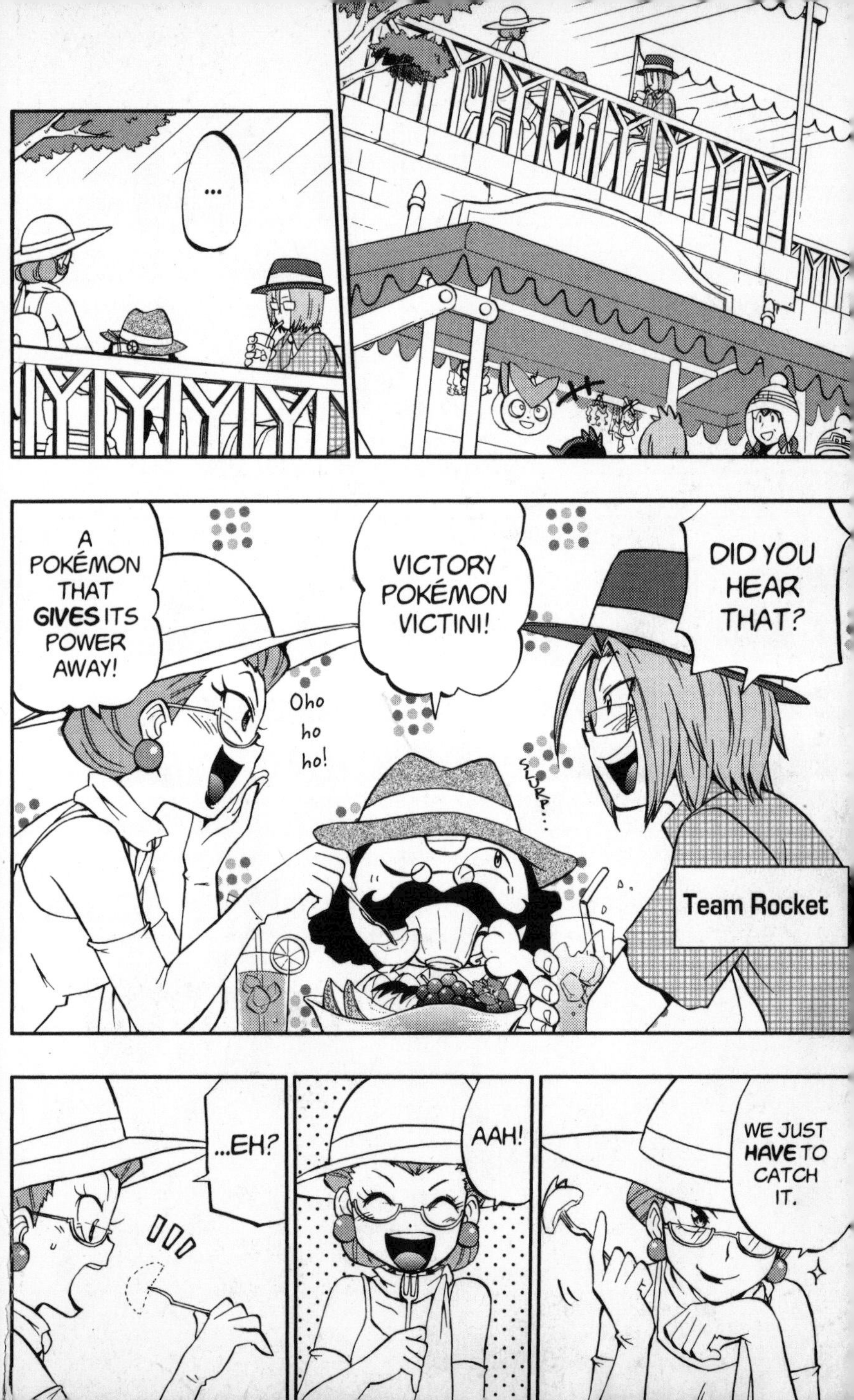
...
DID YOU HEAR THAT?
Team Rocket
VICTORY POKÉMON VICTINI!
SLURP...
Oho ho ho!
A POKÉMON THAT GIVES ITS POWER AWAY!
WE JUST HAVE TO CATCH IT.
AAH!
...EH?

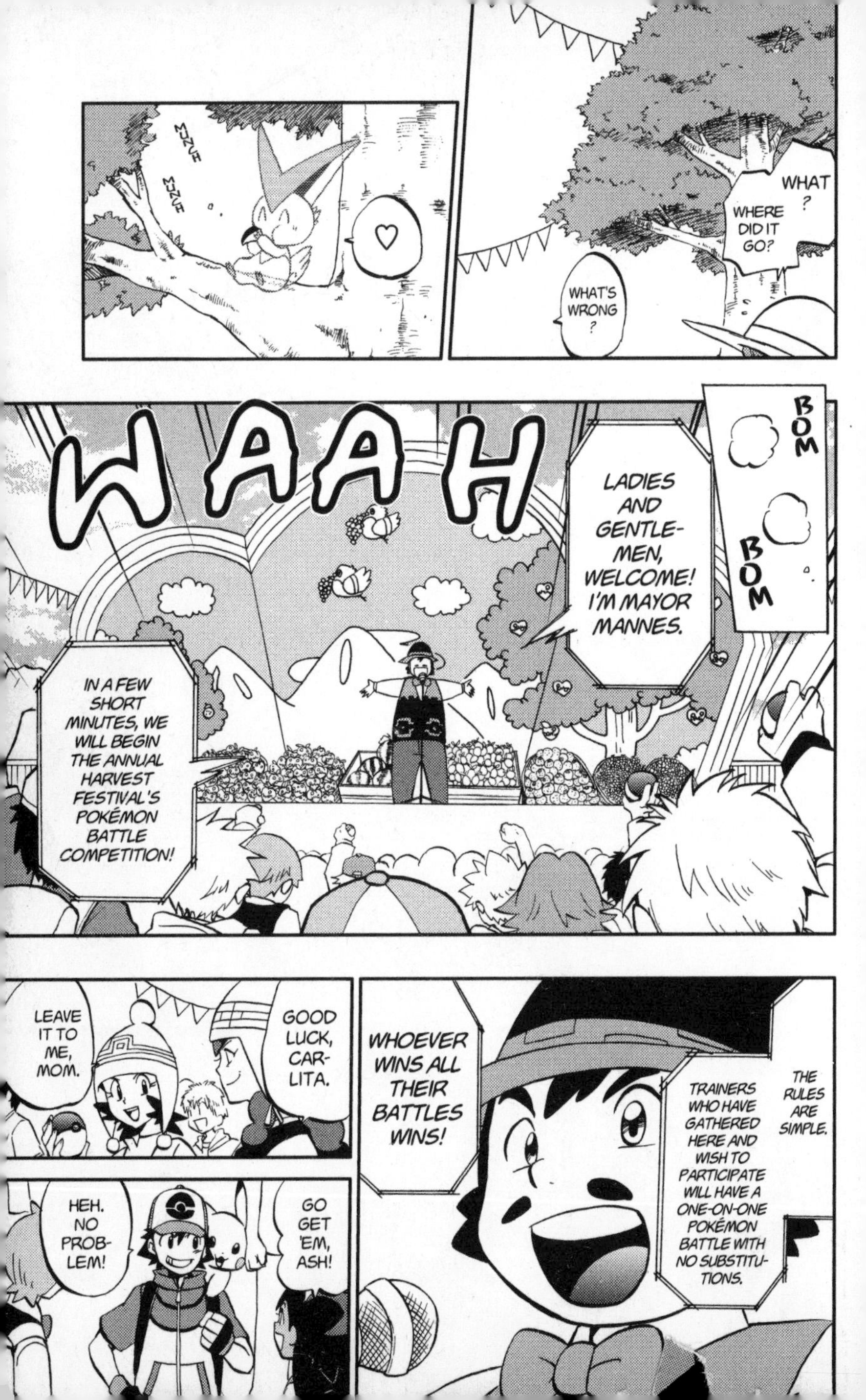
WHAT?
WHERE DID IT GO?
WHAT'S WRONG?
MUNCH
MUNCH
♥
BOM
BOM
BOM
BOM
WAAH
LADIES AND GENTLEMEN, WELCOME! I'M MAYOR MANNES.
IN A FEW SHORT MINUTES, WE WILL BEGIN THE ANNUAL HARVEST FESTIVAL'S POKÉMON BATTLE COMPETITION!
THE RULES ARE SIMPLE.
TRAINERS WHO HAVE GATHERED HERE AND WISH TO PARTICIPATE WILL HAVE A ONE-ON-ONE POKÉMON BATTLE WITH NO SUBSTITUTIONS.
WHOEVER WINS ALL THEIR BATTLES WINS!
GOOD LUCK, CARLITA.
LEAVE IT TO ME, MOM.
GO GET 'EM, ASH!
HEH. NO PROBLEM!

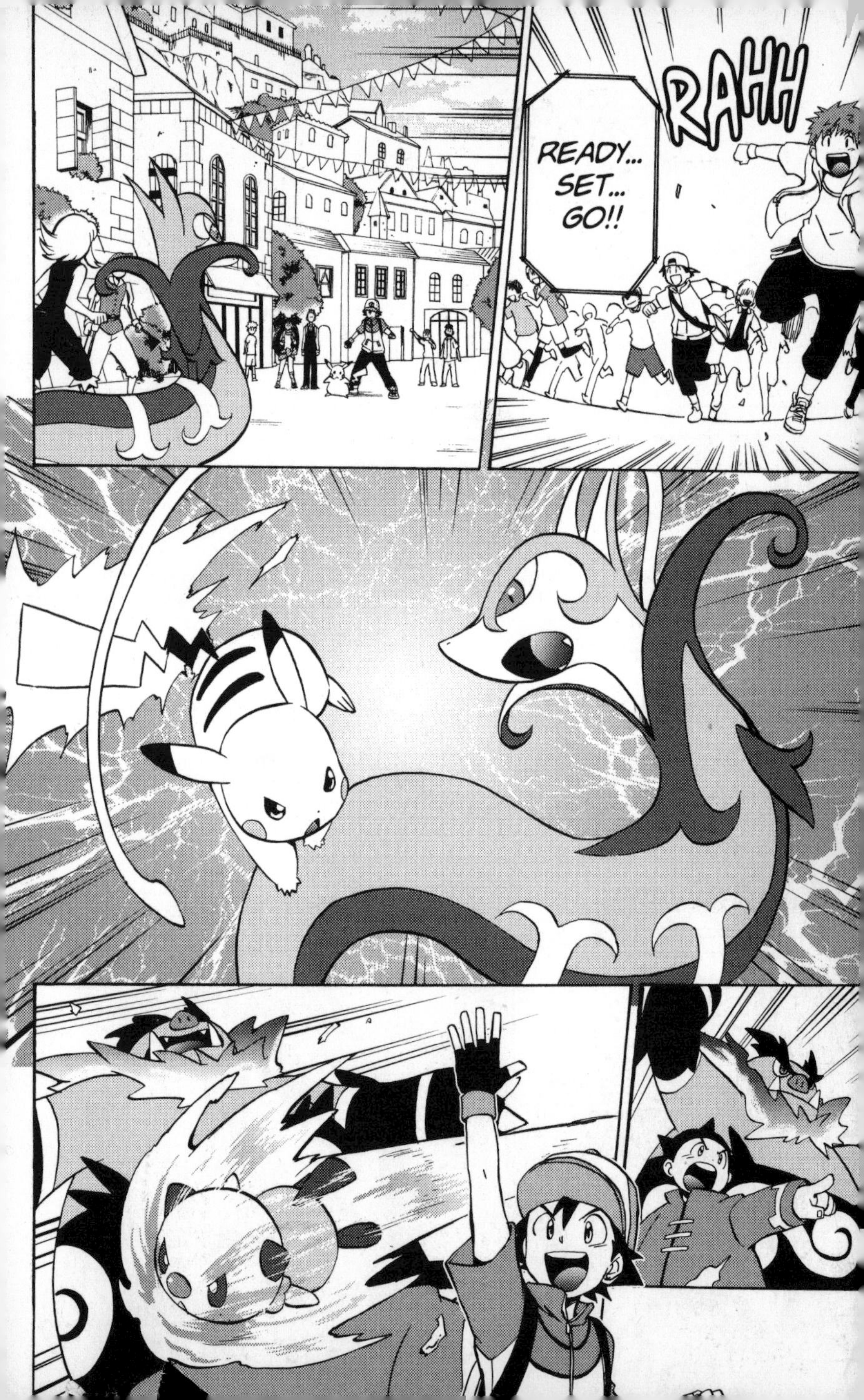
RAHH
READY... SET... GO!!

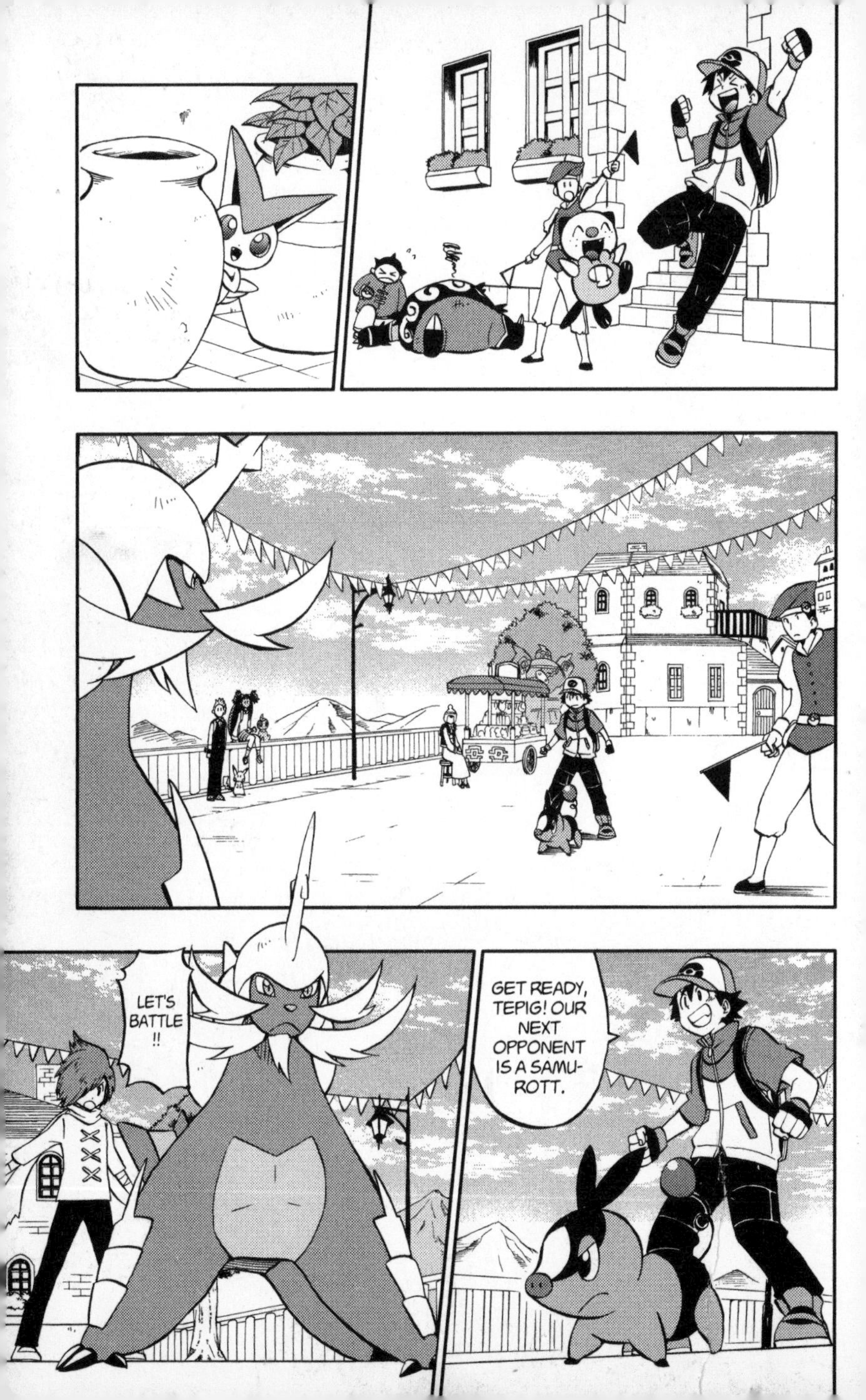
GET READY, TEPIG! OUR NEXT OPPONENT IS A SAMU-ROTT.
LET'S BATTLE !!

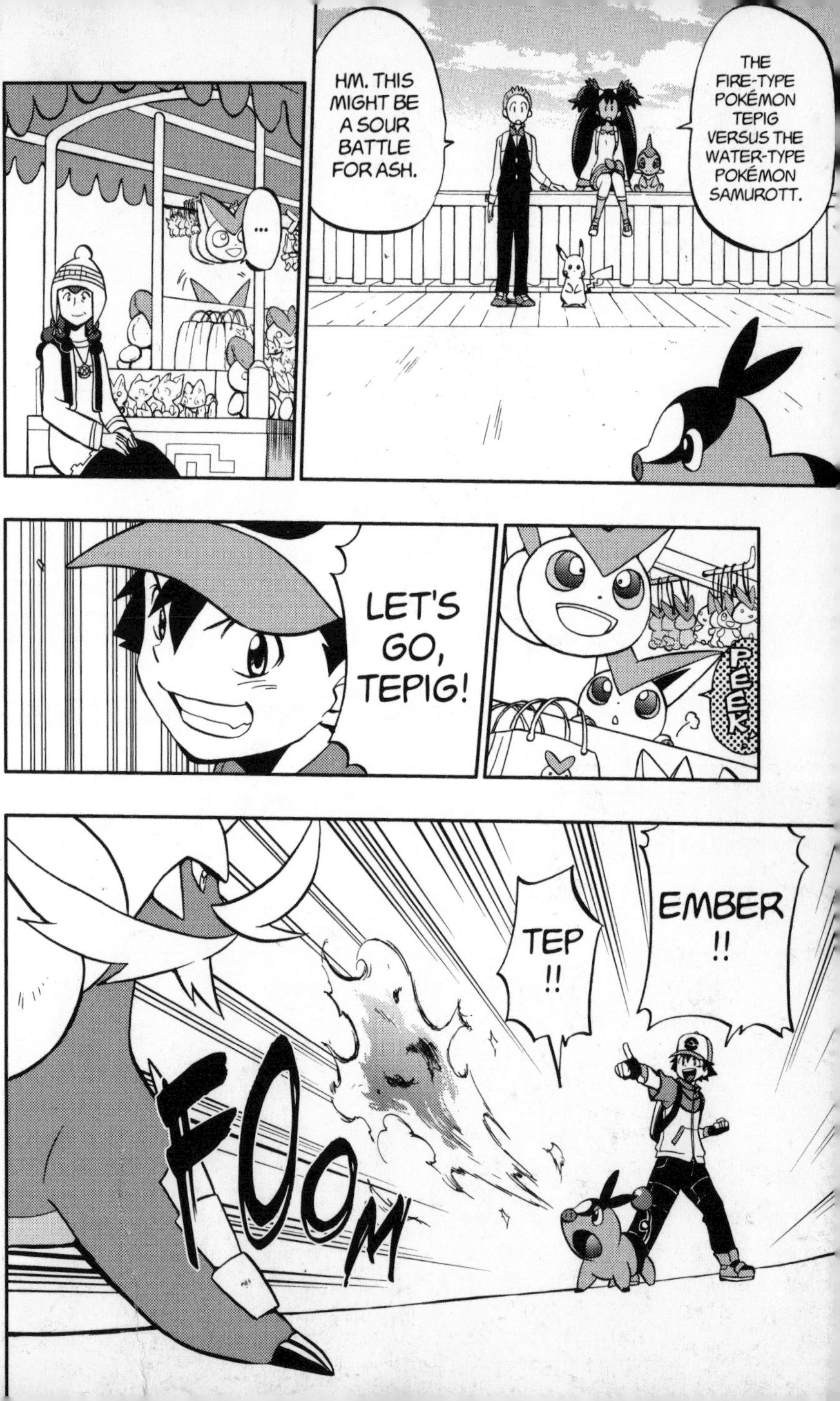
THE FIRE-TYPE POKÉMON TEPIG VERSUS THE WATER-TYPE POKÉMON SAMUROTT.
HM. THIS MIGHT BE A SOUR BATTLE FOR ASH.
...
PEEK
LET'S GO, TEPIG!
EMBER !!
TEP !!
FOOM

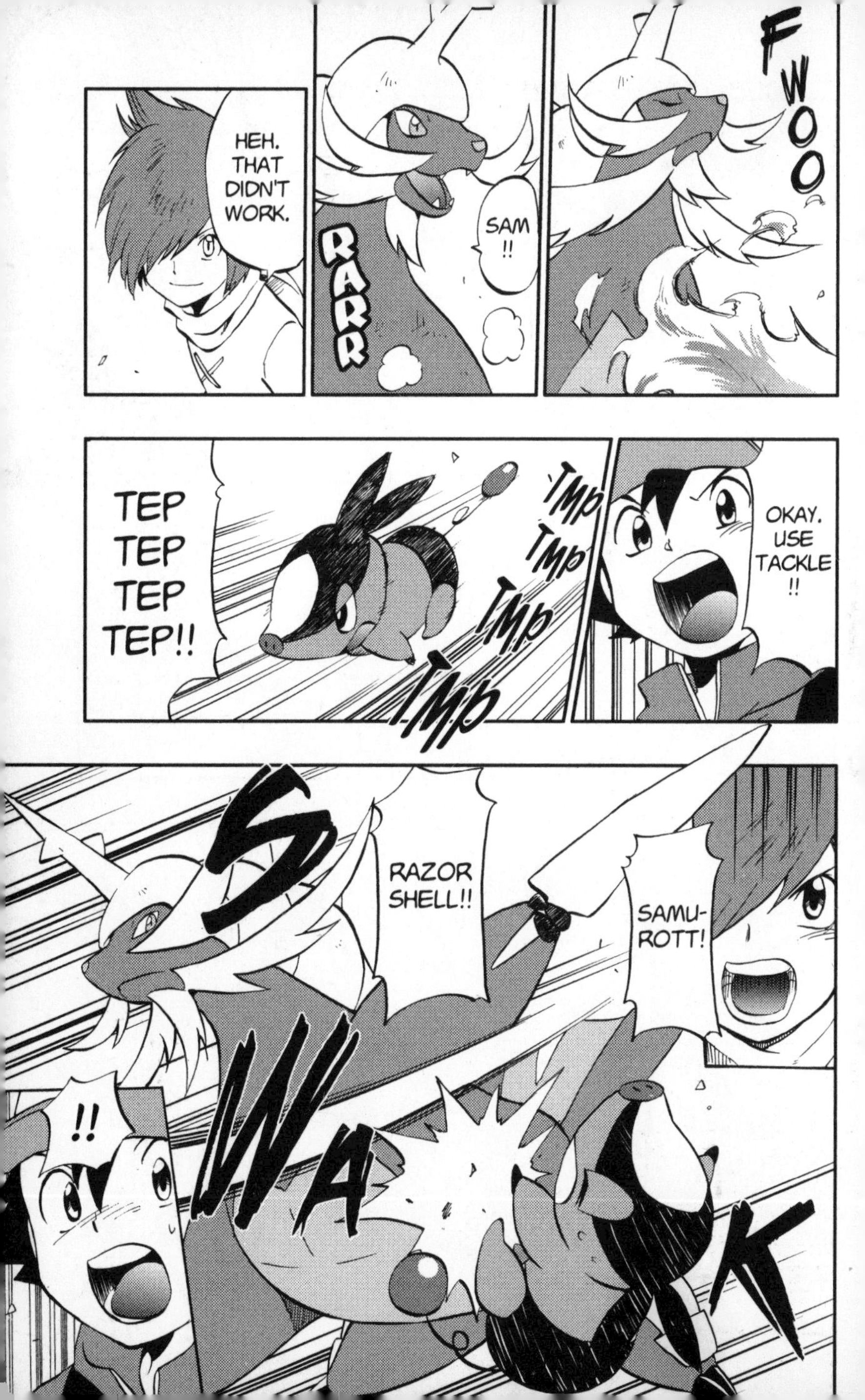
FWOO
SAM!!
RARR
HEH. THAT DIDN'T WORK.
OKAY. USE TACKLE!!
TMP TMP TMP TMP
TEP TEP TEP TEP!!
SAMU-ROTT!
RAZOR SHELL!!
S
WA
K
!!

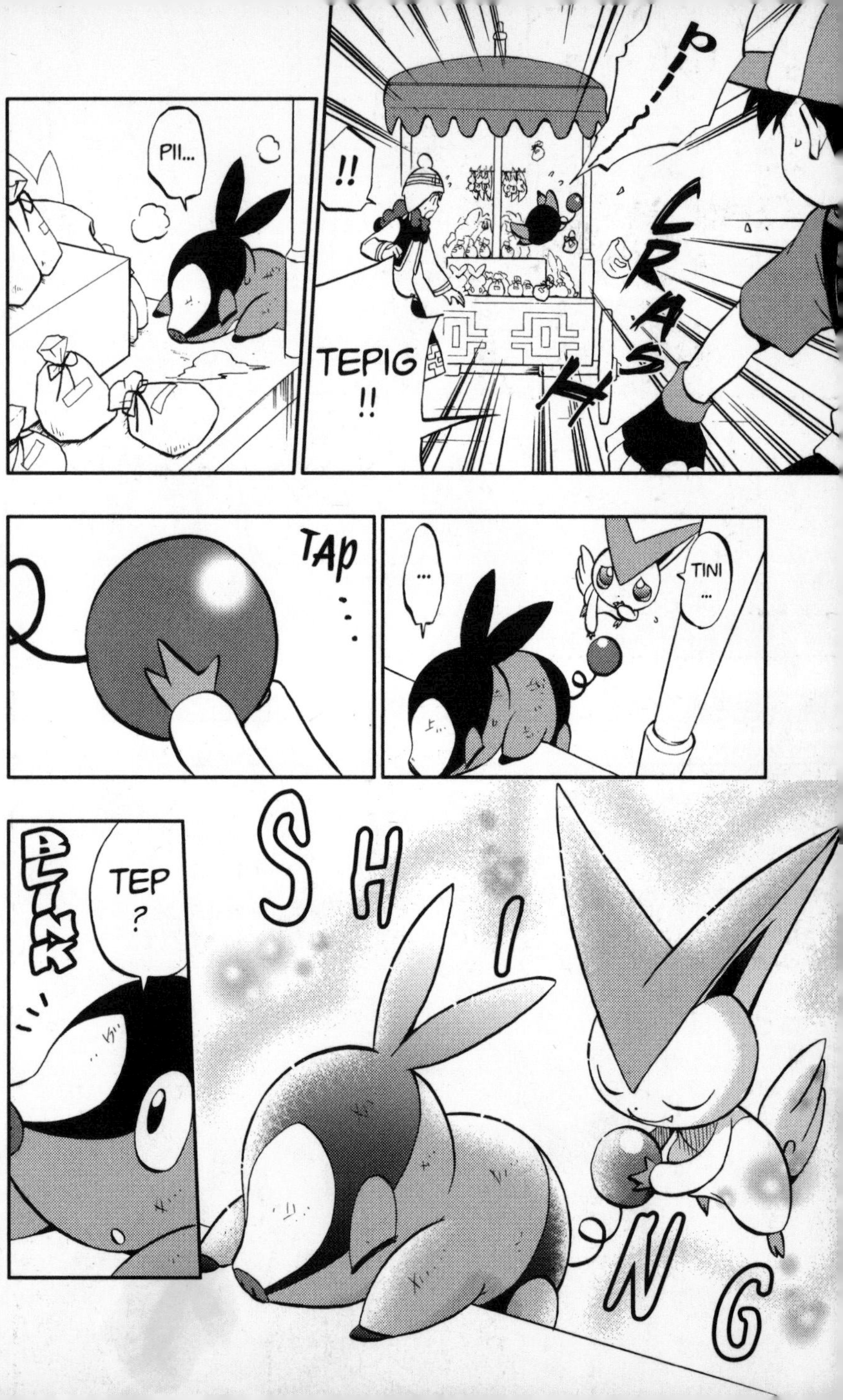

P!!~~
CRASH
!!
TEPIG !!
PII...
...
TINI ...
TAP...
SHING
BLINK
TEP ?

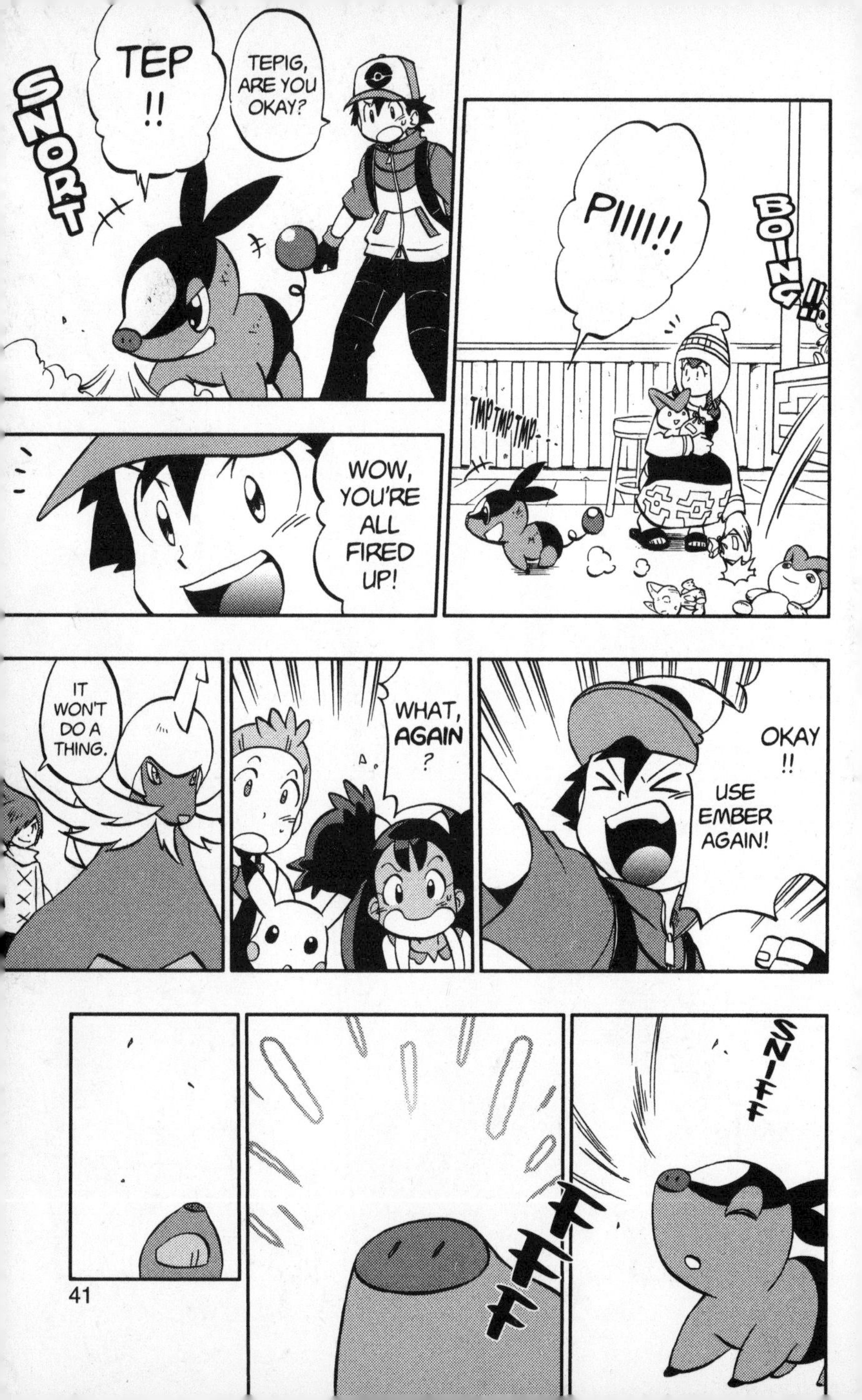
BOING!!
PIIII!!
TMPTMPTMP...
TEPIG, ARE YOU OKAY?
TEP!!
SNORT
WOW, YOU'RE ALL FIRED UP!
OKAY!! USE EMBER AGAIN!
WHAT, **AGAIN**?
IT WON'T DO A THING.
SNIFF

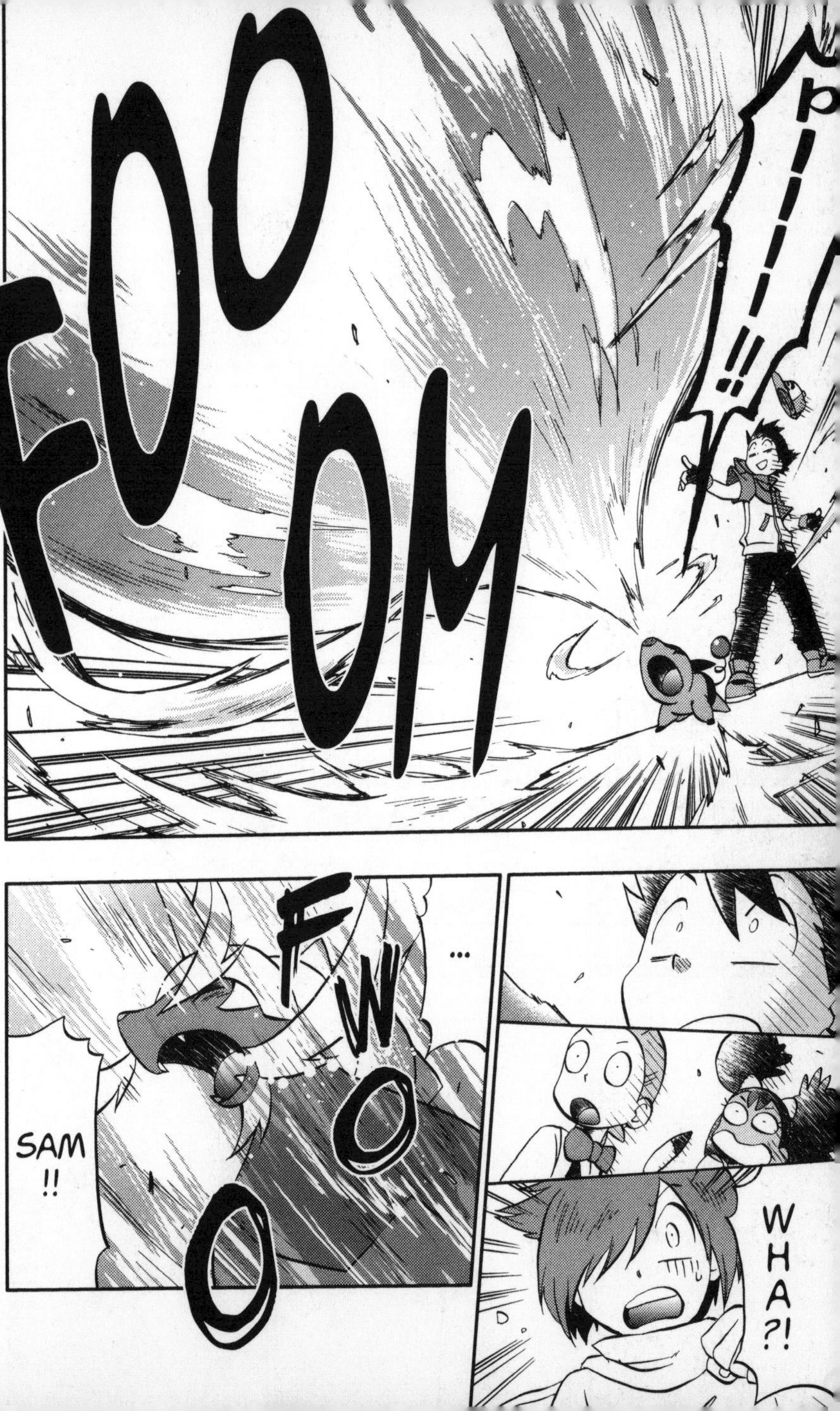
PI—!!
FOOOM
WHA?!
...
FWOOO
SAM!!

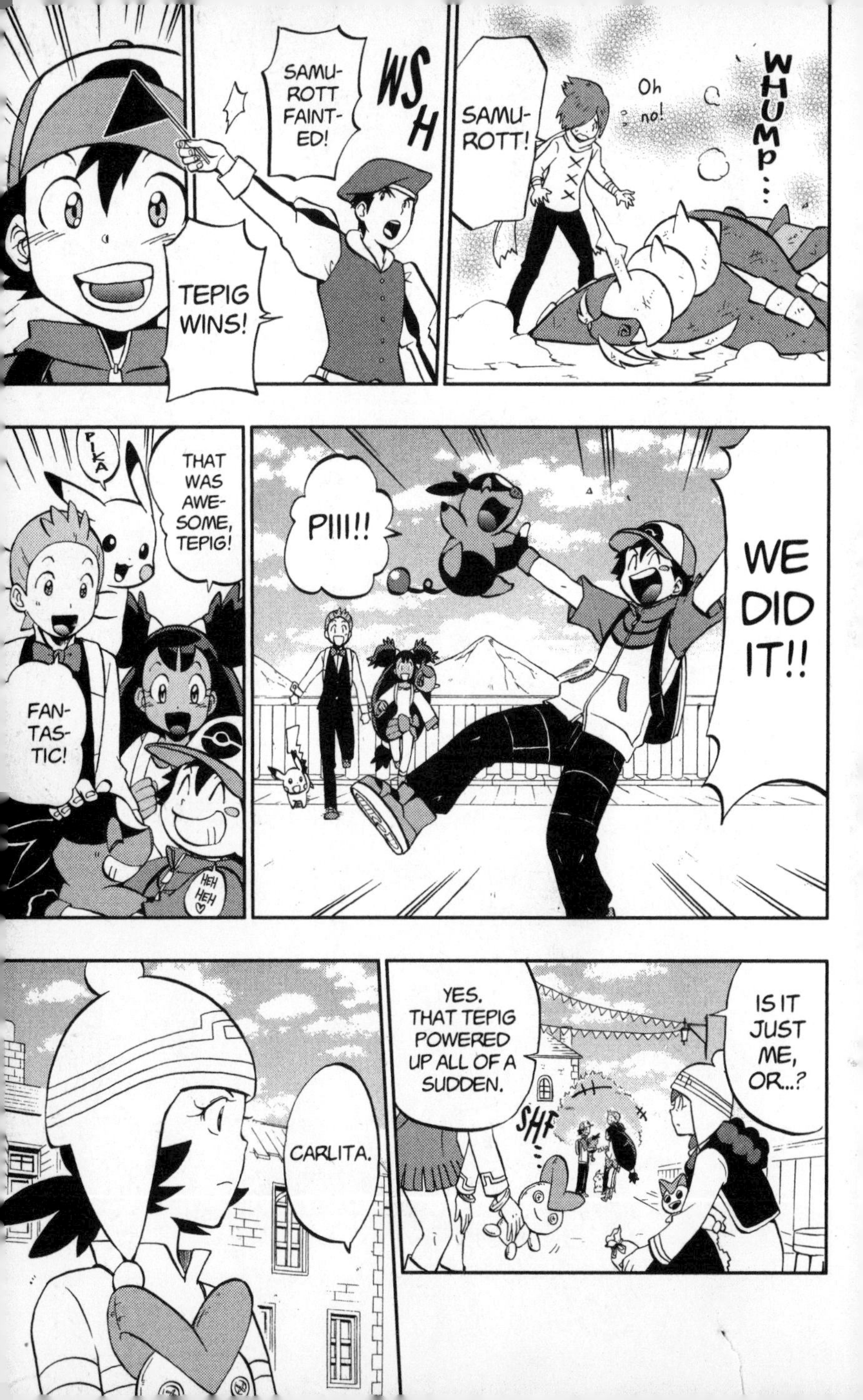
WHUMP...
Oh no!
SAMU-ROTT!
WSH
SAMU-ROTT FAINT-ED!
TEPIG WINS!
WE DID IT!!
PIII!!
THAT WAS AWE-SOME, TEPIG!
PIKA
FAN-TAS-TIC!
HEH HEH ♡
IS IT JUST ME, OR...?
YES. THAT TEPIG POWERED UP ALL OF A SUDDEN.
SHF
CARLITA.

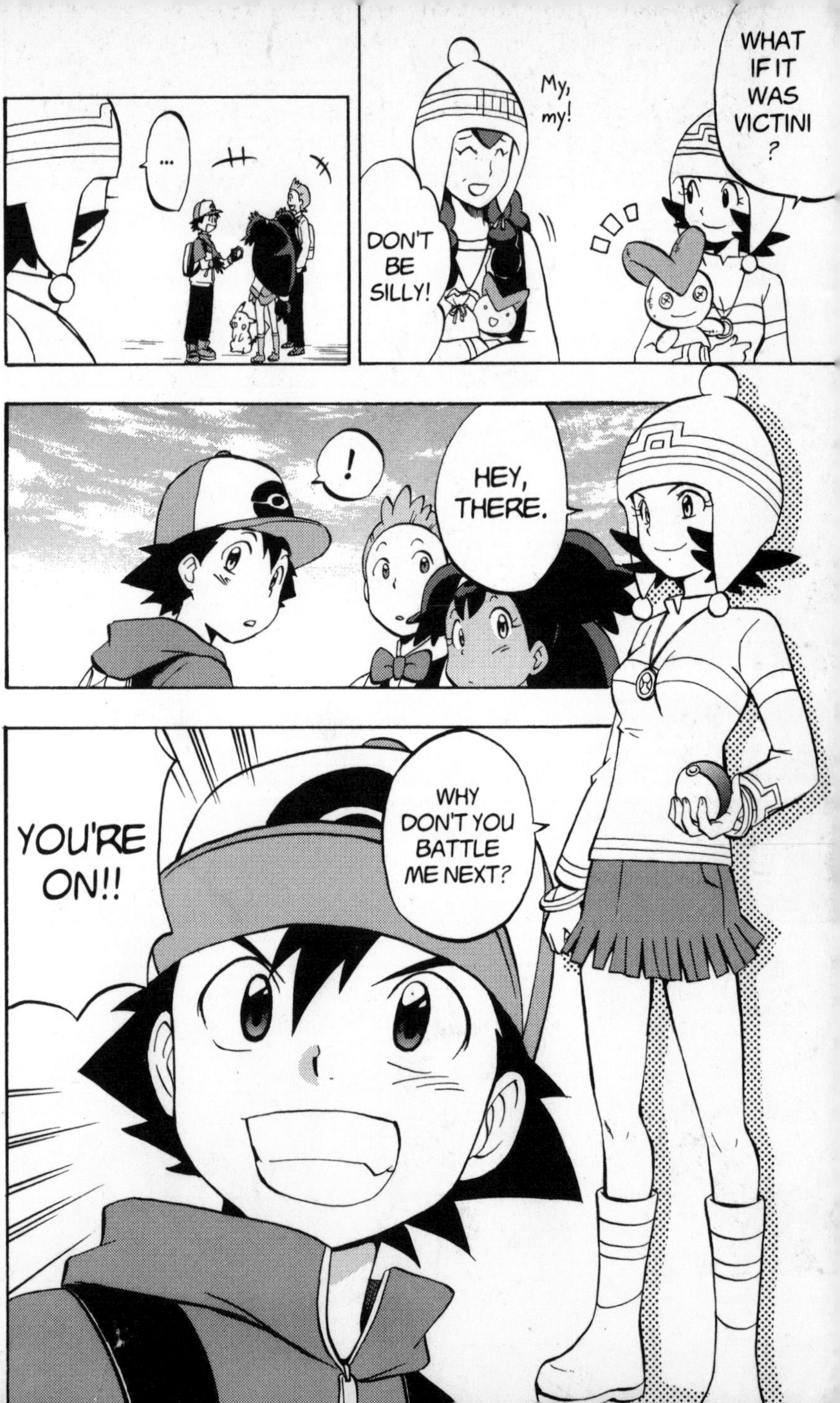
WHAT IF IT WAS VICTINI?
My, my!
DON'T BE SILLY!
...
HEY, THERE.
!
WHY DON'T YOU BATTLE ME NEXT?
YOU'RE ON!!

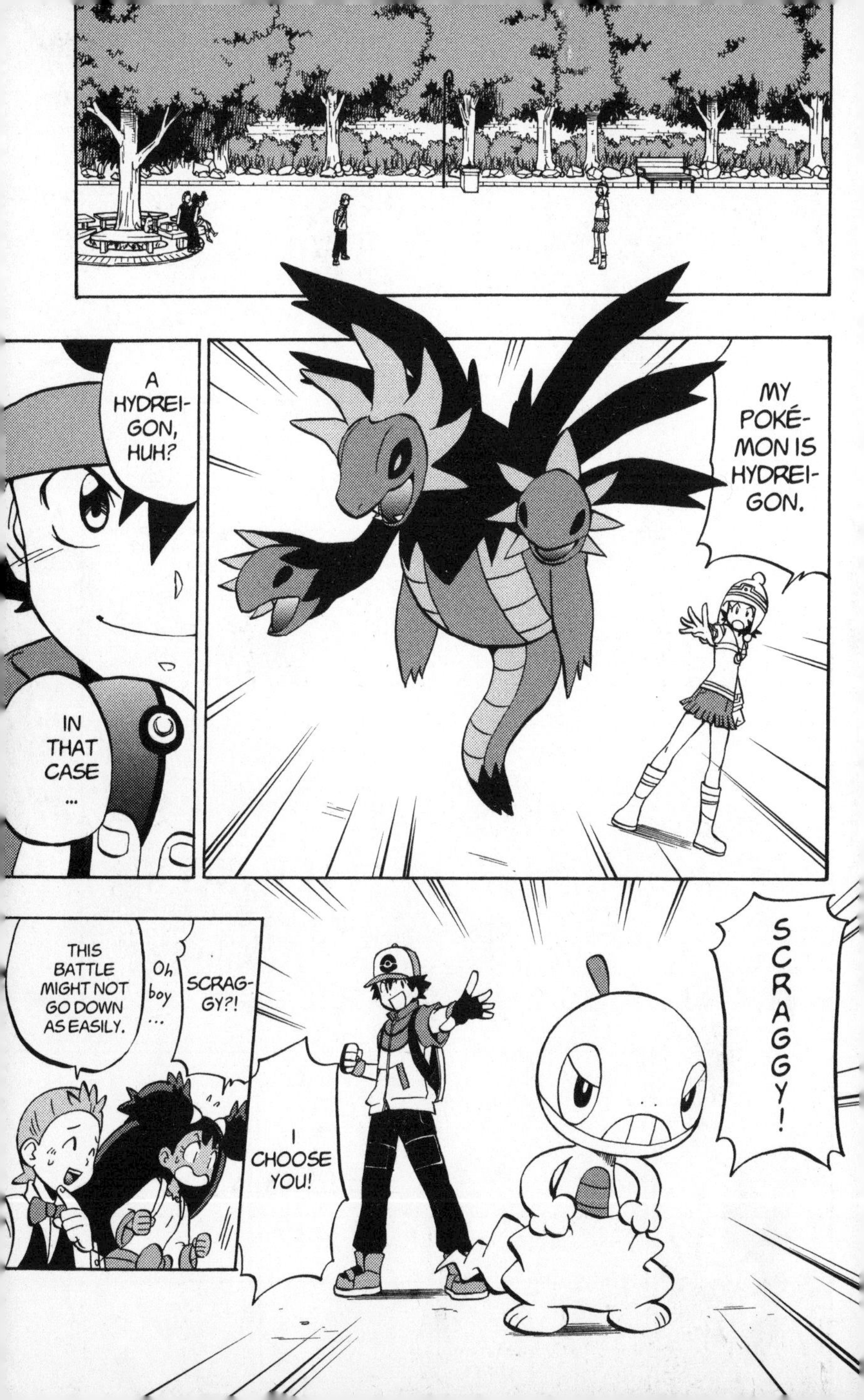
MY POKÉMON IS HYDREIGON.
A HYDREIGON, HUH?
IN THAT CASE...
SCRAGGY!
SCRAGGY?!
Oh boy...
THIS BATTLE MIGHT NOT GO DOWN AS EASILY.
I CHOOSE YOU!

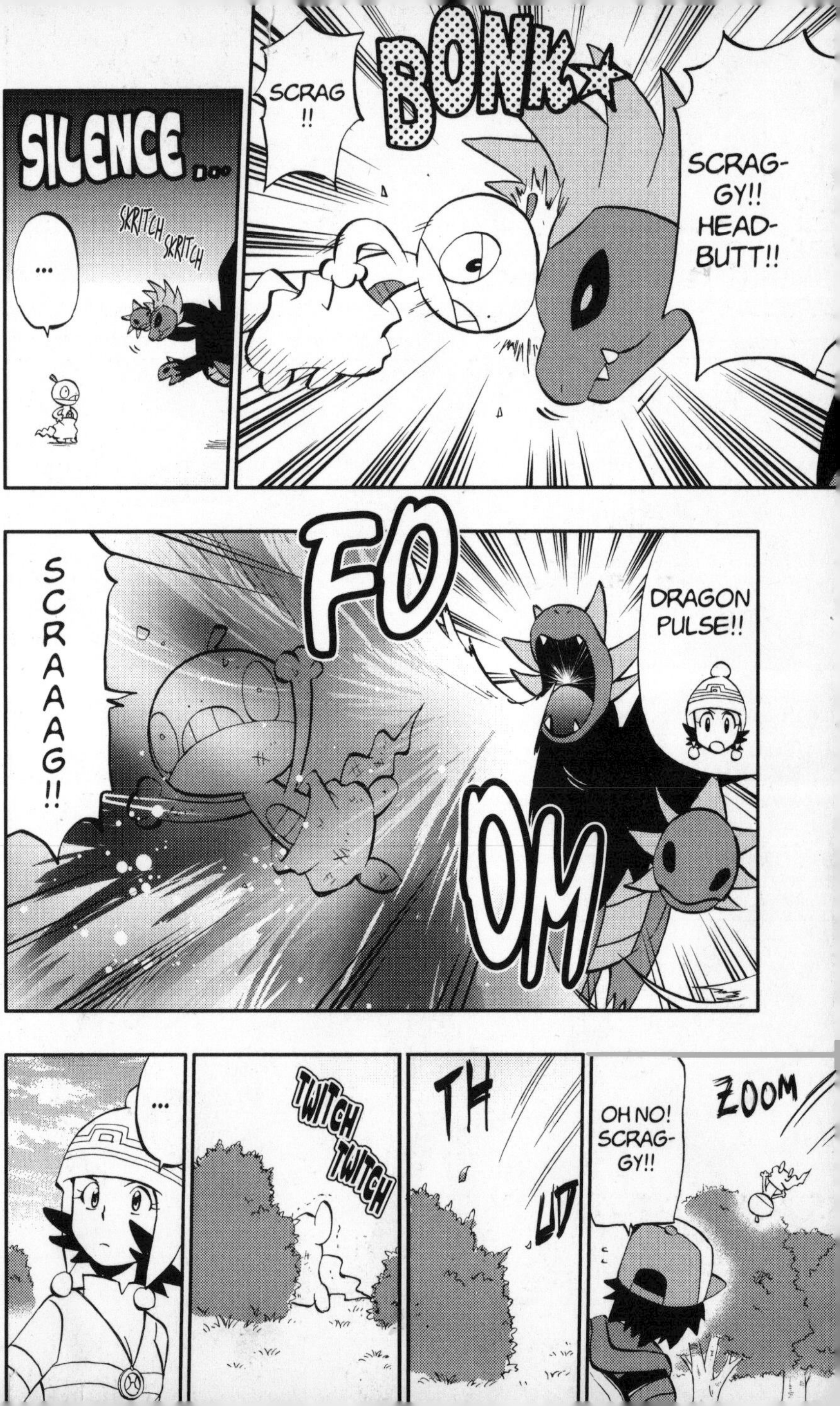
SCRAG-GY!! HEAD-BUTT!!
BONK☆
SCRAG !!
SILENCE
...
SKRITCH SKRITCH
DRAGON PULSE!!
FOOM
SCRAAAAG!!
ZOOM
OH NO! SCRAG-GY!!
THUD
TWITCH TWITCH
...

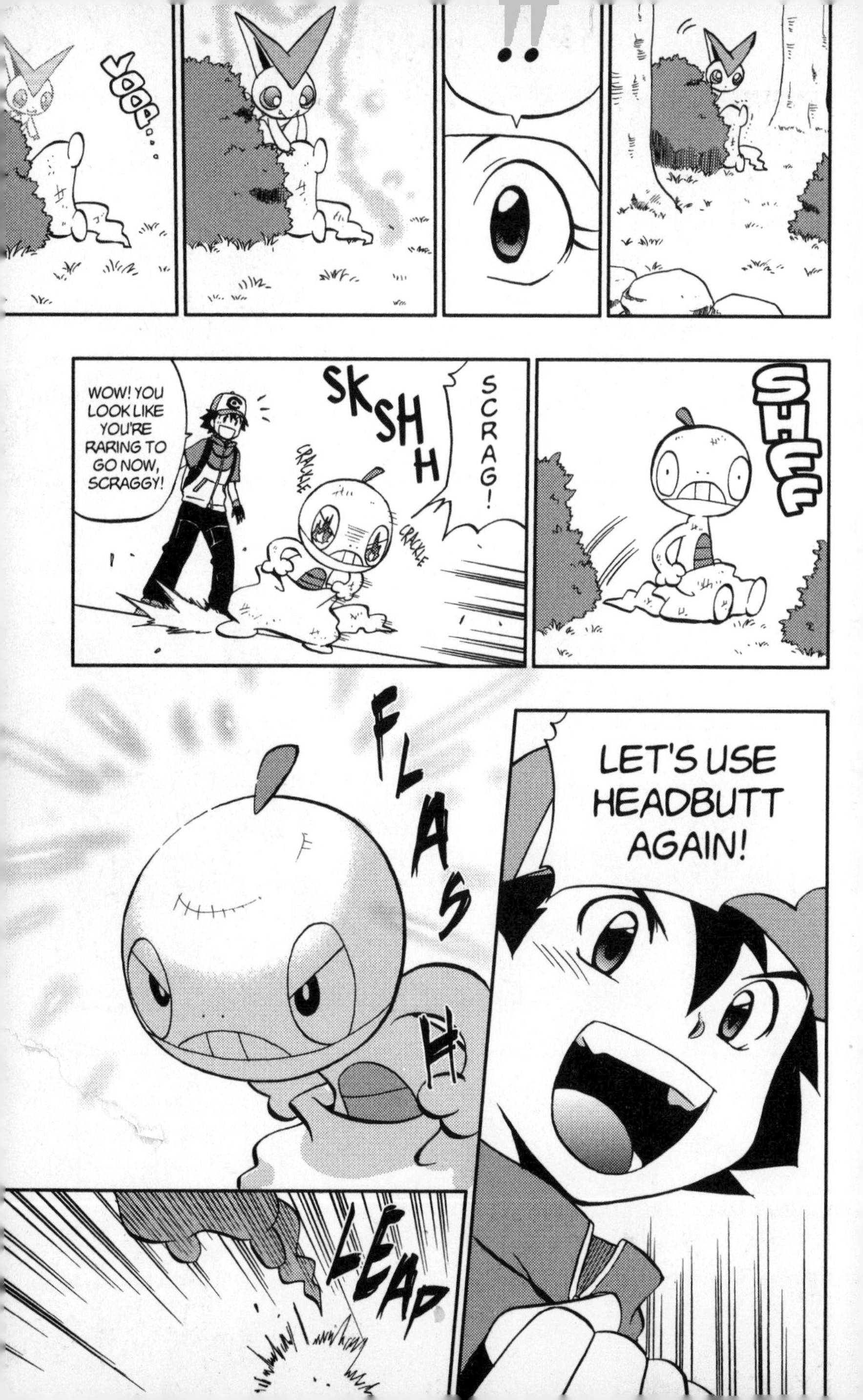

!!
VOOP...
SCRAG!
SKSHH
CRACKLE
CRACKLE
WOW! YOU LOOK LIKE YOU'RE RARING TO GO NOW, SCRAGGY!
SHFF
LET'S USE HEADBUTT AGAIN!
FLASH
LEAP

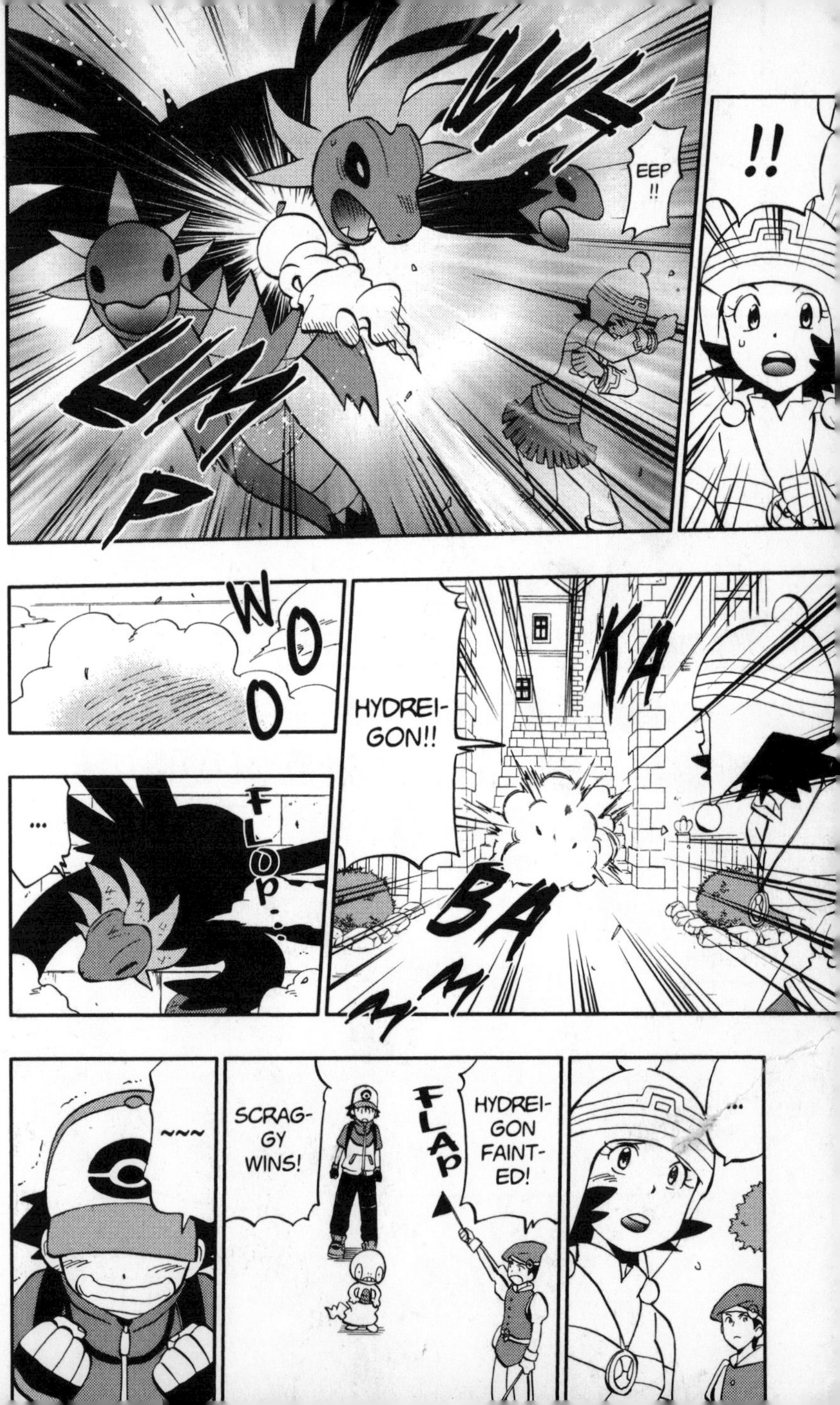
!!
EEP !!
CLUMP
KA
HYDREI-GON!!
BAMM
WOO
...
FLOP...
...
HYDREI-GON FAINT-ED!
FLAP
SCRAG-GY WINS!
~~~
~~~

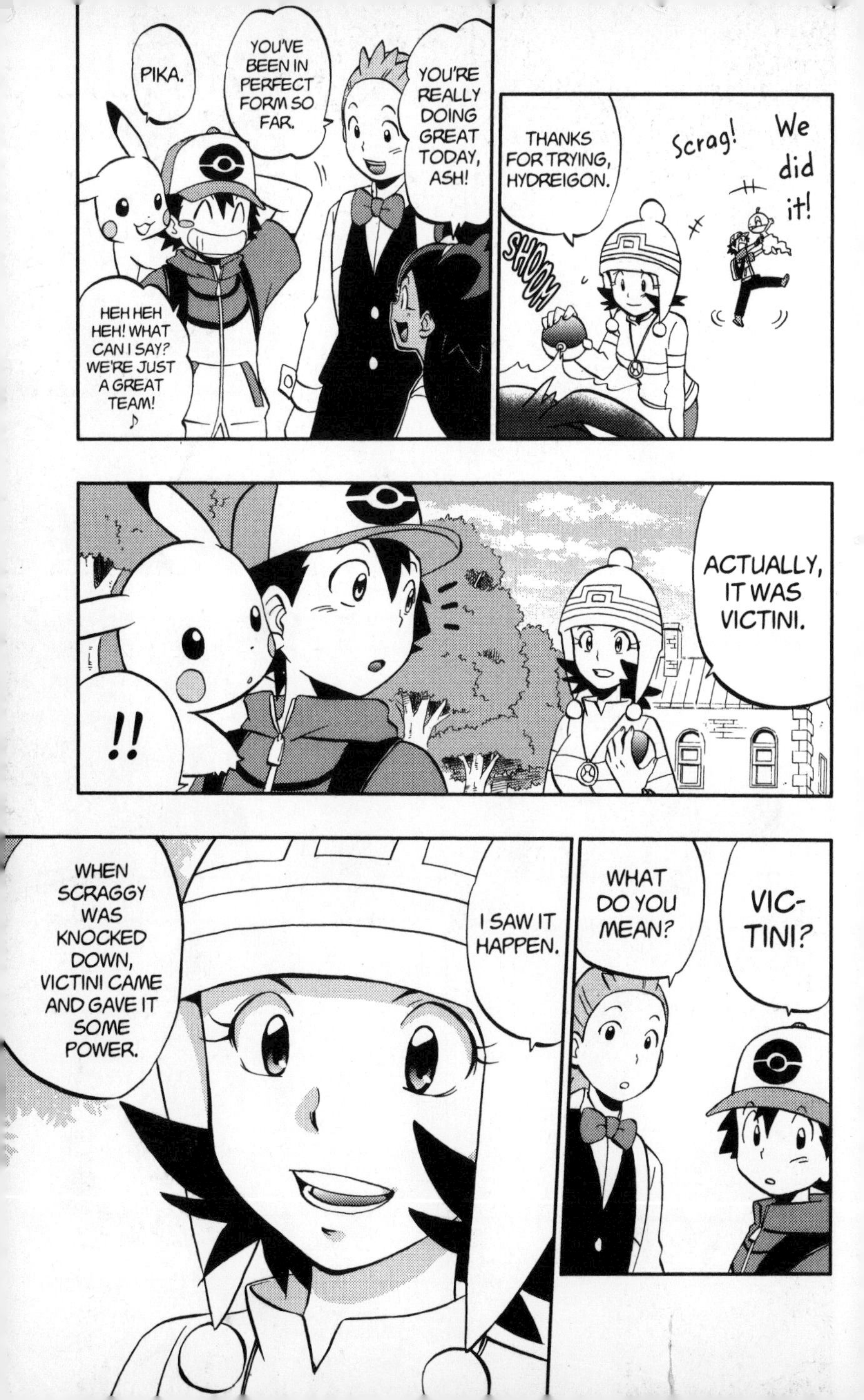
We did it!
Scrag!
THANKS FOR TRYING, HYDREIGON.
SHOOM
YOU'RE REALLY DOING GREAT TODAY, ASH!
YOU'VE BEEN IN PERFECT FORM SO FAR.
PIKA.
HEH HEH HEH! WHAT CAN I SAY? WE'RE JUST A GREAT TEAM! ♪
ACTUALLY, IT WAS VICTINI.
!!
VIC-TINI?
WHAT DO YOU MEAN?
I SAW IT HAPPEN.
WHEN SCRAGGY WAS KNOCKED DOWN, VICTINI CAME AND GAVE IT SOME POWER.

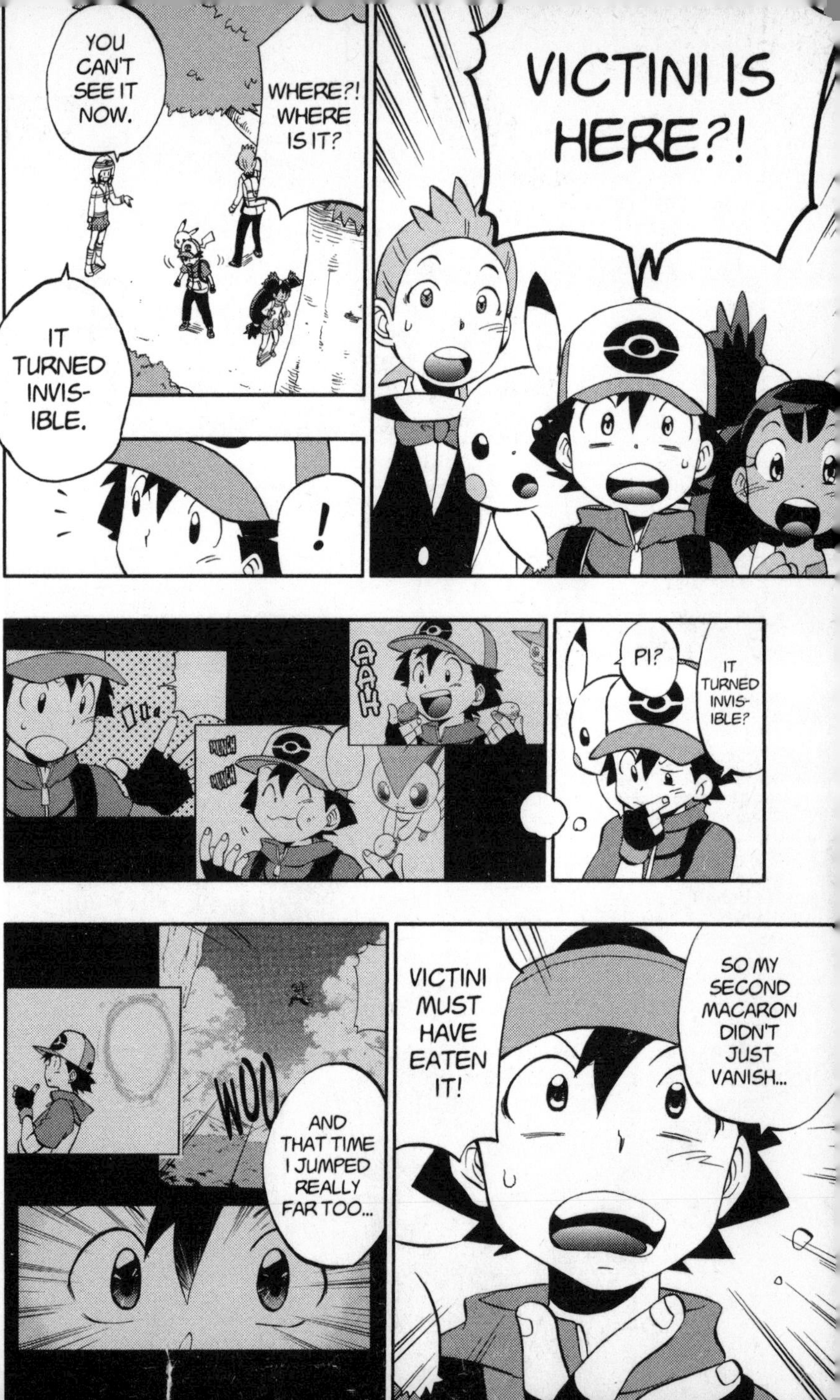
VICTINI IS HERE?!
WHERE?! WHERE IS IT?
YOU CAN'T SEE IT NOW.
IT TURNED INVISIBLE.
!
PI?
IT TURNED INVISIBLE?
AAAH
MUNCH
MUNCH
SO MY SECOND MACARON DIDN'T JUST VANISH...
VICTINI MUST HAVE EATEN IT!
WOO
AND THAT TIME I JUMPED REALLY FAR TOO...

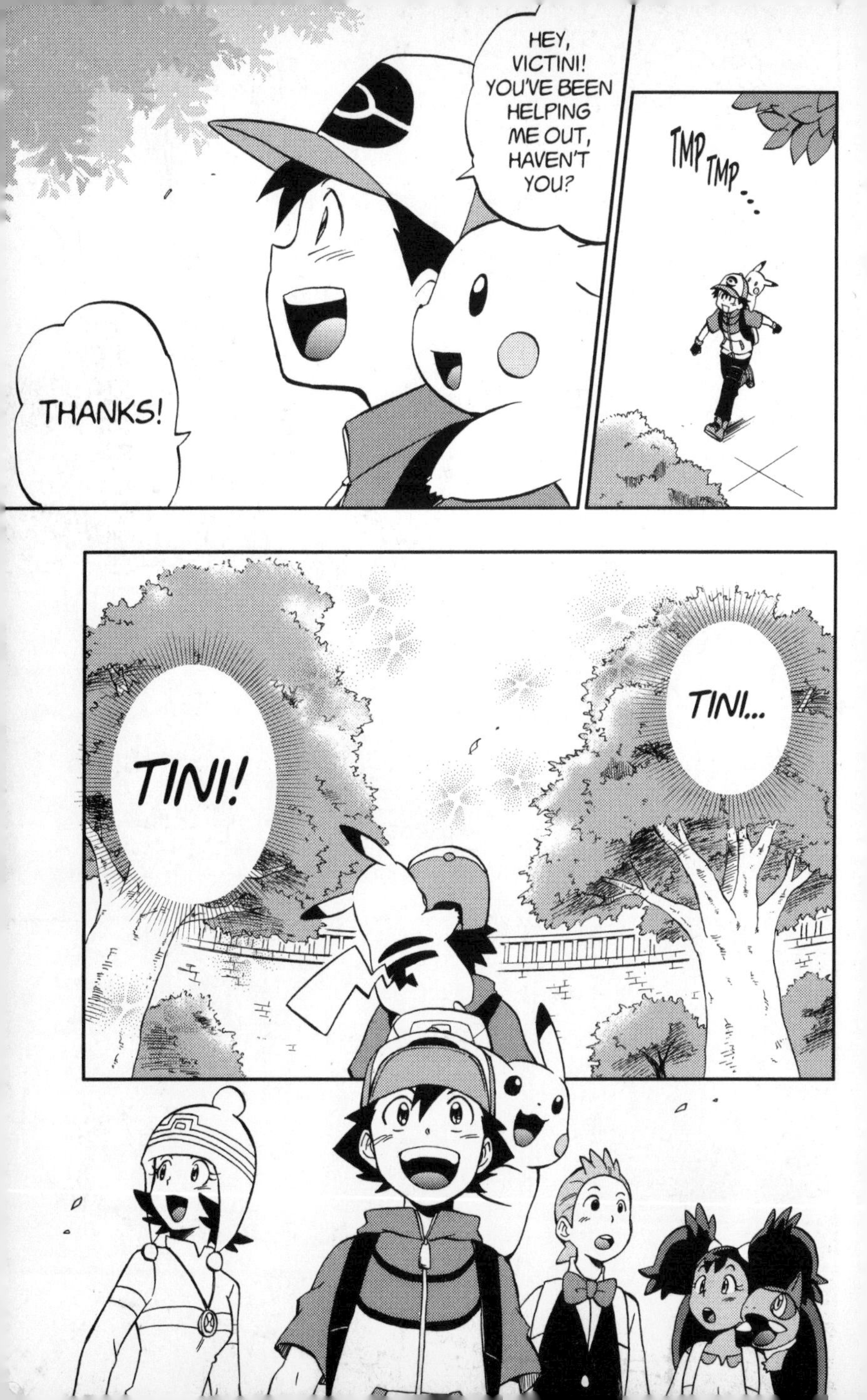
TMP TMP...
HEY, VICTINI! YOU'VE BEEN HELPING ME OUT, HAVEN'T YOU?
THANKS!
TINI...
TINI!

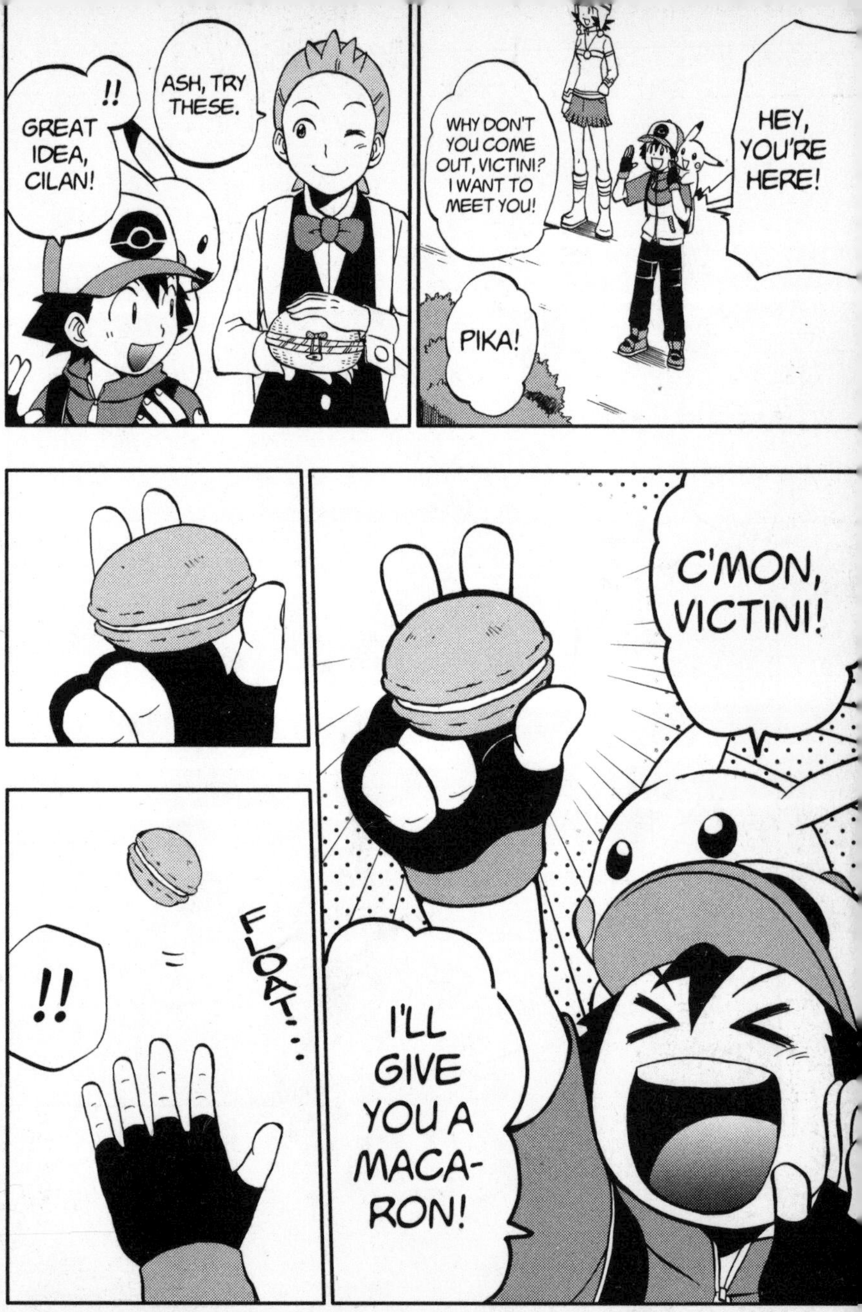
HEY, YOU'RE HERE!
WHY DON'T YOU COME OUT, VICTINI? I WANT TO MEET YOU!
PIKA!
ASH, TRY THESE.
!! GREAT IDEA, CILAN!
C'MON, VICTINI!
I'LL GIVE YOU A MACA-RON!
FLOAT...
!!

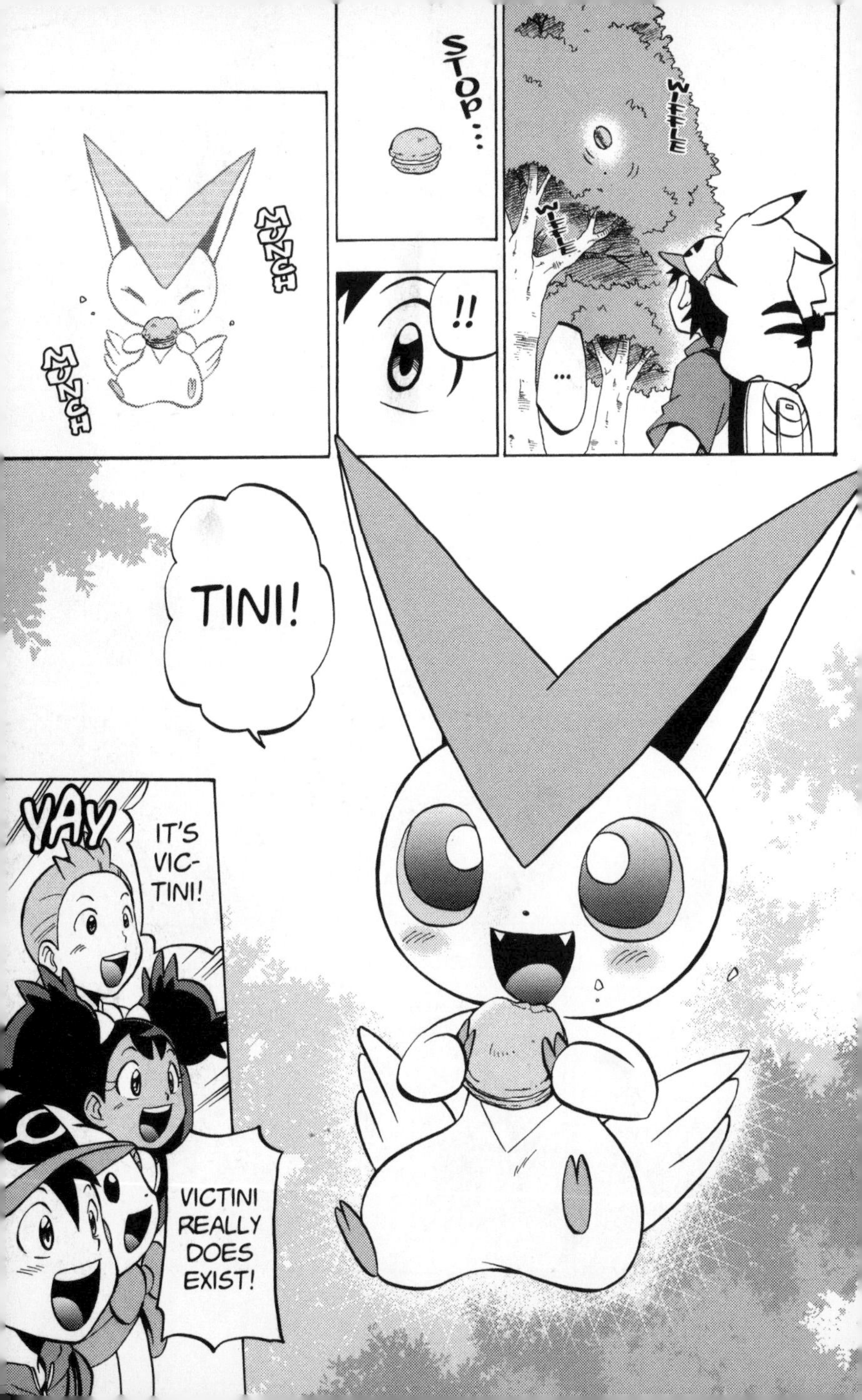
WIFFLE
WIFFLE
...
STOP...
!!
MUNCH
MUNCH
TINI!
YAY
IT'S VIC-TINI!
VICTINI REALLY DOES EXIST!

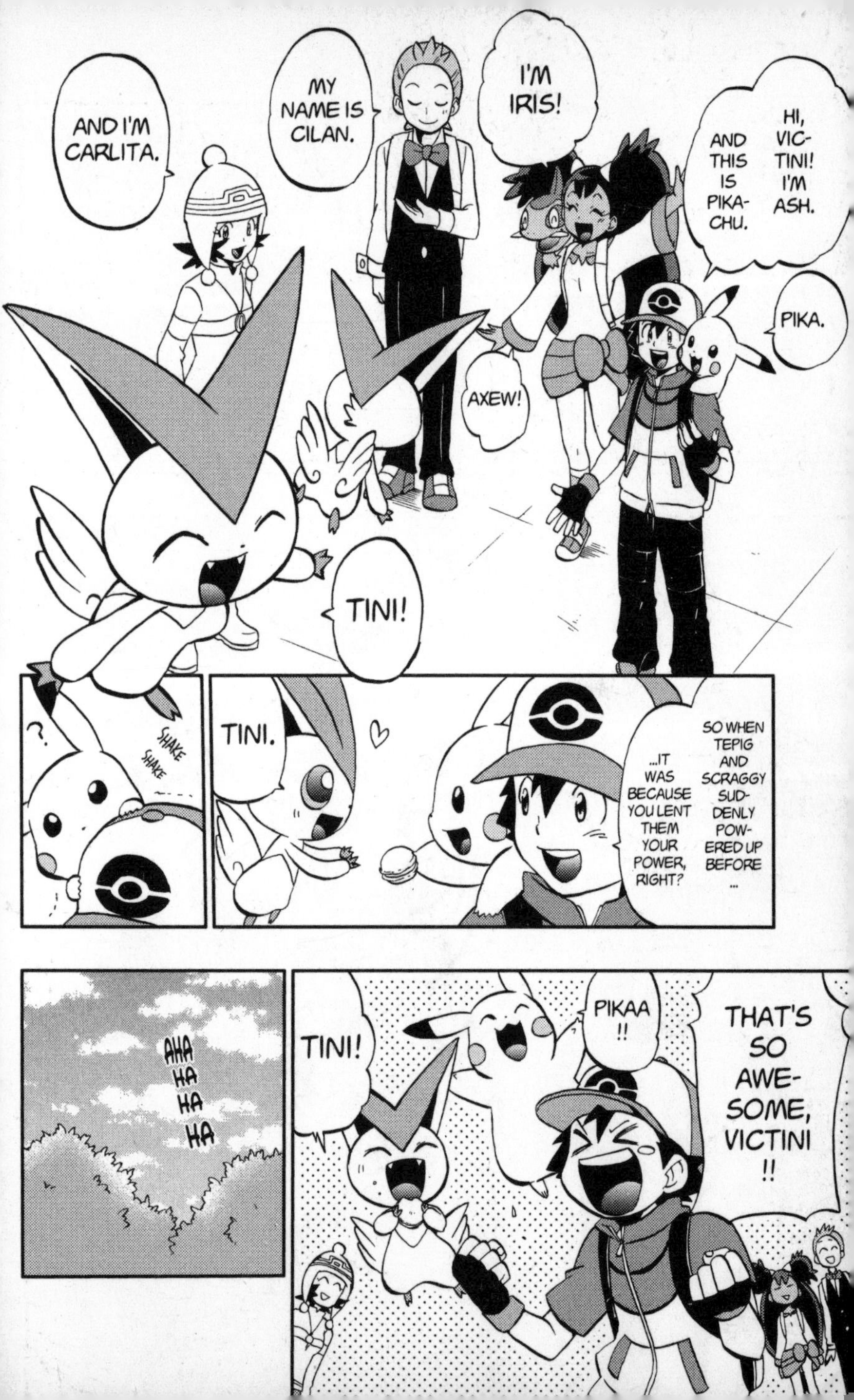
HI, VICTINI! I'M ASH.
AND THIS IS PIKACHU.
I'M IRIS!
MY NAME IS CILAN.
AND I'M CARLITA.
PIKA.
AXEW!
TINI!
SO WHEN TEPIG AND SCRAGGY SUDDENLY POWERED UP BEFORE...
...IT WAS BECAUSE YOU LENT THEM YOUR POWER, RIGHT?
TINI.
?
SHAKE SHAKE
THAT'S SO AWESOME, VICTINI!!
PIKAA!!
TINI!
AHA HA HA HA

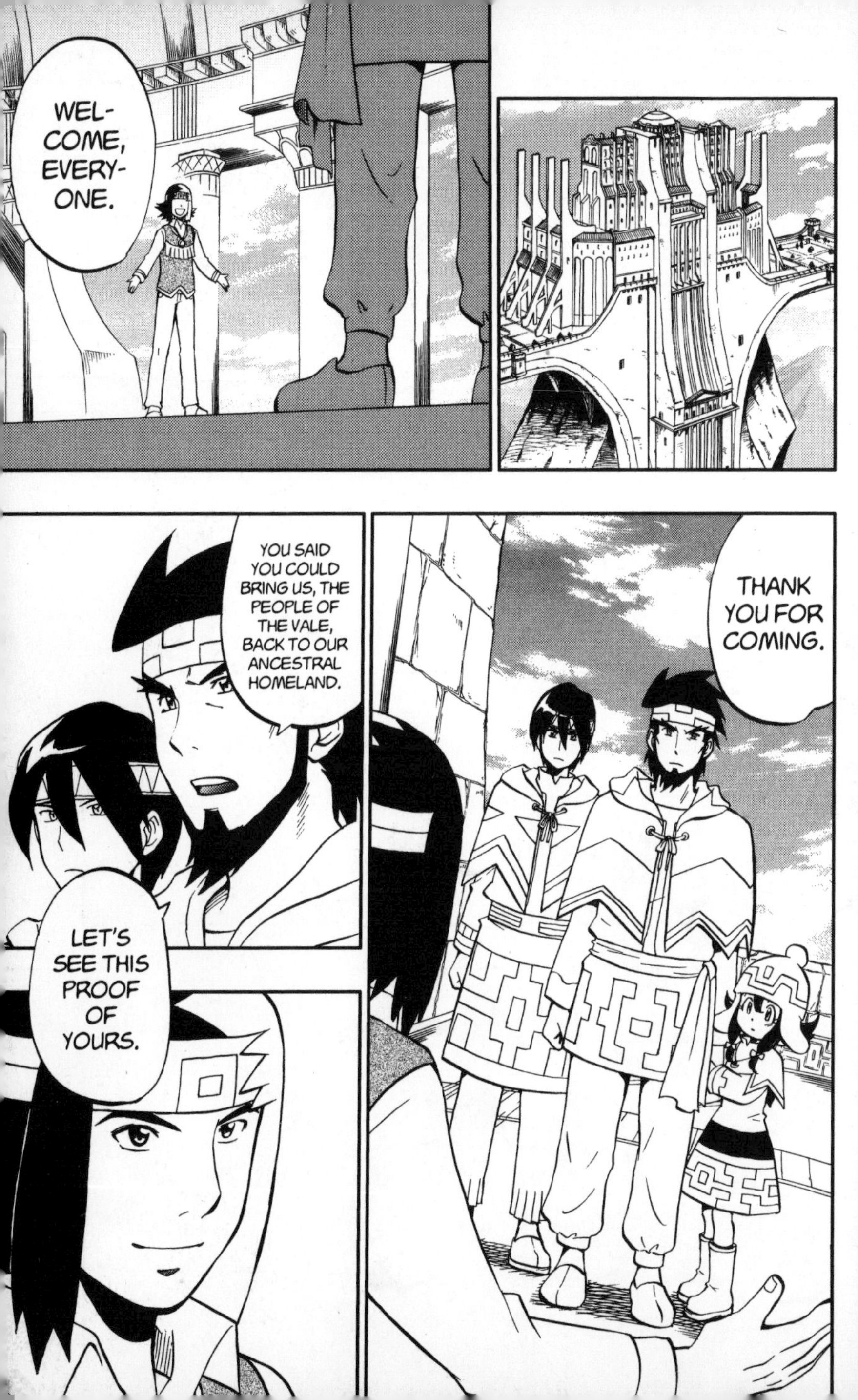
WEL-COME, EVERY-ONE.
THANK YOU FOR COMING.
YOU SAID YOU COULD BRING US, THE PEOPLE OF THE VALE, BACK TO OUR ANCESTRAL HOMELAND.
LET'S SEE THIS PROOF OF YOURS.

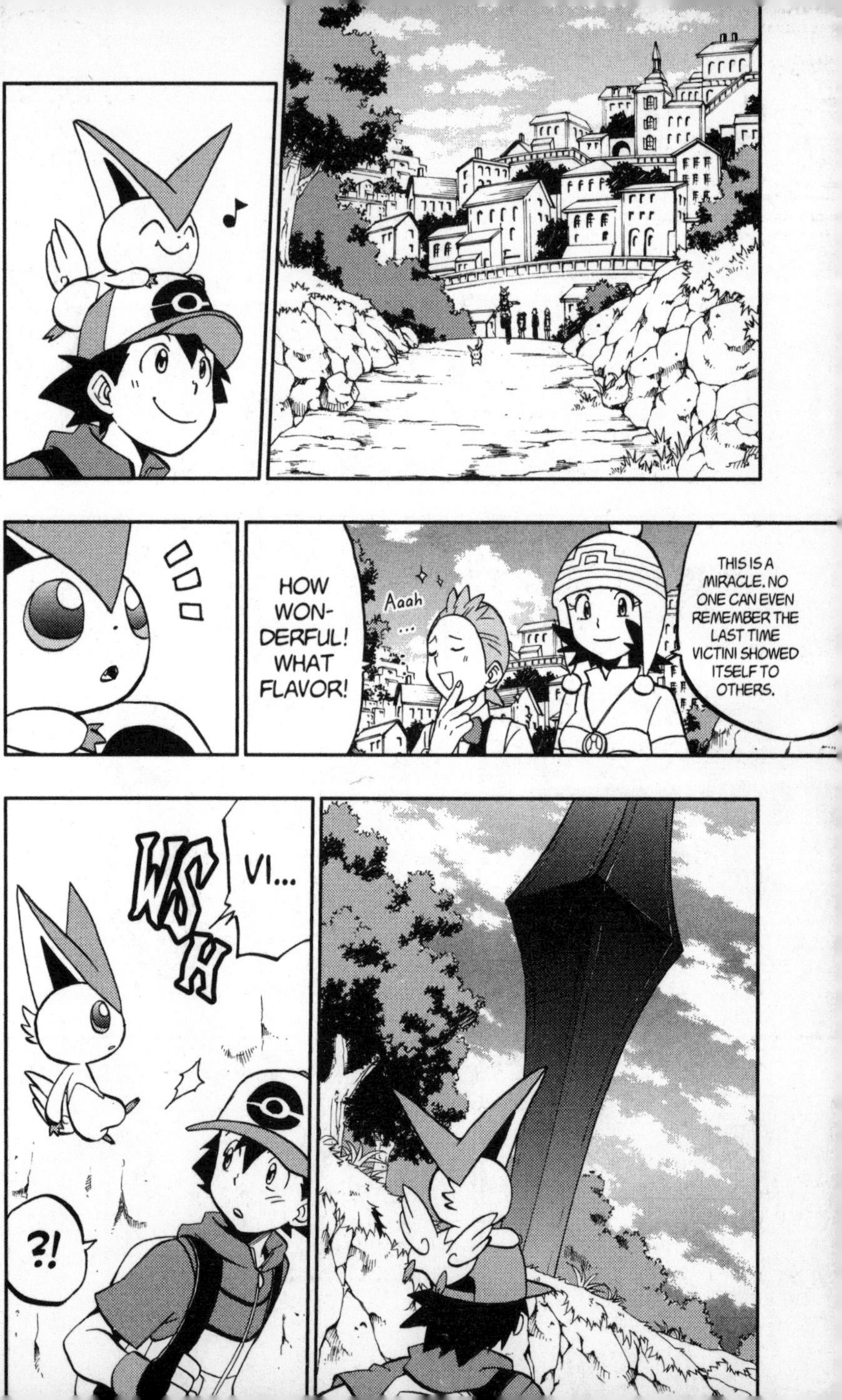
THIS IS A MIRACLE. NO ONE CAN EVEN REMEMBER THE LAST TIME VICTINI SHOWED ITSELF TO OTHERS.
Aaah...
HOW WON-DERFUL! WHAT FLAVOR!
VI...
WSH
?!

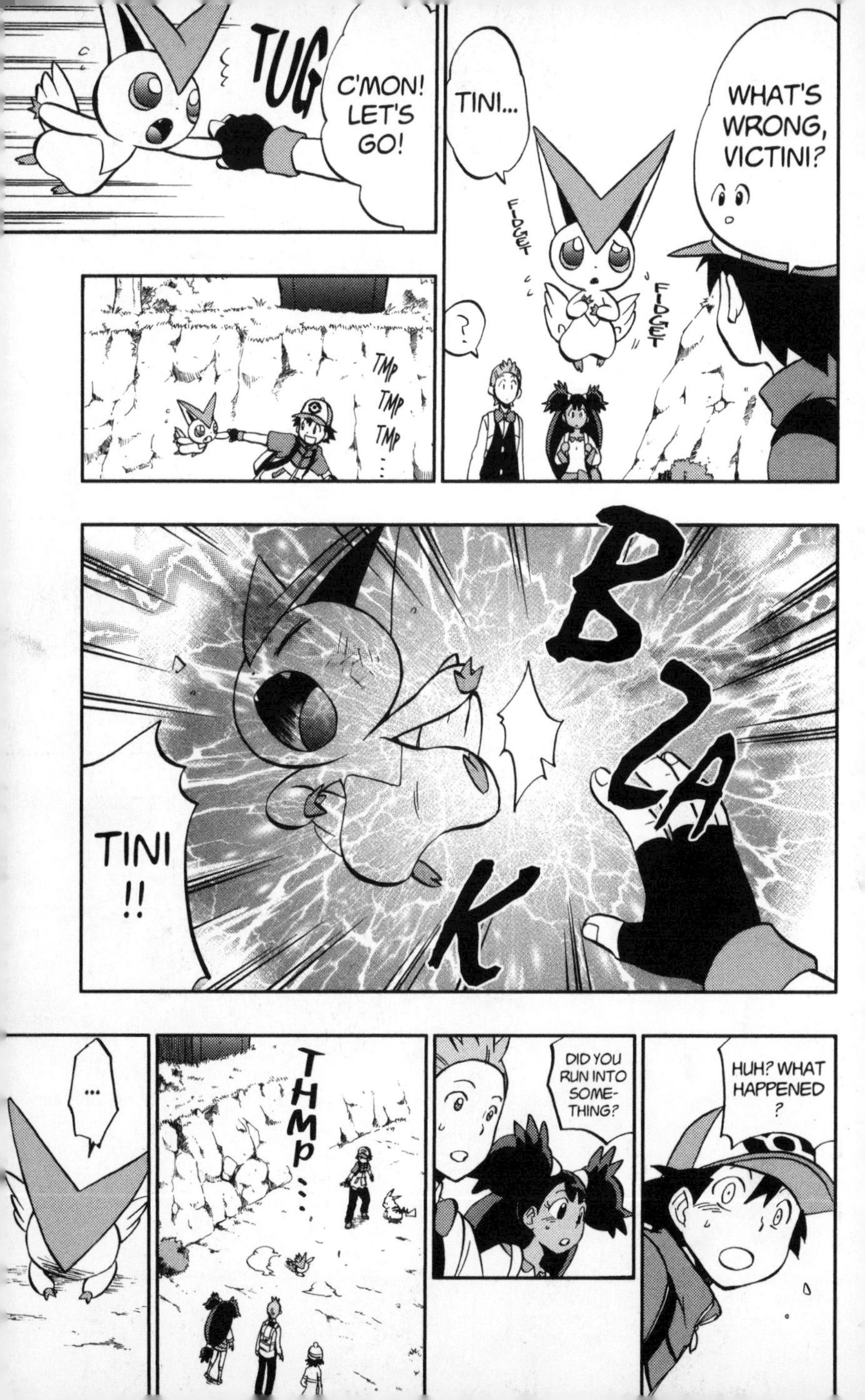

WHAT'S WRONG, VICTINI?
TINI...
FIDGET
FIDGET
?
C'MON! LET'S GO!
TUG
TMP TMP TMP...
BLAK
TINI !!
HUH? WHAT HAPPENED?
DID YOU RUN INTO SOME-THING?
THMP...
...

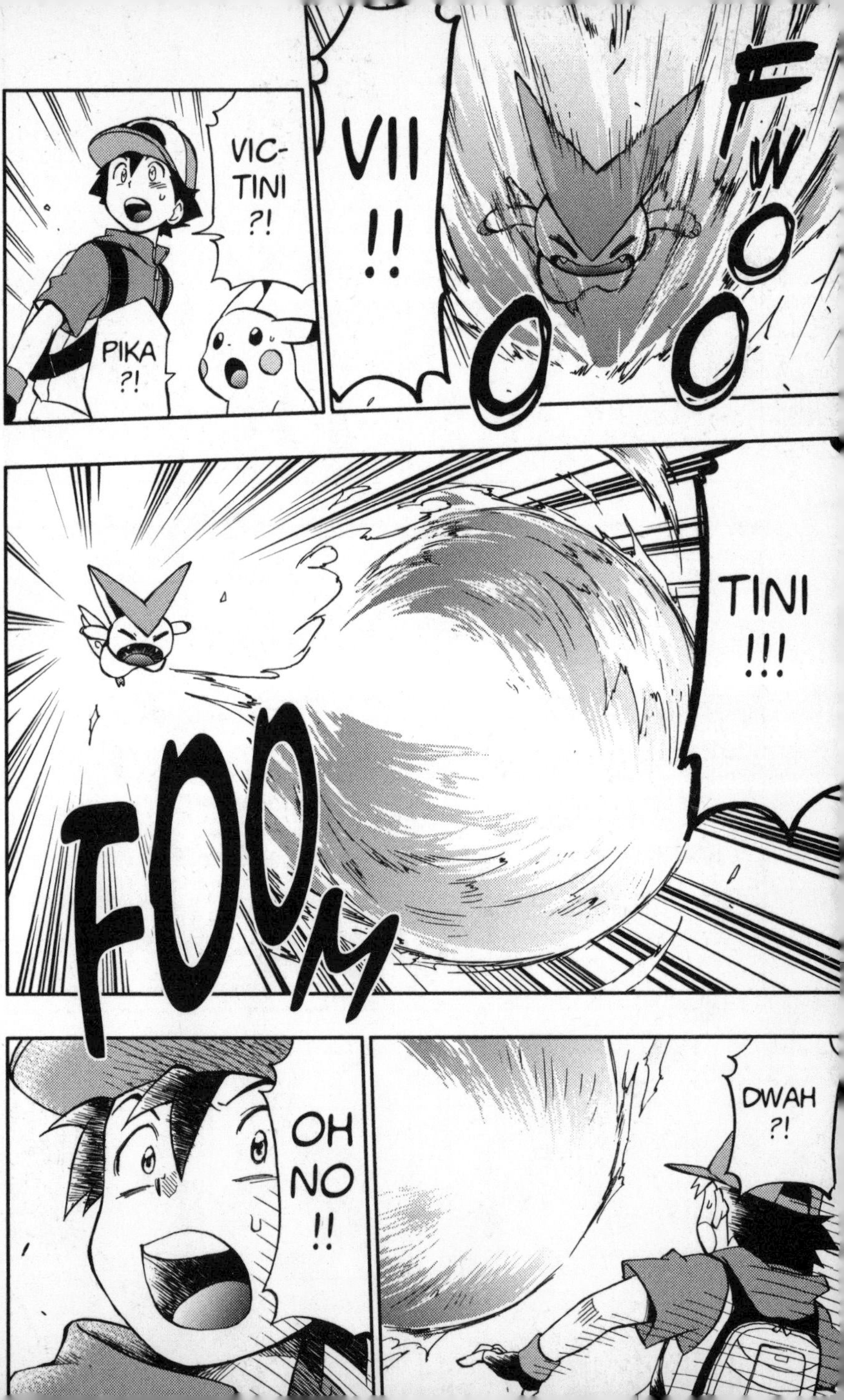
VII !!
FWOOOO
VIC-TINI ?!
PIKA ?!
TINI !!!
FOOM
DWAH ?!
OH NO !!

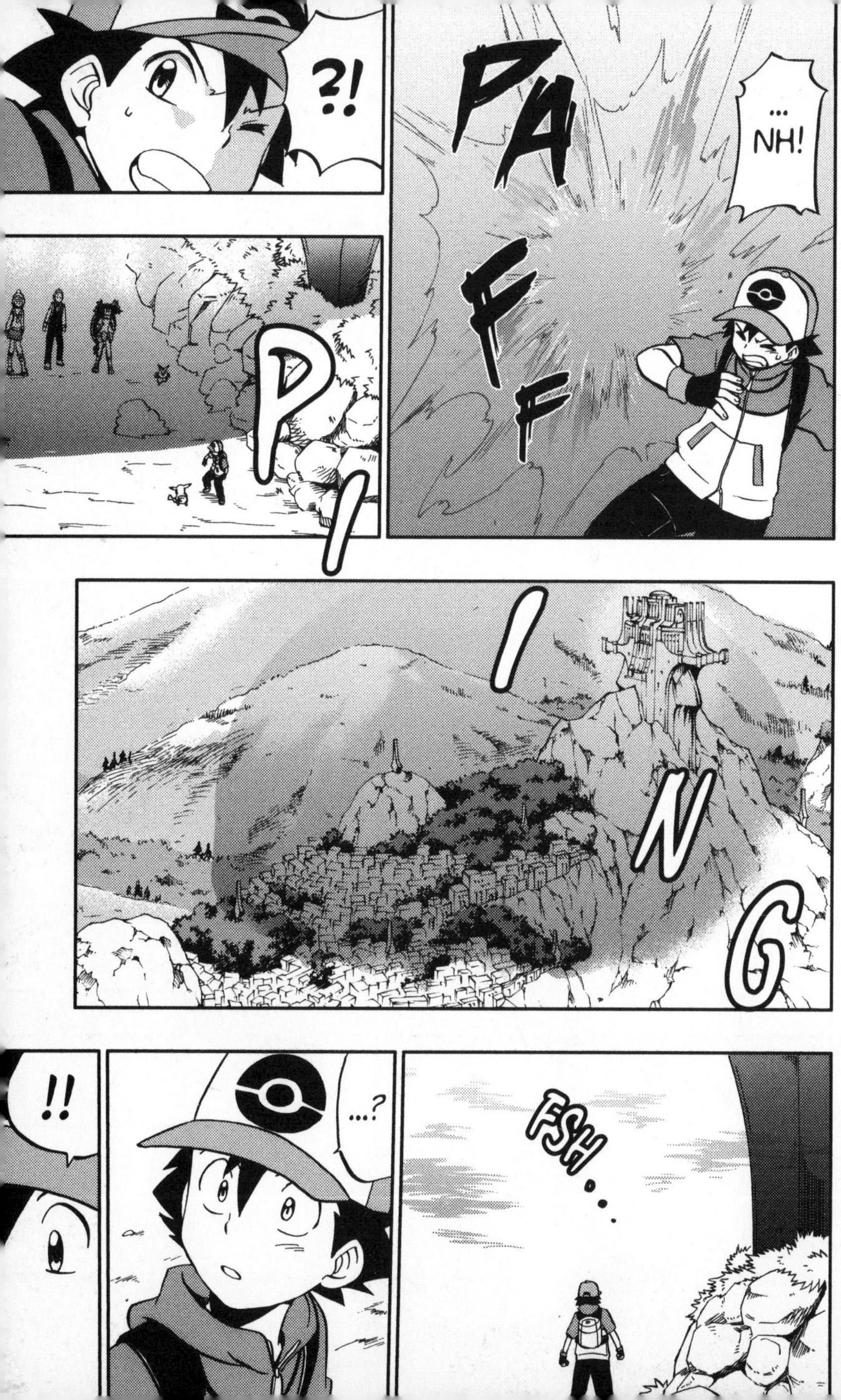
PAFFF
... NH!
?!
PIING
FSH...
...?
!!

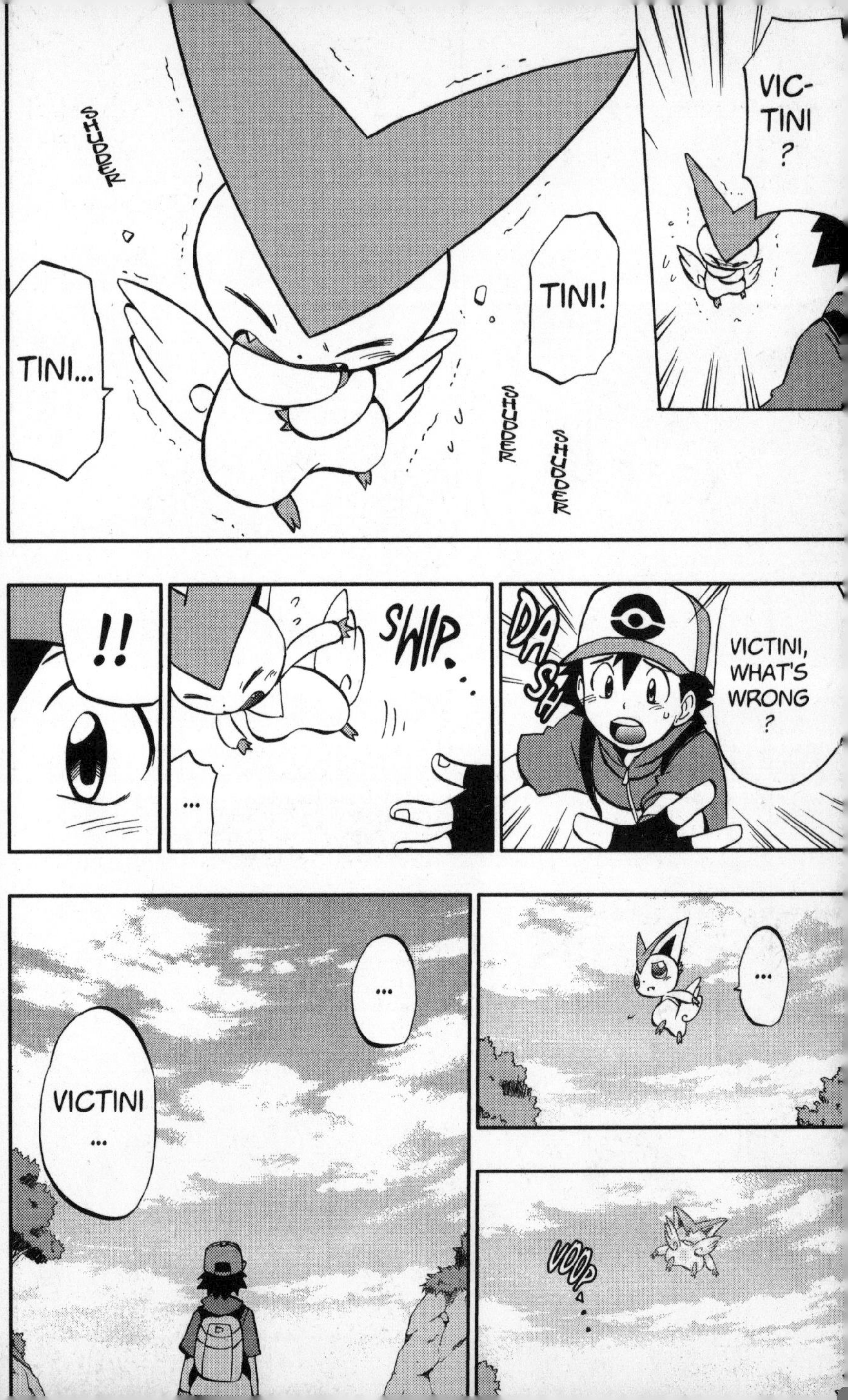
VIC-TINI?
TINI!
SHUDDER
SHUDDER
SHUDDER
TINI...
DASH
VICTINI, WHAT'S WRONG?
SWIP
...
!!
...
VOOP
...
VICTINI...

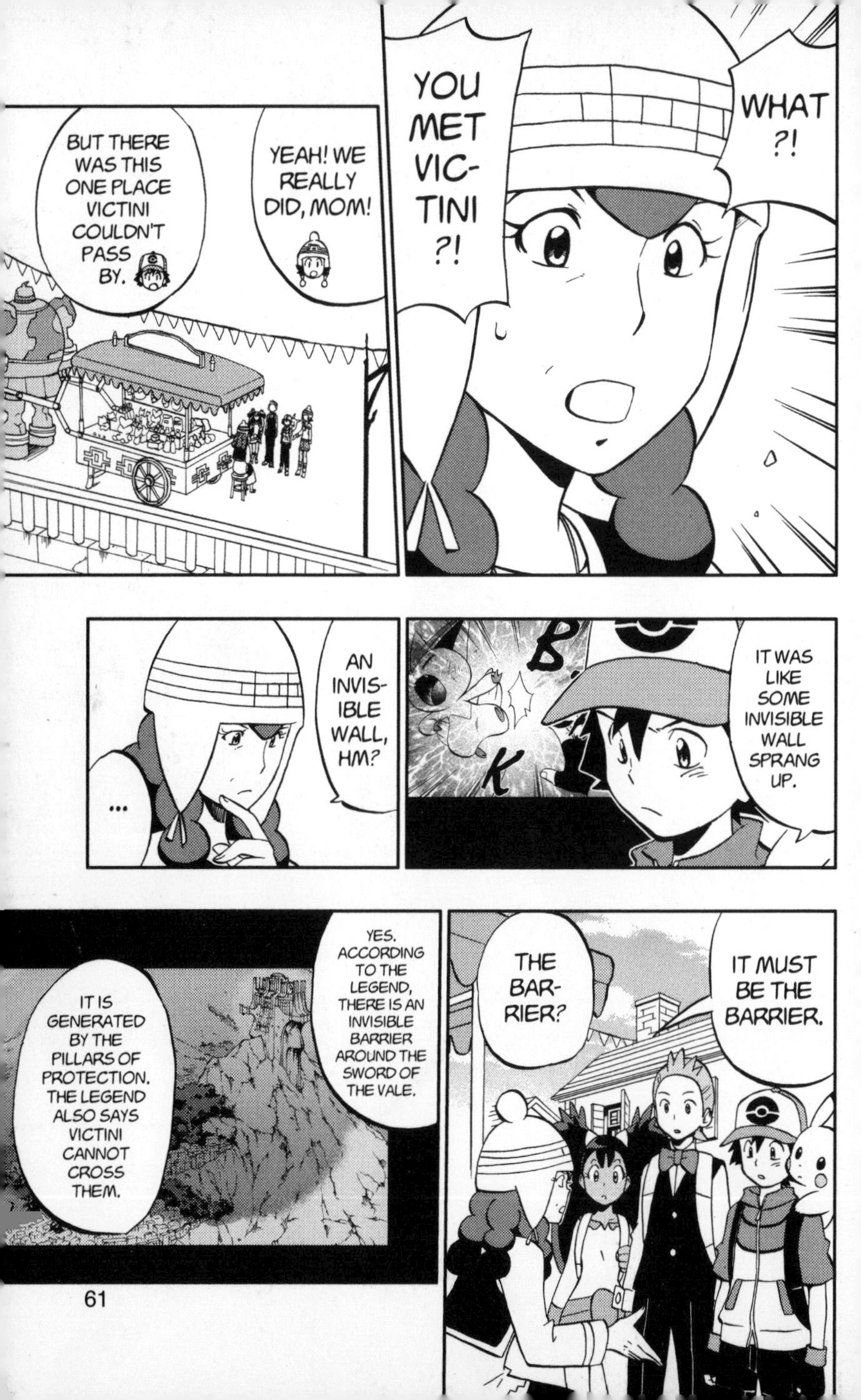
WHAT?!
YOU MET VICTINI?!
YEAH! WE REALLY DID, MOM!
BUT THERE WAS THIS ONE PLACE VICTINI COULDN'T PASS BY.
IT WAS LIKE SOME INVISIBLE WALL SPRANG UP.
B...K
AN INVISIBLE WALL, HM?
...
IT MUST BE THE BARRIER.
THE BARRIER?
YES. ACCORDING TO THE LEGEND, THERE IS AN INVISIBLE BARRIER AROUND THE SWORD OF THE VALE.
IT IS GENERATED BY THE PILLARS OF PROTECTION. THE LEGEND ALSO SAYS VICTINI CANNOT CROSS THEM.

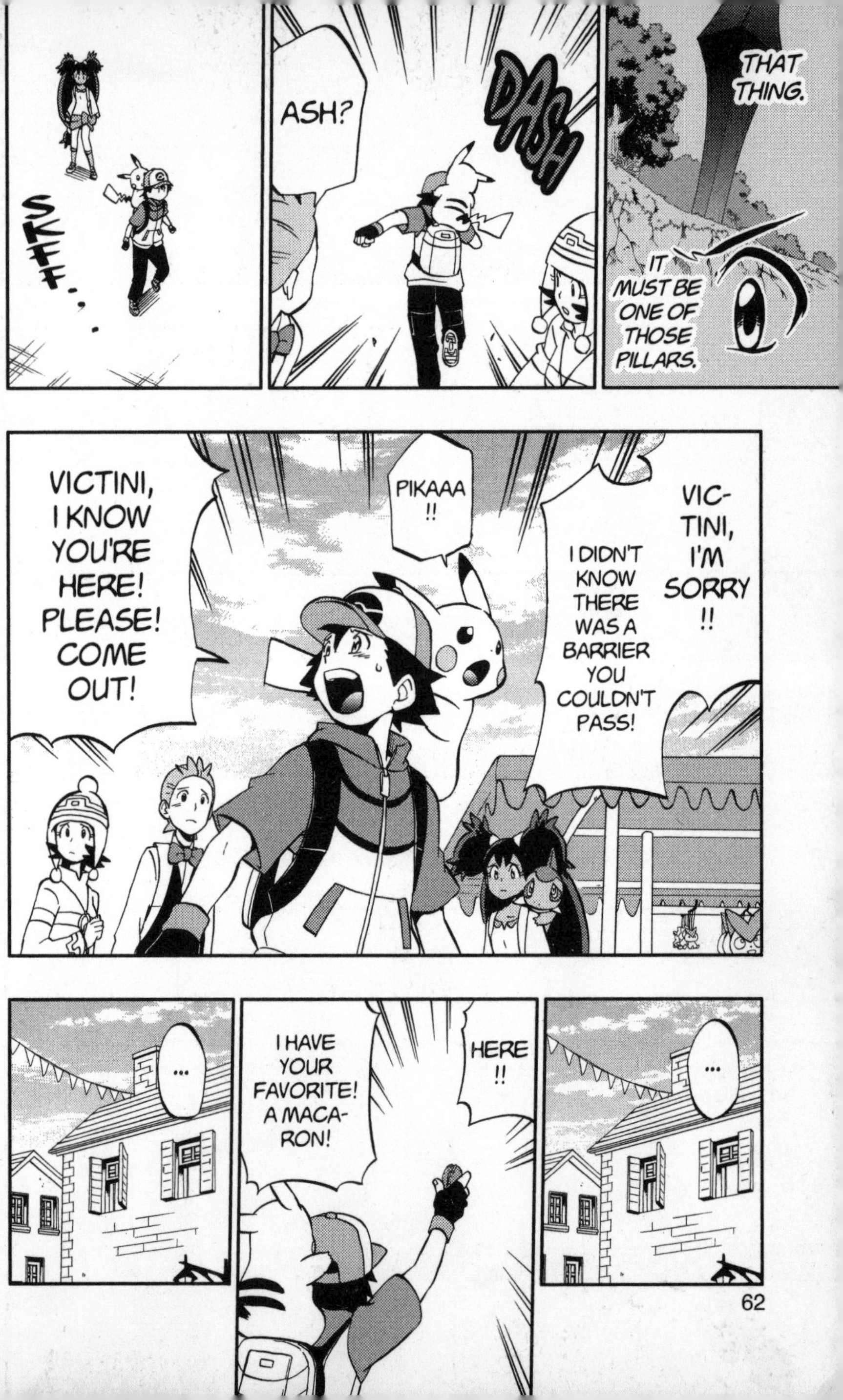
THAT THING.
IT MUST BE ONE OF THOSE PILLARS.
ASH?
DASH
SKFFF...
VIC-TINI, I'M SORRY!!
I DIDN'T KNOW THERE WAS A BARRIER YOU COULDN'T PASS!
PIKAAA!!
VICTINI, I KNOW YOU'RE HERE! PLEASE! COME OUT!
...
HERE!!
I HAVE YOUR FAVORITE! A MACA-RON!
...

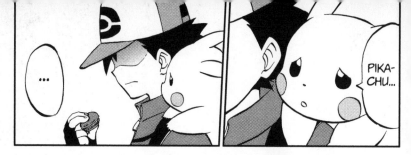

...

PIKA-CHU...

TINI!

POP

CHU! ♡

OH, WELL. HERE, PIKACHU. YOU CAN HAVE IT.

Aha ha ha! C'mon, Victini! Let's be friends again!

Tiniiii!

GASP

HEE!

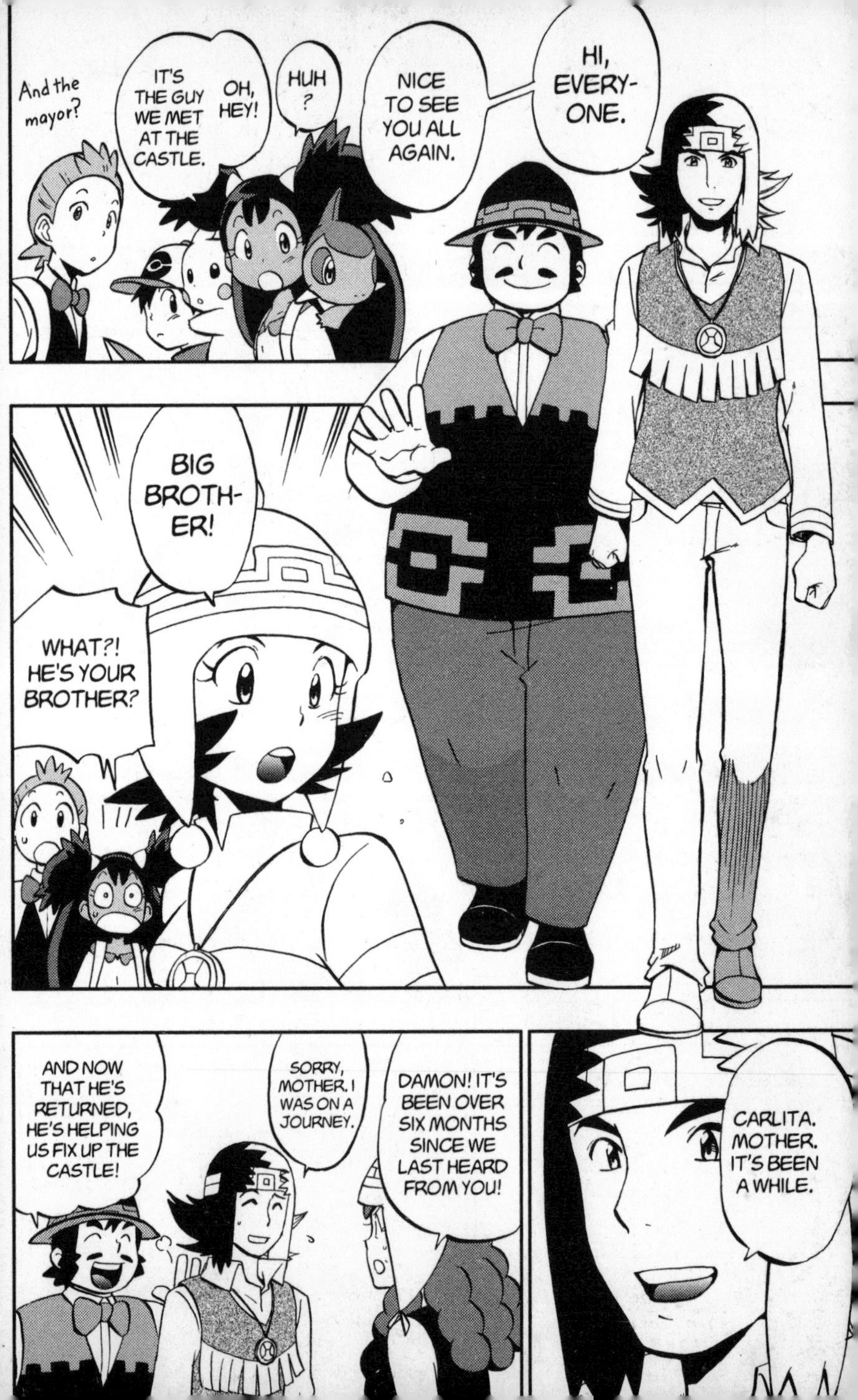
HI, EVERYONE.
NICE TO SEE YOU ALL AGAIN.
HUH?
OH, HEY!
IT'S THE GUY WE MET AT THE CASTLE.
And the mayor?
BIG BROTHER!
WHAT?! HE'S YOUR BROTHER?
CARLITA. MOTHER. IT'S BEEN A WHILE.
DAMON! IT'S BEEN OVER SIX MONTHS SINCE WE LAST HEARD FROM YOU!
SORRY, MOTHER. I WAS ON A JOURNEY.
AND NOW THAT HE'S RETURNED, HE'S HELPING US FIX UP THE CASTLE!

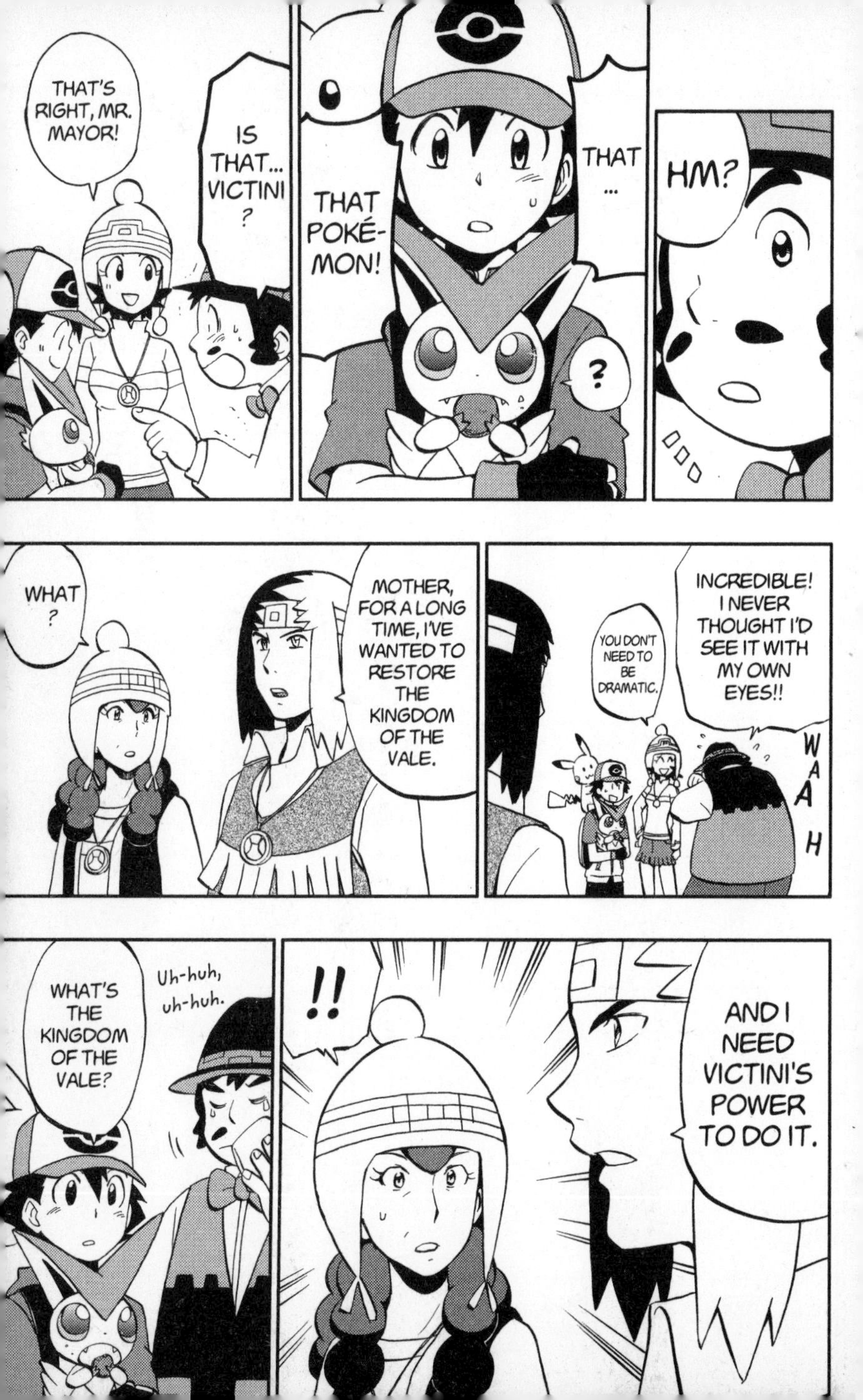
HM?
THAT ...
THAT POKÉMON!
?
IS THAT... VICTINI?
THAT'S RIGHT, MR. MAYOR!
INCREDIBLE! I NEVER THOUGHT I'D SEE IT WITH MY OWN EYES!!
YOU DON'T NEED TO BE DRAMATIC.
WAAH
MOTHER, FOR A LONG TIME, I'VE WANTED TO RESTORE THE KINGDOM OF THE VALE.
WHAT?
AND I NEED VICTINI'S POWER TO DO IT.
!!
Uh-huh, uh-huh.
WHAT'S THE KINGDOM OF THE VALE?

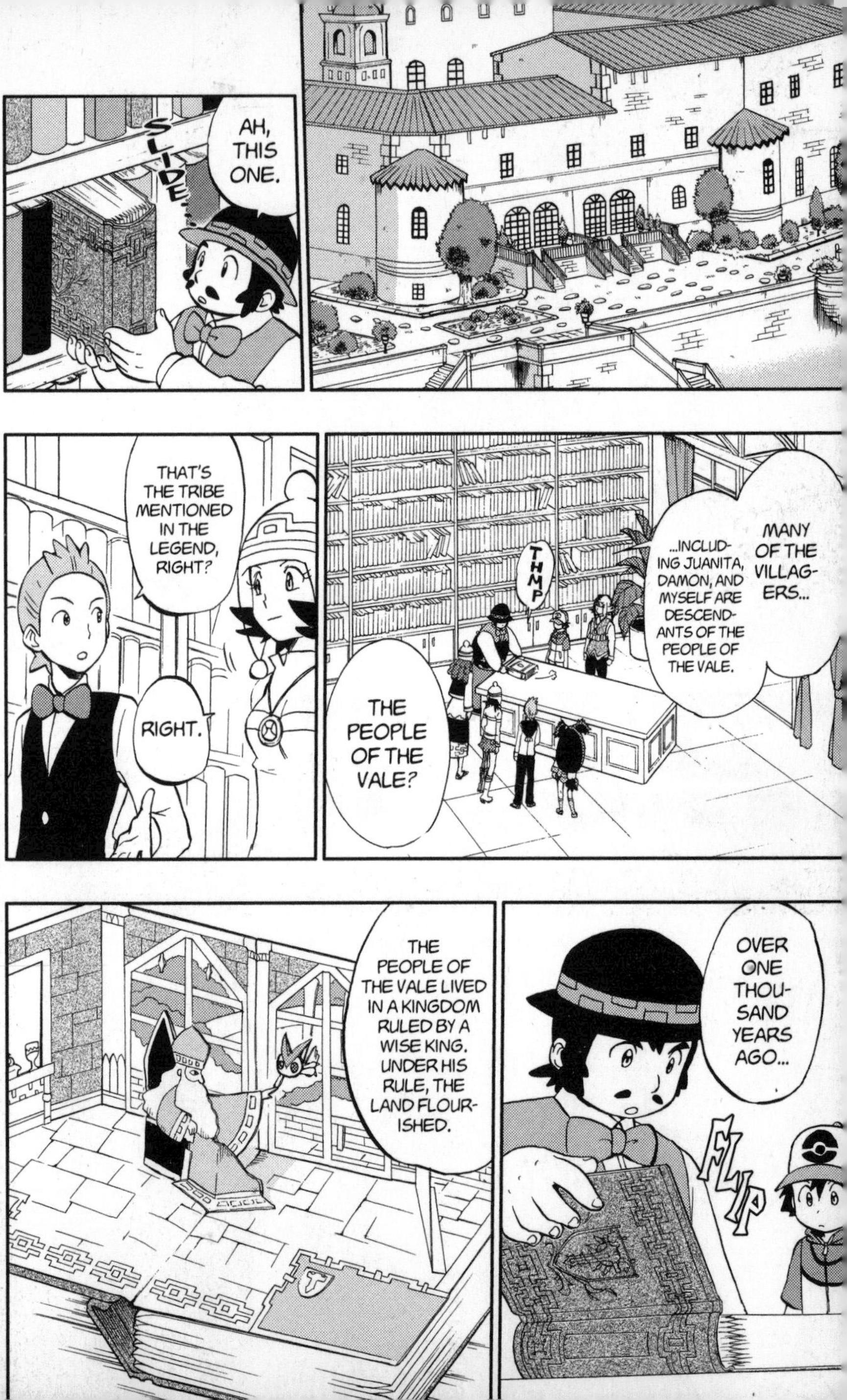
SLIDE
AH, THIS ONE.
MANY OF THE VILLAG-ERS...
...INCLUD-ING JUANITA, DAMON, AND MYSELF ARE DESCEND-ANTS OF THE PEOPLE OF THE VALE.
THMP
THE PEOPLE OF THE VALE?
THAT'S THE TRIBE MENTIONED IN THE LEGEND, RIGHT?
RIGHT.
OVER ONE THOU-SAND YEARS AGO...
FLIP
THE PEOPLE OF THE VALE LIVED IN A KINGDOM RULED BY A WISE KING. UNDER HIS RULE, THE LAND FLOUR-ISHED.

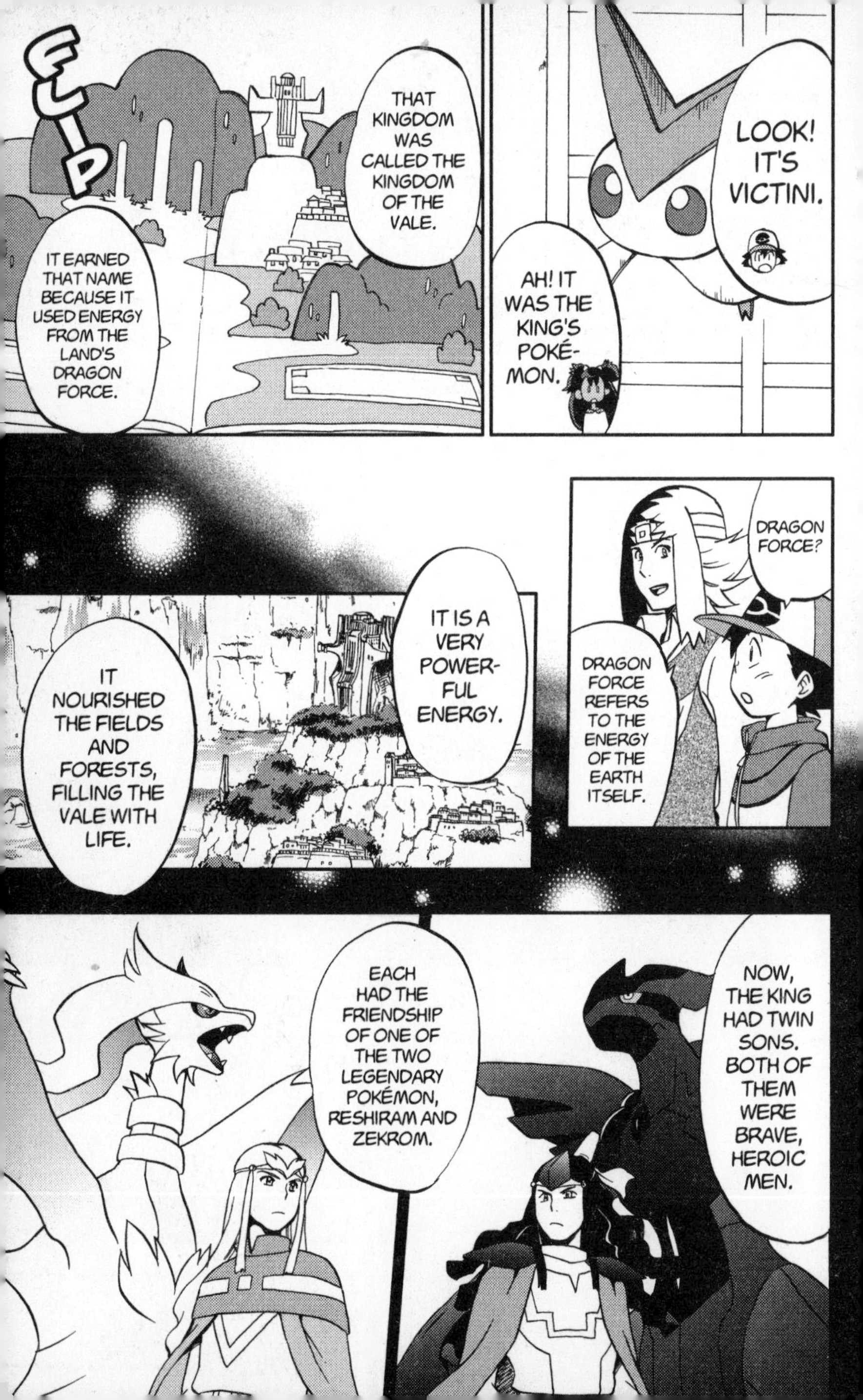
LOOK! IT'S VICTINI.
AH! IT WAS THE KING'S POKÉMON.
FLIP
THAT KINGDOM WAS CALLED THE KINGDOM OF THE VALE.
IT EARNED THAT NAME BECAUSE IT USED ENERGY FROM THE LAND'S DRAGON FORCE.
DRAGON FORCE?
DRAGON FORCE REFERS TO THE ENERGY OF THE EARTH ITSELF.
IT IS A VERY POWERFUL ENERGY.
IT NOURISHED THE FIELDS AND FORESTS, FILLING THE VALE WITH LIFE.
NOW, THE KING HAD TWIN SONS. BOTH OF THEM WERE BRAVE, HEROIC MEN.
EACH HAD THE FRIENDSHIP OF ONE OF THE TWO LEGENDARY POKÉMON, RESHIRAM AND ZEKROM.

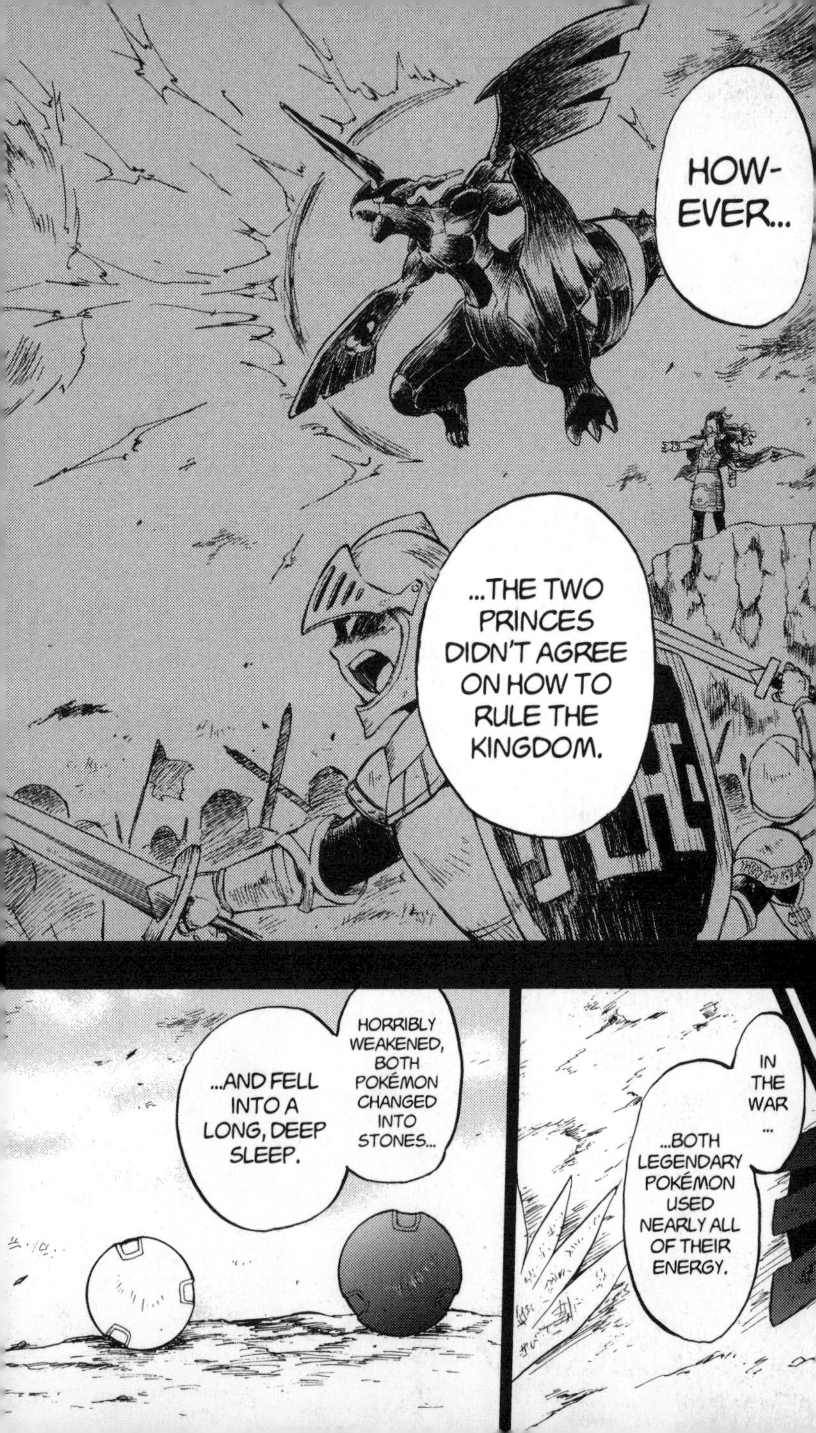
HOW-EVER...
...THE TWO PRINCES DIDN'T AGREE ON HOW TO RULE THE KINGDOM.
IN THE WAR...
...BOTH LEGENDARY POKÉMON USED NEARLY ALL OF THEIR ENERGY.
HORRIBLY WEAKENED, BOTH POKÉMON CHANGED INTO STONES...
...AND FELL INTO A LONG, DEEP SLEEP.

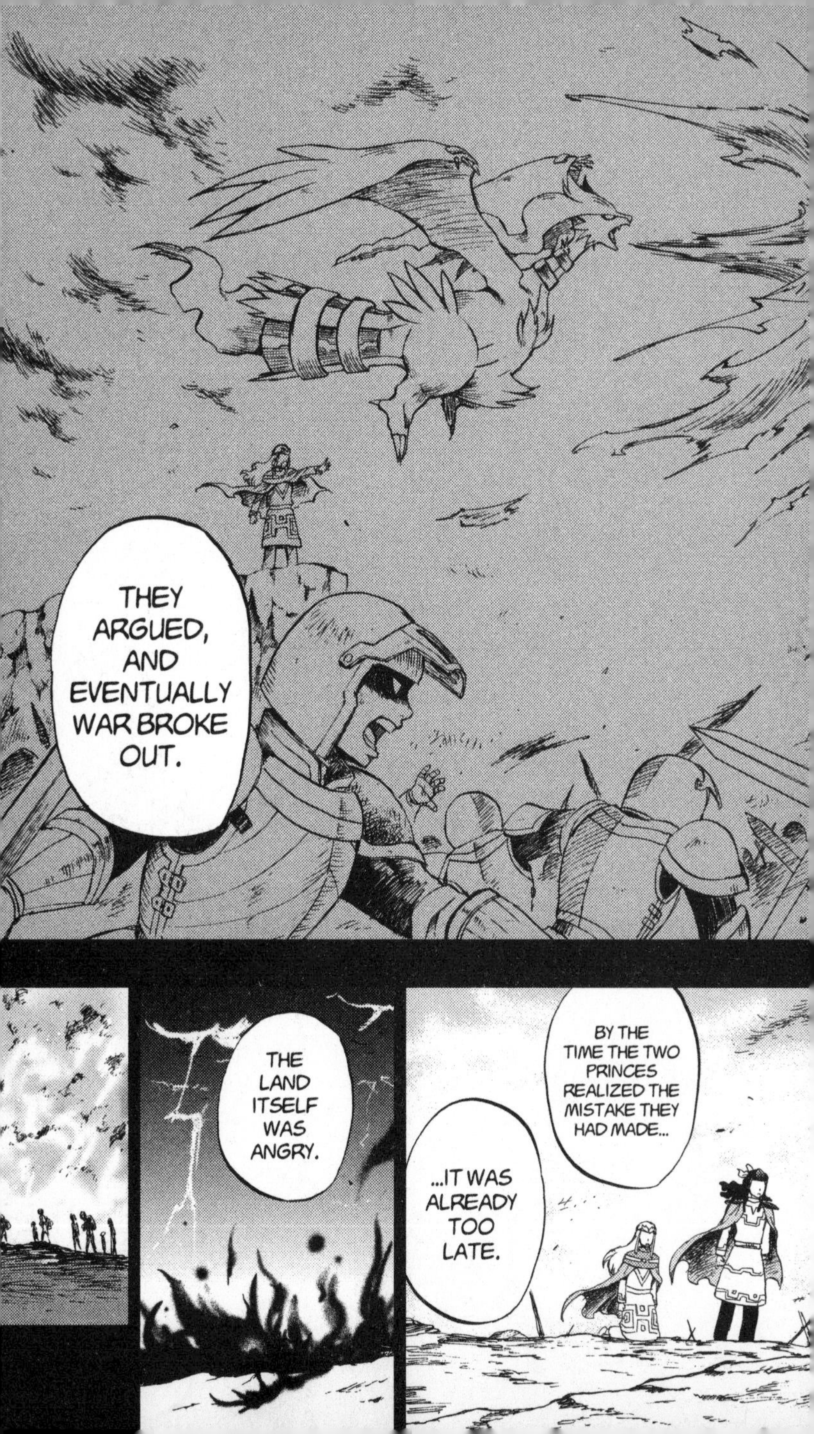
THEY ARGUED, AND EVENTUALLY WAR BROKE OUT.
BY THE TIME THE TWO PRINCES REALIZED THE MISTAKE THEY HAD MADE...
...IT WAS ALREADY TOO LATE.
THE LAND ITSELF WAS ANGRY.

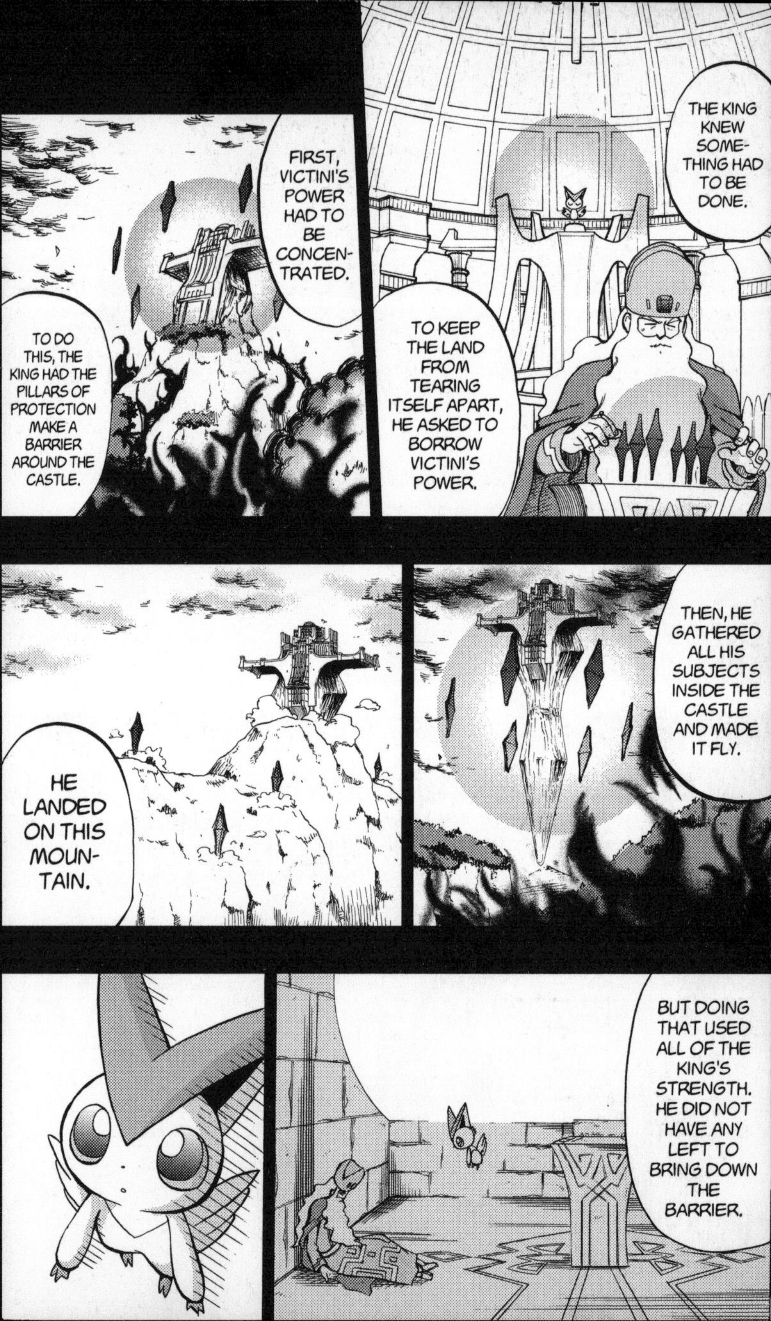
THE KING KNEW SOMETHING HAD TO BE DONE.
TO KEEP THE LAND FROM TEARING ITSELF APART, HE ASKED TO BORROW VICTINI'S POWER.
FIRST, VICTINI'S POWER HAD TO BE CONCENTRATED.
TO DO THIS, THE KING HAD THE PILLARS OF PROTECTION MAKE A BARRIER AROUND THE CASTLE.
THEN, HE GATHERED ALL HIS SUBJECTS INSIDE THE CASTLE AND MADE IT FLY.
HE LANDED ON THIS MOUNTAIN.
BUT DOING THAT USED ALL OF THE KING'S STRENGTH. HE DID NOT HAVE ANY LEFT TO BRING DOWN THE BARRIER.

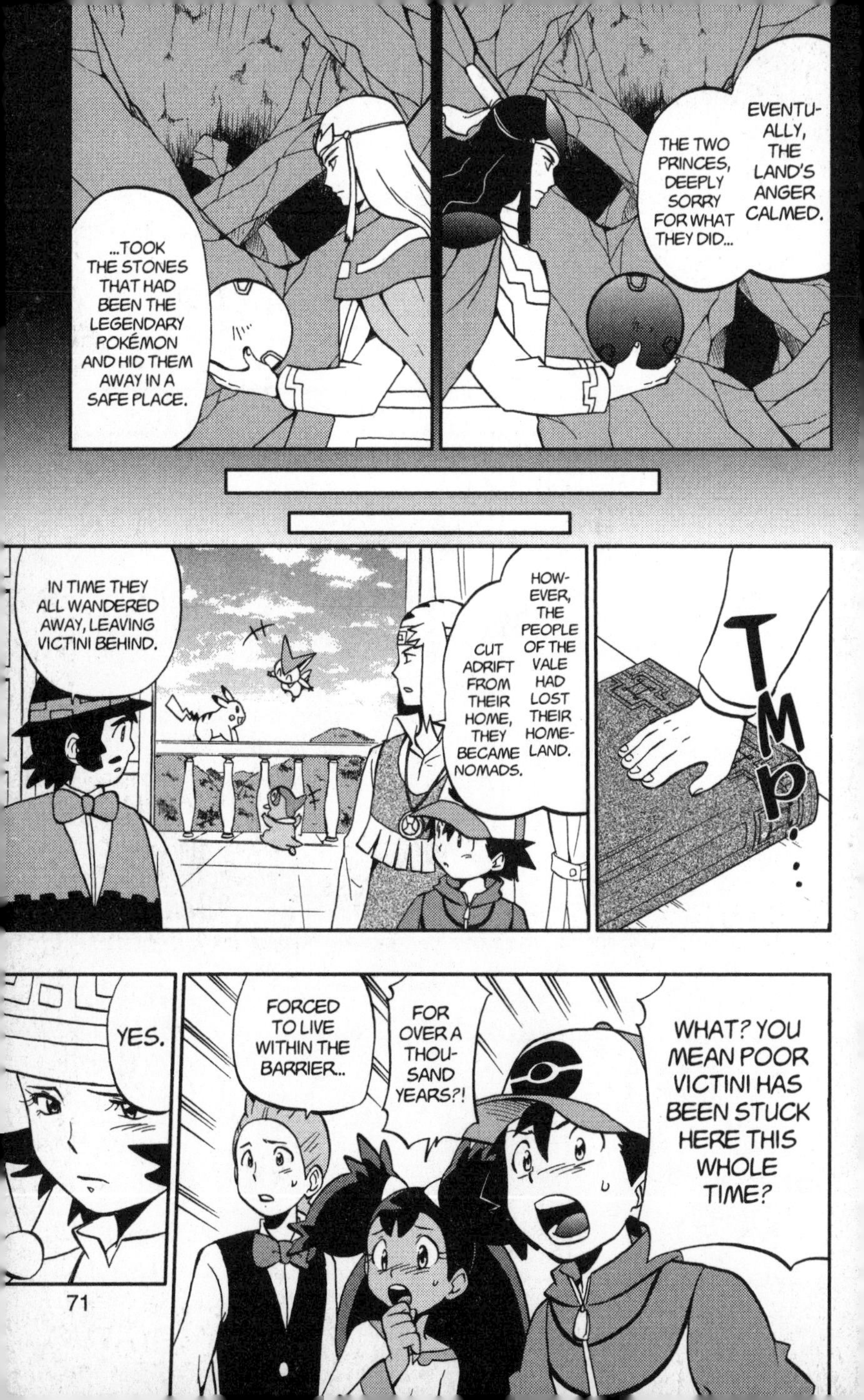
EVENTUALLY, THE LAND'S ANGER CALMED.
THE TWO PRINCES, DEEPLY SORRY FOR WHAT THEY DID...
...TOOK THE STONES THAT HAD BEEN THE LEGENDARY POKÉMON AND HID THEM AWAY IN A SAFE PLACE.
TMP
HOWEVER, THE PEOPLE OF THE VALE HAD LOST THEIR HOMELAND.
CUT ADRIFT FROM THEIR HOME, THEY BECAME NOMADS.
IN TIME THEY ALL WANDERED AWAY, LEAVING VICTINI BEHIND.
WHAT? YOU MEAN POOR VICTINI HAS BEEN STUCK HERE THIS WHOLE TIME?
FOR OVER A THOUSAND YEARS?!
FORCED TO LIVE WITHIN THE BARRIER...
YES.

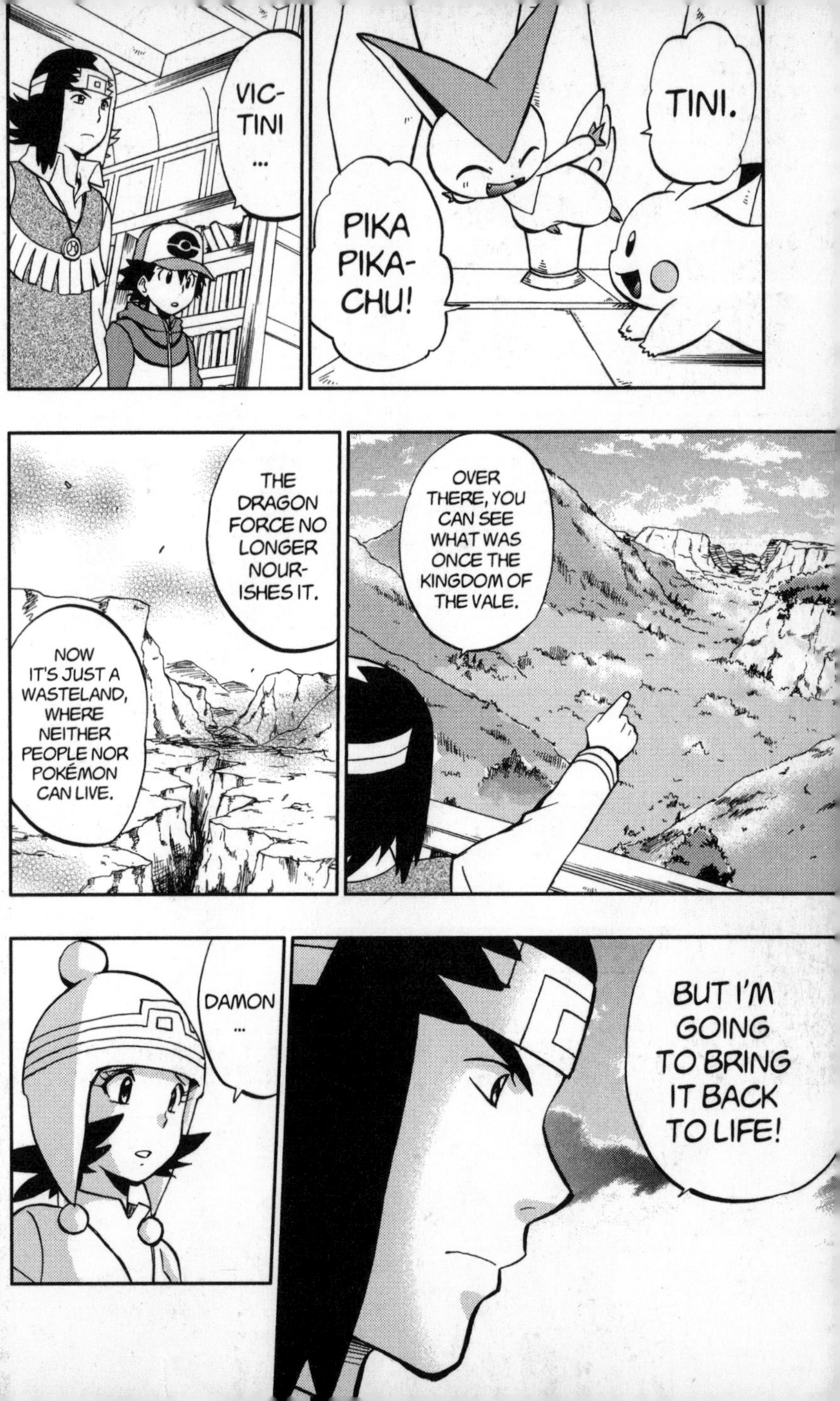
TINI.
PIKA PIKA-CHU!
VIC-TINI ...
OVER THERE, YOU CAN SEE WHAT WAS ONCE THE KINGDOM OF THE VALE.
THE DRAGON FORCE NO LONGER NOURISHES IT.
NOW IT'S JUST A WASTELAND, WHERE NEITHER PEOPLE NOR POKÉMON CAN LIVE.
BUT I'M GOING TO BRING IT BACK TO LIFE!
DAMON ...

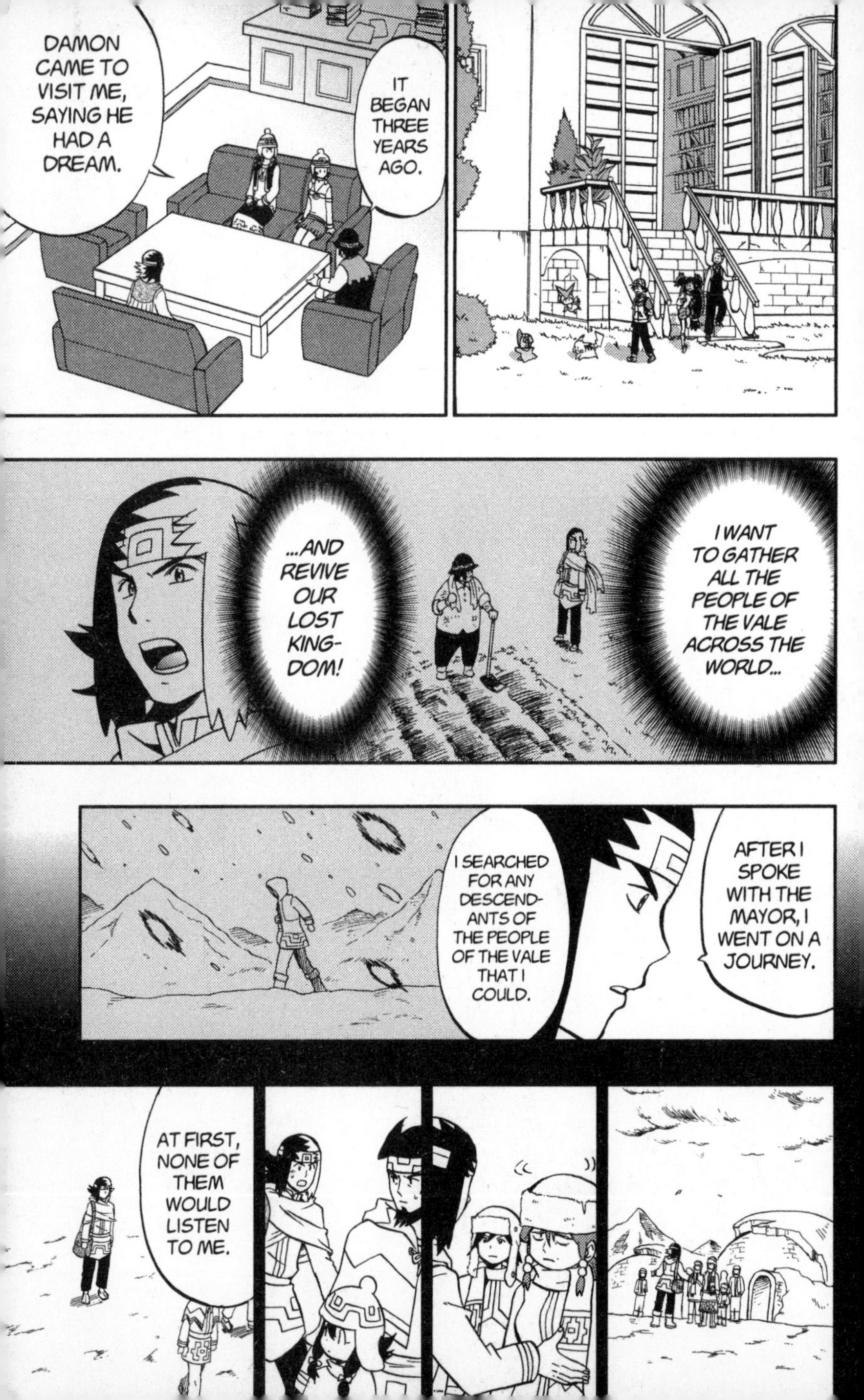

IT BEGAN THREE YEARS AGO.
DAMON CAME TO VISIT ME, SAYING HE HAD A DREAM.
I WANT TO GATHER ALL THE PEOPLE OF THE VALE ACROSS THE WORLD...
...AND REVIVE OUR LOST KING-DOM!
AFTER I SPOKE WITH THE MAYOR, I WENT ON A JOURNEY.
I SEARCHED FOR ANY DESCEND-ANTS OF THE PEOPLE OF THE VALE THAT I COULD.
AT FIRST, NONE OF THEM WOULD LISTEN TO ME.

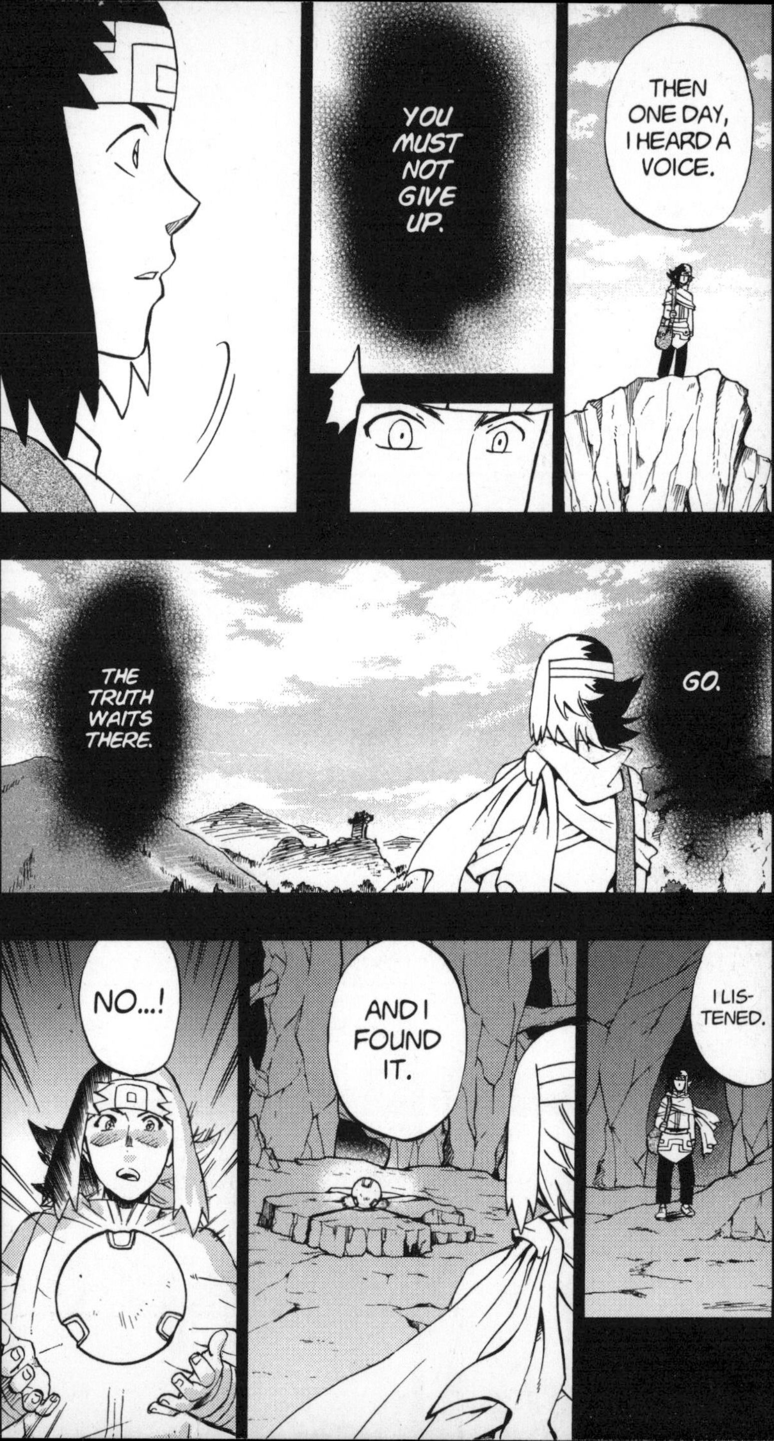
THEN ONE DAY, I HEARD A VOICE.
YOU MUST NOT GIVE UP.
GO.
THE TRUTH WAITS THERE.
I LISTENED.
AND I FOUND IT.
NO...!

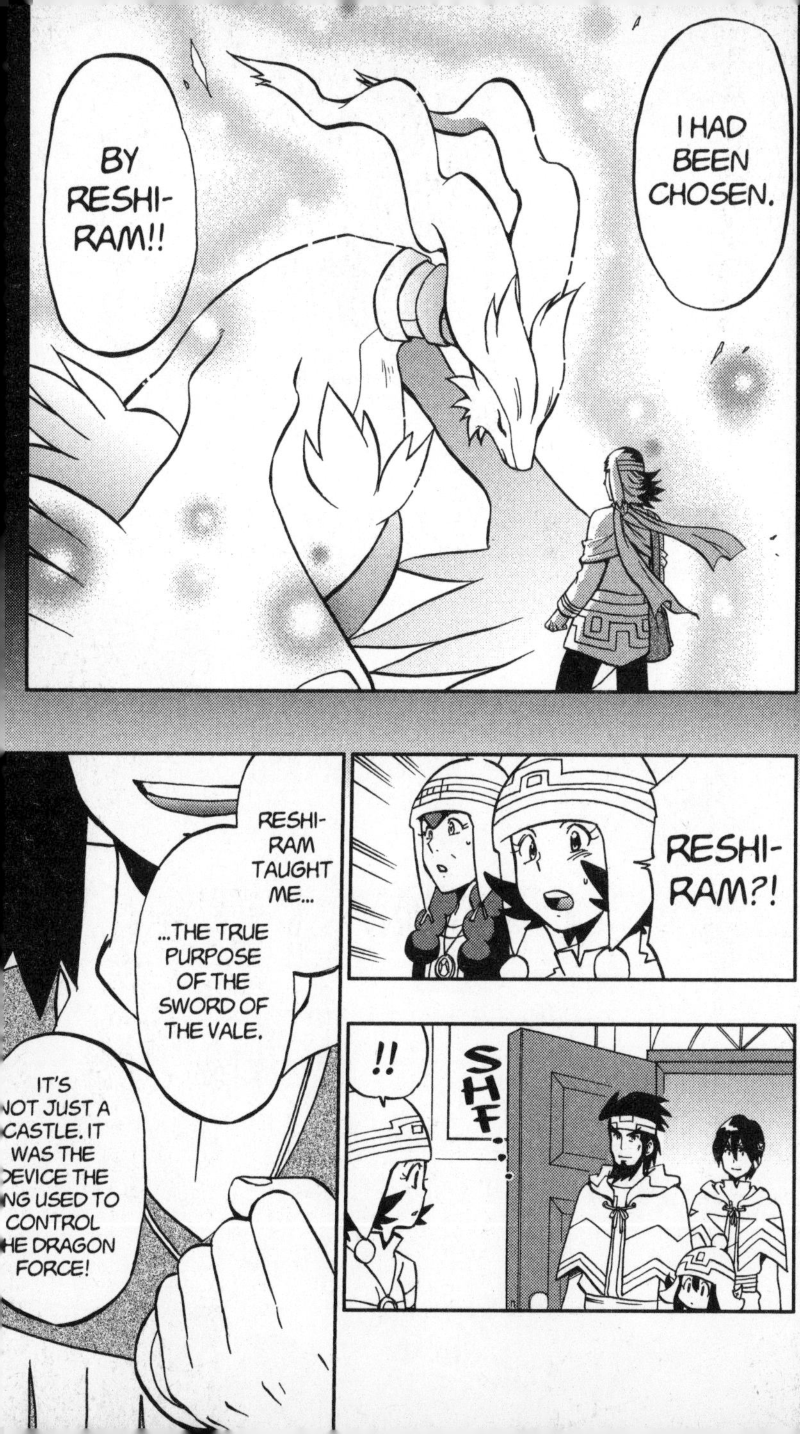

I HAD BEEN CHOSEN.
BY RESHI-RAM!!
RESHI-RAM?!
SHF
!!
RESHI-RAM TAUGHT ME...
...THE TRUE PURPOSE OF THE SWORD OF THE VALE.
IT'S NOT JUST A CASTLE. IT WAS THE DEVICE THE NG USED TO CONTROL HE DRAGON FORCE!

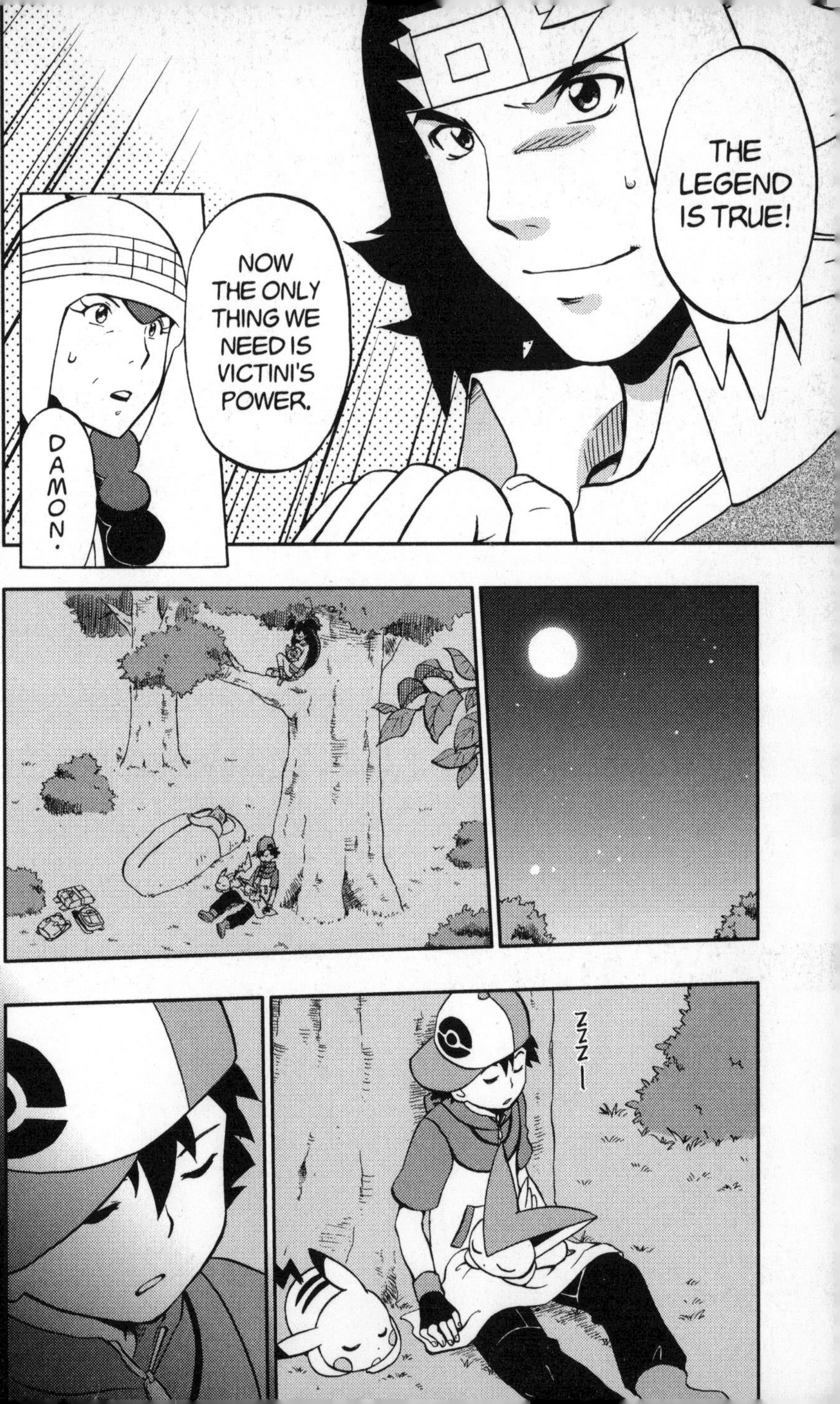
THE LEGEND IS TRUE!
NOW THE ONLY THING WE NEED IS VICTINI'S POWER.
DAMON.
ZZZ—

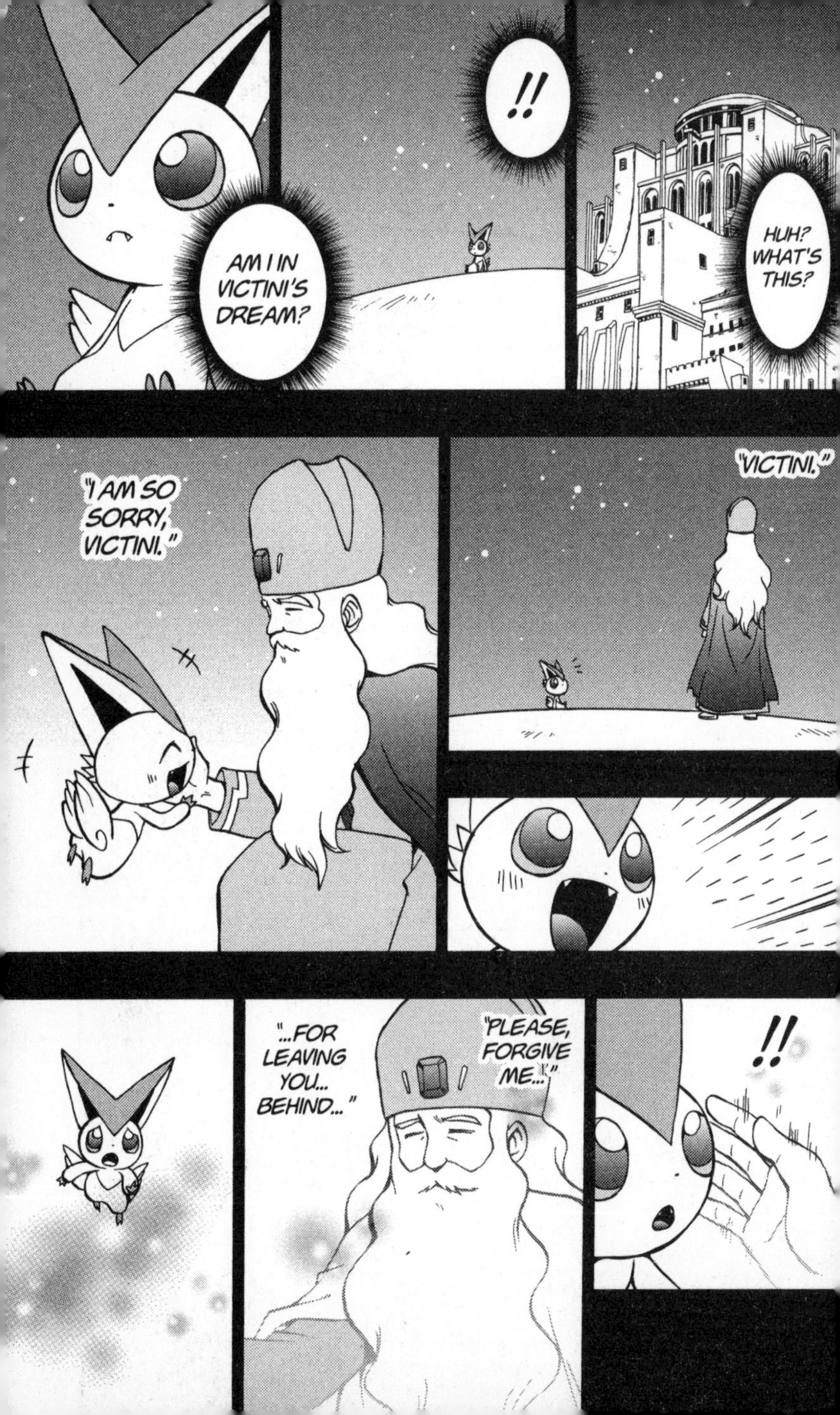
HUH? WHAT'S THIS?
!!
AM I IN VICTINI'S DREAM?
"VICTINI."
"I AM SO SORRY, VICTINI."
!!
"PLEASE, FORGIVE ME..."
"...FOR LEAVING YOU... BEHIND..."

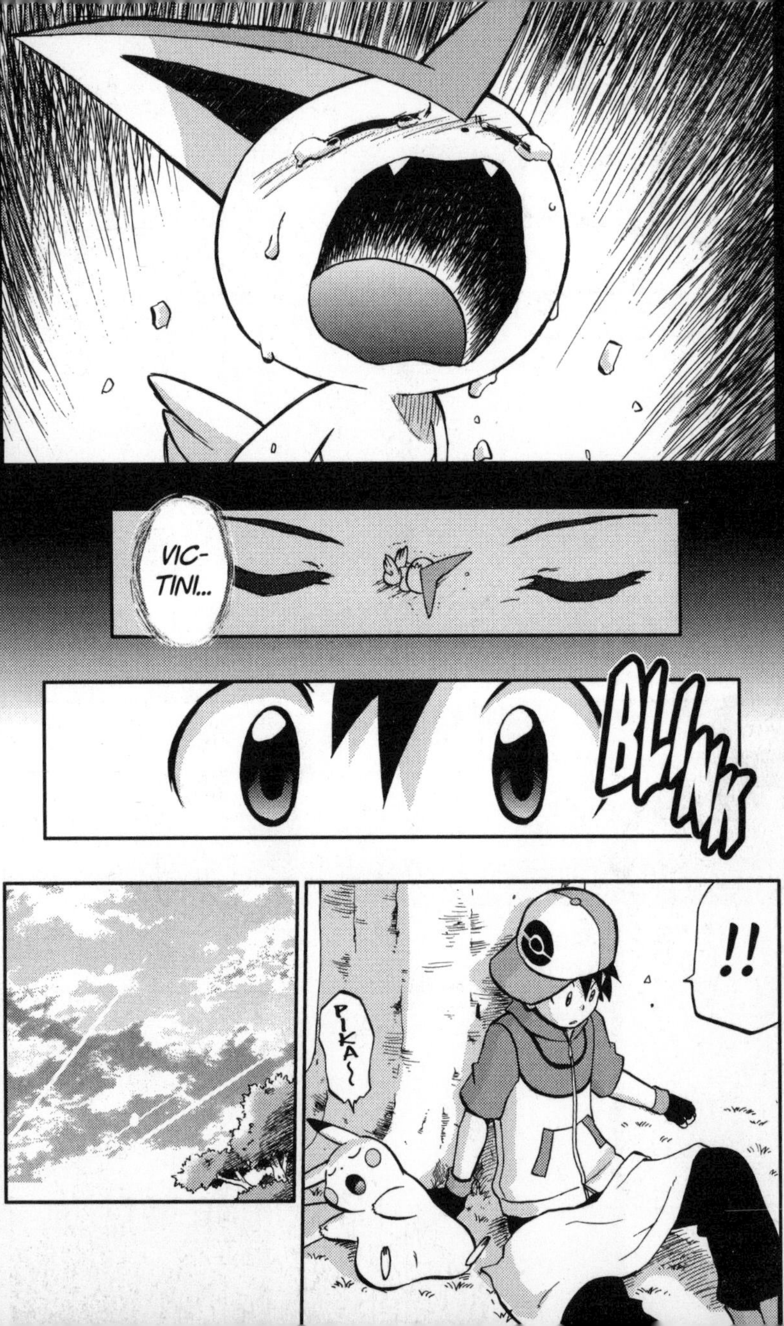
VIC-TINI...
BLINK
!!
PIKA~

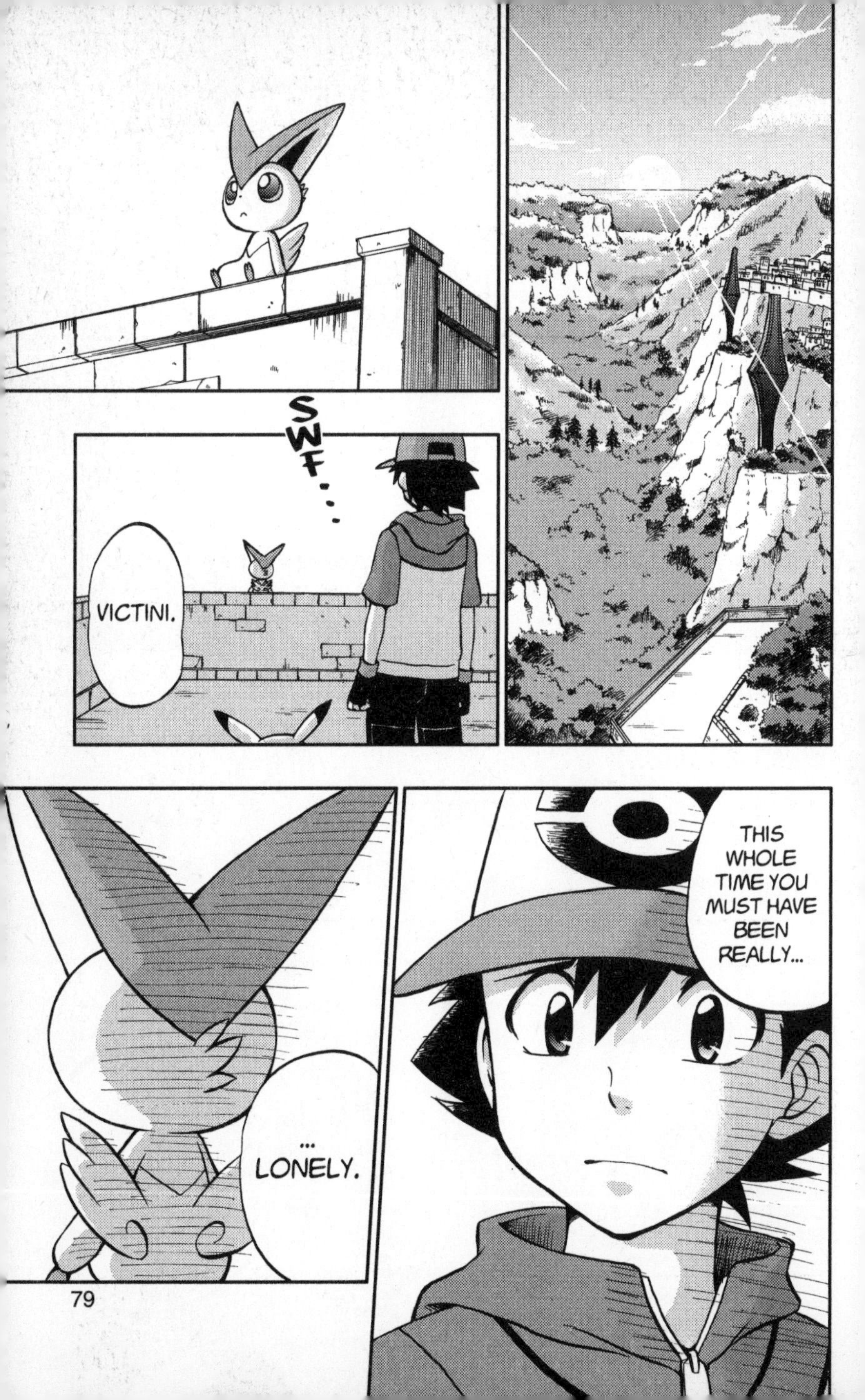
SWF...
VICTINI.
THIS WHOLE TIME YOU MUST HAVE BEEN REALLY...
... LONELY.

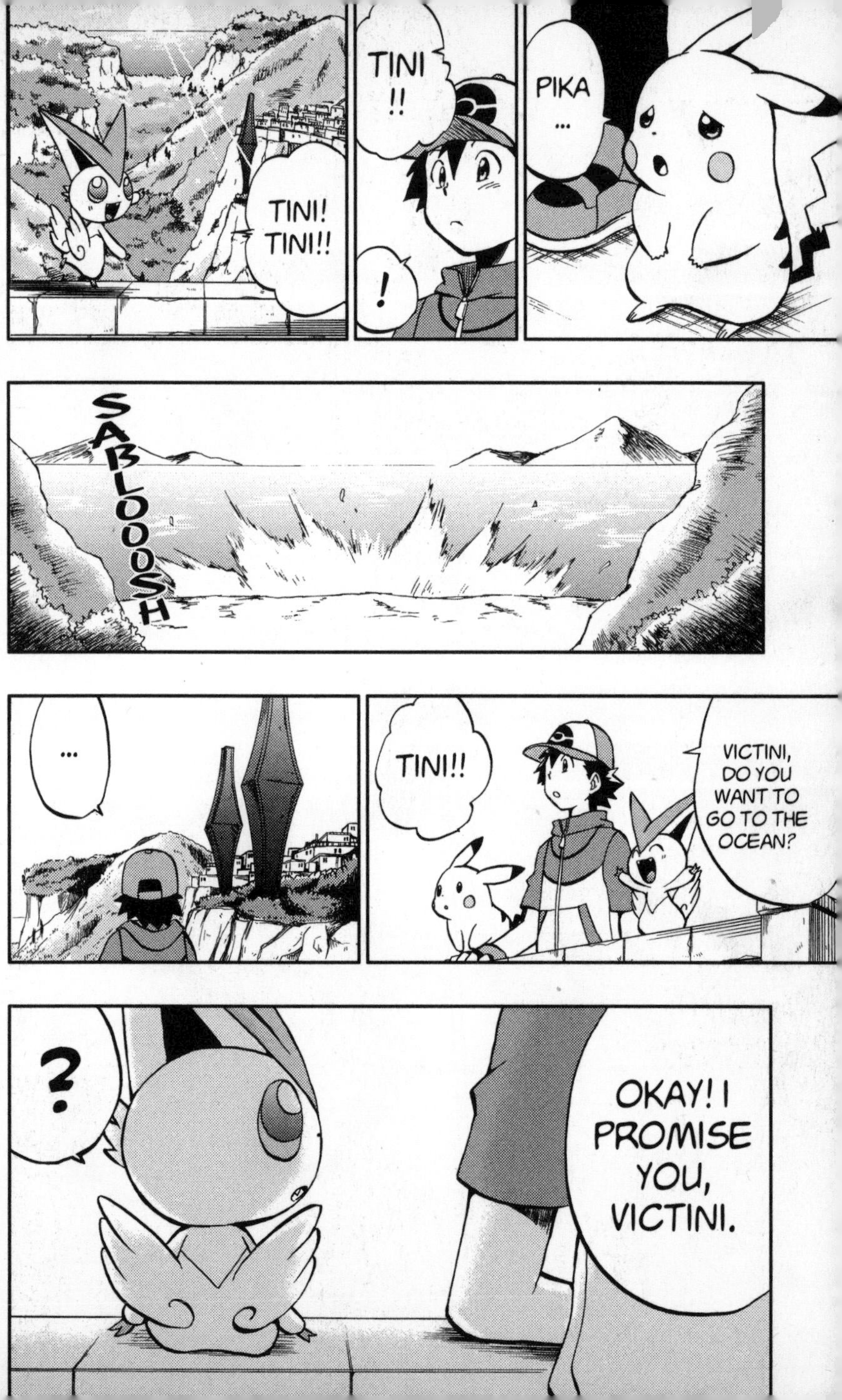
PIKA ...
TINI !!
!
TINI! TINI!!
SABLOOOSH
VICTINI, DO YOU WANT TO GO TO THE OCEAN?
TINI!!
...
OKAY! I PROMISE YOU, VICTINI.
?

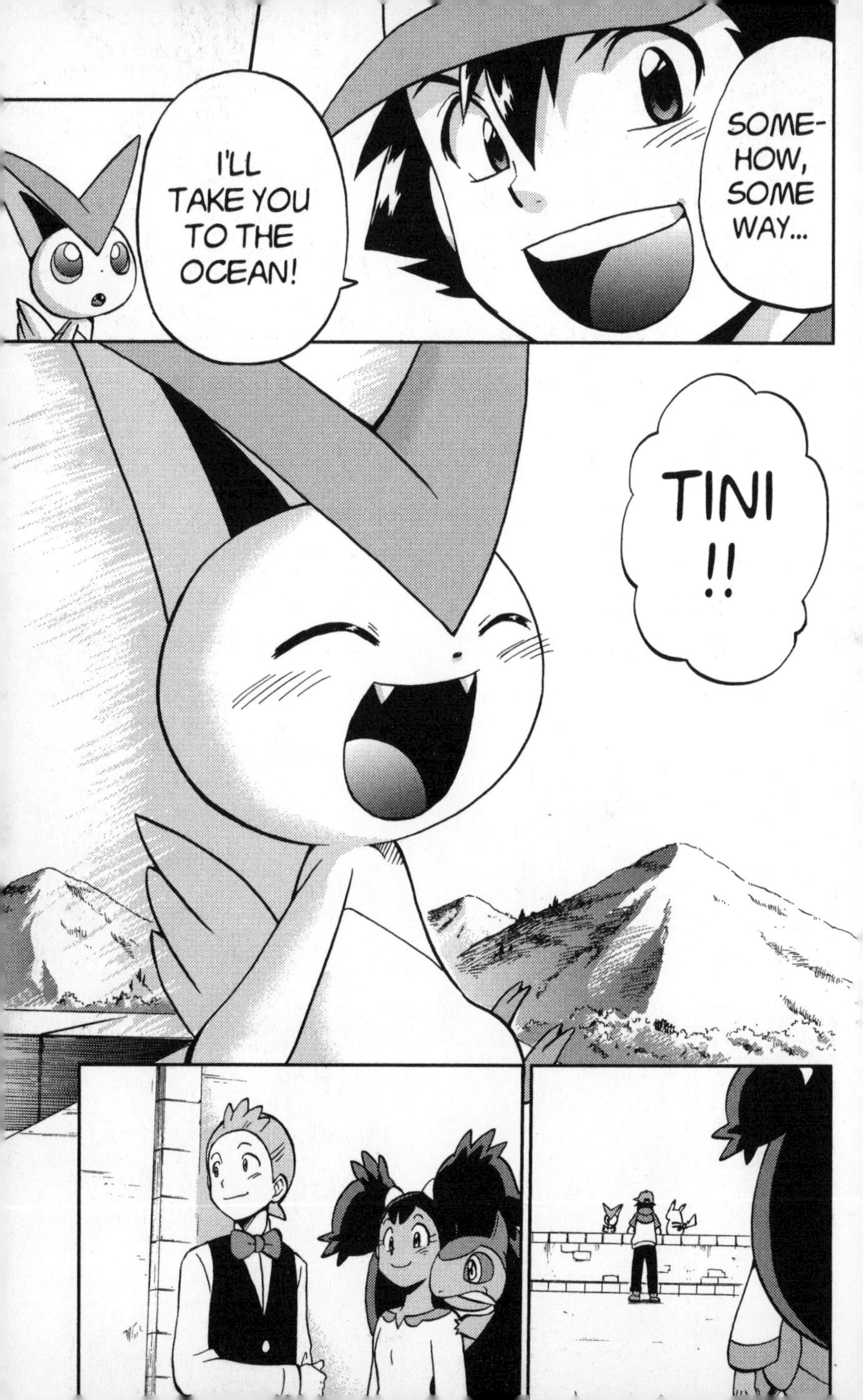
SOME-HOW, SOME WAY...
I'LL TAKE YOU TO THE OCEAN!
TINI !!

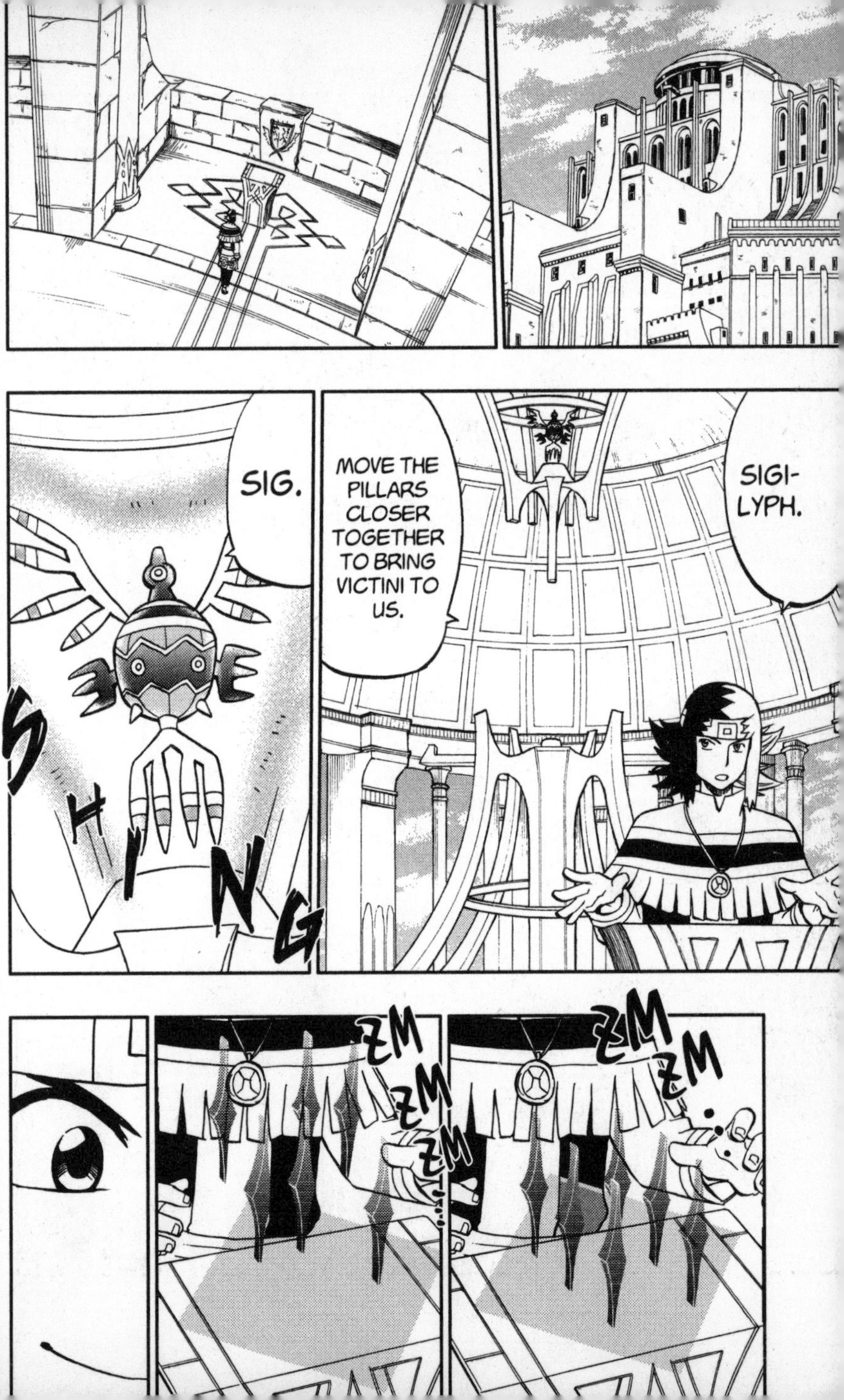
SIGI-LYPH.
MOVE THE PILLARS CLOSER TOGETHER TO BRING VICTINI TO US.
SIG.
SHING
ZM ZM
ZM ZM ZM ZM

READ THIS WAY

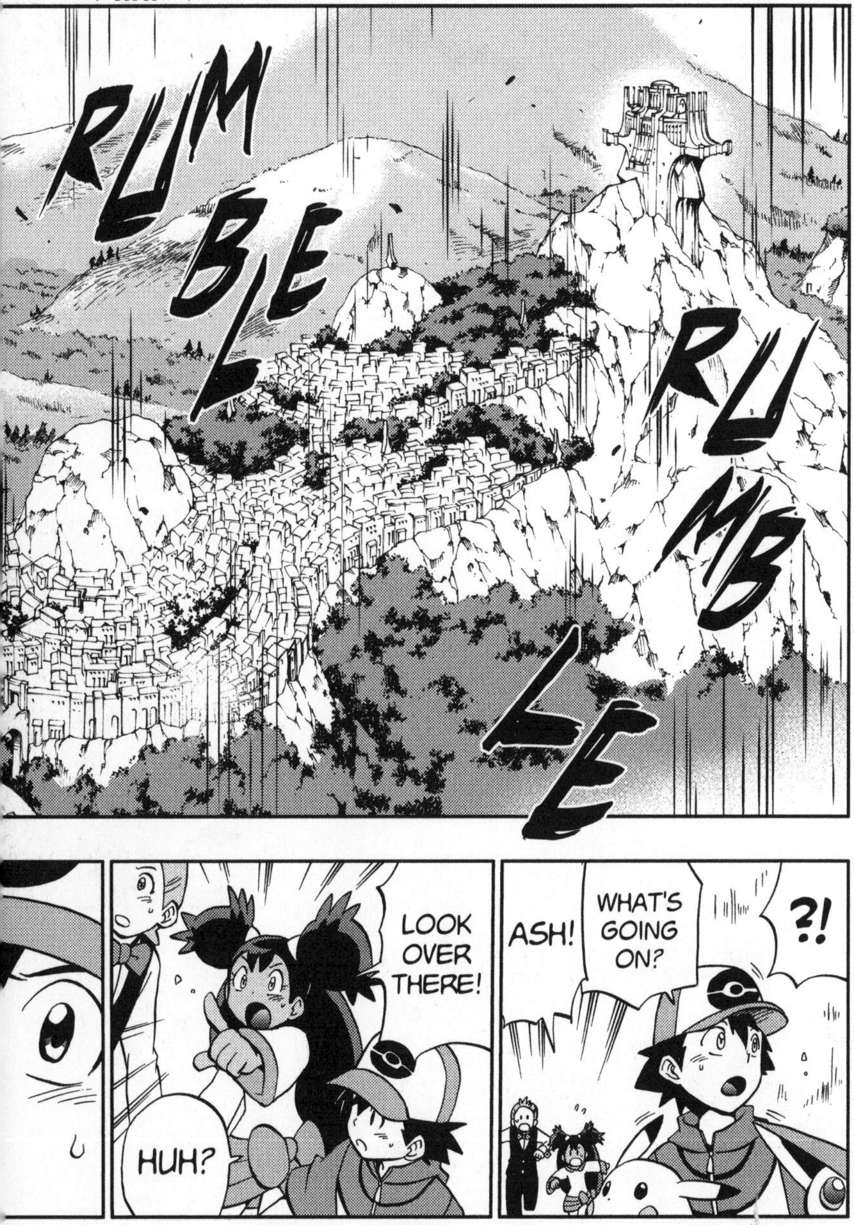
RUMBLE
RUMBLE
?!
WHAT'S GOING ON?
ASH!
LOOK OVER THERE!
HUH?

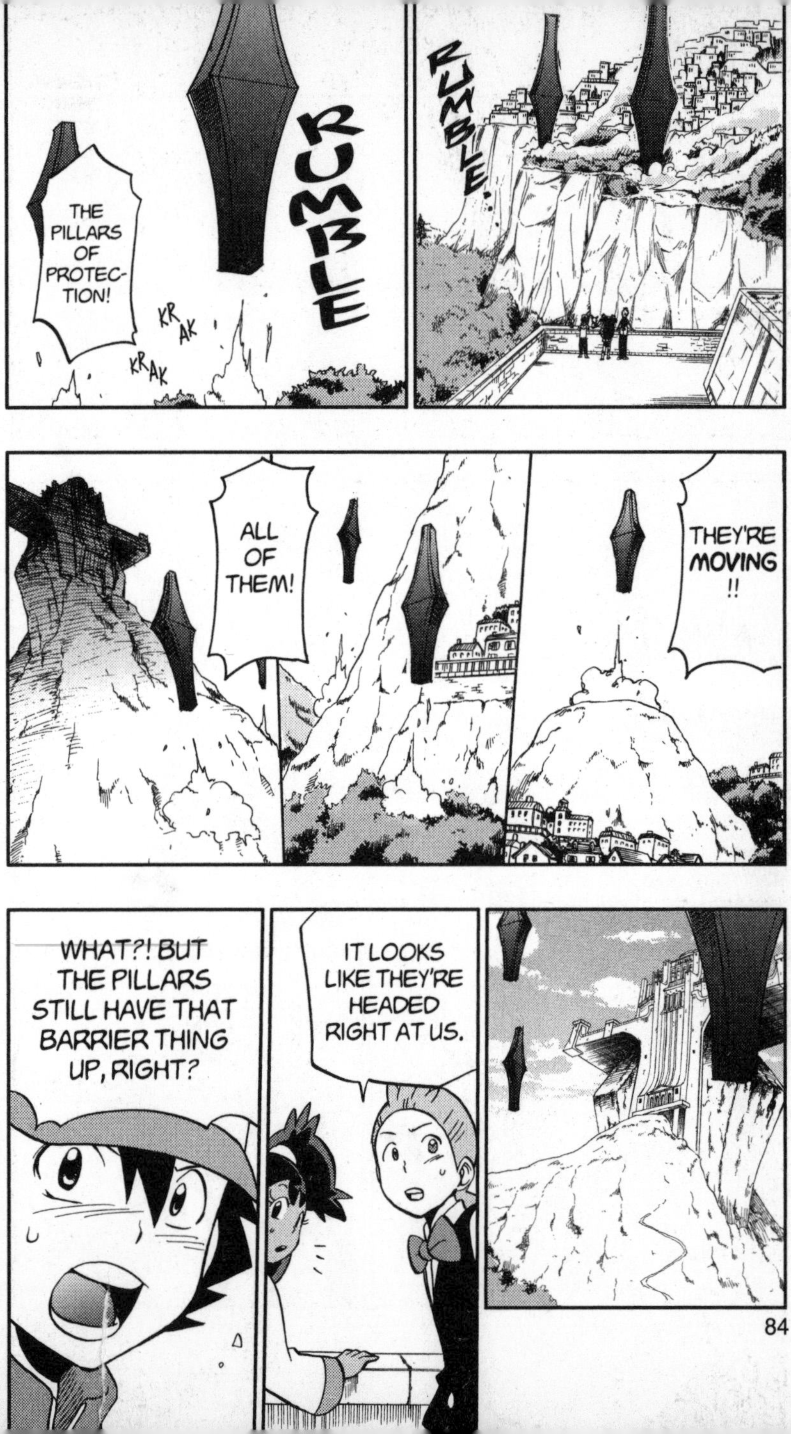
RUMBLE
THE PILLARS OF PROTECTION!
RUMBLE
KRAK
KRAK
THEY'RE **MOVING** !!
ALL OF THEM!
IT LOOKS LIKE THEY'RE HEADED RIGHT AT US.
WHAT?! BUT THE PILLARS STILL HAVE THAT BARRIER THING UP, RIGHT?

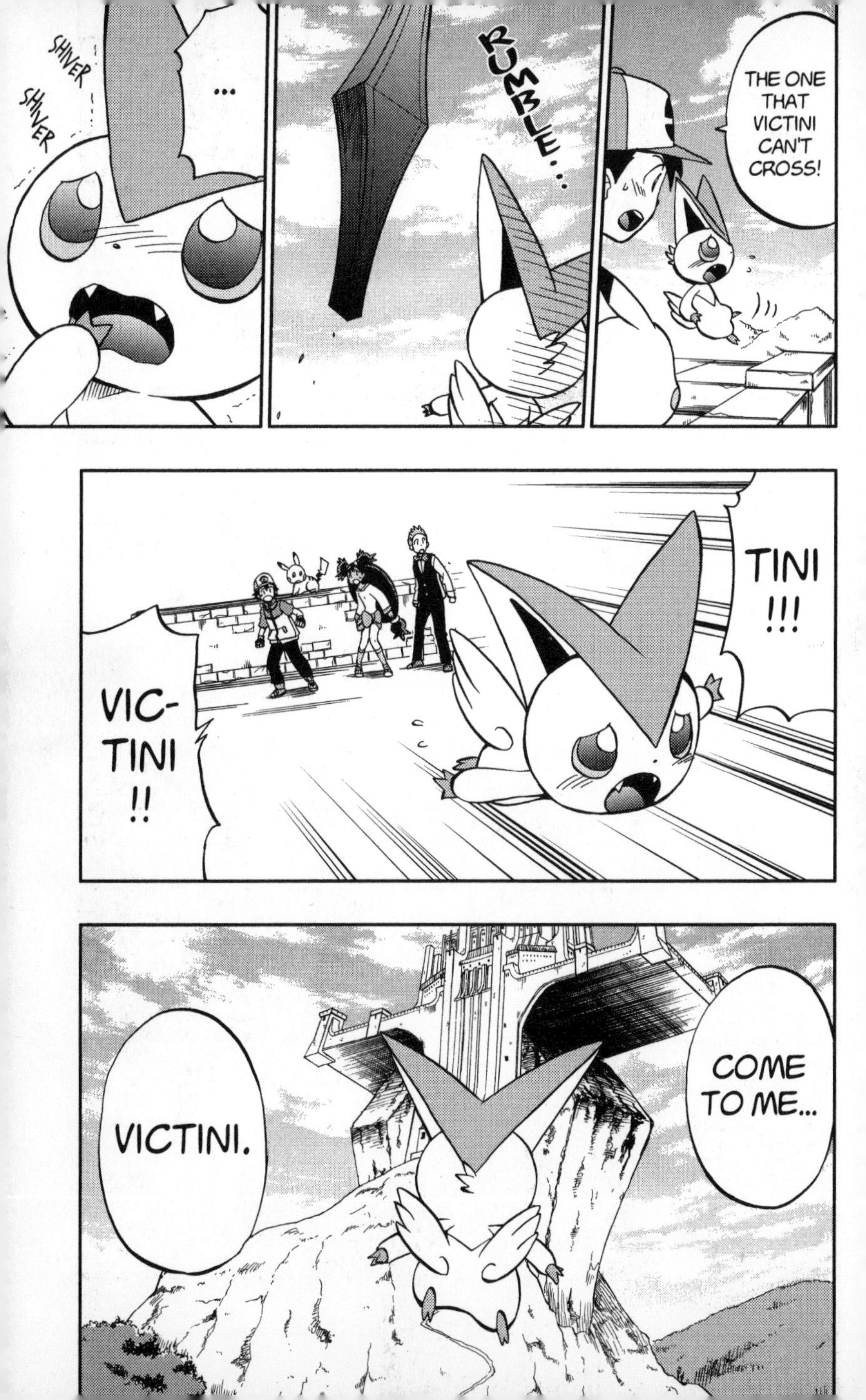
THE ONE THAT VICTINI CAN'T CROSS!
RUMBLE...
...
SHIVER SHIVER
TINI !!!
VIC-TINI !!
COME TO ME...
VICTINI.

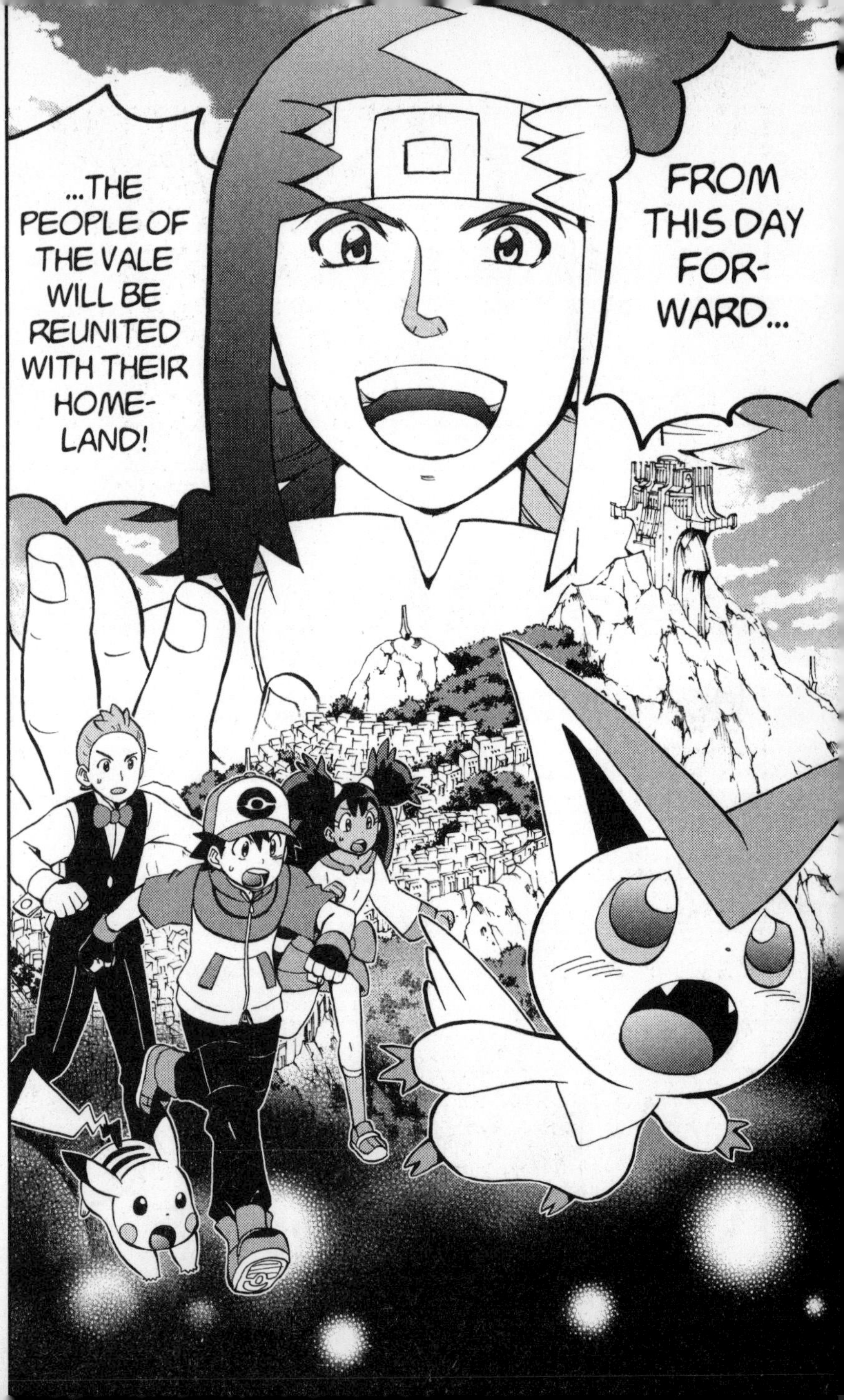
FROM THIS DAY FOR-WARD...
...THE PEOPLE OF THE VALE WILL BE REUNITED WITH THEIR HOME-LAND!

READ THIS WAY

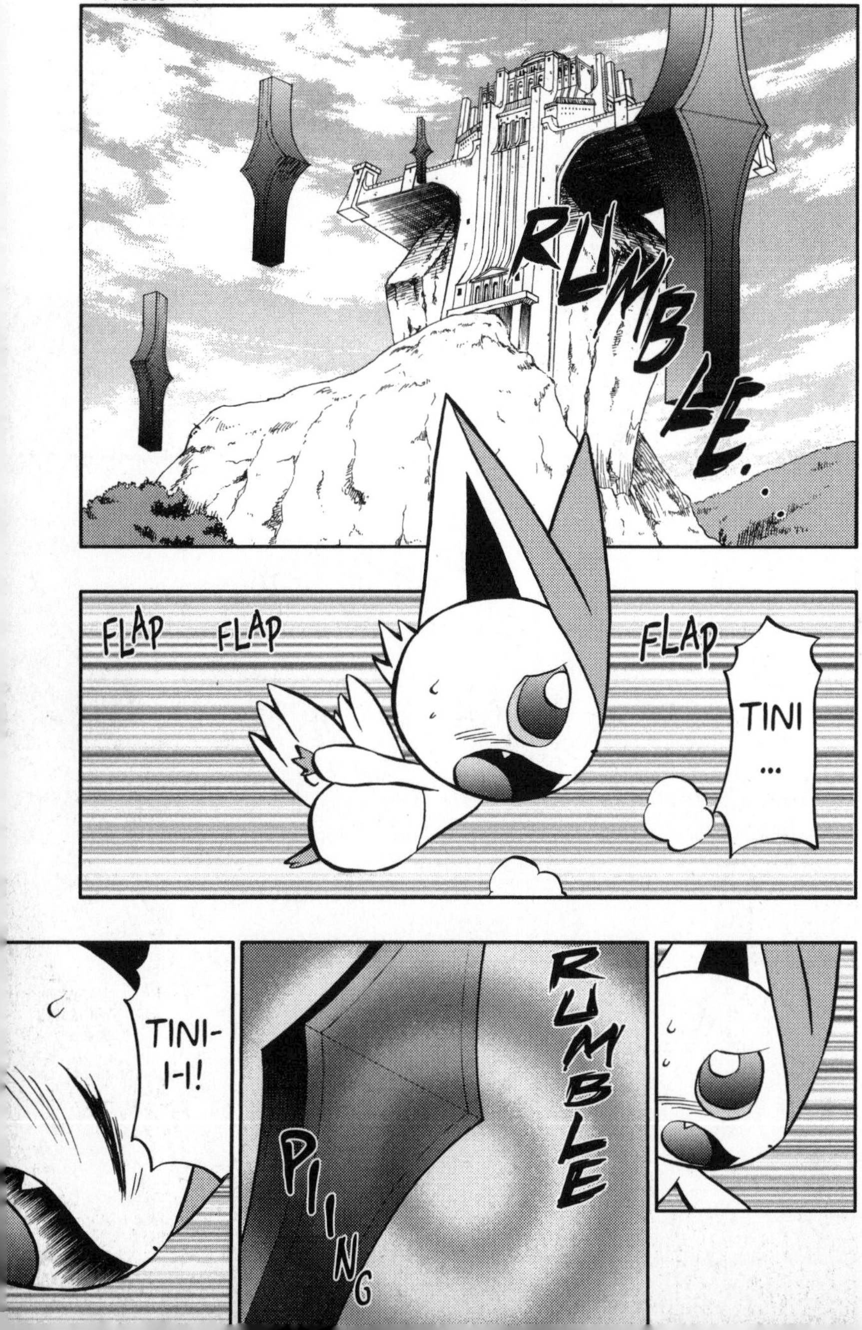
RUMBLE.
TINI ...
FLAP
FLAP
FLAP
RUMBLE
PIING
TINI-I-I!

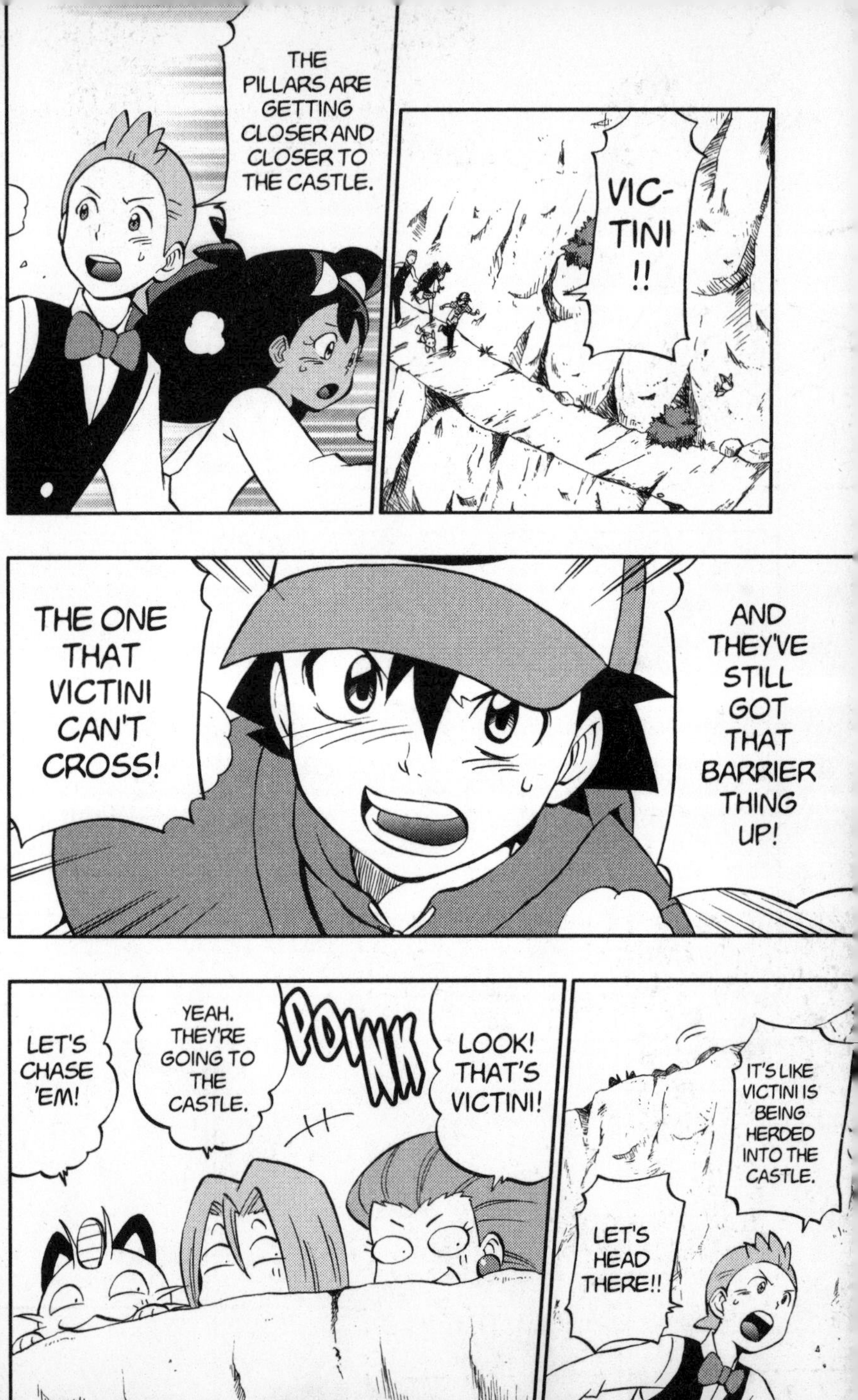
VICTINI!!
THE PILLARS ARE GETTING CLOSER AND CLOSER TO THE CASTLE.
AND THEY'VE STILL GOT THAT BARRIER THING UP!
THE ONE THAT VICTINI CAN'T CROSS!
IT'S LIKE VICTINI IS BEING HERDED INTO THE CASTLE.
LET'S HEAD THERE!!
LOOK! THAT'S VICTINI!
POINK
YEAH. THEY'RE GOING TO THE CASTLE.
LET'S CHASE 'EM!

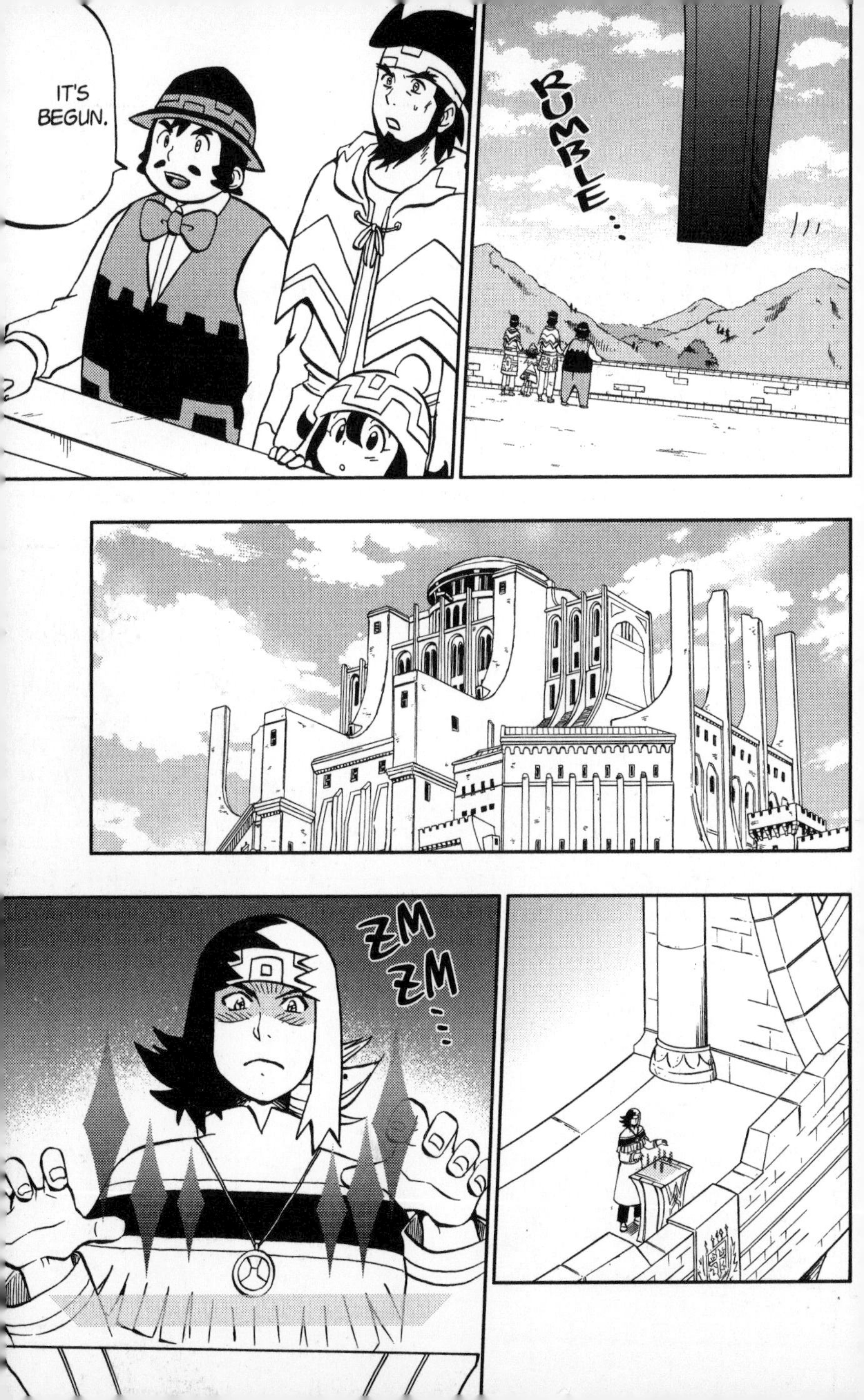
RUMBLE...
IT'S BEGUN.
ZM ZM...

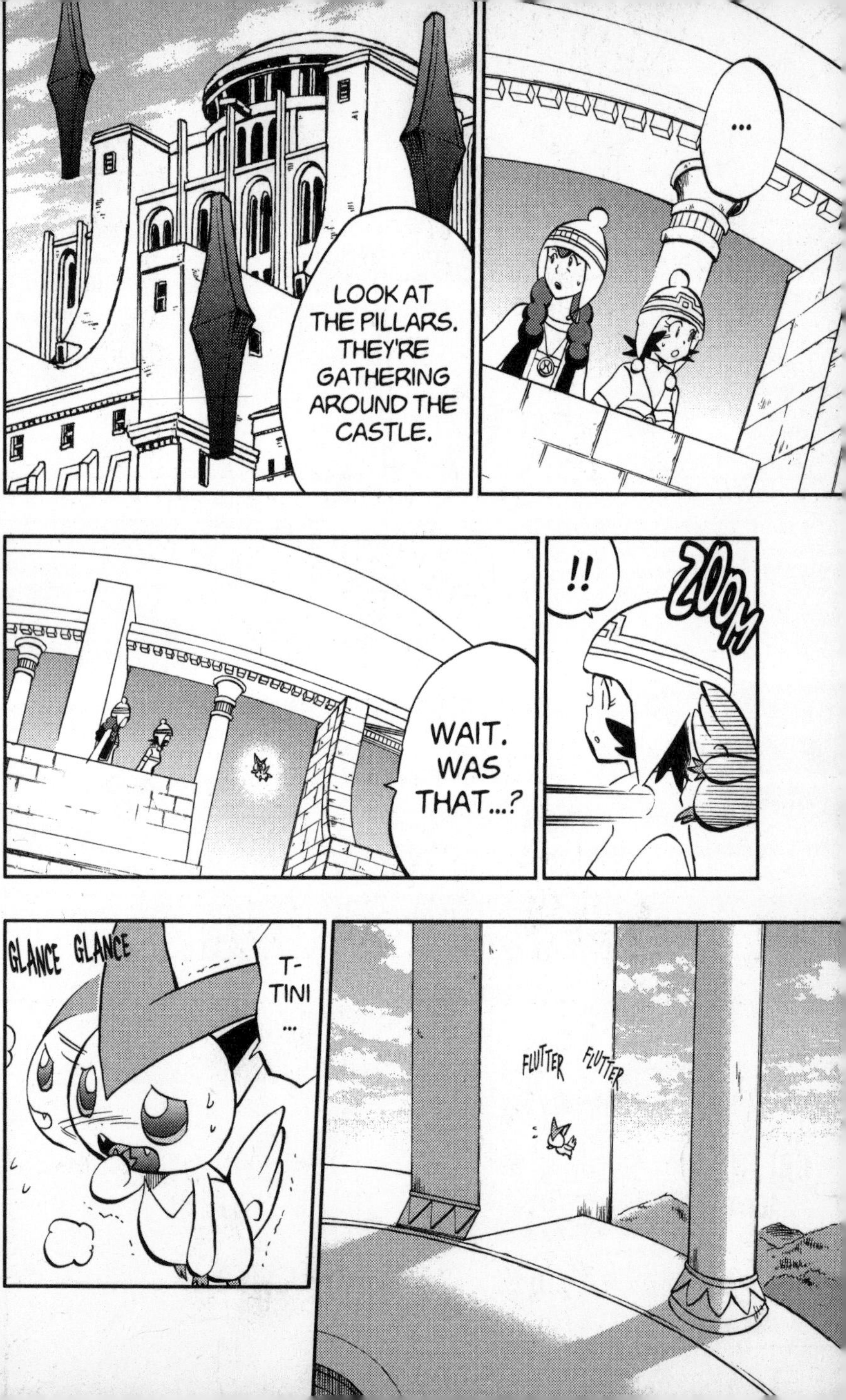
...
LOOK AT THE PILLARS. THEY'RE GATHERING AROUND THE CASTLE.
!!
ZOOM
WAIT. WAS THAT...?
FLUTTER FLUTTER
GLANCE GLANCE
T-TINI...

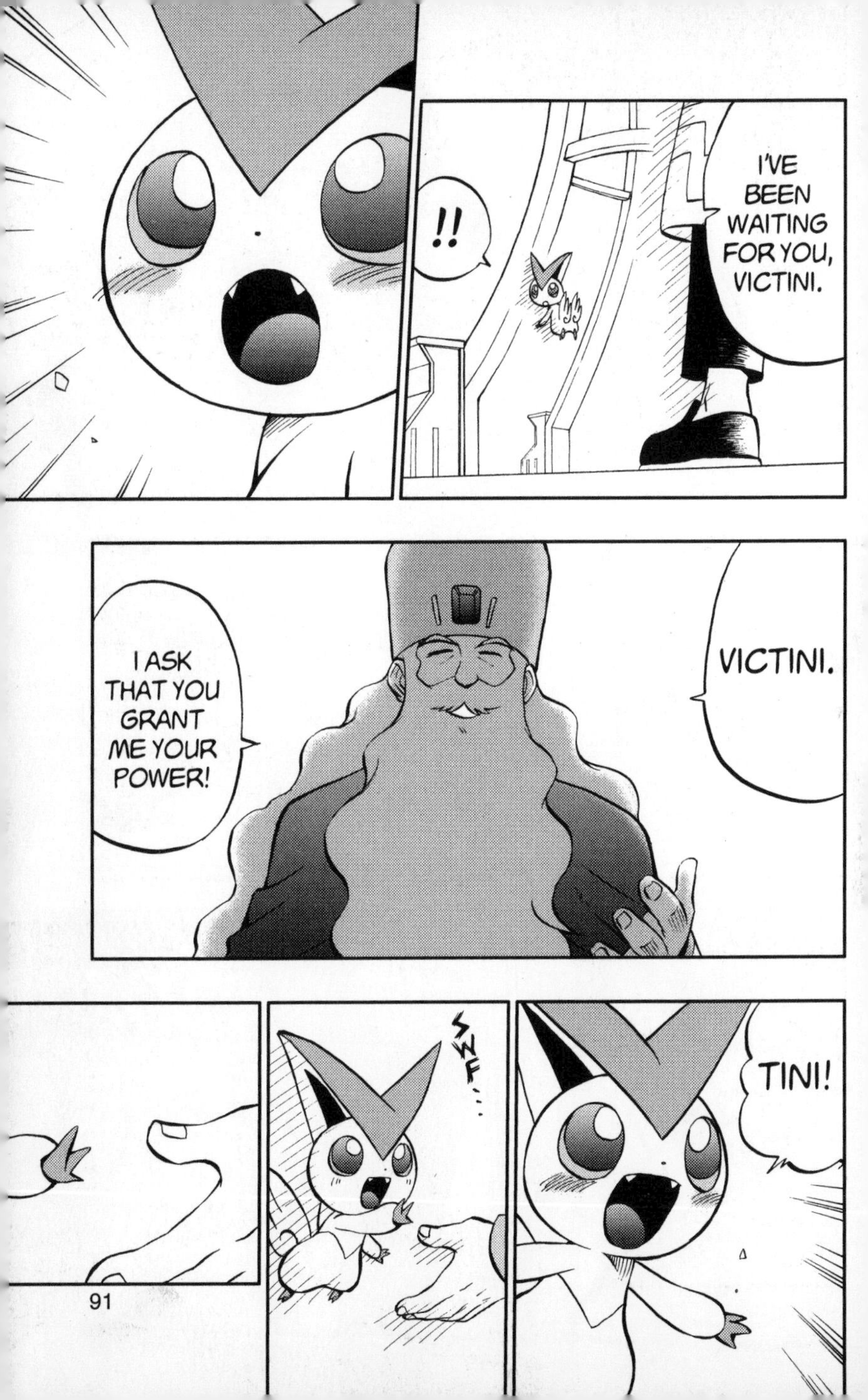
I'VE BEEN WAITING FOR YOU, VICTINI.
!!
VICTINI.
I ASK THAT YOU GRANT ME YOUR POWER!
TINI!
SWF

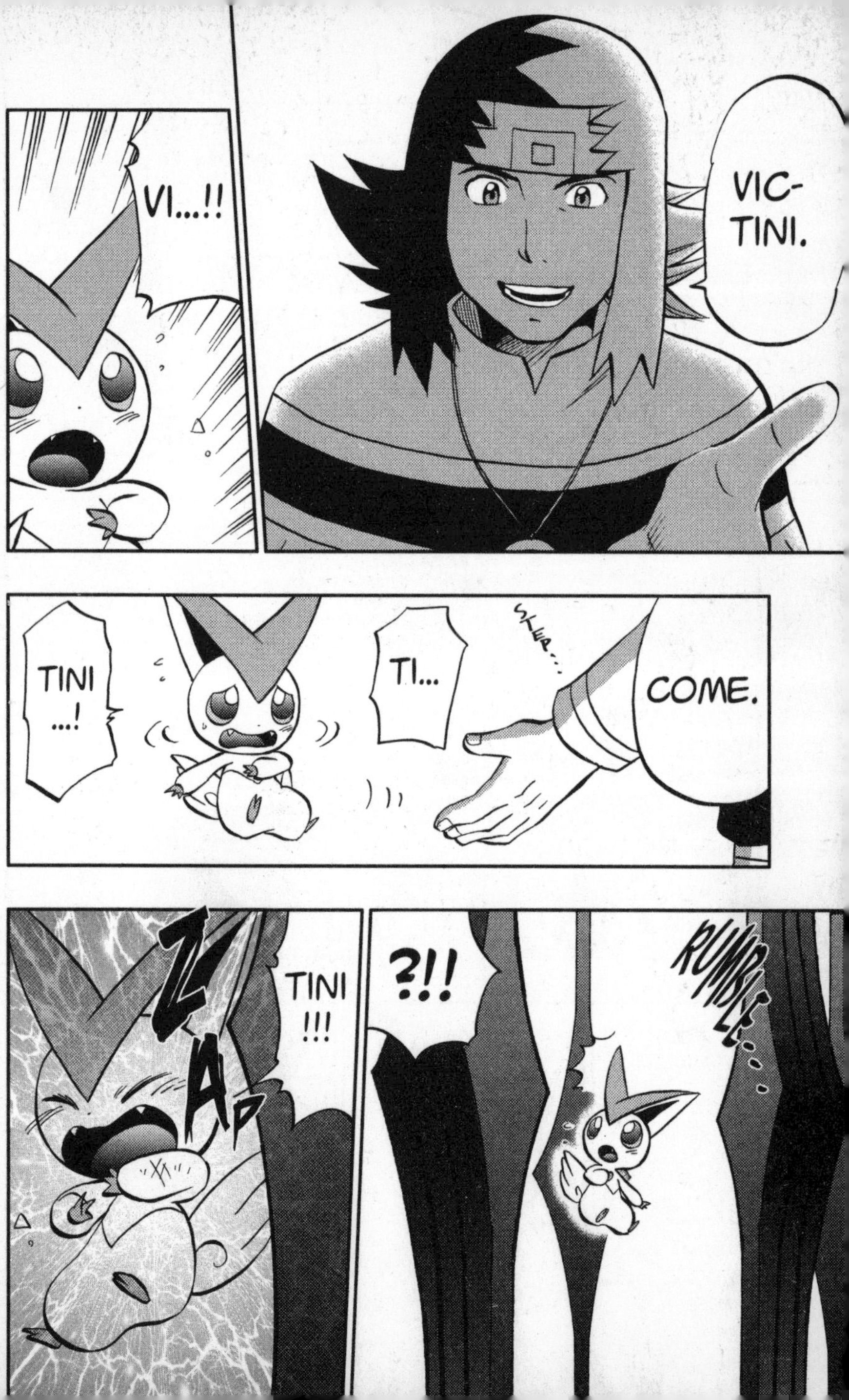
VIC-TINI.
VI...!!
COME.
TI...
TINI ...!
RUMBLE...
?!!
TINI !!!
ZAP

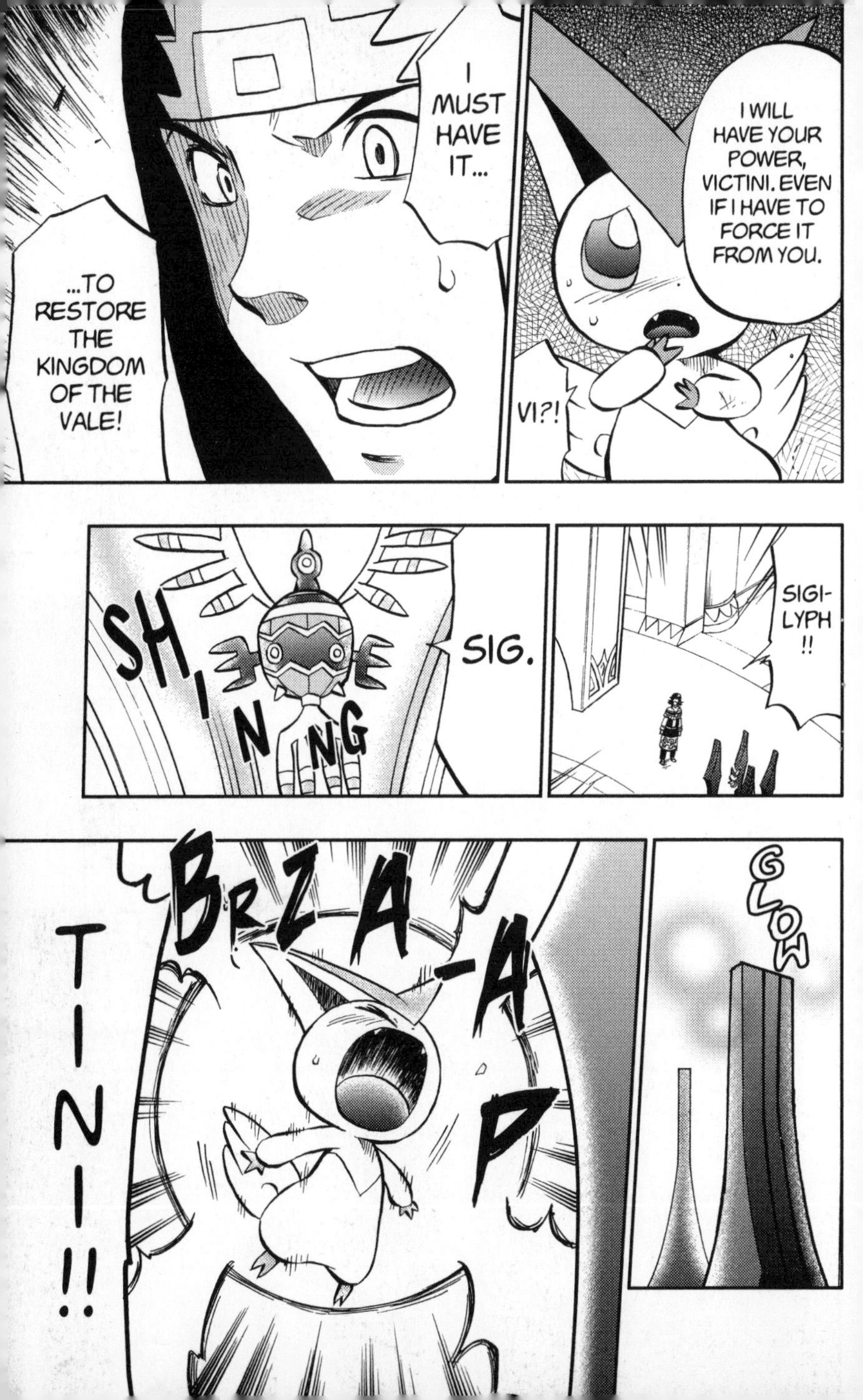

I WILL HAVE YOUR POWER, VICTINI. EVEN IF I HAVE TO FORCE IT FROM YOU.
VI?!
I MUST HAVE IT...
...TO RESTORE THE KINGDOM OF THE VALE!
SIGI-LYPH !!
SHINNG
SIG.
GLOW
BRZA-AP
TINI!!

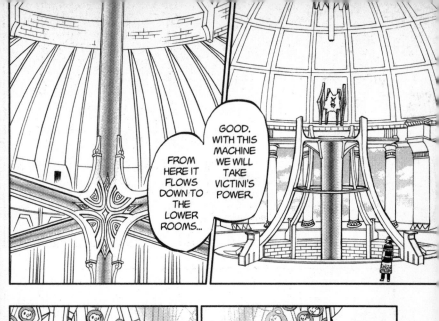

GOOD. WITH THIS MACHINE WE WILL TAKE VICTINI'S POWER.

FROM HERE IT FLOWS DOWN TO THE LOWER ROOMS...

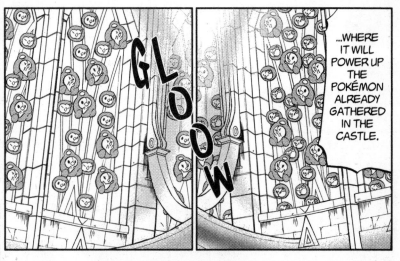

GLOOW

...WHERE IT WILL POWER UP THE POKÉMON ALREADY GATHERED IN THE CASTLE.

TI...!

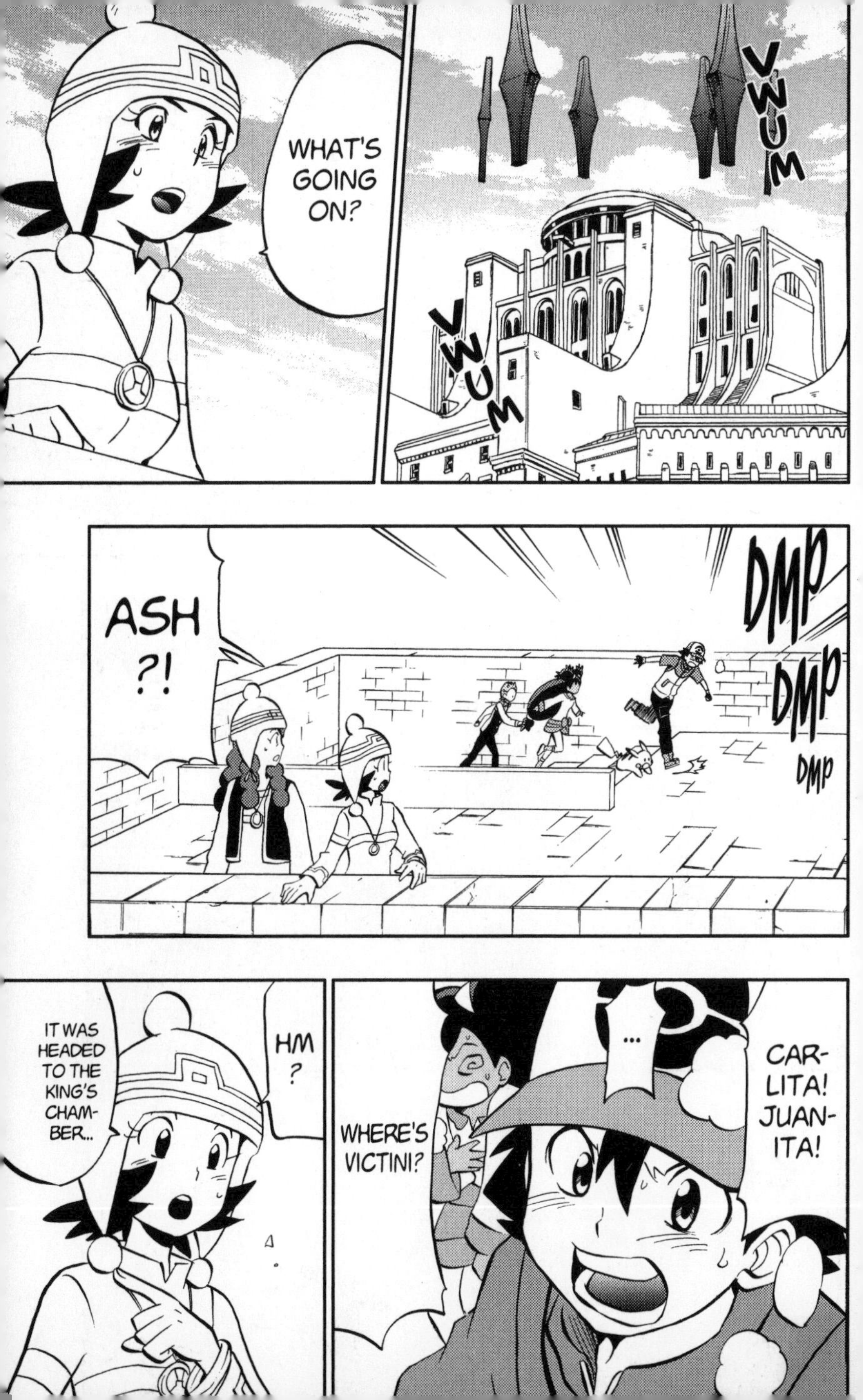
VWUM
VWUM
WHAT'S GOING ON?
DMP
DMP
DMP
ASH ?!
CAR-LITA! JUAN-ITA!
...
WHERE'S VICTINI?
HM ?
IT WAS HEADED TO THE KING'S CHAM-BER...

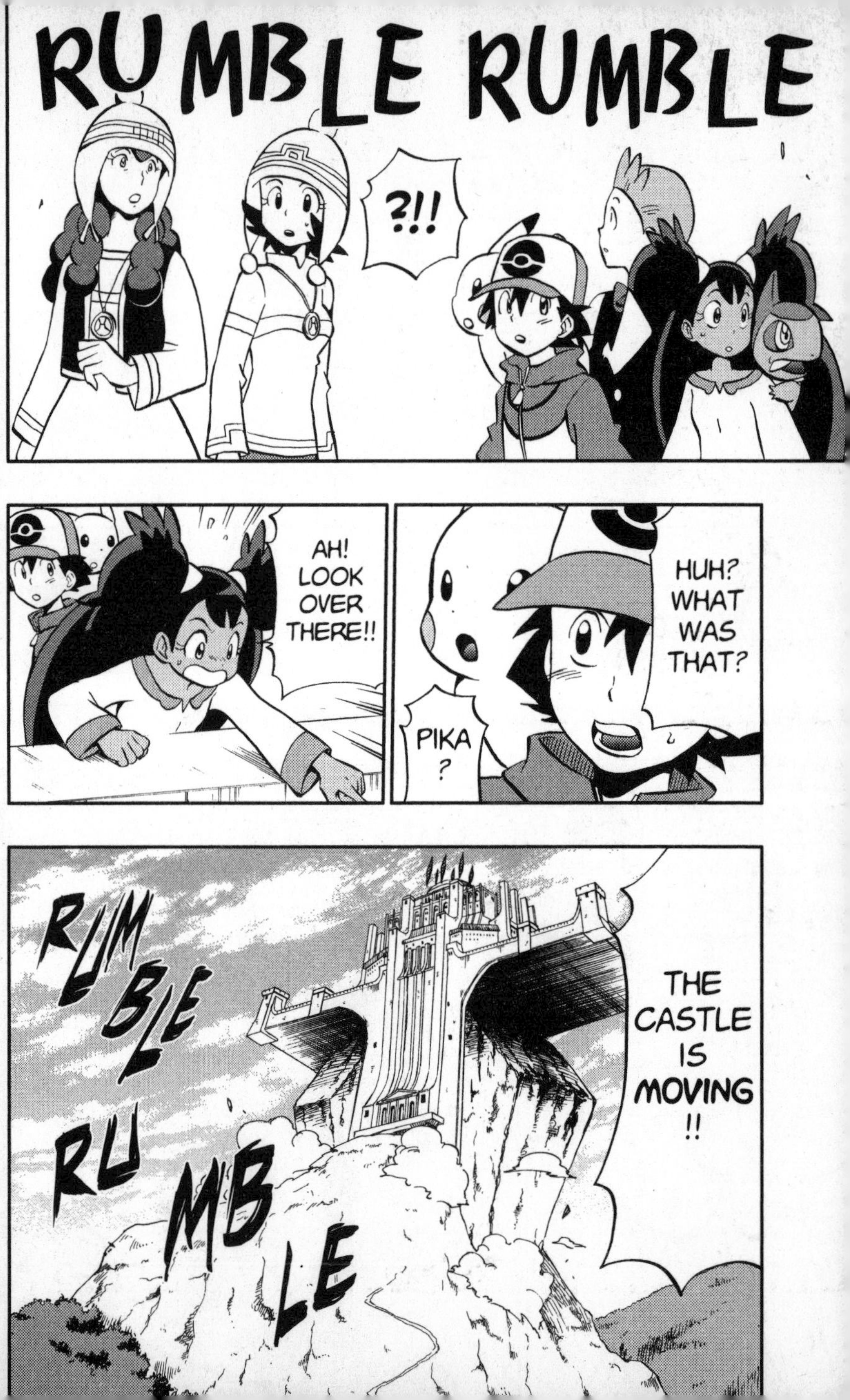
RUMBLE RUMBLE
?!!
HUH? WHAT WAS THAT?
PIKA?
AH! LOOK OVER THERE!!
THE CASTLE IS MOVING!!
RUMBLE RUMBLE

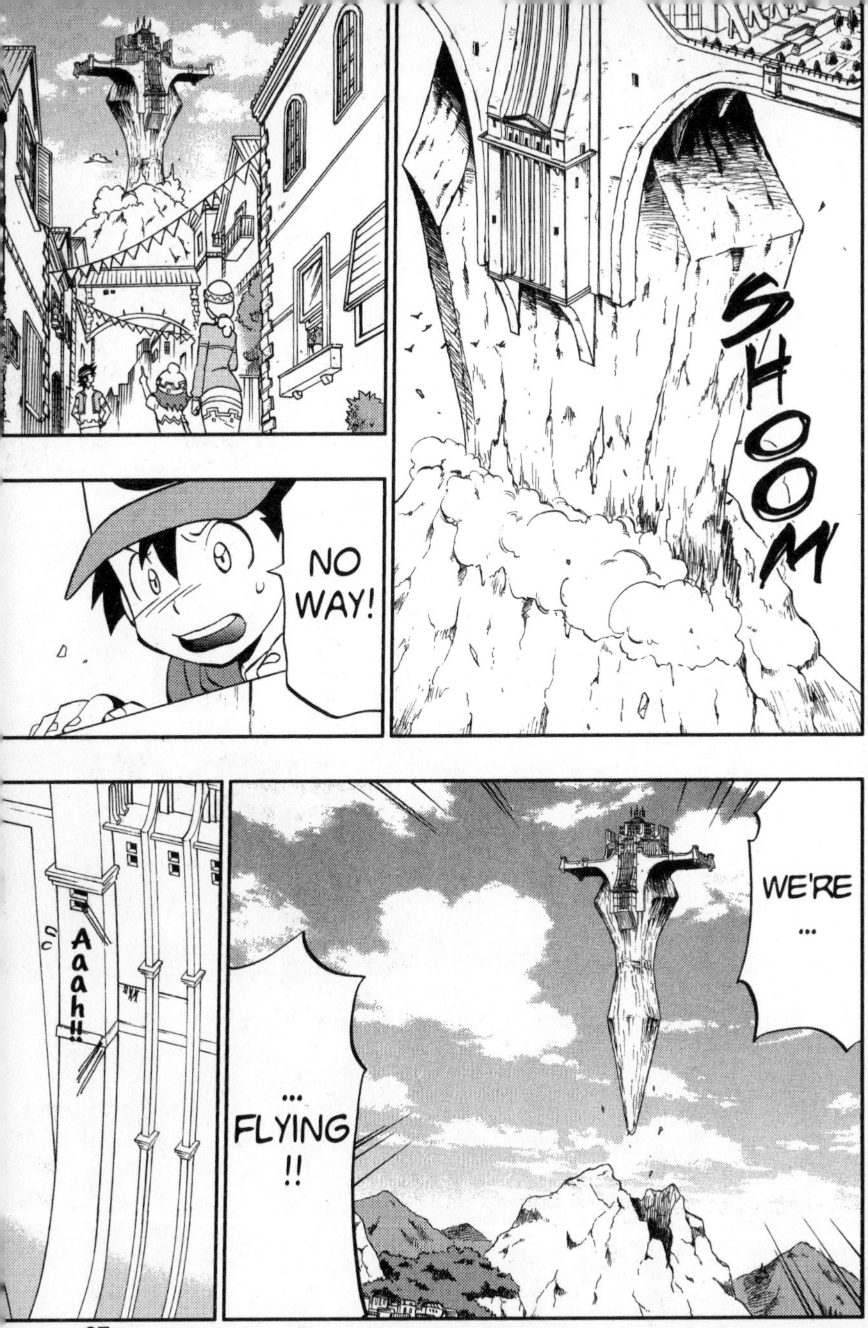
SHOOM
NO WAY!
WE'RE ...
... FLYING !!
Aaah!!

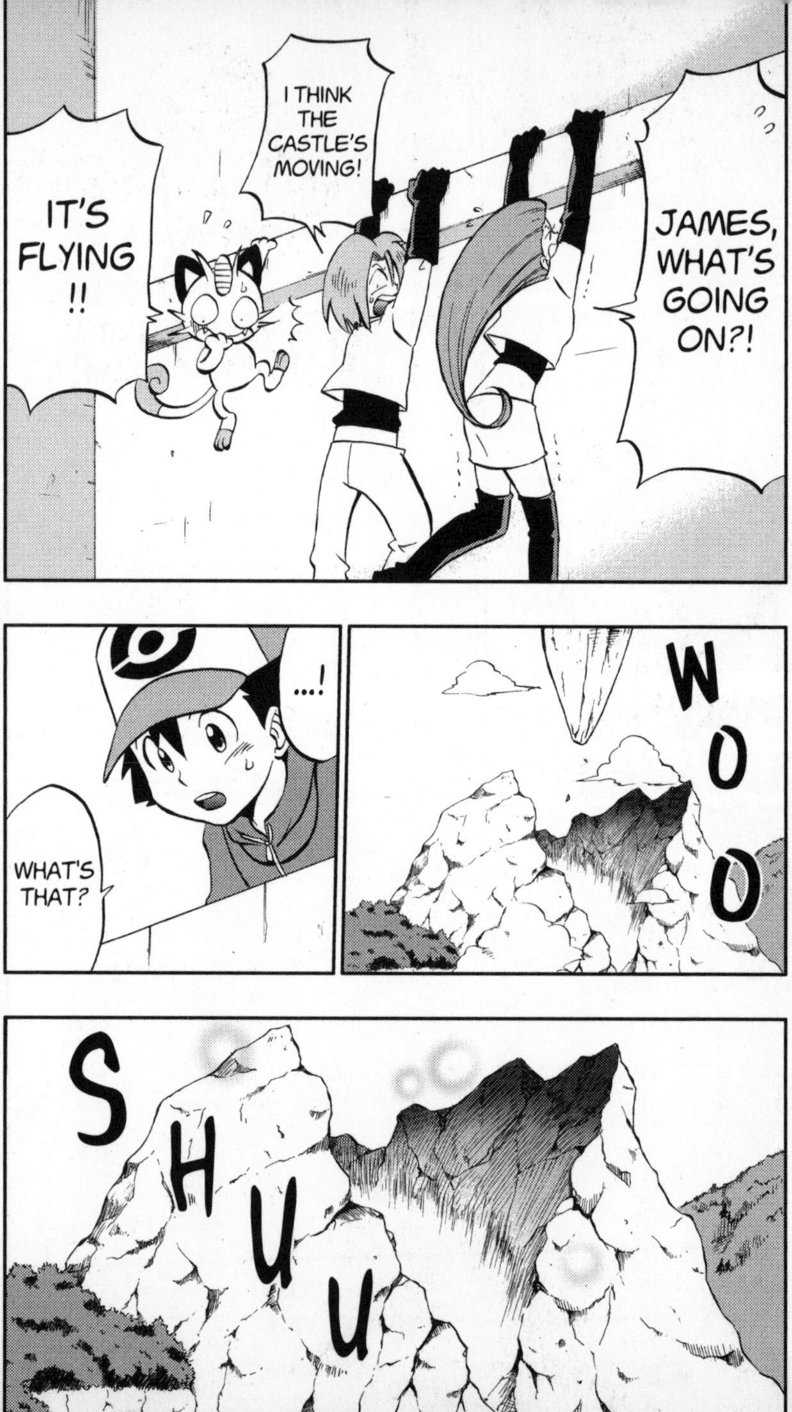
JAMES, WHAT'S GOING ON?!
I THINK THE CASTLE'S MOVING!
IT'S FLYING !!
WOOO
...!
WHAT'S THAT?
SHUUU

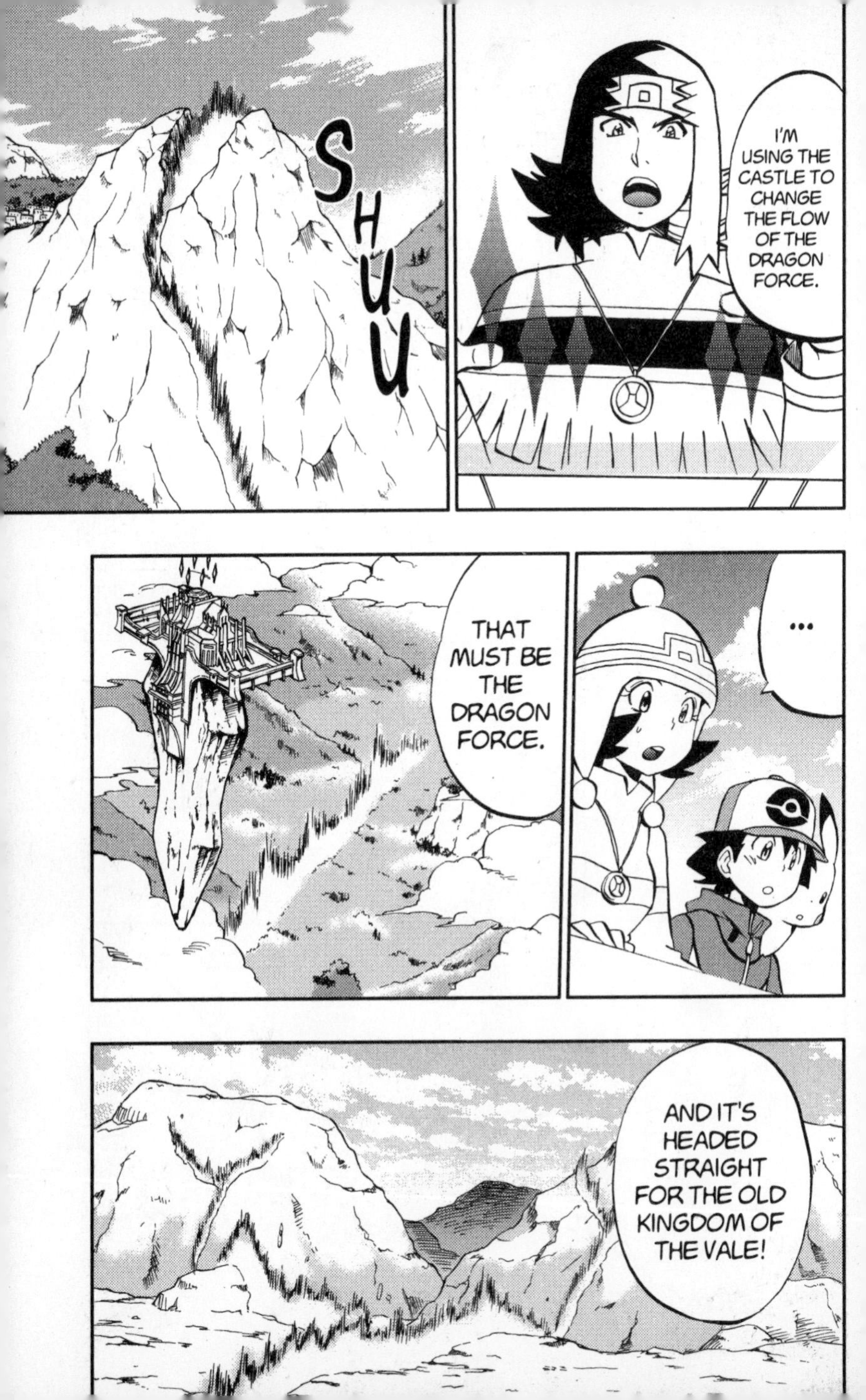

I'M USING THE CASTLE TO CHANGE THE FLOW OF THE DRAGON FORCE.
SHUUU
...
THAT MUST BE THE DRAGON FORCE.
AND IT'S HEADED STRAIGHT FOR THE OLD KINGDOM OF THE VALE!

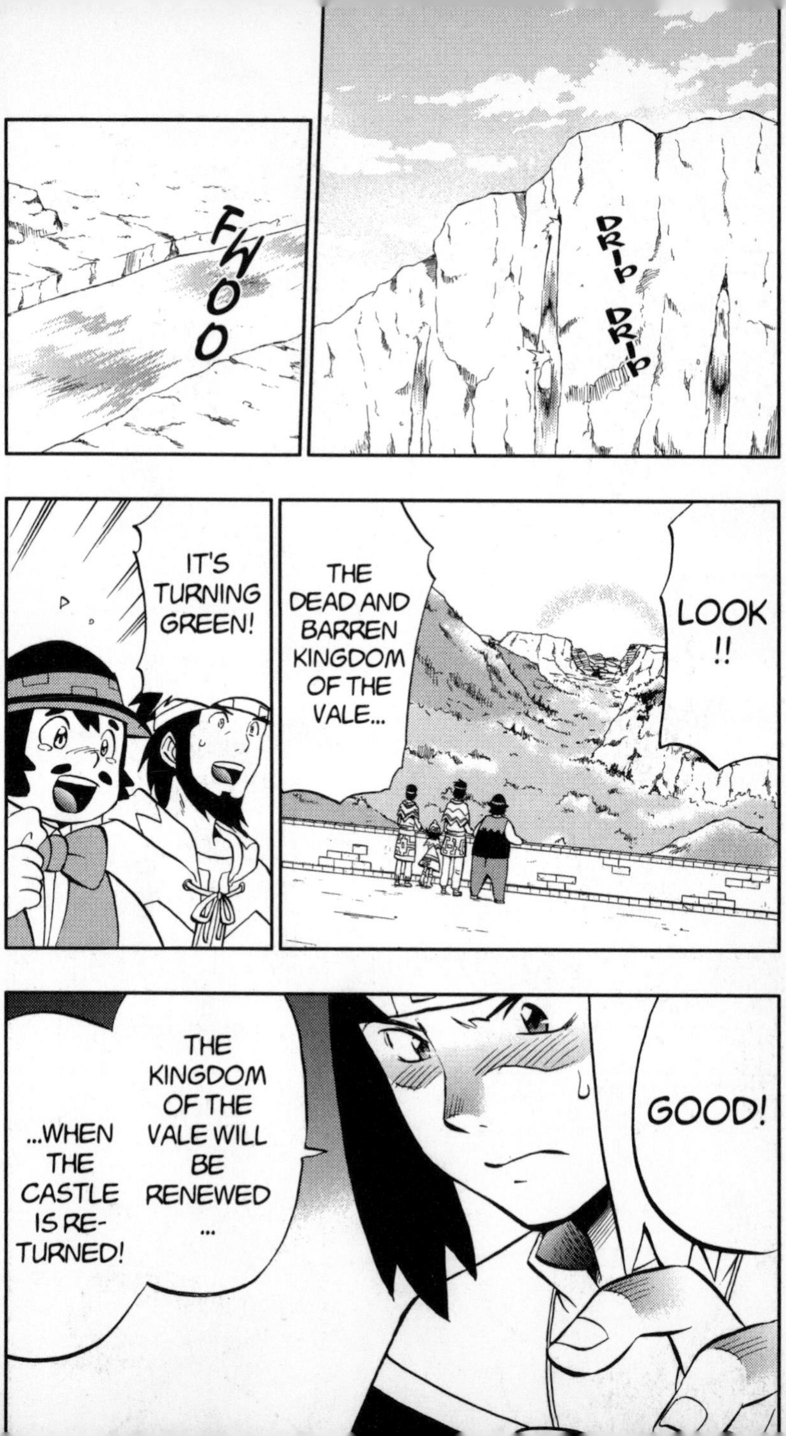
DRIP DRIP
FWOOO
LOOK!!
THE DEAD AND BARREN KINGDOM OF THE VALE...
IT'S TURNING GREEN!
GOOD!
THE KINGDOM OF THE VALE WILL BE RENEWED...
...WHEN THE CASTLE IS RE-TURNED!

READ THIS WAY

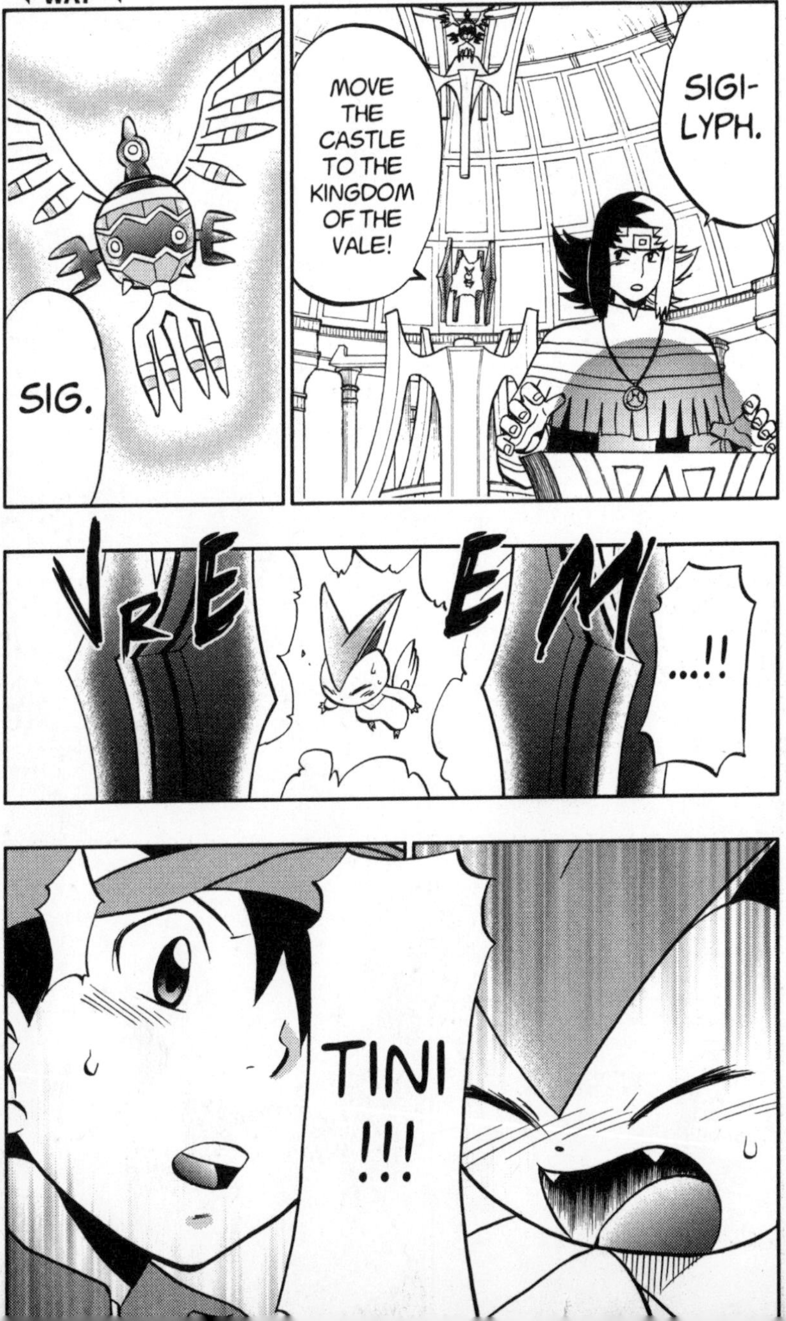
SIGI-LYPH.
MOVE THE CASTLE TO THE KINGDOM OF THE VALE!
SIG.
VREEM
...!!
TINI!!!

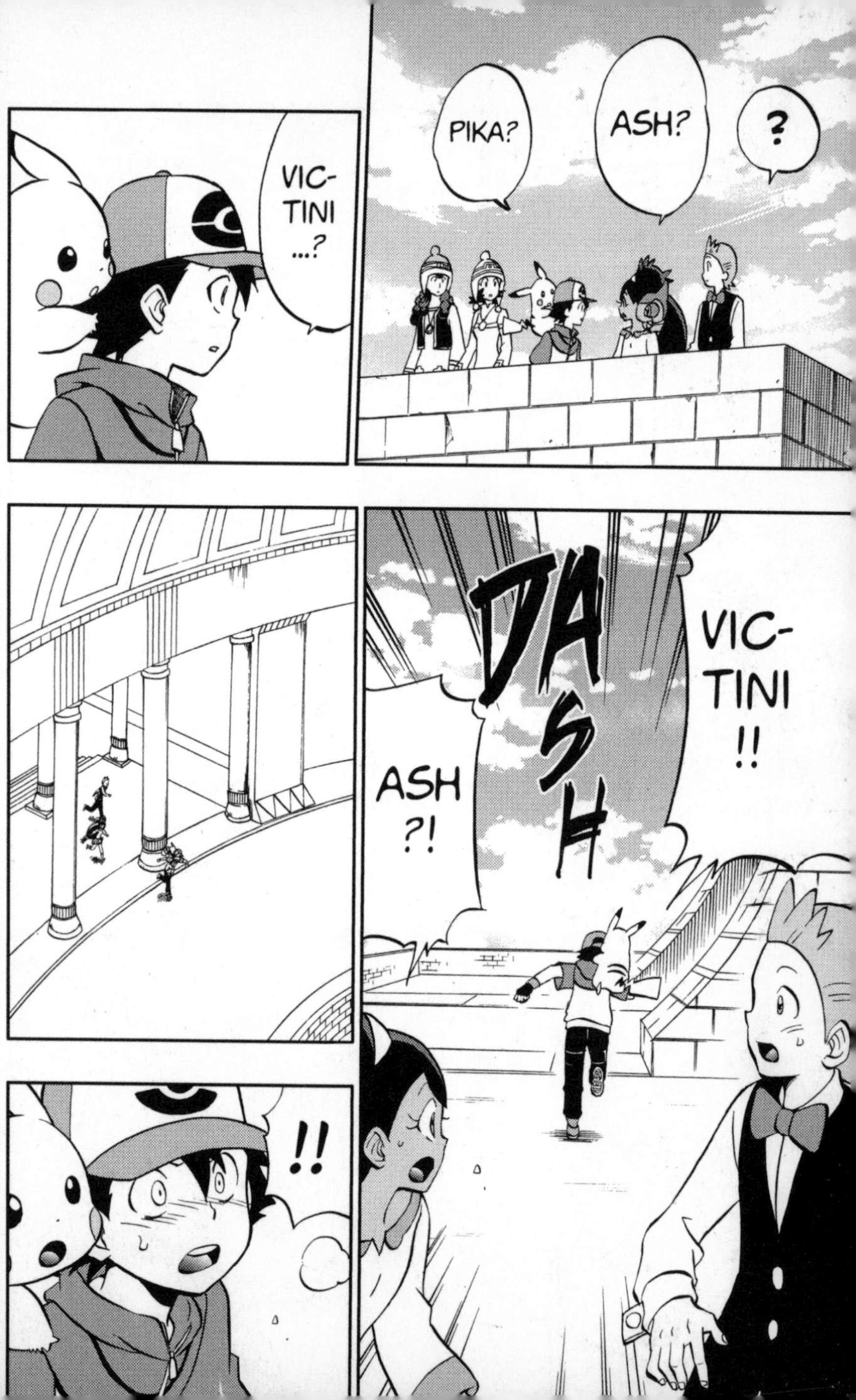
VIC-TINI ...?
PIKA?
ASH?
?
!!
VIC-TINI !!
DASH
ASH ?!

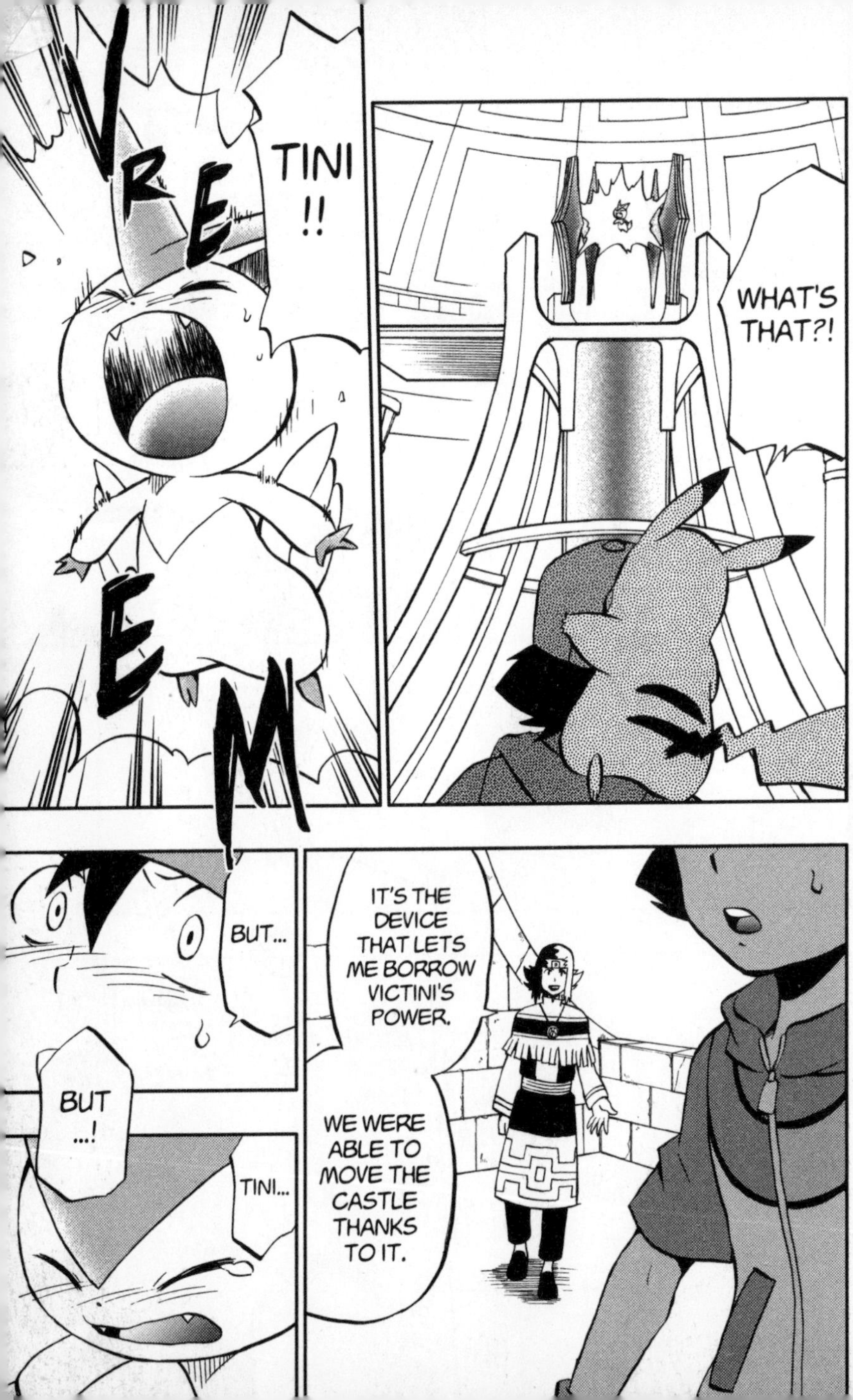
WHAT'S THAT?!
TINI !!
VREEM
IT'S THE DEVICE THAT LETS ME BORROW VICTINI'S POWER.
WE WERE ABLE TO MOVE THE CASTLE THANKS TO IT.
BUT...
BUT ...!
TINI...

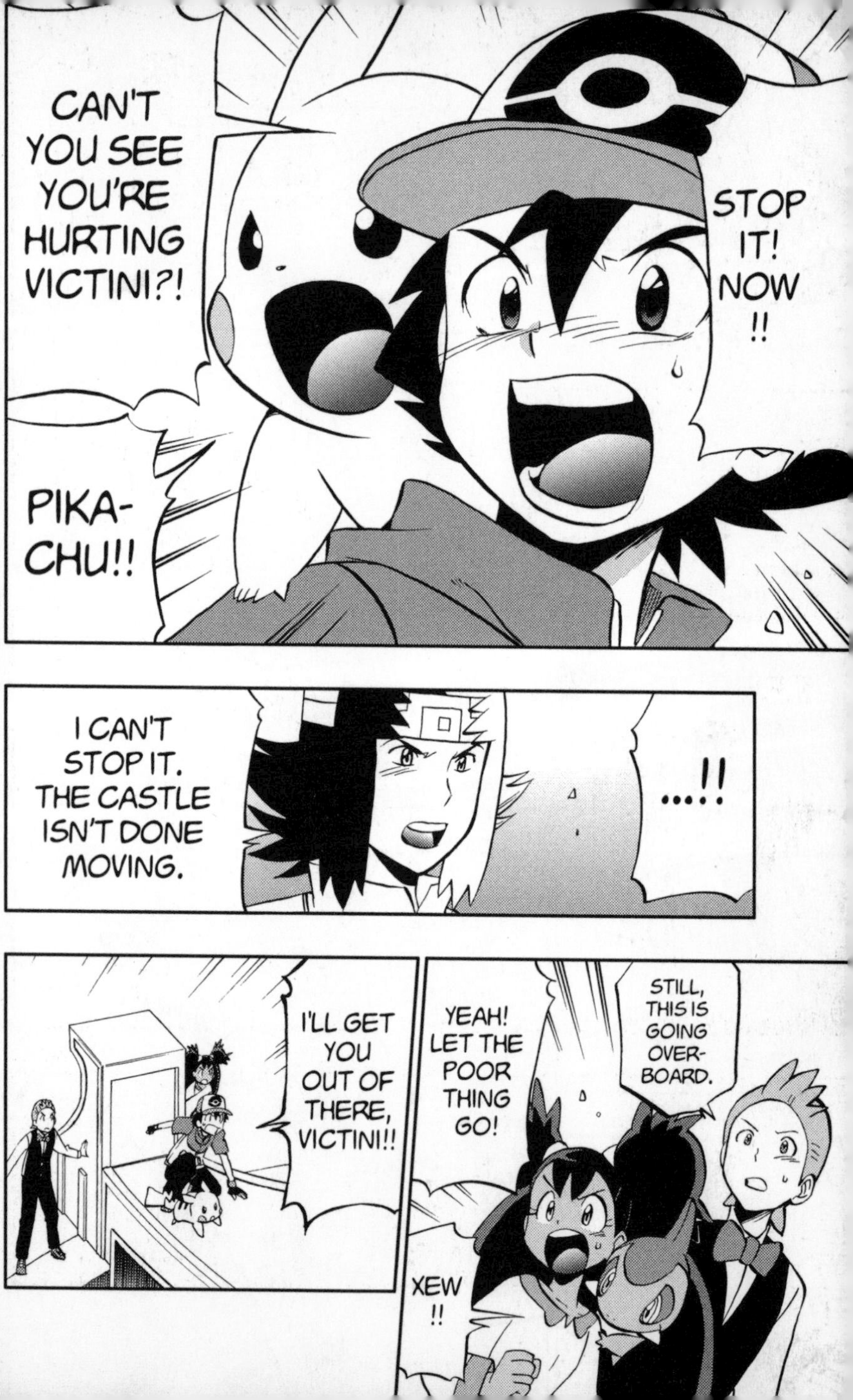
STOP IT! NOW!!
CAN'T YOU SEE YOU'RE HURTING VICTINI?!
PIKA-CHU!!
...!!
I CAN'T STOP IT. THE CASTLE ISN'T DONE MOVING.
STILL, THIS IS GOING OVER-BOARD.
YEAH! LET THE POOR THING GO!
XEW!!
I'LL GET YOU OUT OF THERE, VICTINI!!

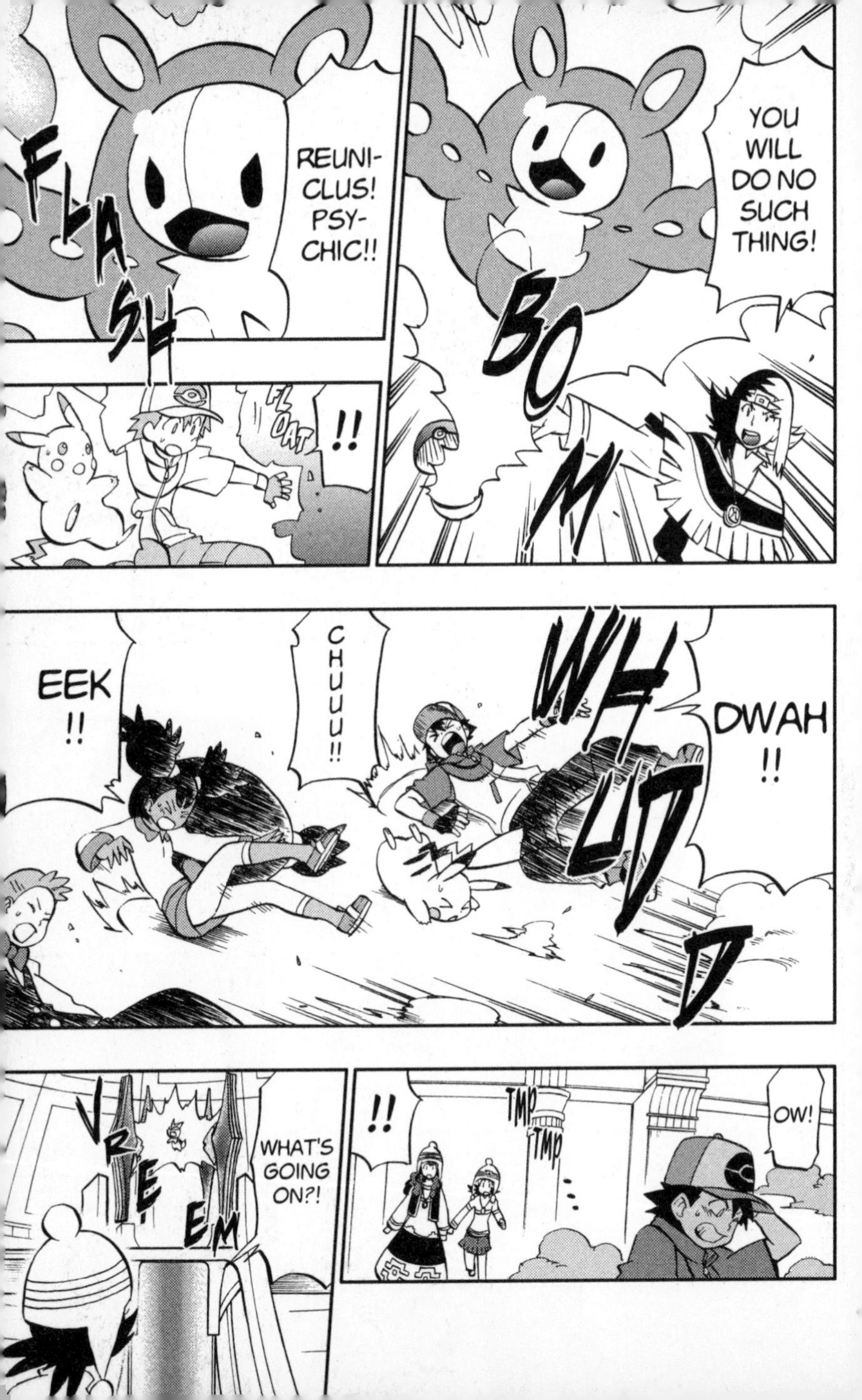
YOU WILL DO NO SUCH THING!
BOOM
REUNI-CLUS! PSY-CHIC!!
FLASH
!!
FLOAT
DWAH!!
WHUD
CHUUUU!!
EEK!!
OW!
TMP
TMP
!!
WHAT'S GOING ON?!
VREEM

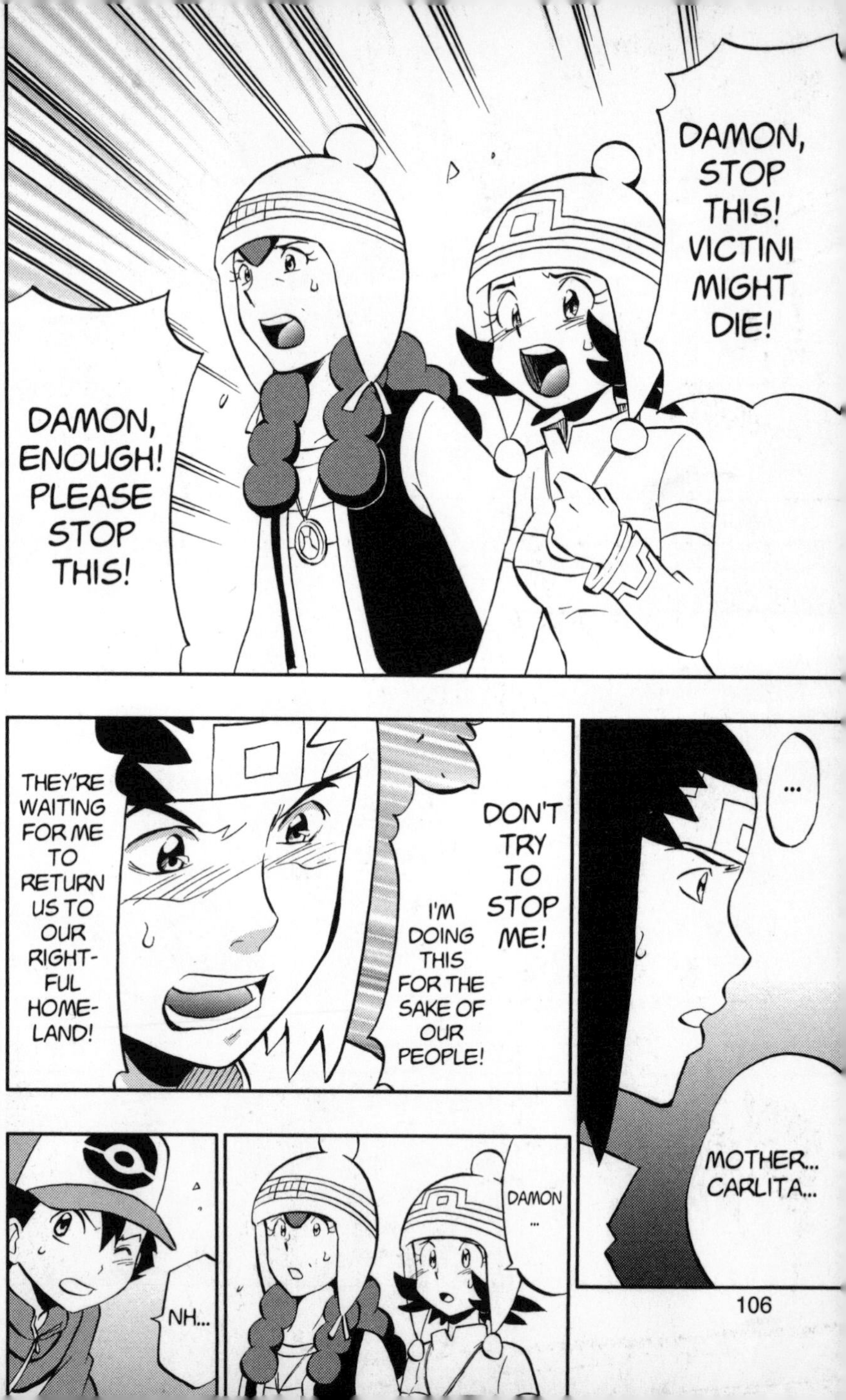
DAMON, STOP THIS! VICTINI MIGHT DIE!
DAMON, ENOUGH! PLEASE STOP THIS!
...
MOTHER... CARLITA...
DON'T TRY TO STOP ME!
I'M DOING THIS FOR THE SAKE OF OUR PEOPLE!
THEY'RE WAITING FOR ME TO RETURN US TO OUR RIGHTFUL HOMELAND!
DAMON...
NH...

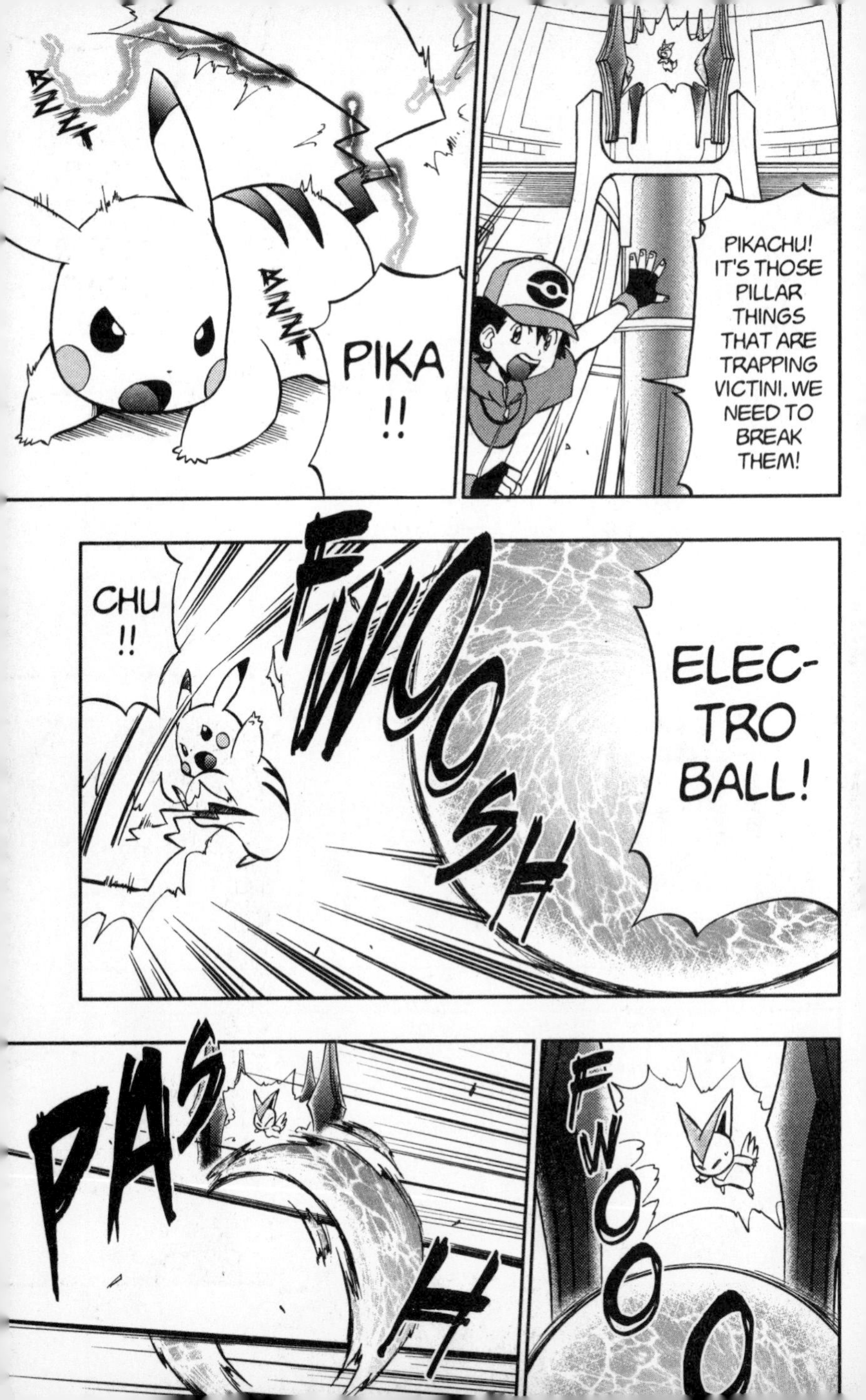
PIKACHU! IT'S THOSE PILLAR THINGS THAT ARE TRAPPING VICTINI. WE NEED TO BREAK THEM!
BZZZT
BZZZT
PIKA !!
ELEC-TRO BALL!
FWOOSH
CHU !!
FWOOO
PASH

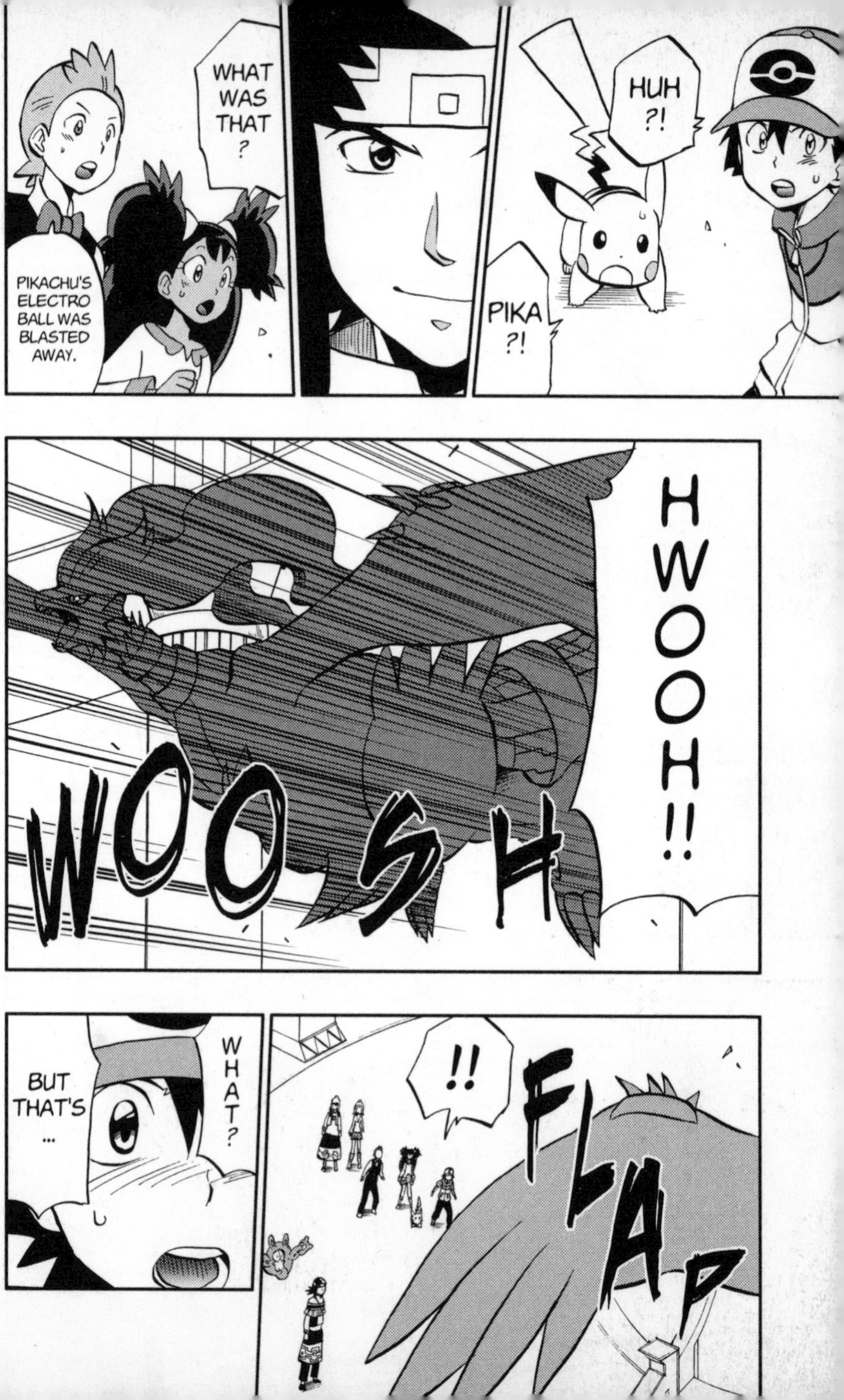
HUH?!
PIKA?!
WHAT WAS THAT?
PIKACHU'S ELECTRO BALL WAS BLASTED AWAY.
HWOOOH!!
WOOSH
!!
FLAP
WHAT?
BUT THAT'S ...

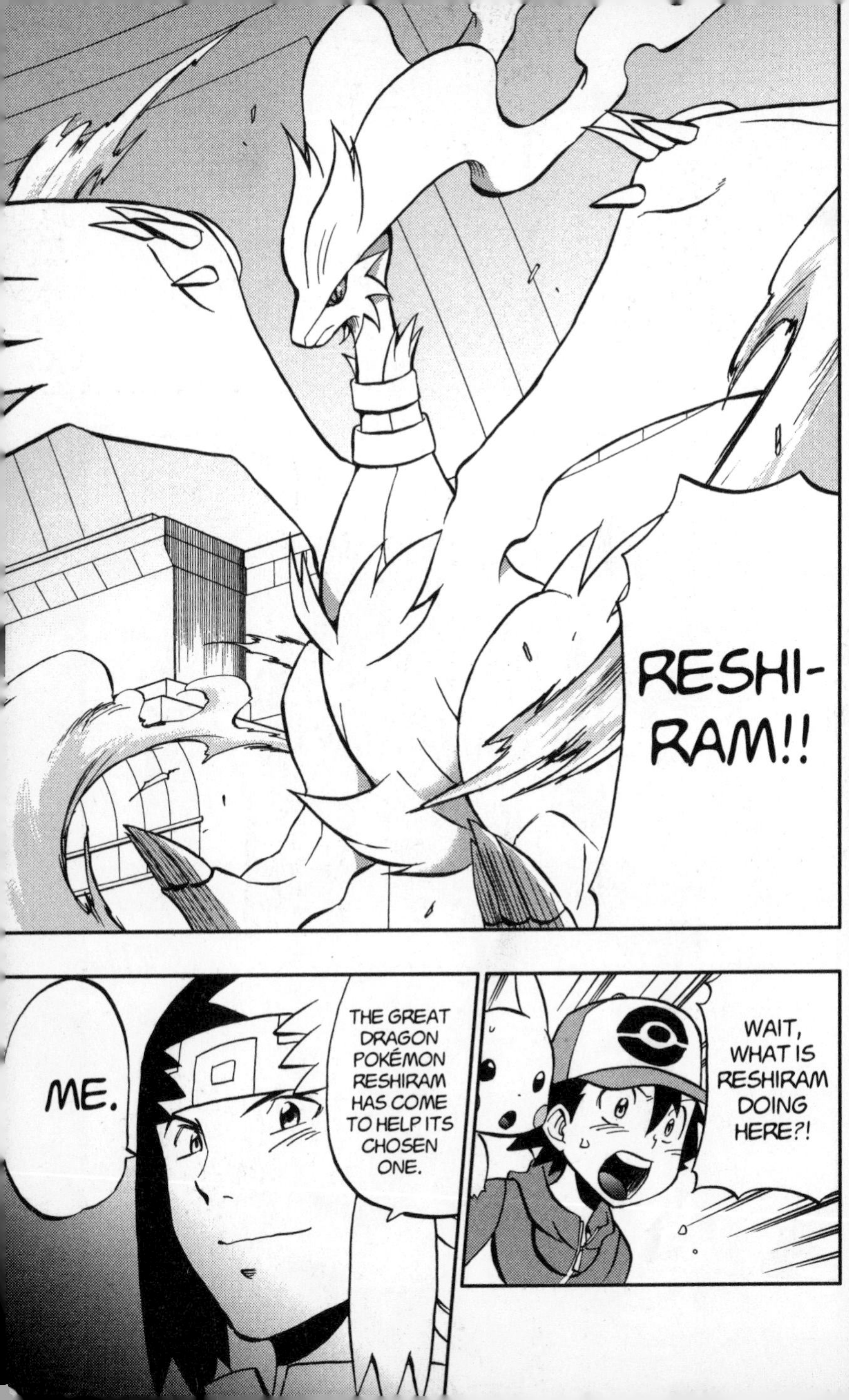
RESHI-RAM!!
WAIT, WHAT IS RESHIRAM DOING HERE?!
THE GREAT DRAGON POKÉMON RESHIRAM HAS COME TO HELP ITS CHOSEN ONE.
ME.

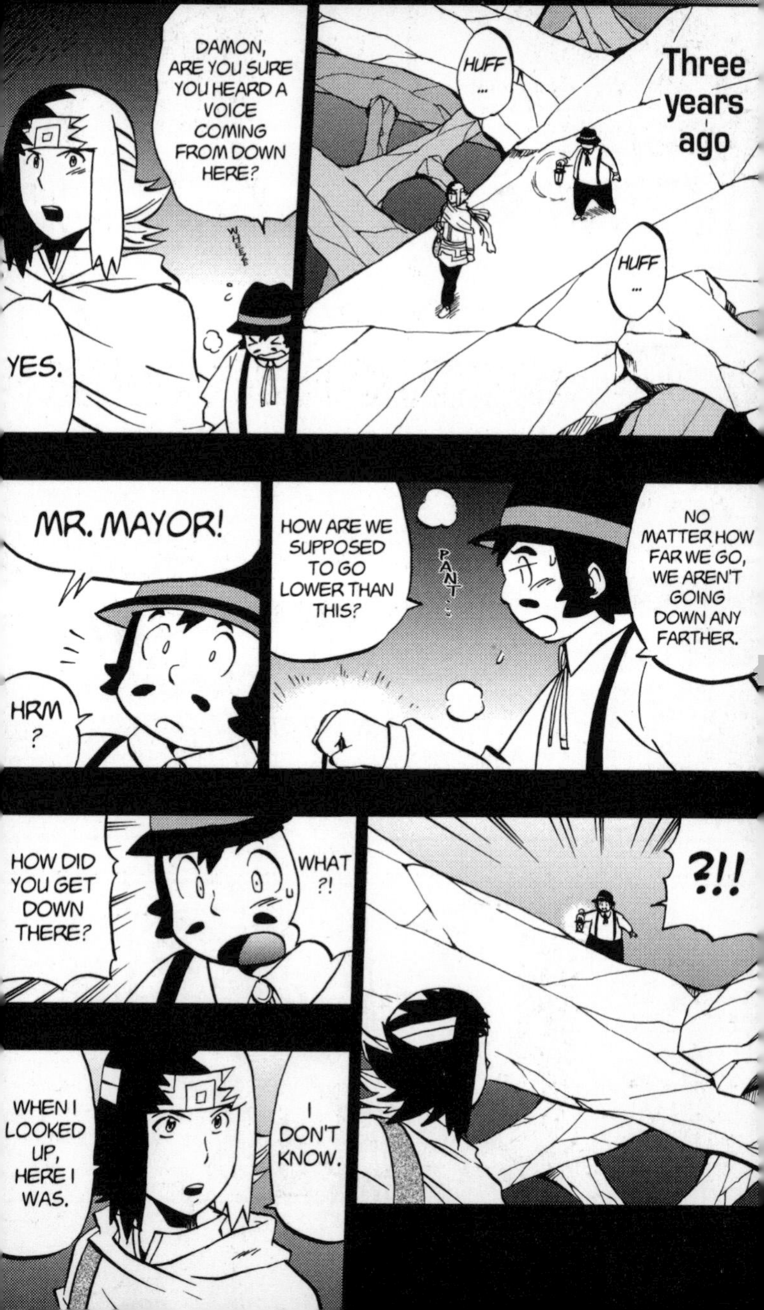
Three years ago
HUFF ...
HUFF ...
DAMON, ARE YOU SURE YOU HEARD A VOICE COMING FROM DOWN HERE?
YES.
NO MATTER HOW FAR WE GO, WE AREN'T GOING DOWN ANY FARTHER.
PANT
HOW ARE WE SUPPOSED TO GO LOWER THAN THIS?
MR. MAYOR!
HRM ?
?!!
WHAT ?!
HOW DID YOU GET DOWN THERE?
I DON'T KNOW.
WHEN I LOOKED UP, HERE I WAS.

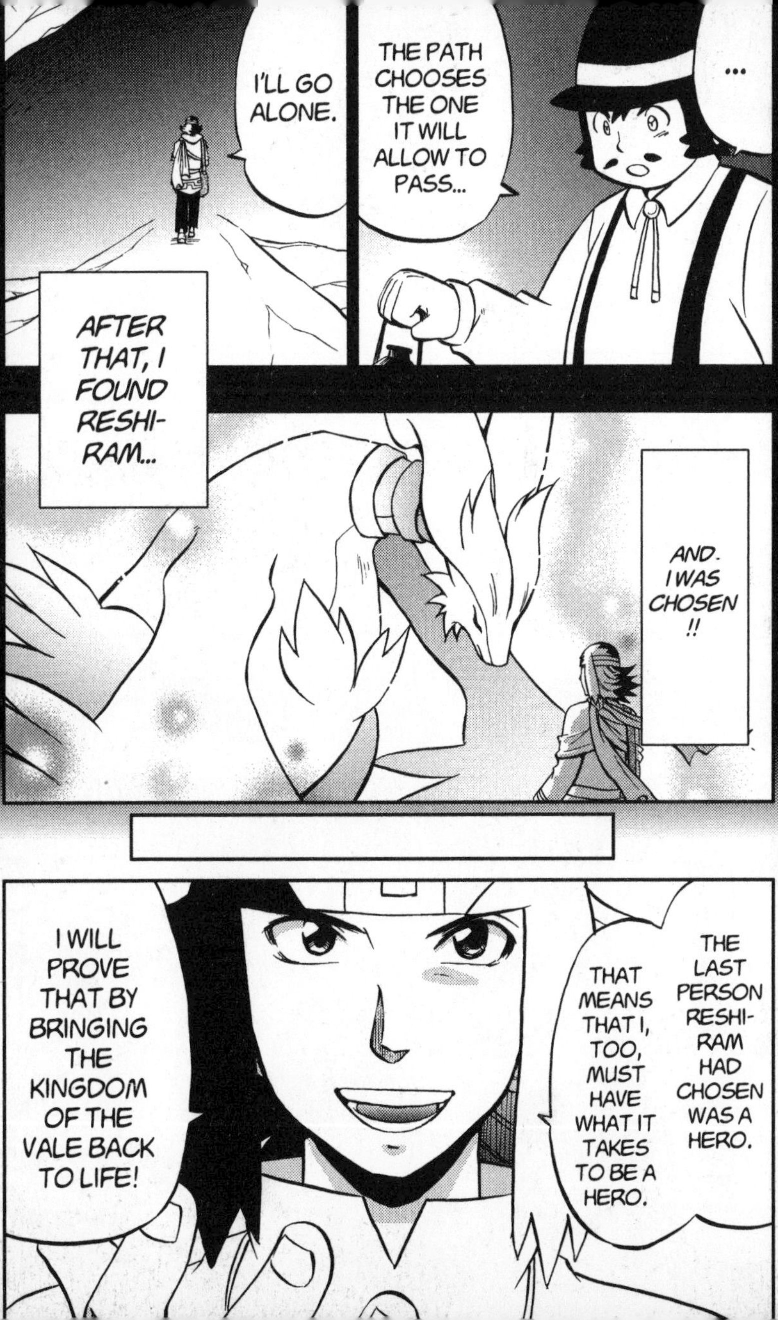
...
THE PATH CHOOSES THE ONE IT WILL ALLOW TO PASS...
I'LL GO ALONE.
AFTER THAT, I FOUND RESHI-RAM...
AND I WAS CHOSEN!!
THE LAST PERSON RESHI-RAM HAD CHOSEN WAS A HERO.
THAT MEANS THAT I, TOO, MUST HAVE WHAT IT TAKES TO BE A HERO.
I WILL PROVE THAT BY BRINGING THE KINGDOM OF THE VALE BACK TO LIFE!

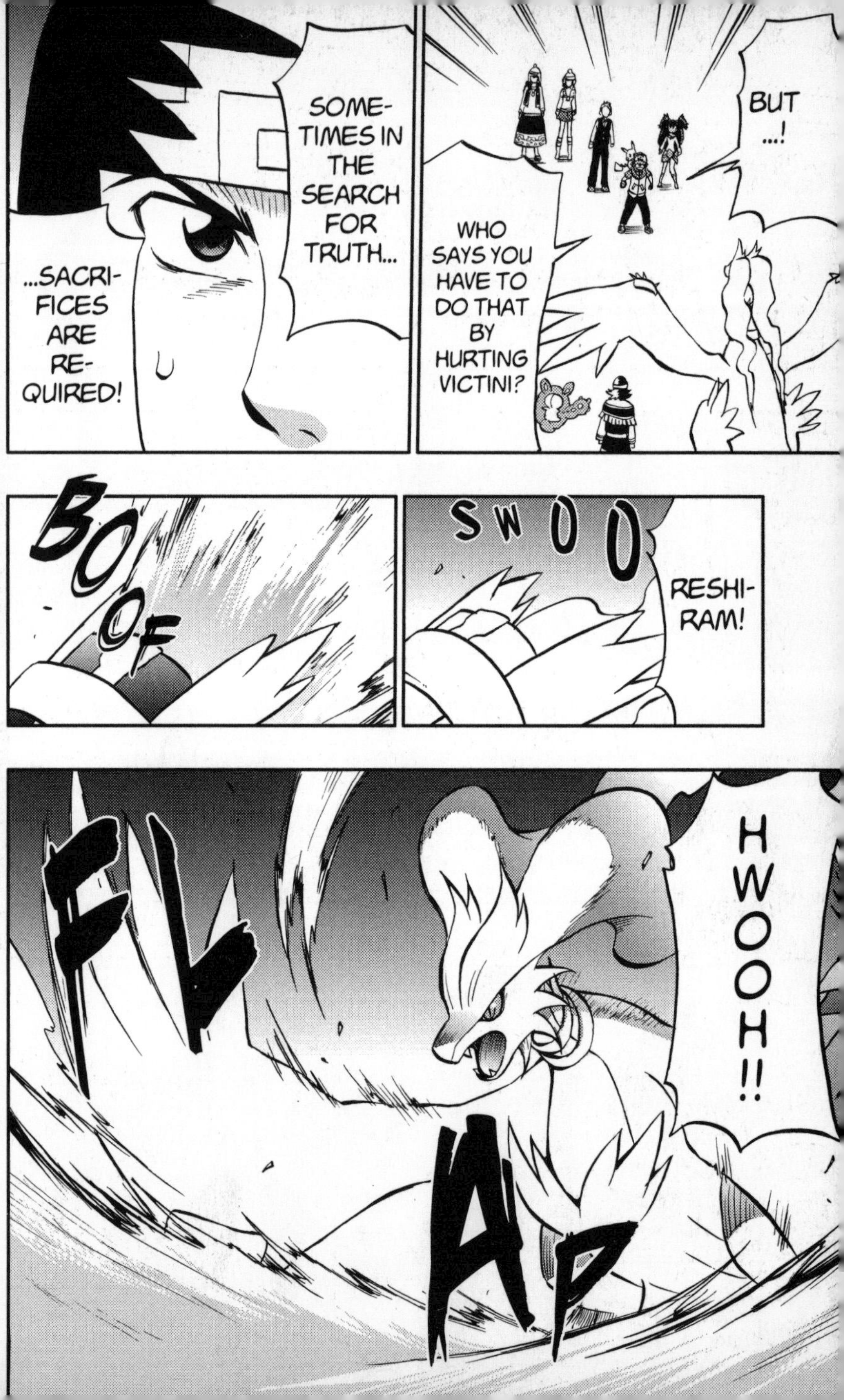
BUT ...!
WHO SAYS YOU HAVE TO DO THAT BY HURTING VICTINI?
SOMETIMES IN THE SEARCH FOR TRUTH...
...SACRIFICES ARE REQUIRED!
SWOO
RESHIRAM!
BOOOF
HWOOOH!!
FLAP

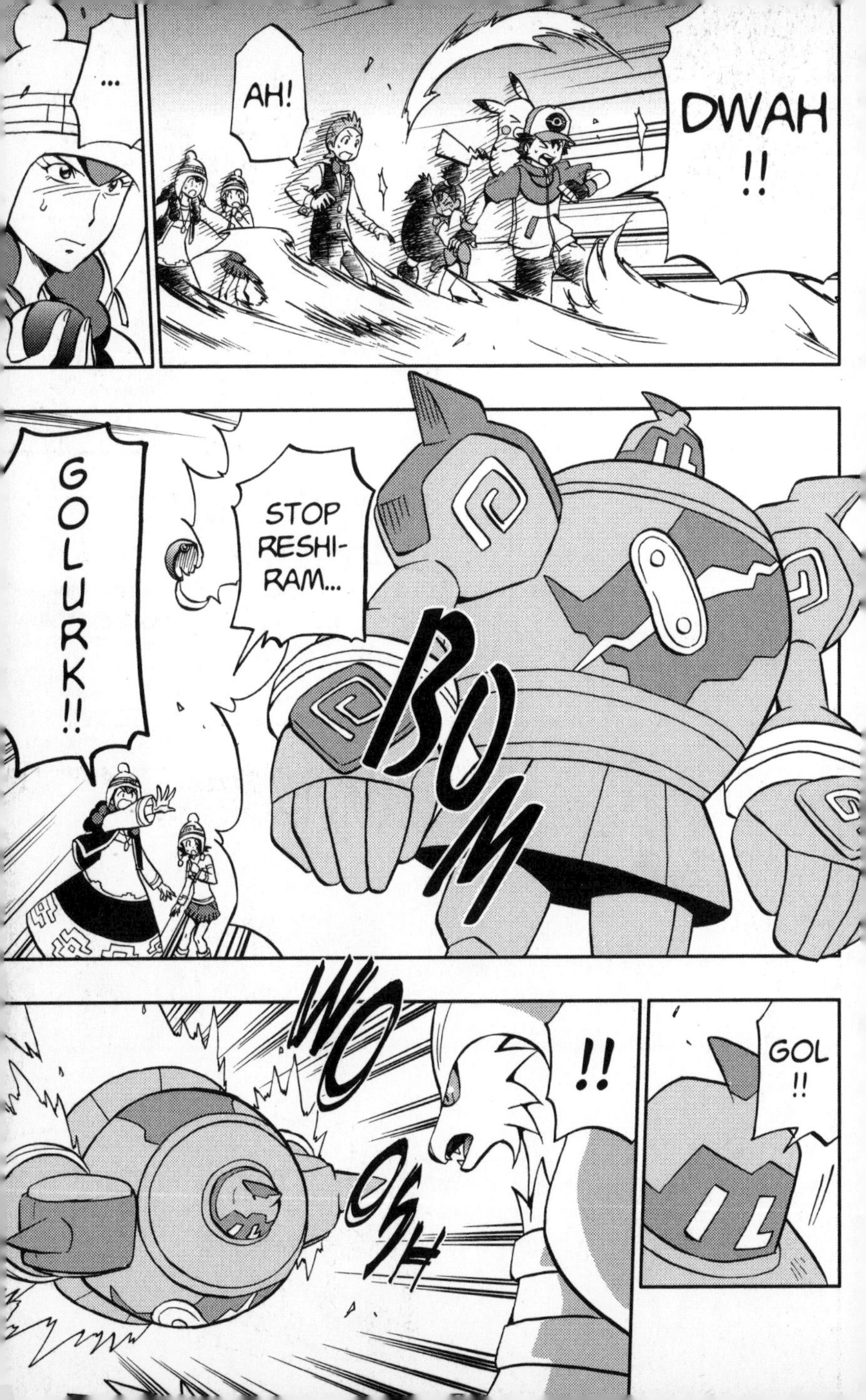
DWAH !!
AH!
...
STOP RESHI-RAM...
GOLURK!!
BOM
GOL !!
!!
WOOSH

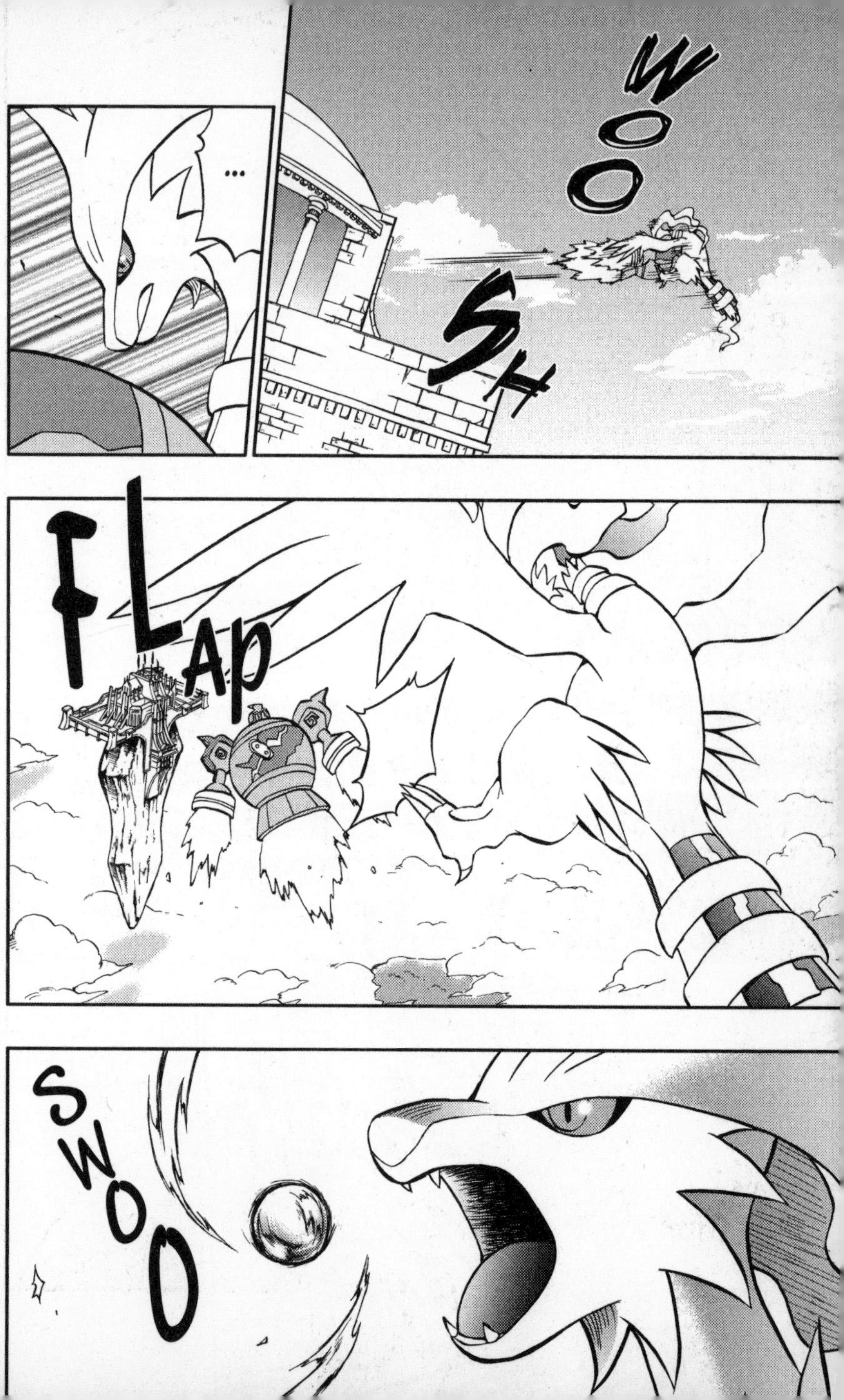
WOOSH
...
FLAP
SWOO

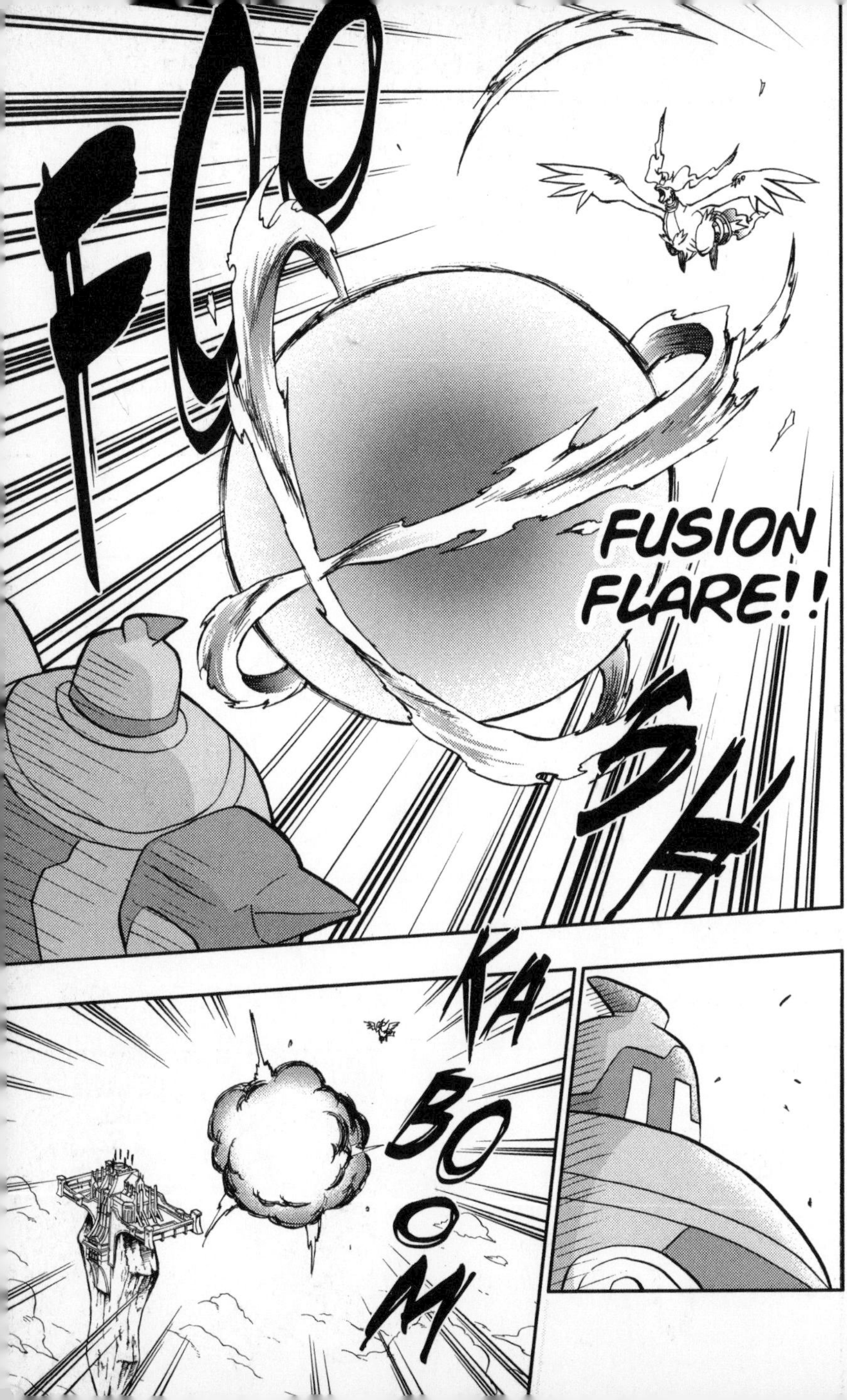
FUSION FLARE!!
SHH
FOOO
KA BOOM

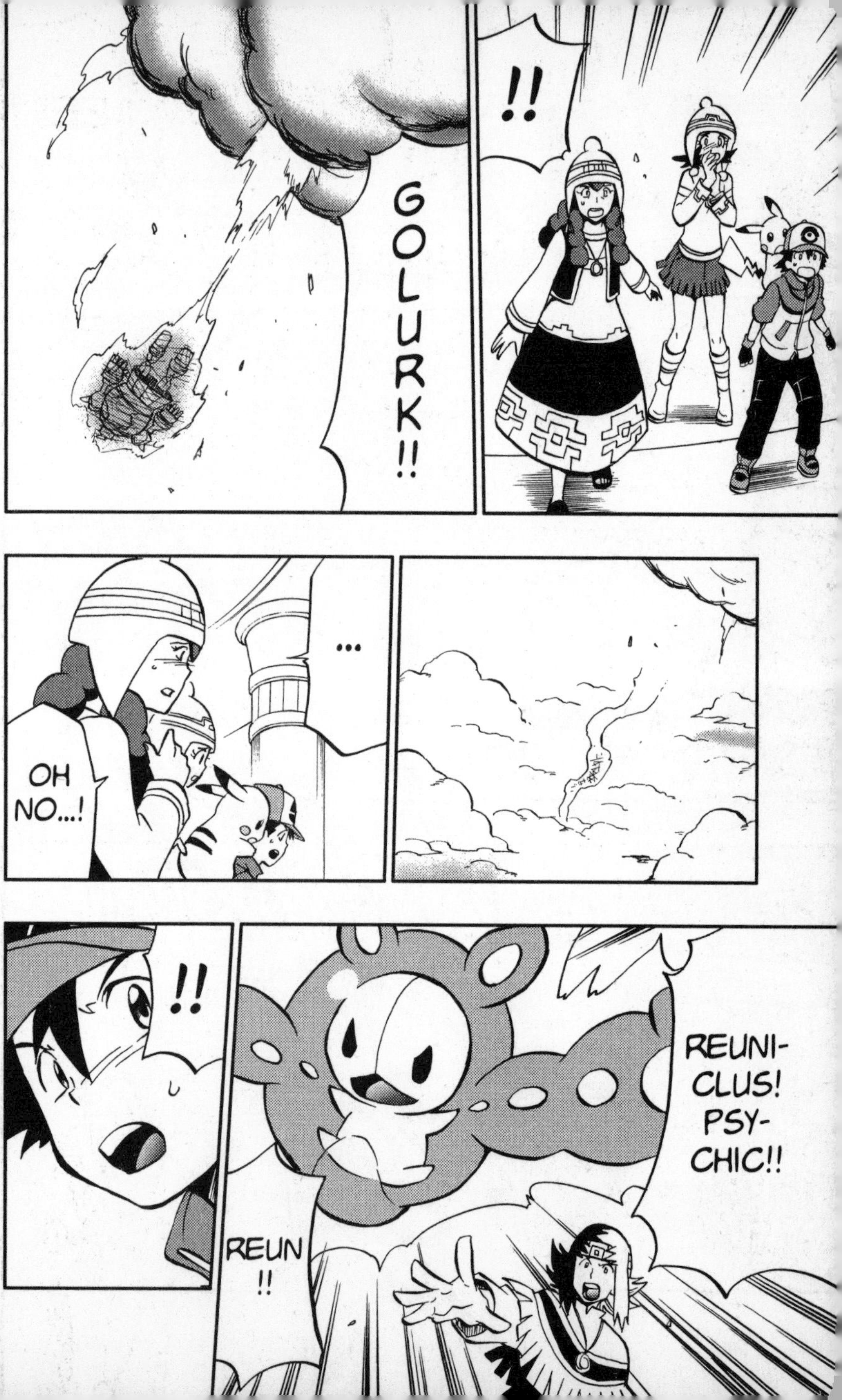
!!
GOLURK!!
...
OH NO...!
!!
REUNICLUS! PSYCHIC!!
REUN!!

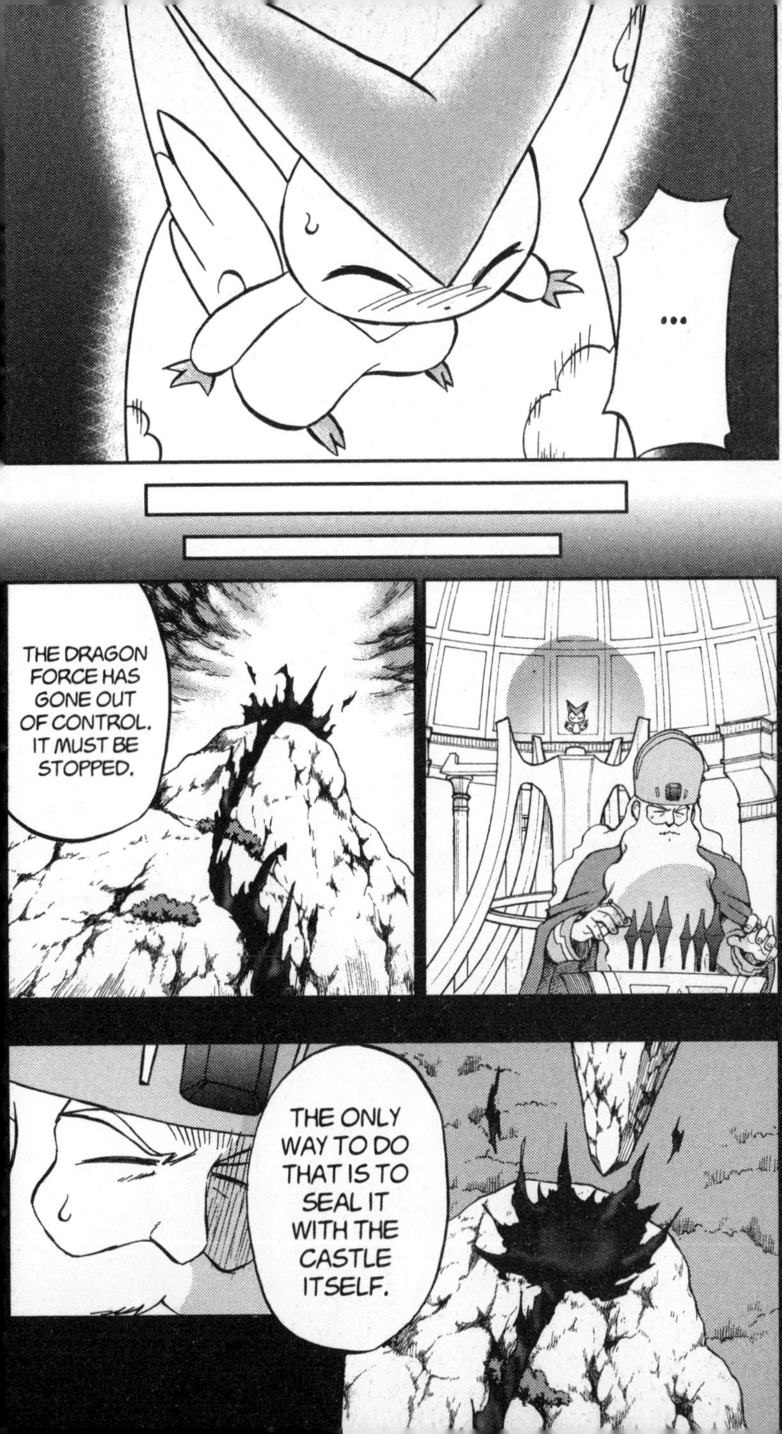
...
THE DRAGON FORCE HAS GONE OUT OF CONTROL. IT MUST BE STOPPED.
THE ONLY WAY TO DO THAT IS TO SEAL IT WITH THE CASTLE ITSELF.

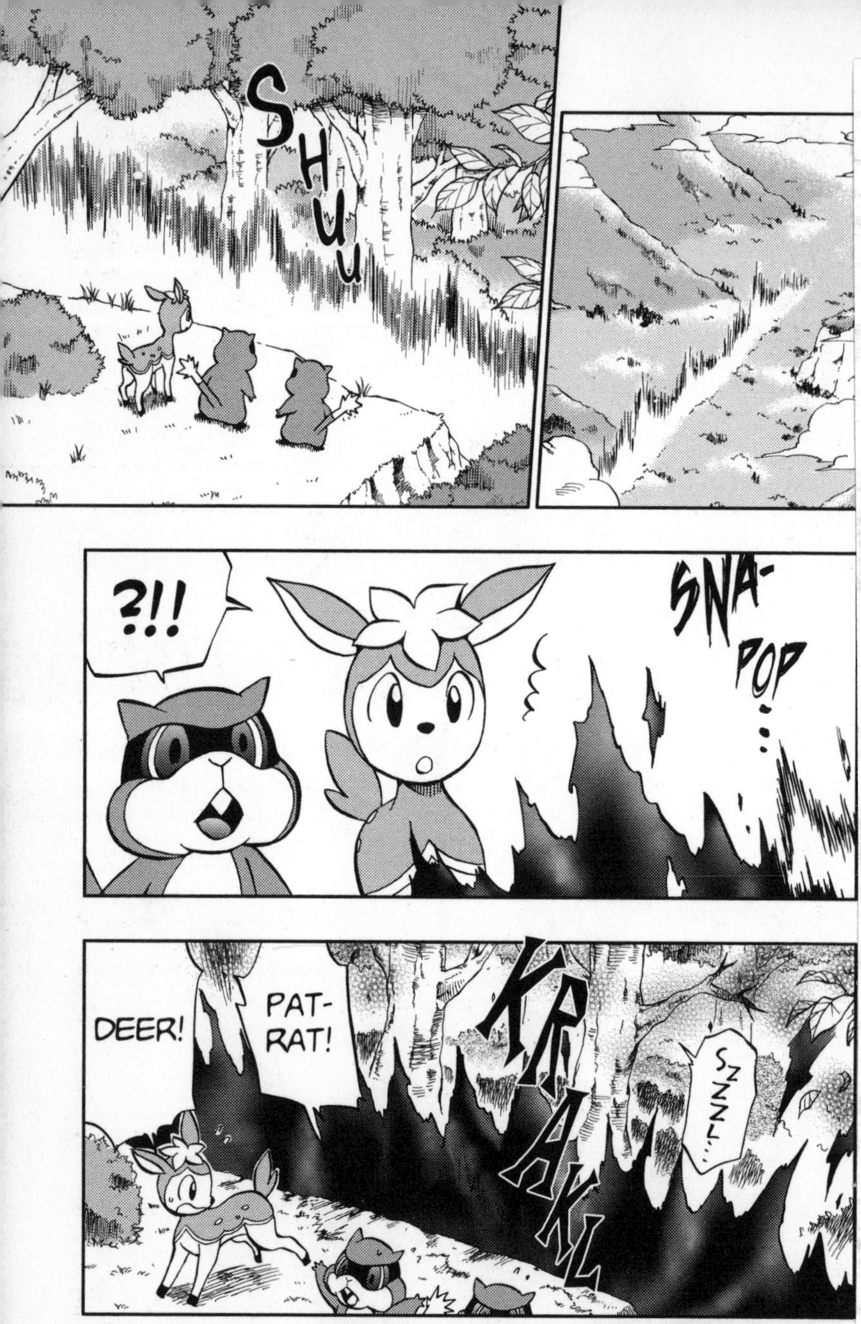
SHUUU
SNA-POP...
?!!
SZZZL...
KRAKL
PAT-RAT!
DEER!

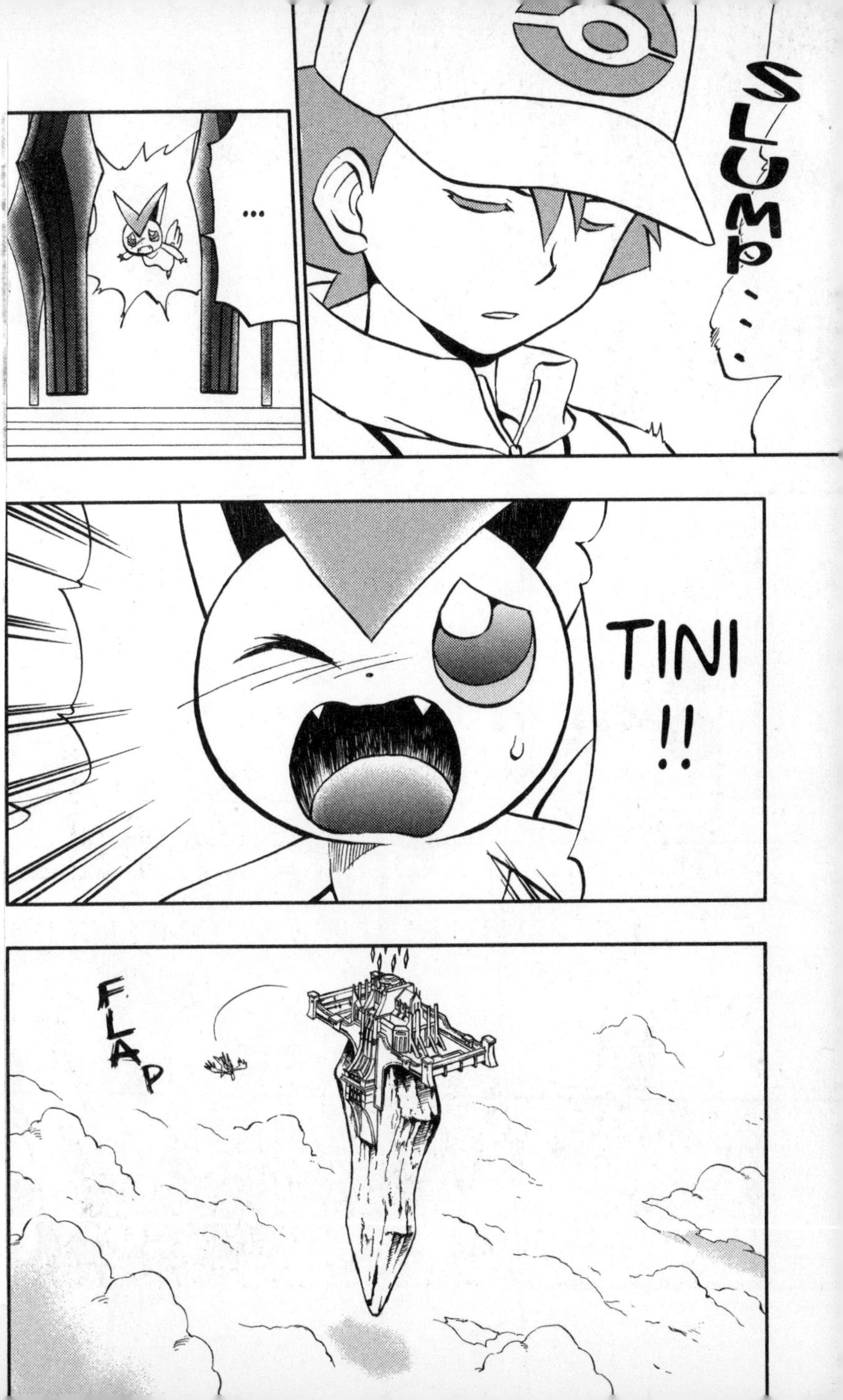
SLUMP...
...
TINI!!
FLAP

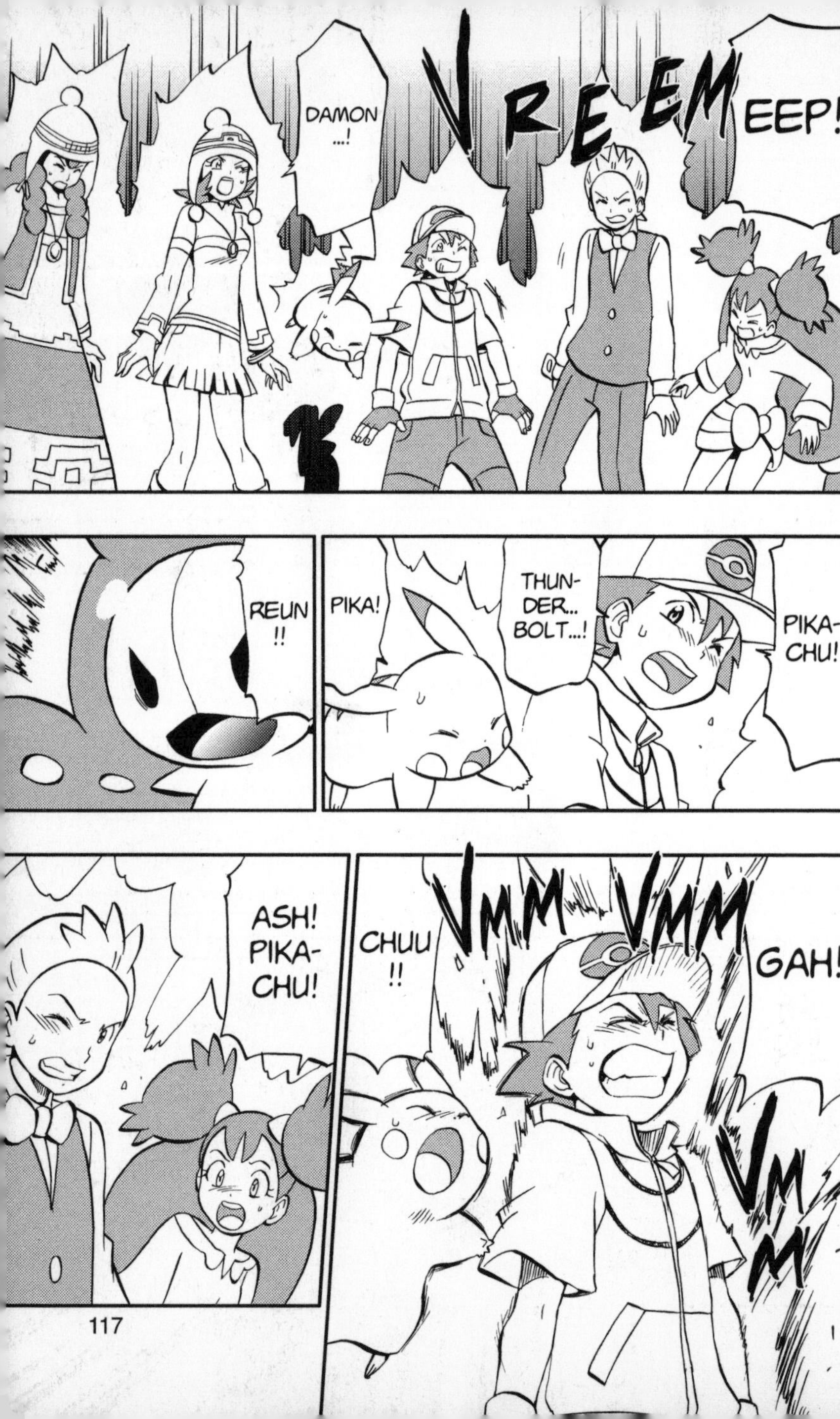
EEP!
VREEM
DAMON ...!
PIKA-CHU!
THUN-DER... BOLT...!
PIKA!
REUN !!
GAH!
VMM VMM
CHUU !!
VMM
ASH! PIKA-CHU!

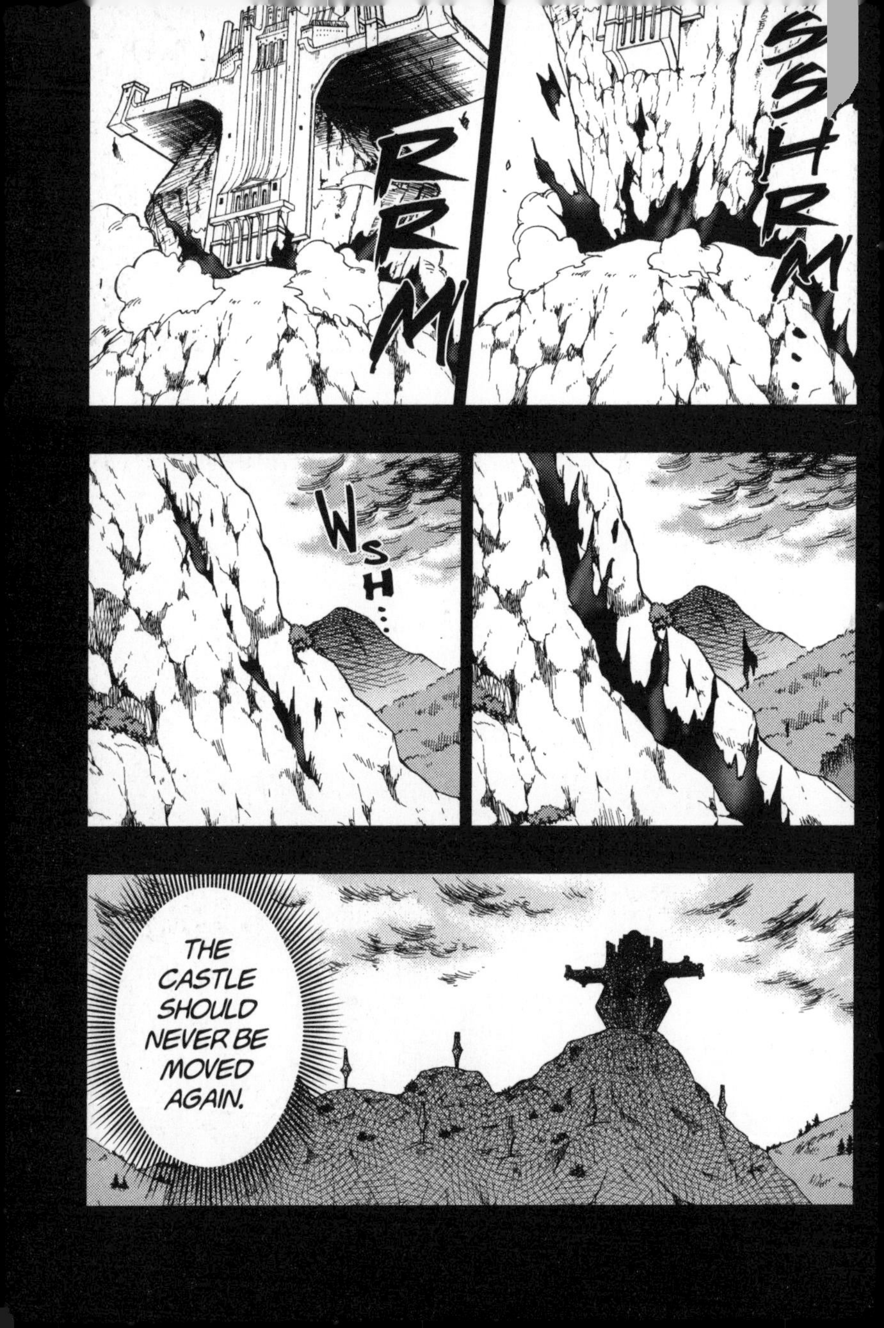
SSHRM...
RRM
WSH...
THE CASTLE SHOULD NEVER BE MOVED AGAIN.

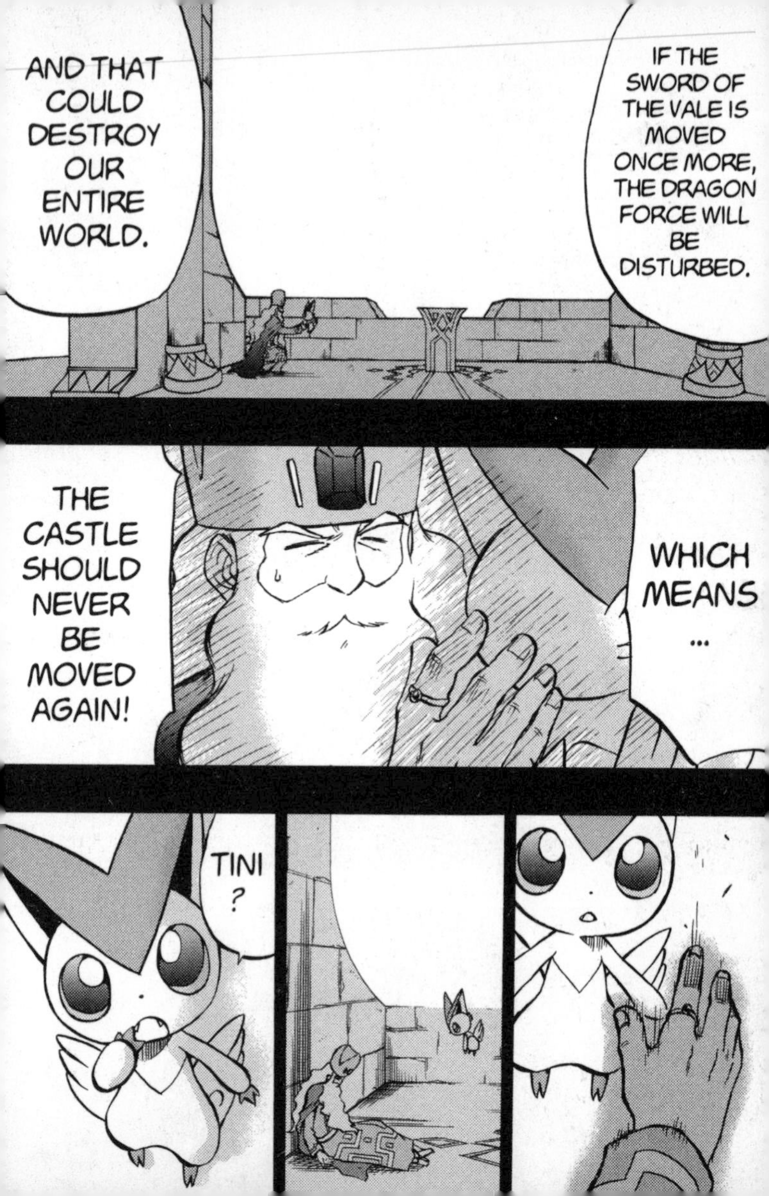
IF THE SWORD OF THE VALE IS MOVED ONCE MORE, THE DRAGON FORCE WILL BE DISTURBED.
AND THAT COULD DESTROY OUR ENTIRE WORLD.
WHICH MEANS ...
THE CASTLE SHOULD NEVER BE MOVED AGAIN!
TINI ?

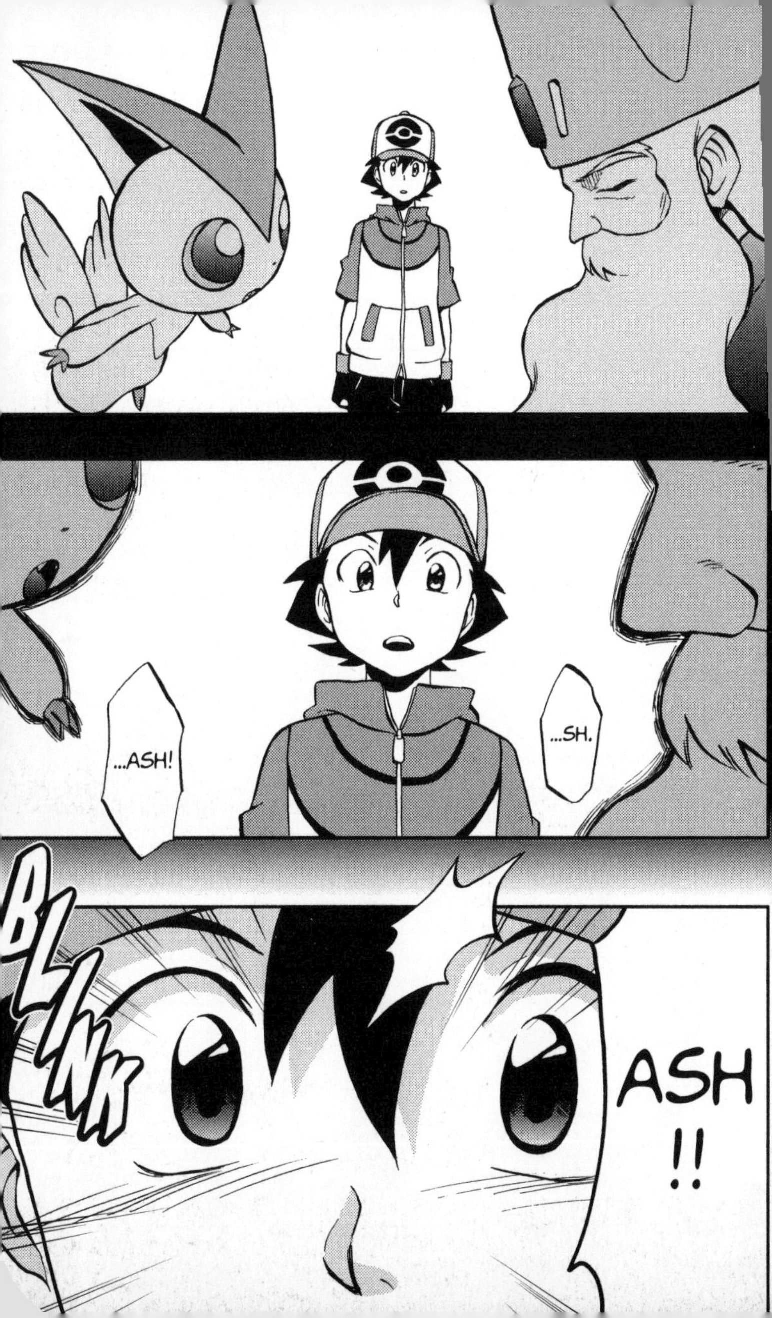
...SH.
...ASH!
ASH !!
BLINK

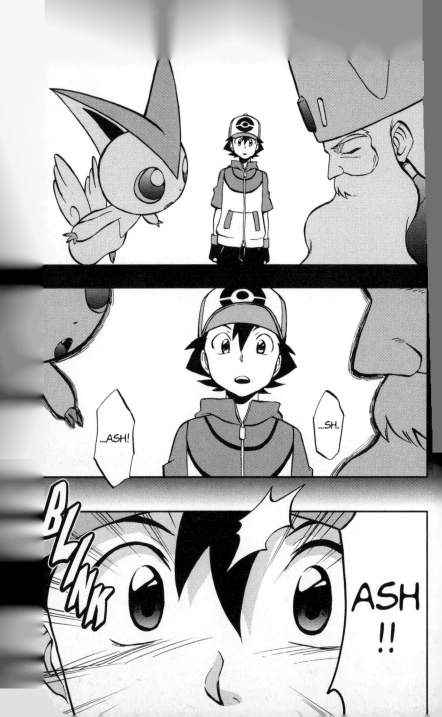

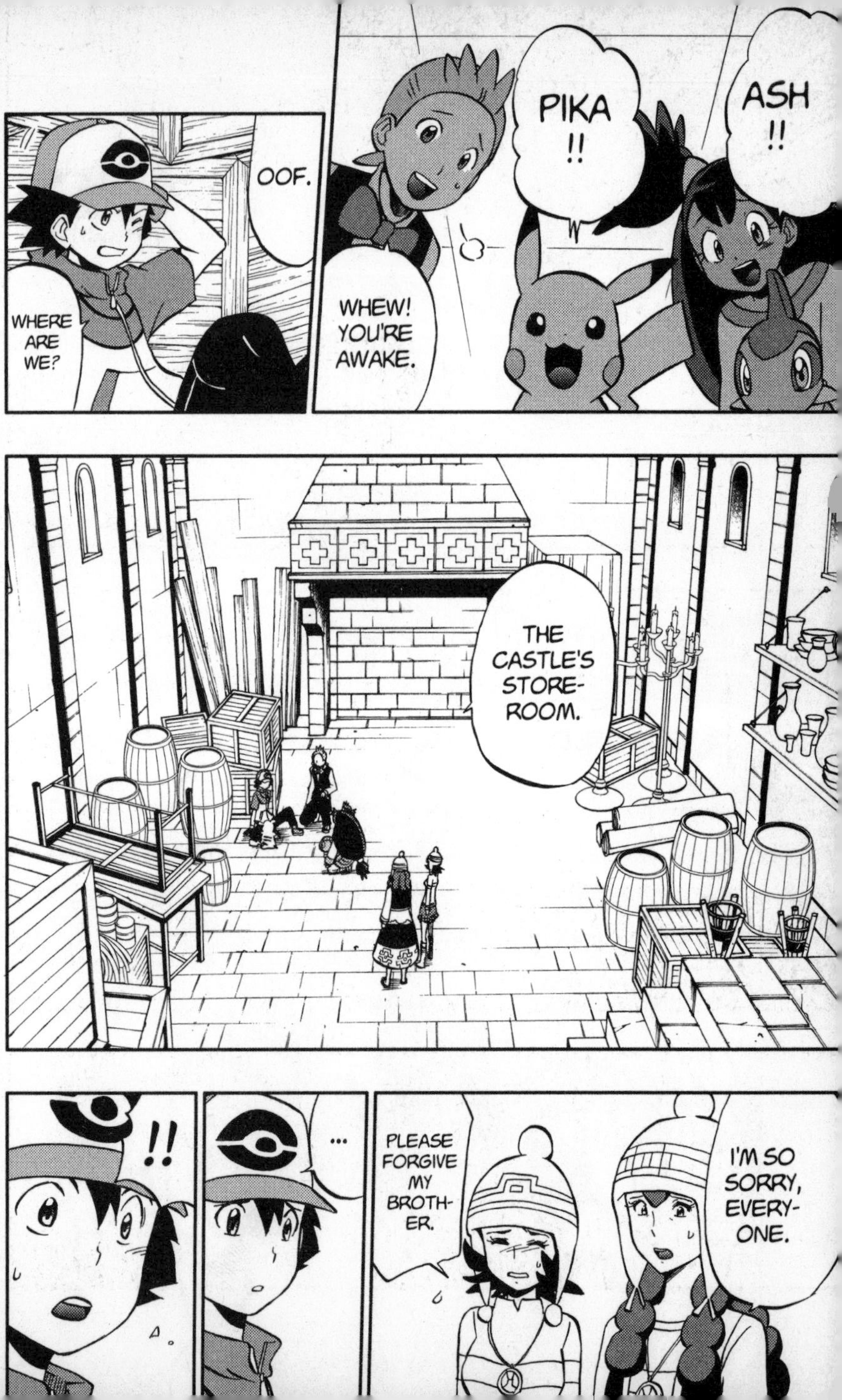
ASH !!
PIKA !!
WHEW! YOU'RE AWAKE.
OOF.
WHERE ARE WE?
THE CASTLE'S STORE-ROOM.
I'M SO SORRY, EVERY-ONE.
PLEASE FORGIVE MY BROTH-ER.
...
!!

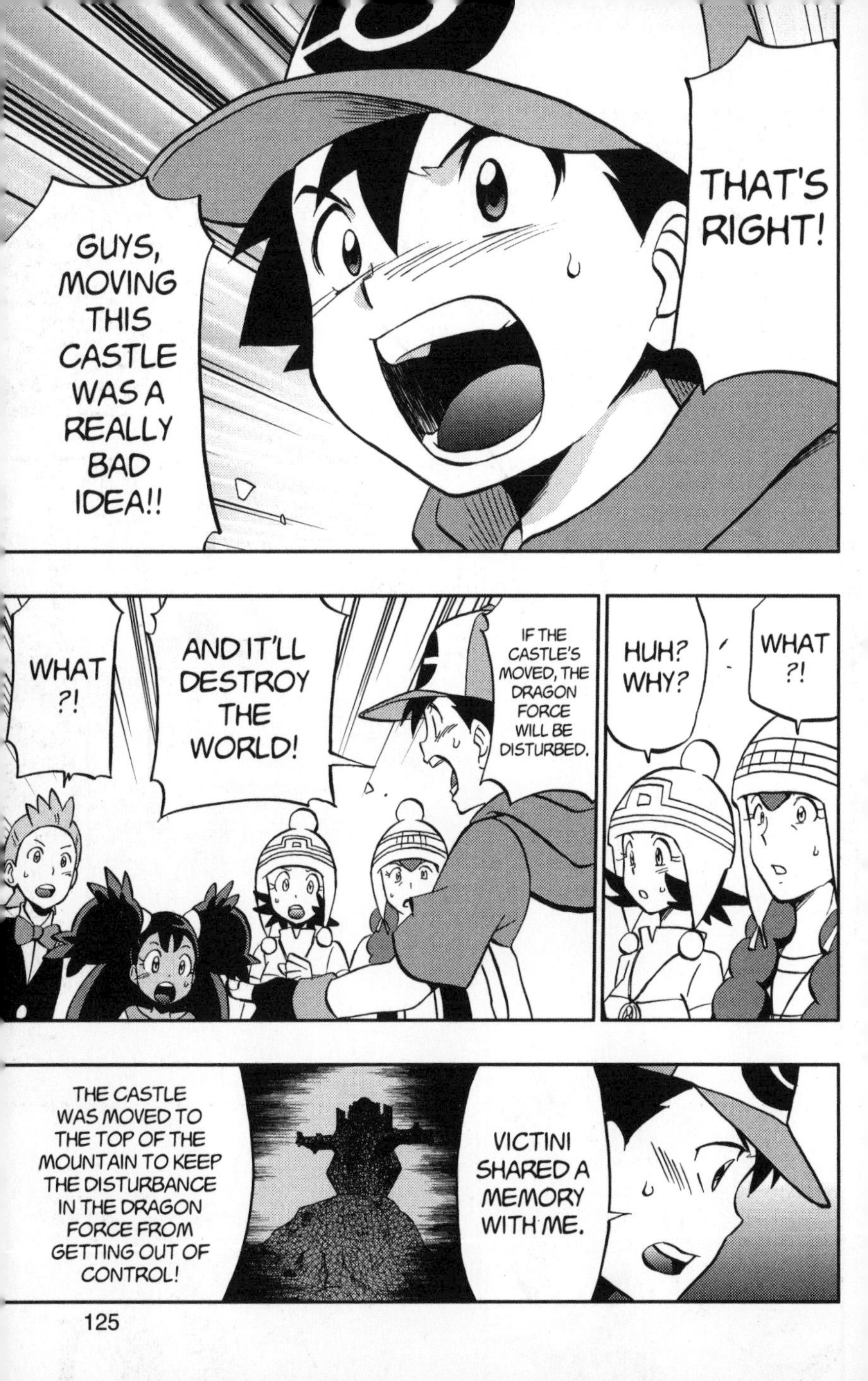
THAT'S RIGHT!
GUYS, MOVING THIS CASTLE WAS A REALLY BAD IDEA!!
WHAT?!
HUH? WHY?
IF THE CASTLE'S MOVED, THE DRAGON FORCE WILL BE DISTURBED.
AND IT'LL DESTROY THE WORLD!
WHAT?!
VICTINI SHARED A MEMORY WITH ME.
THE CASTLE WAS MOVED TO THE TOP OF THE MOUNTAIN TO KEEP THE DISTURBANCE IN THE DRAGON FORCE FROM GETTING OUT OF CONTROL!

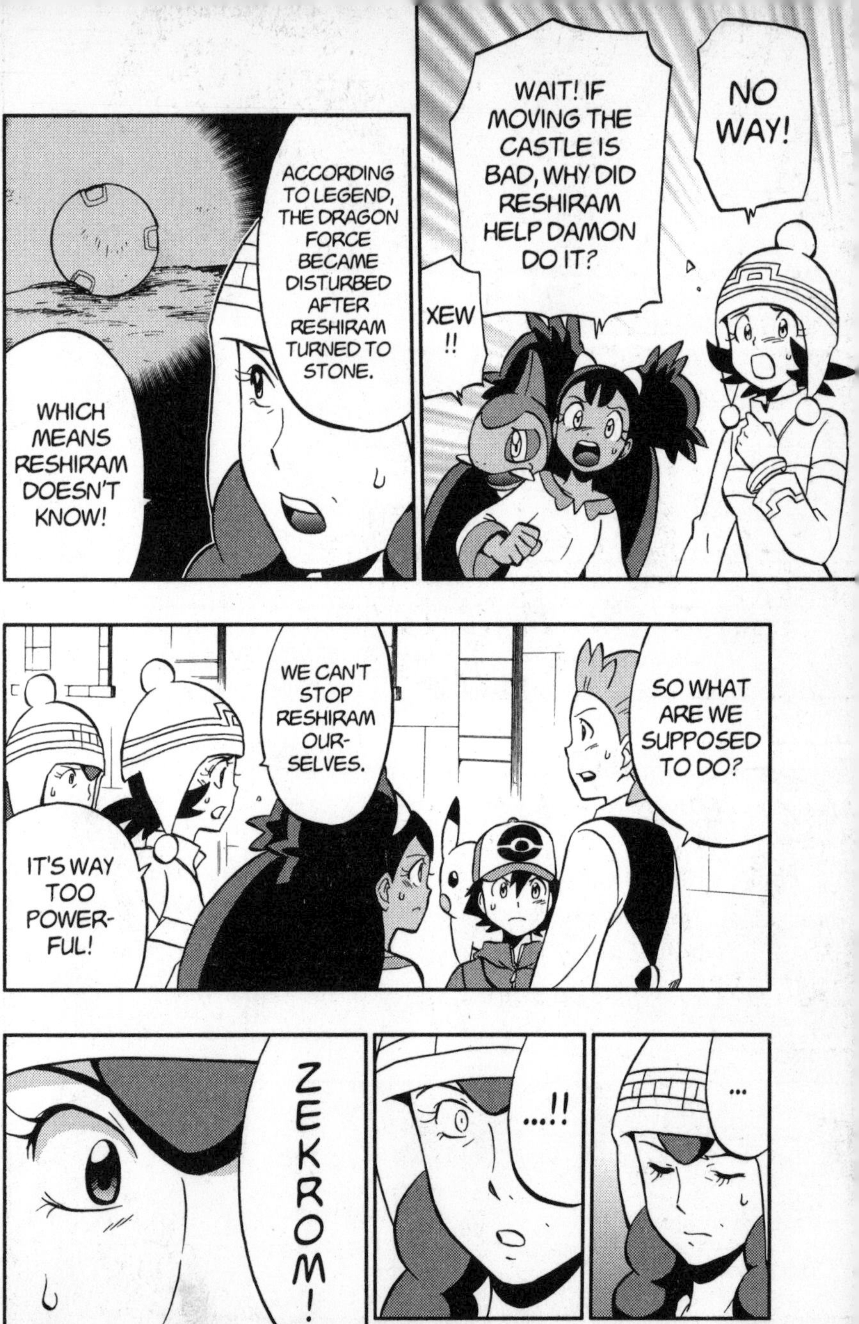
NO WAY!
WAIT! IF MOVING THE CASTLE IS BAD, WHY DID RESHIRAM HELP DAMON DO IT?
XEW!!
ACCORDING TO LEGEND, THE DRAGON FORCE BECAME DISTURBED AFTER RESHIRAM TURNED TO STONE.
WHICH MEANS RESHIRAM DOESN'T KNOW!
SO WHAT ARE WE SUPPOSED TO DO?
WE CAN'T STOP RESHIRAM OUR-SELVES.
IT'S WAY TOO POWER-FUL!
...
...!!
ZEKROM!

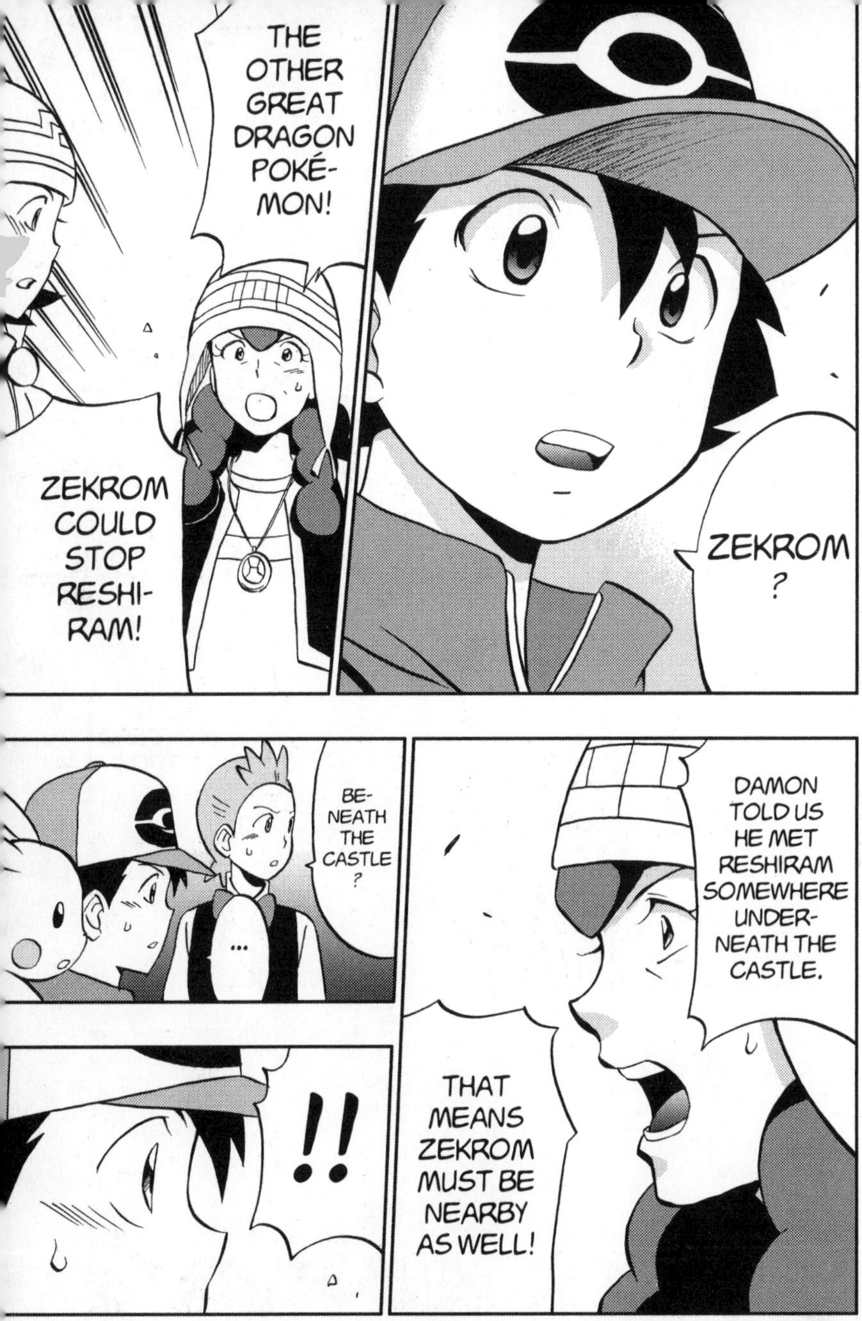
ZEKROM ?
THE OTHER GREAT DRAGON POKÉ-MON!
ZEKROM COULD STOP RESHI-RAM!
DAMON TOLD US HE MET RESHIRAM SOMEWHERE UNDER-NEATH THE CASTLE.
THAT MEANS ZEKROM MUST BE NEARBY AS WELL!
BE-NEATH THE CASTLE ?
...
!!

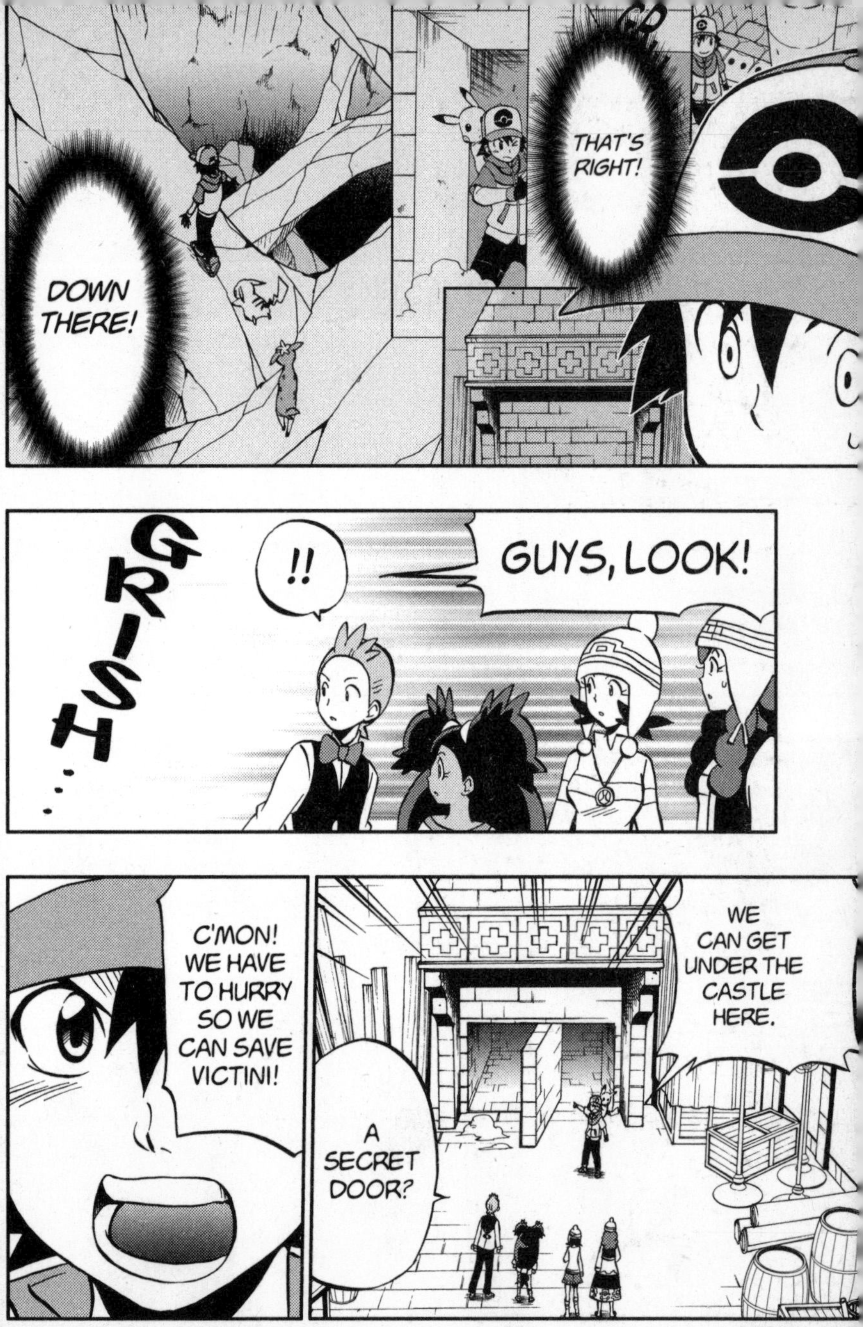
THAT'S RIGHT!
DOWN THERE!
GUYS, LOOK!
!!
GRISH...
WE CAN GET UNDER THE CASTLE HERE.
A SECRET DOOR?
C'MON! WE HAVE TO HURRY SO WE CAN SAVE VICTINI!

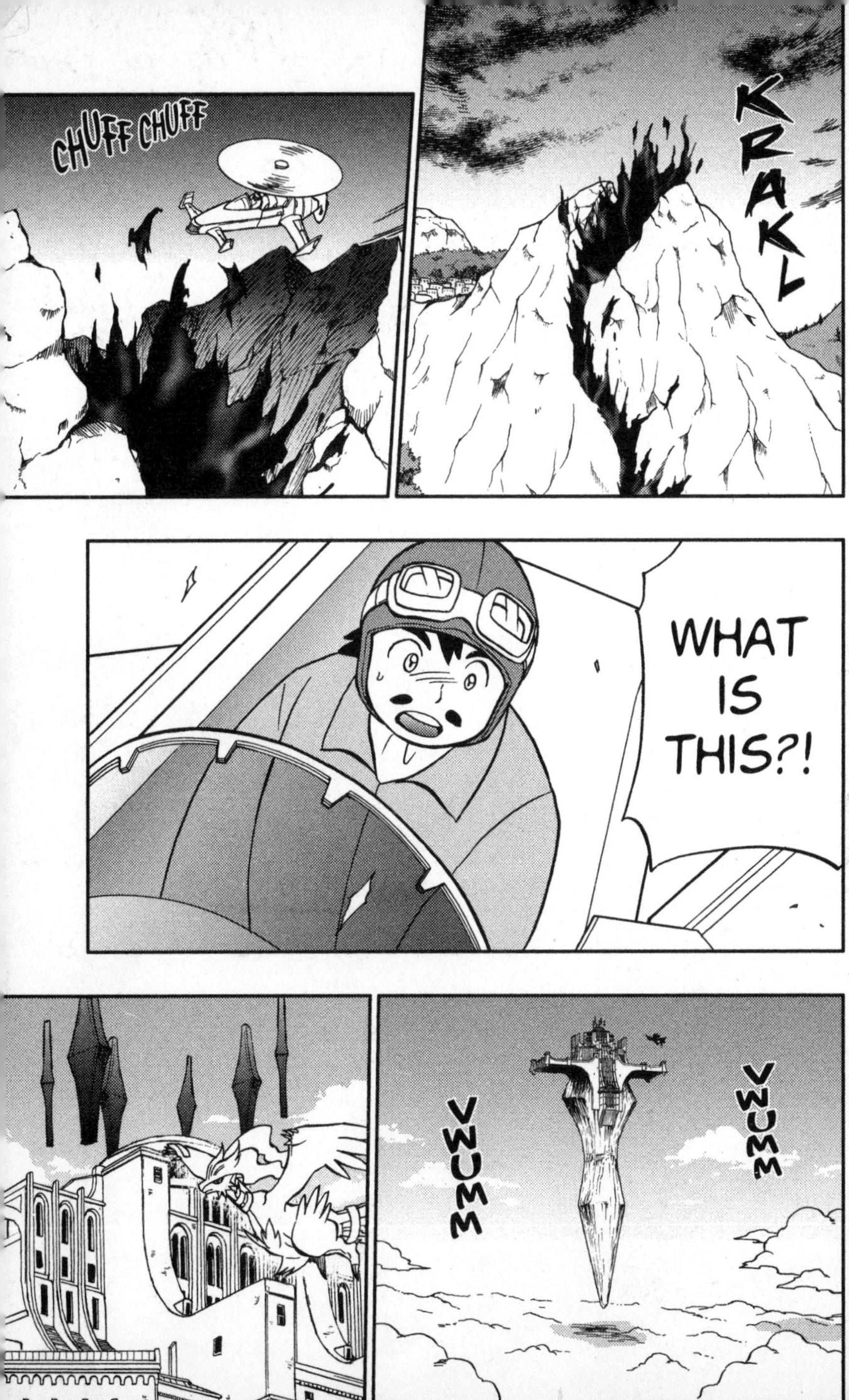
KRAKL
CHUFF CHUFF
WHAT IS THIS?!
VWUMM
VWUMM

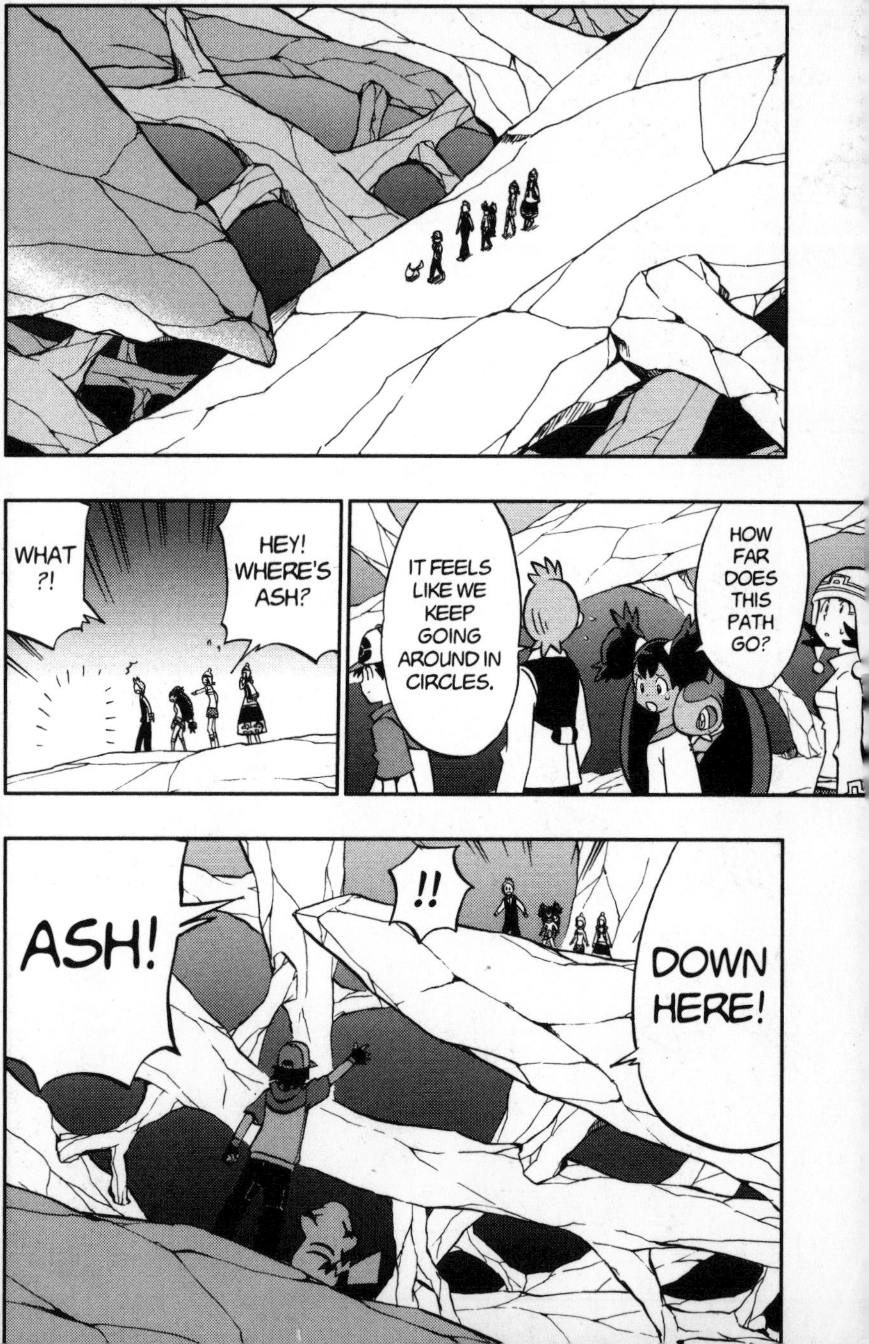
HOW FAR DOES THIS PATH GO?
IT FEELS LIKE WE KEEP GOING AROUND IN CIRCLES.
HEY! WHERE'S ASH?
WHAT ?!
DOWN HERE!
!!
ASH!

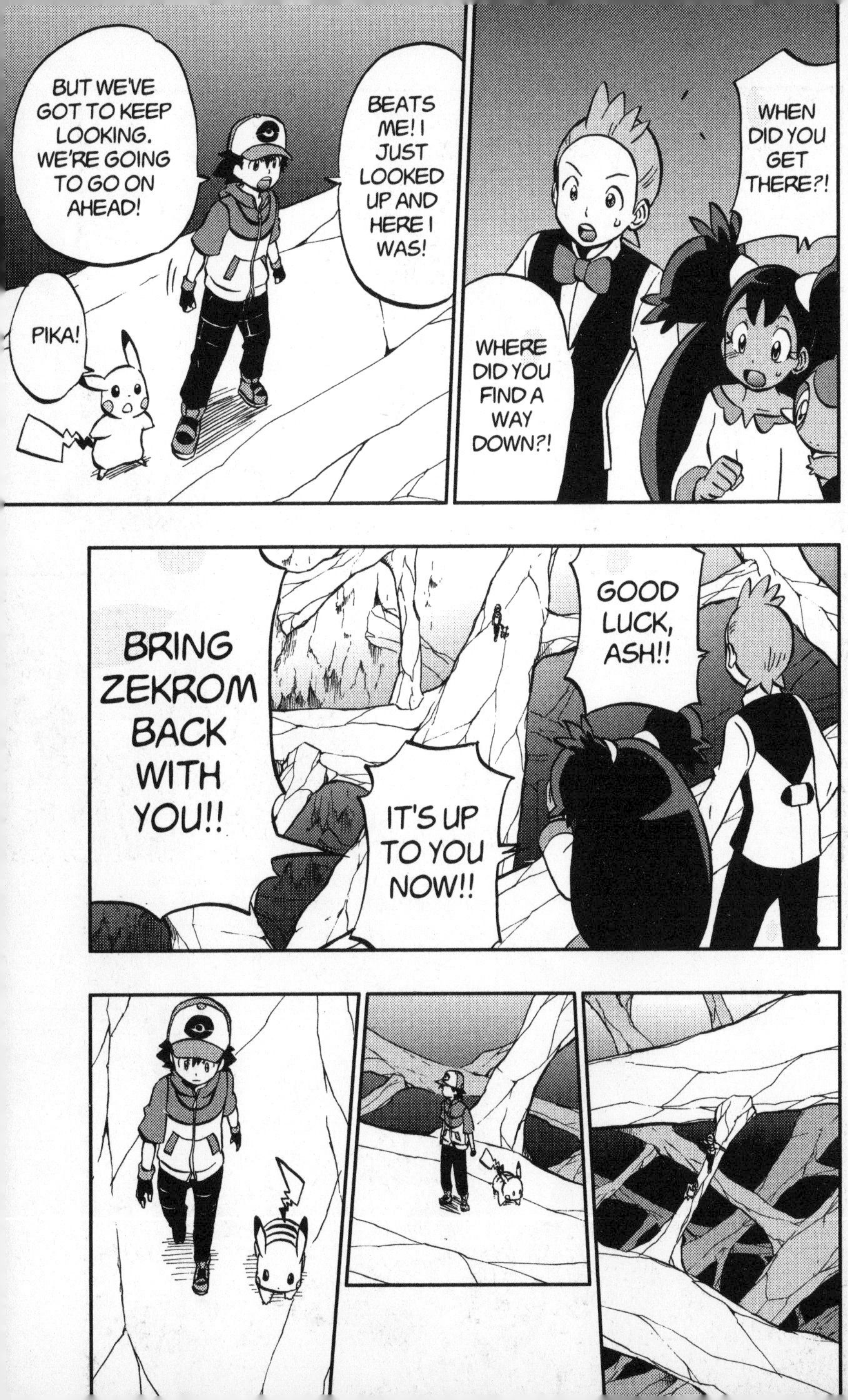
WHEN DID YOU GET THERE?!
WHERE DID YOU FIND A WAY DOWN?!
BEATS ME! I JUST LOOKED UP AND HERE I WAS!
BUT WE'VE GOT TO KEEP LOOKING. WE'RE GOING TO GO ON AHEAD!
PIKA!
GOOD LUCK, ASH!!
IT'S UP TO YOU NOW!!
BRING ZEKROM BACK WITH YOU!!

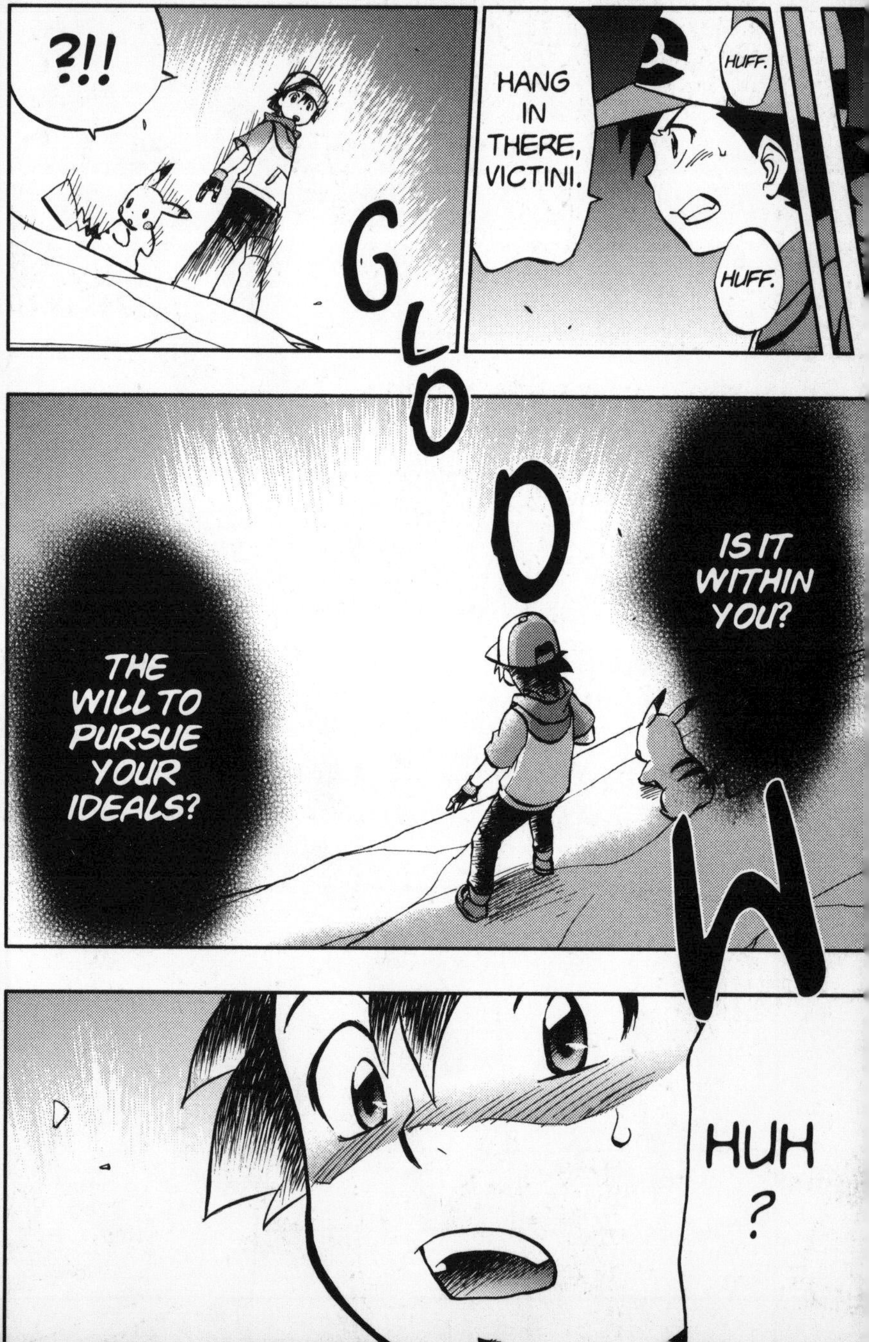

HUFF.
HANG IN THERE, VICTINI.
HUFF.
?!!
GLOOW
IS IT WITHIN YOU?
THE WILL TO PURSUE YOUR IDEALS?
HUH?

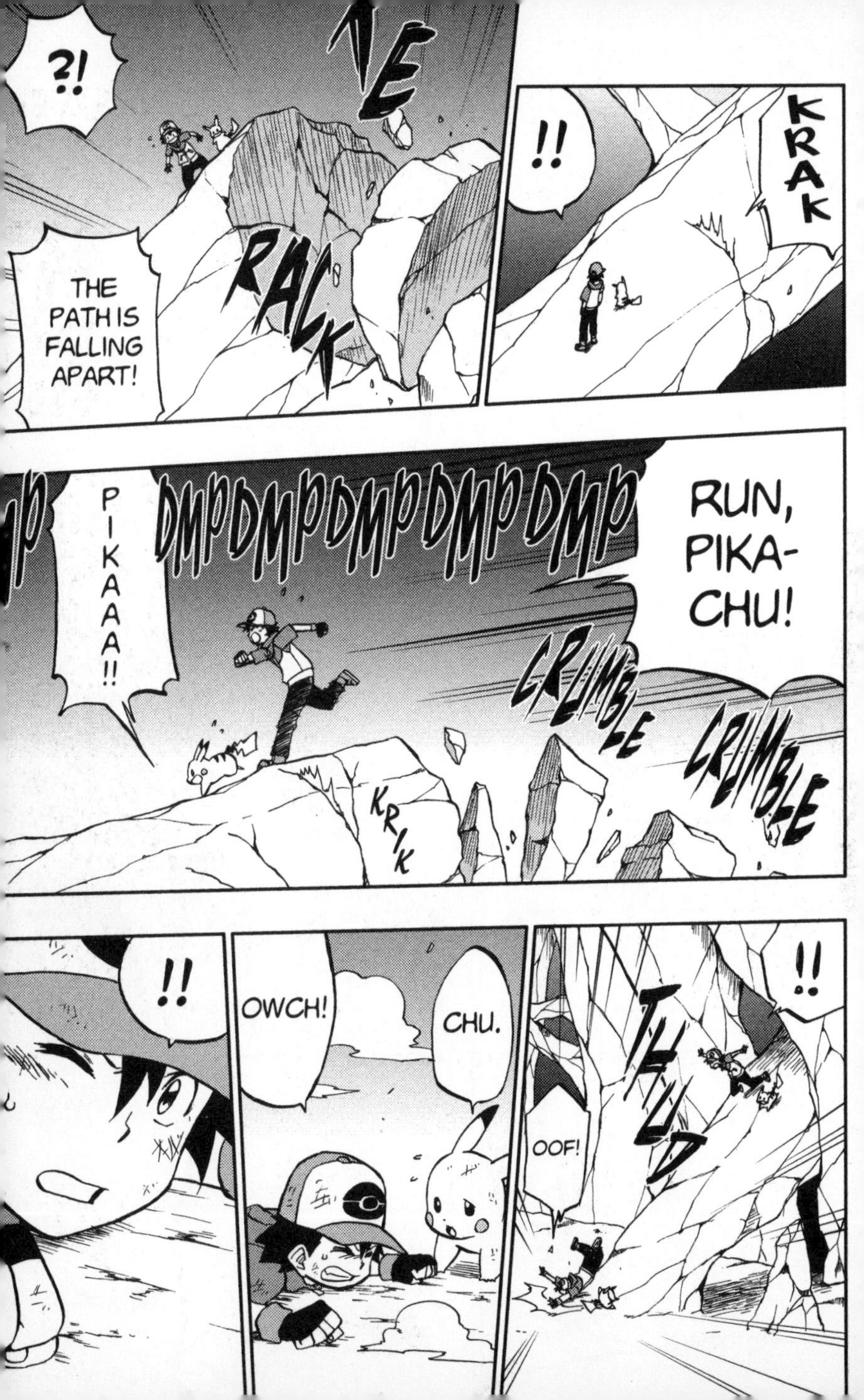

!!
KRAK
?!
RACK
THE PATH IS FALLING APART!
RUN, PIKA-CHU!
CRUMBLE
CRUMBLE
DMPDMPDMPDMPDMPDMP
PIKAAAA!!
KRIK
!!
THUD
OOF!
CHU.
OWCH!
!!

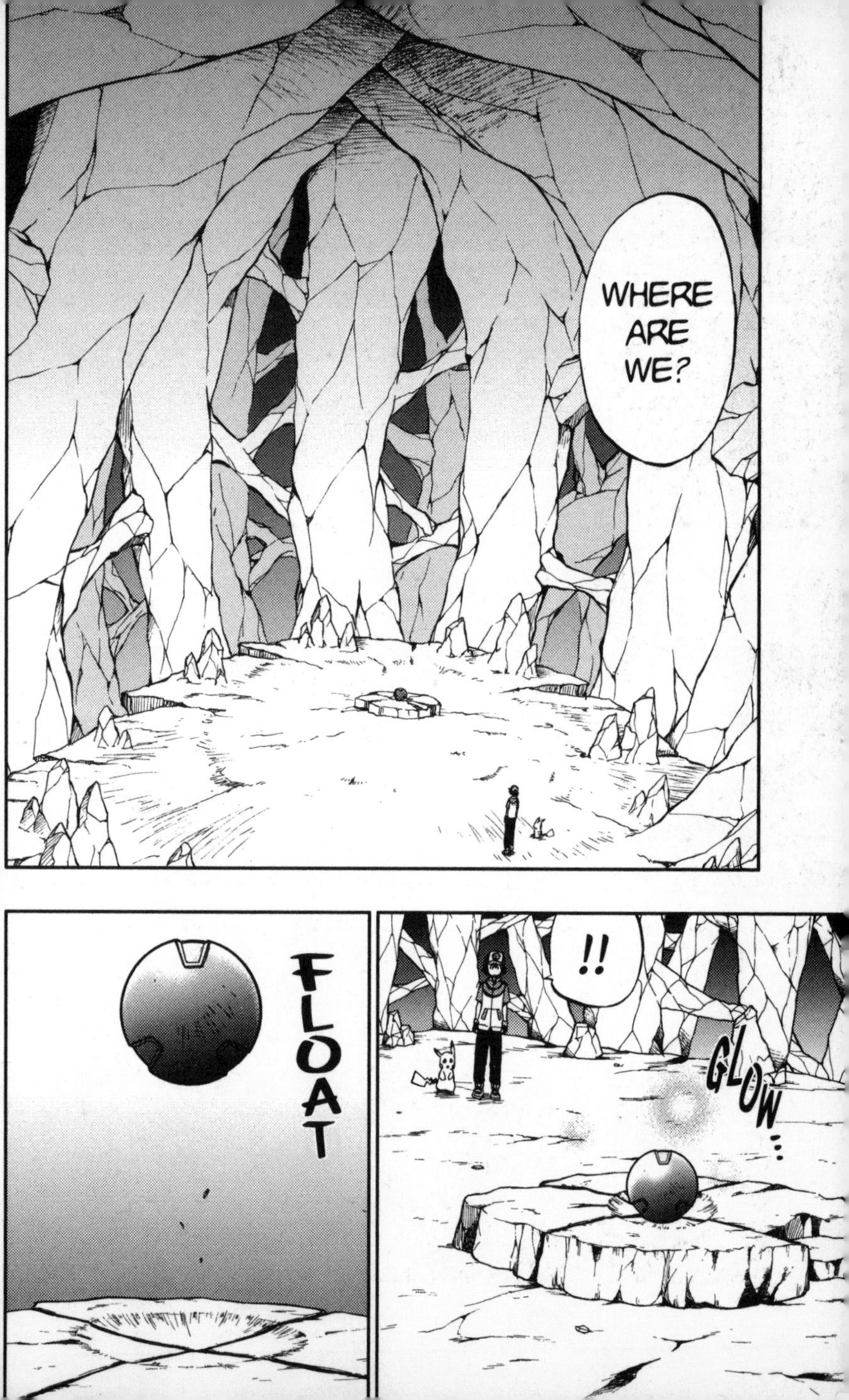
WHERE ARE WE?
!!
GLOW...
FLOAT

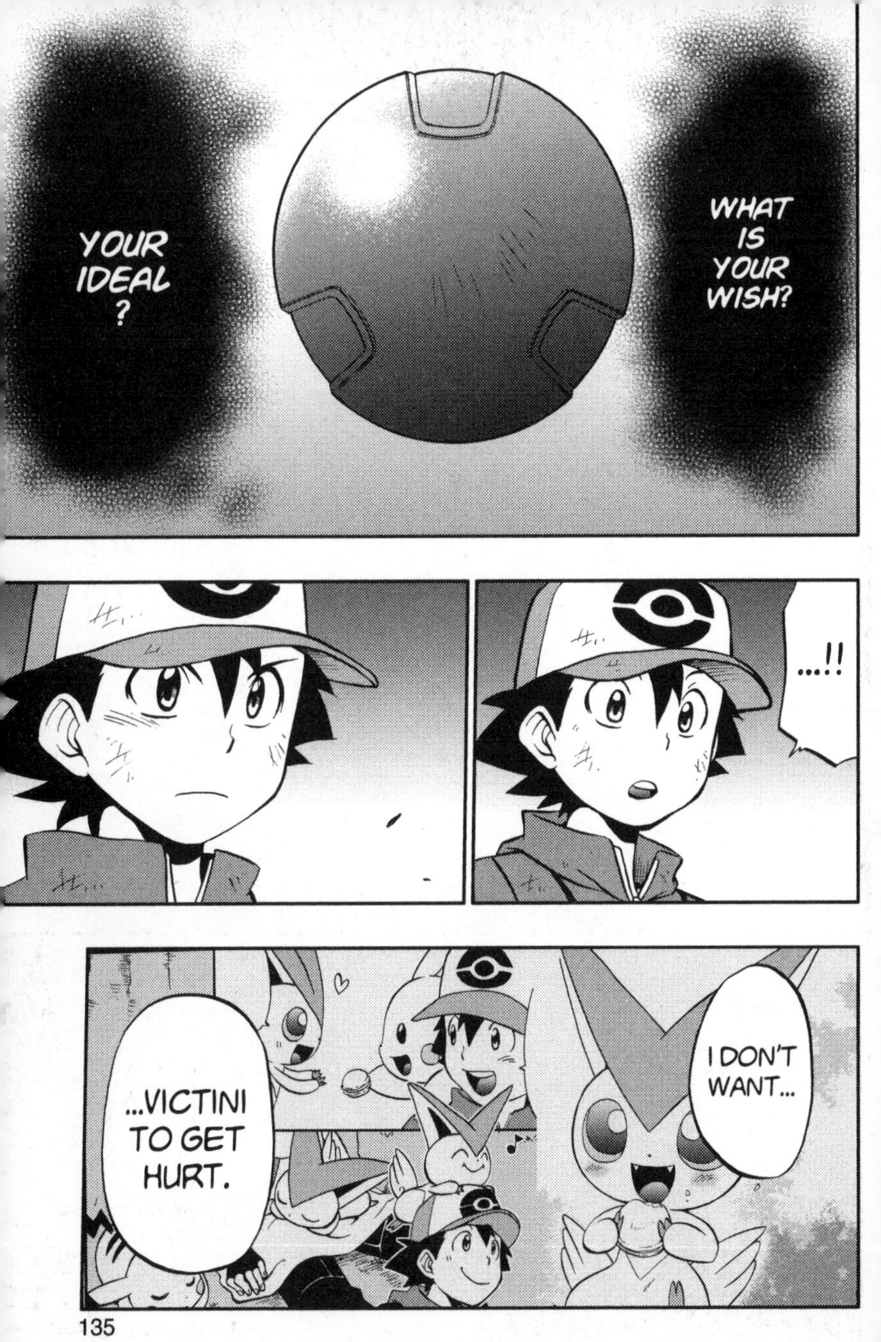
WHAT IS YOUR WISH?
YOUR IDEAL?
...!!
I DON'T WANT...
...VICTINI TO GET HURT.

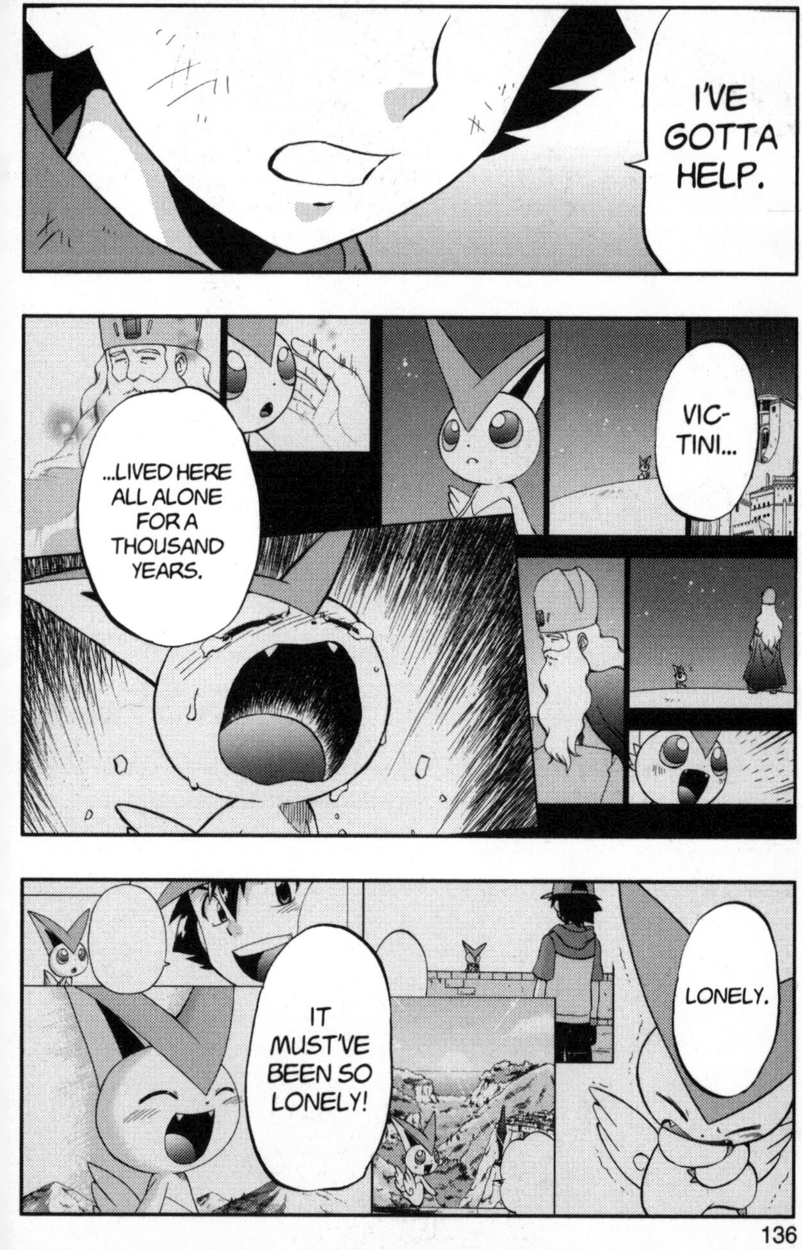
I'VE GOTTA HELP.
VIC-TINI...
...LIVED HERE ALL ALONE FOR A THOUSAND YEARS.
LONELY.
IT MUST'VE BEEN SO LONELY!

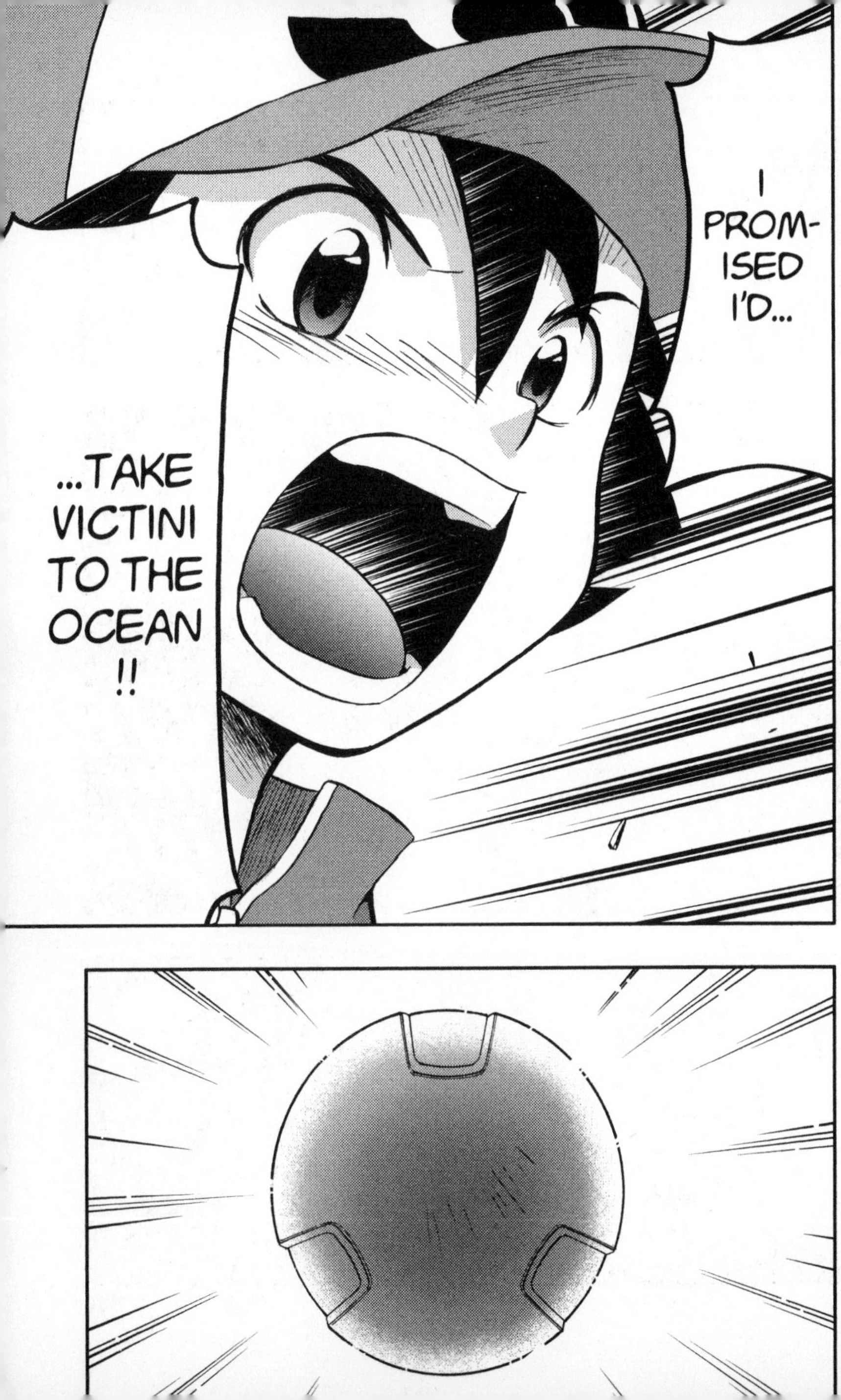
I PROM-
ISED
I'D...
...TAKE
VICTINI
TO THE
OCEAN
!!

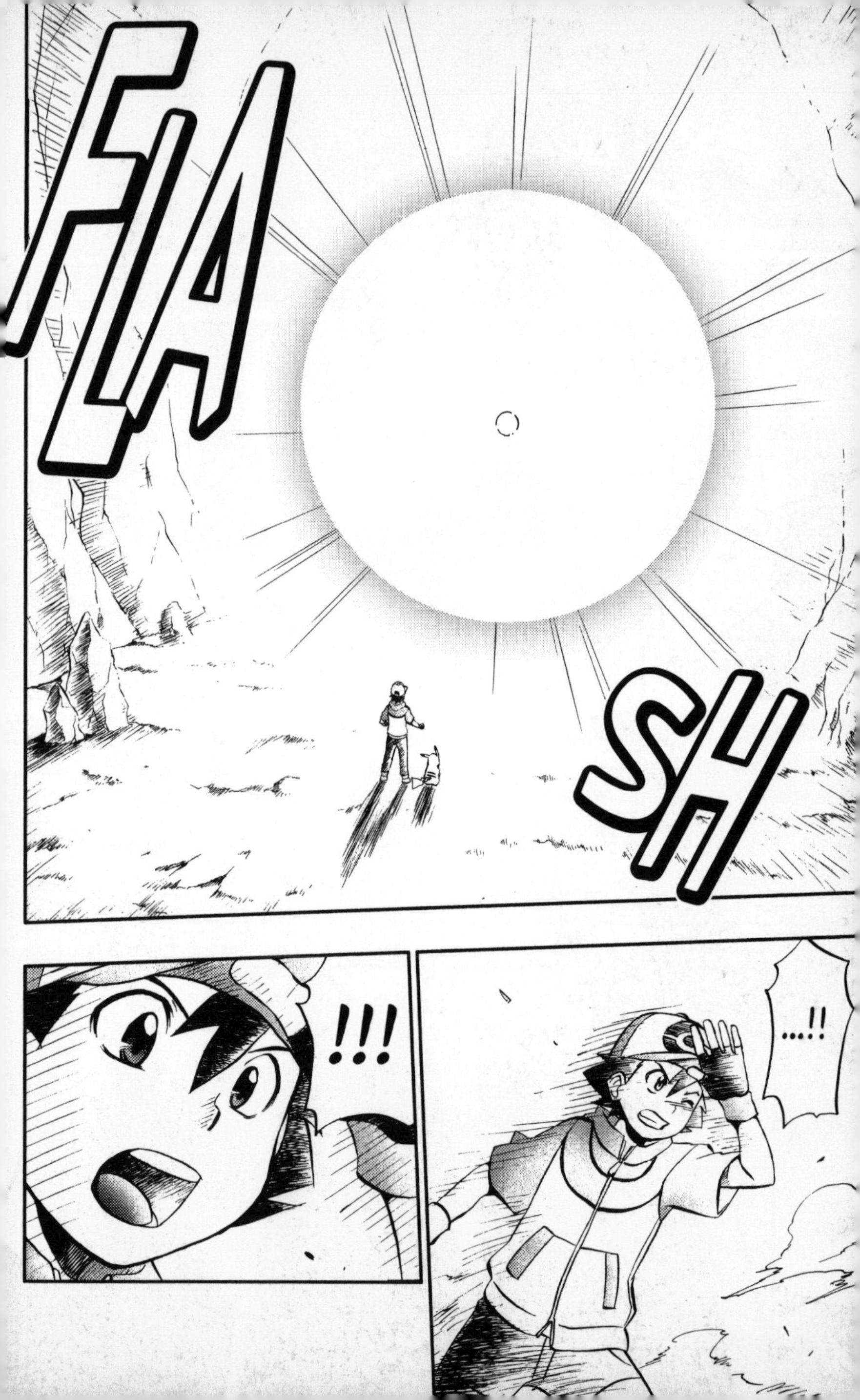
FLASH
...!!
!!!

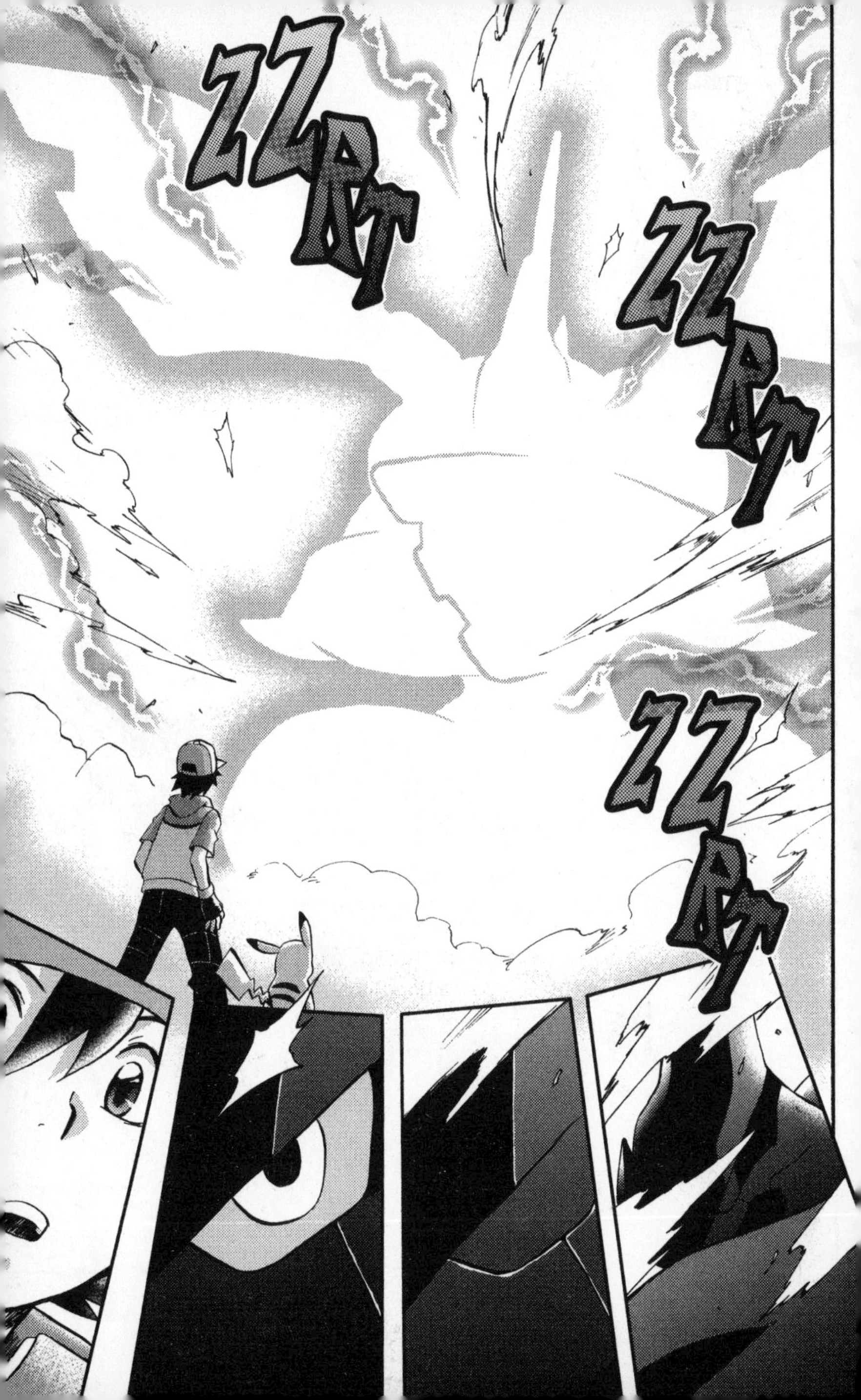
ZZRT
ZZRT
ZZRT

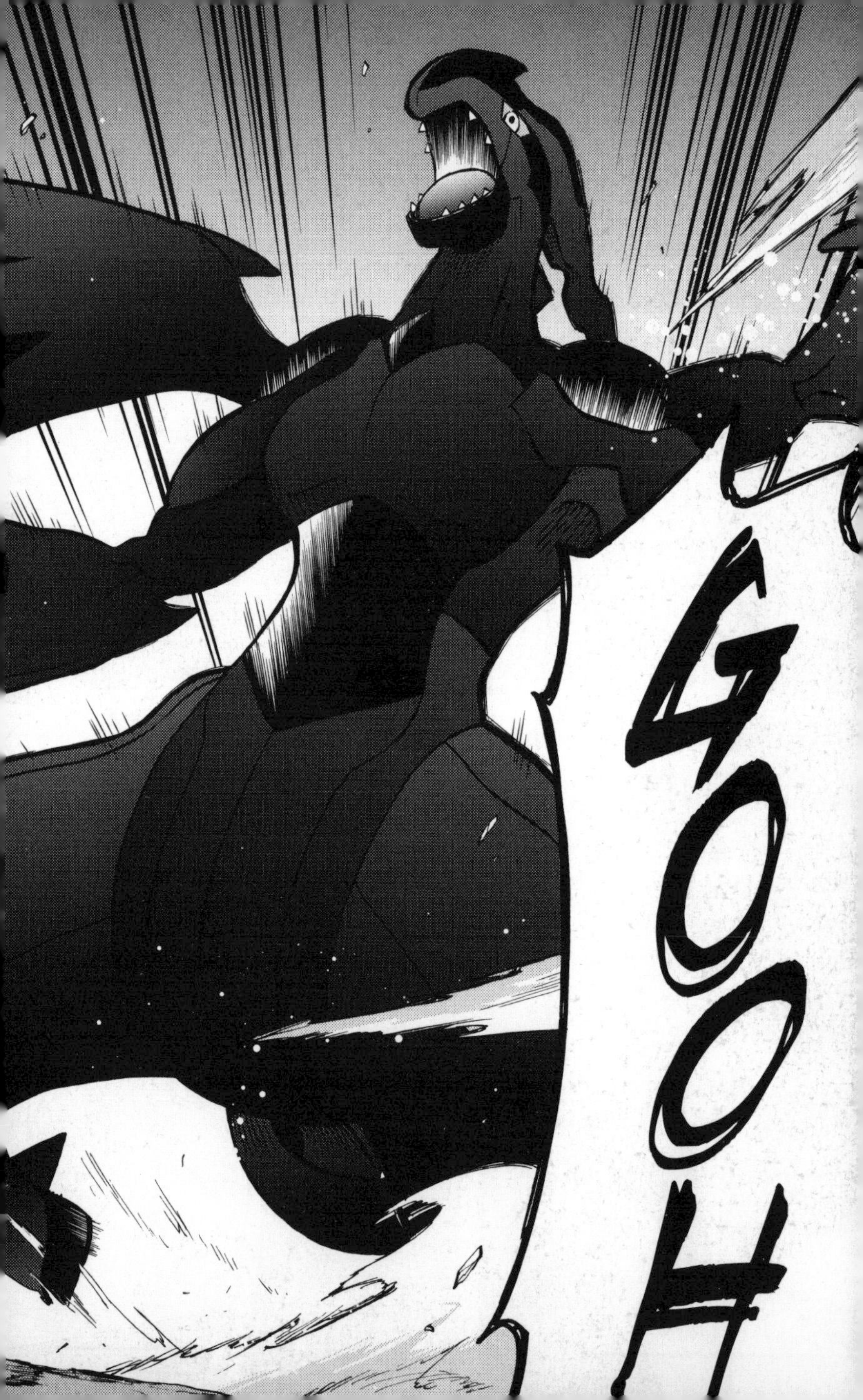
GOOH

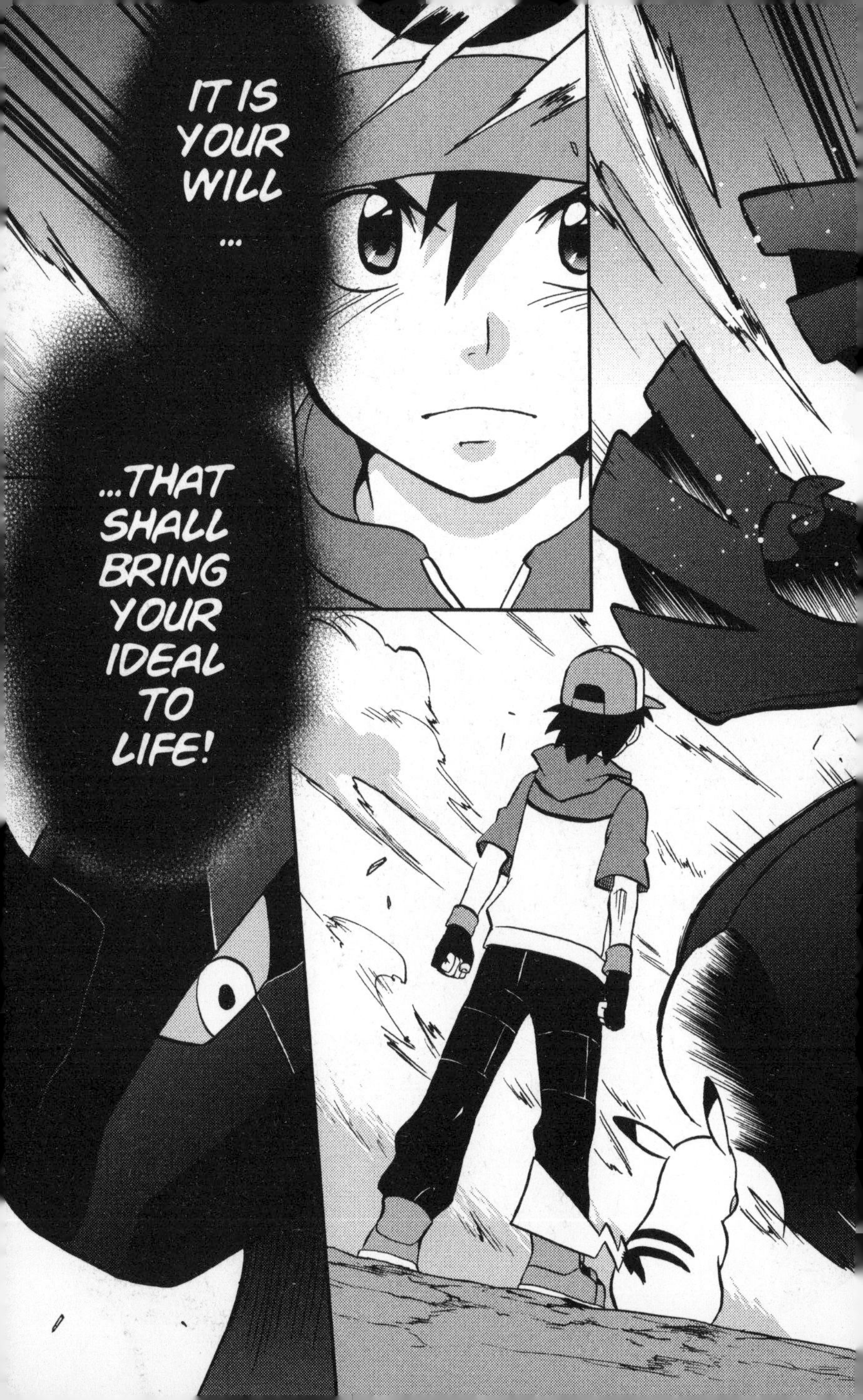
IT IS YOUR WILL ...
...THAT SHALL BRING YOUR IDEAL TO LIFE!

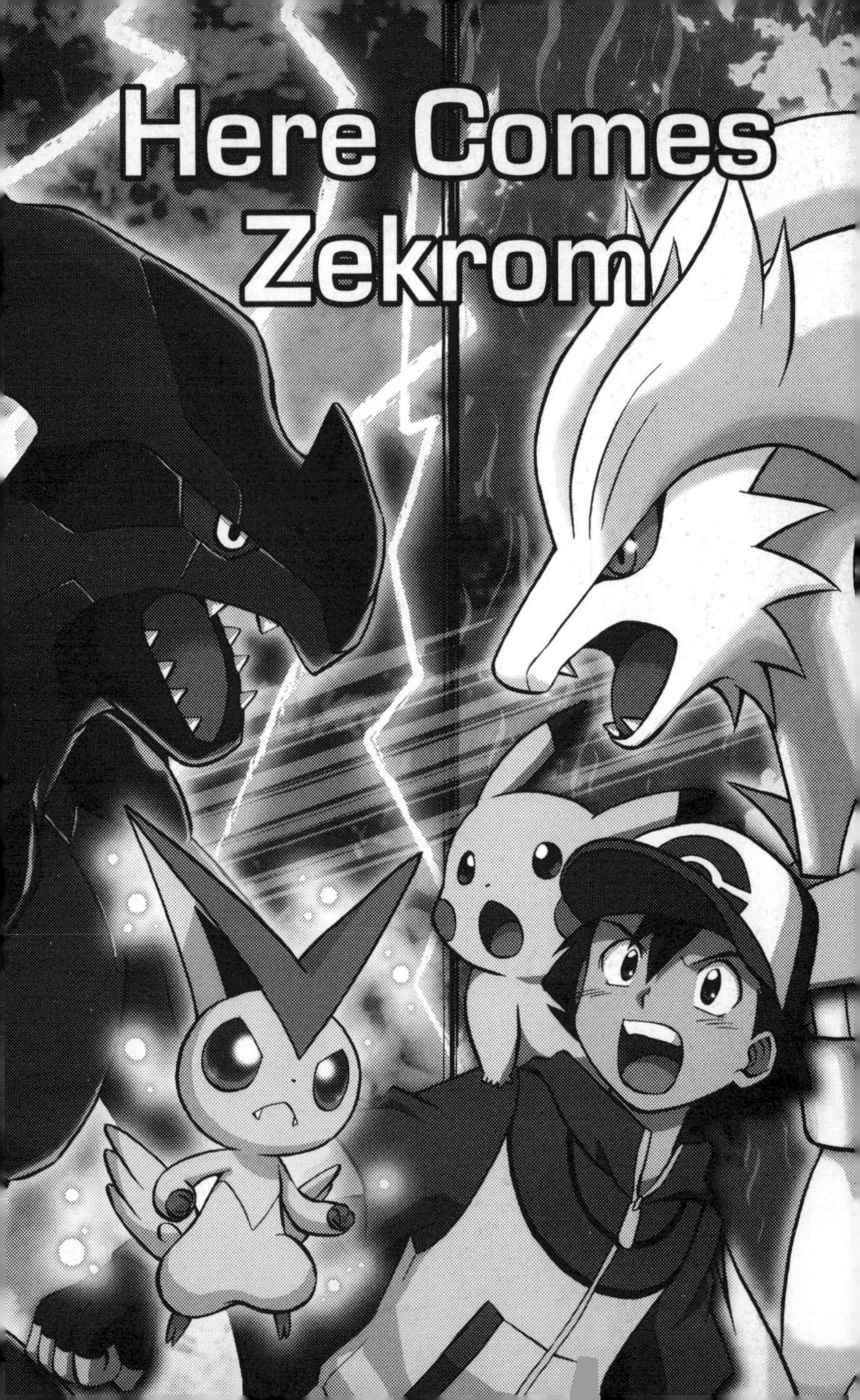
Here Comes
Zekrom

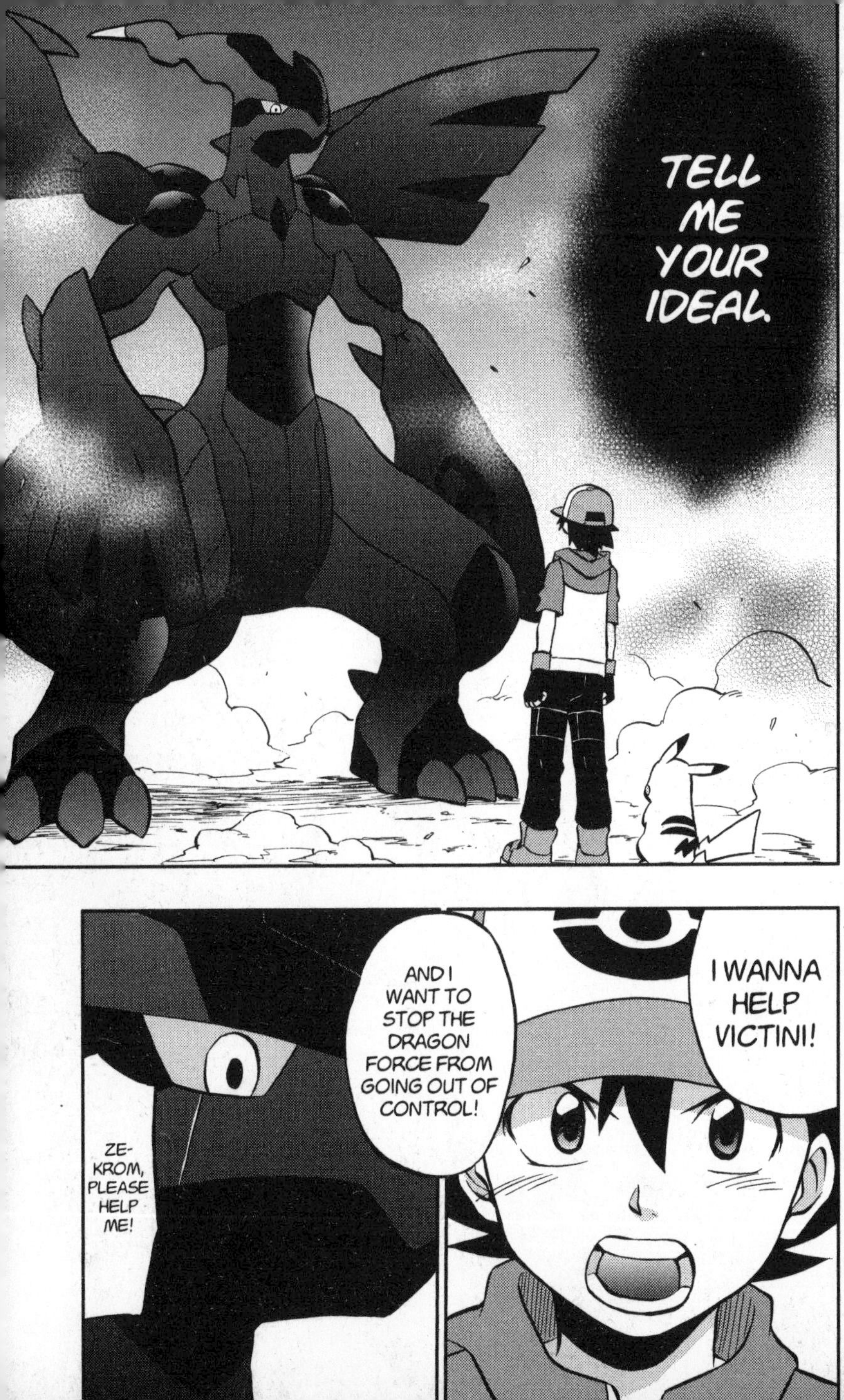
TELL ME YOUR IDEAL.
I WANNA HELP VICTINI!
AND I WANT TO STOP THE DRAGON FORCE FROM GOING OUT OF CONTROL!
ZE-KROM, PLEASE HELP ME!

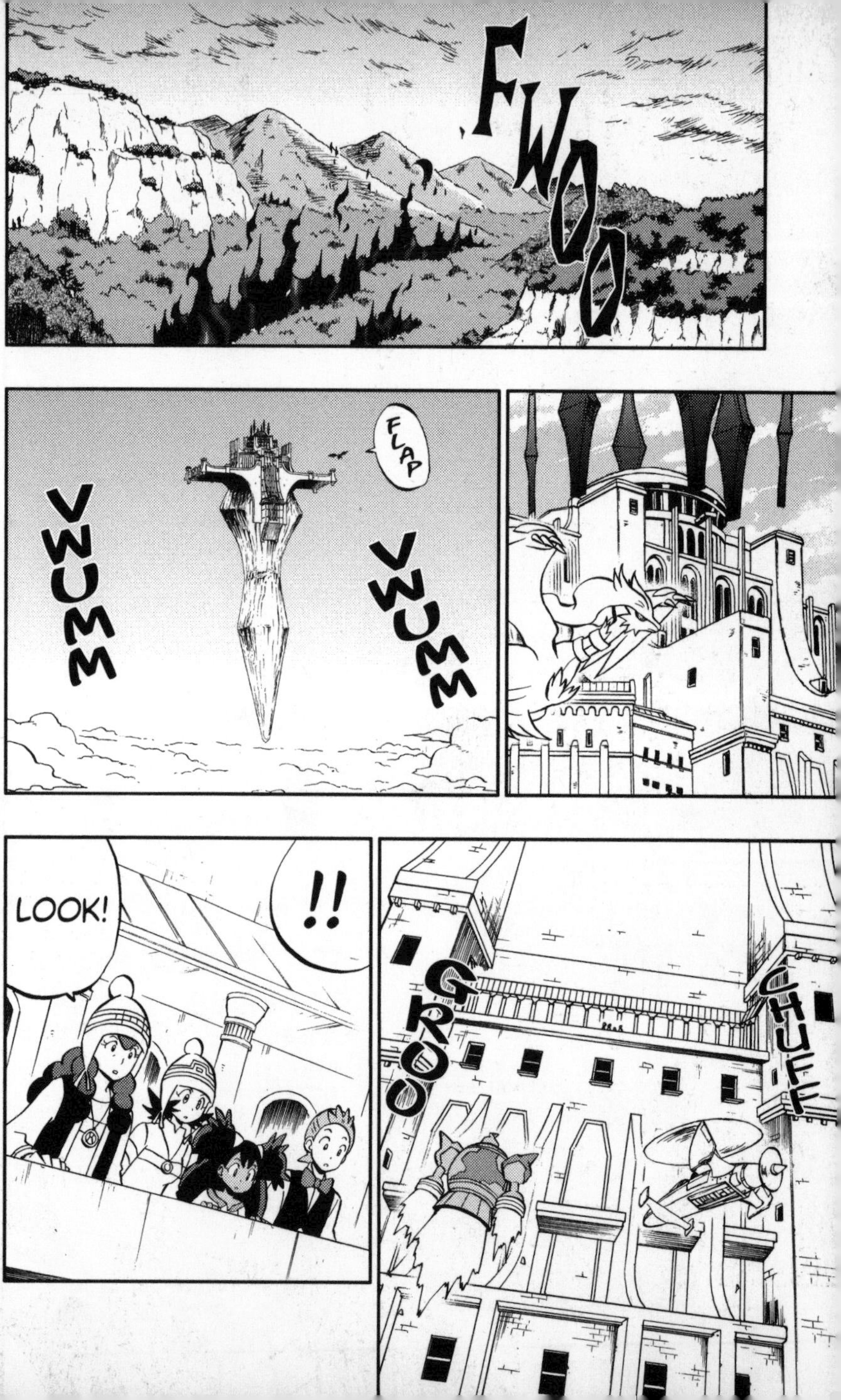
FWOO
FLAP
VWUMM
VWUMM
CHUFF
GROO
!!
LOOK!

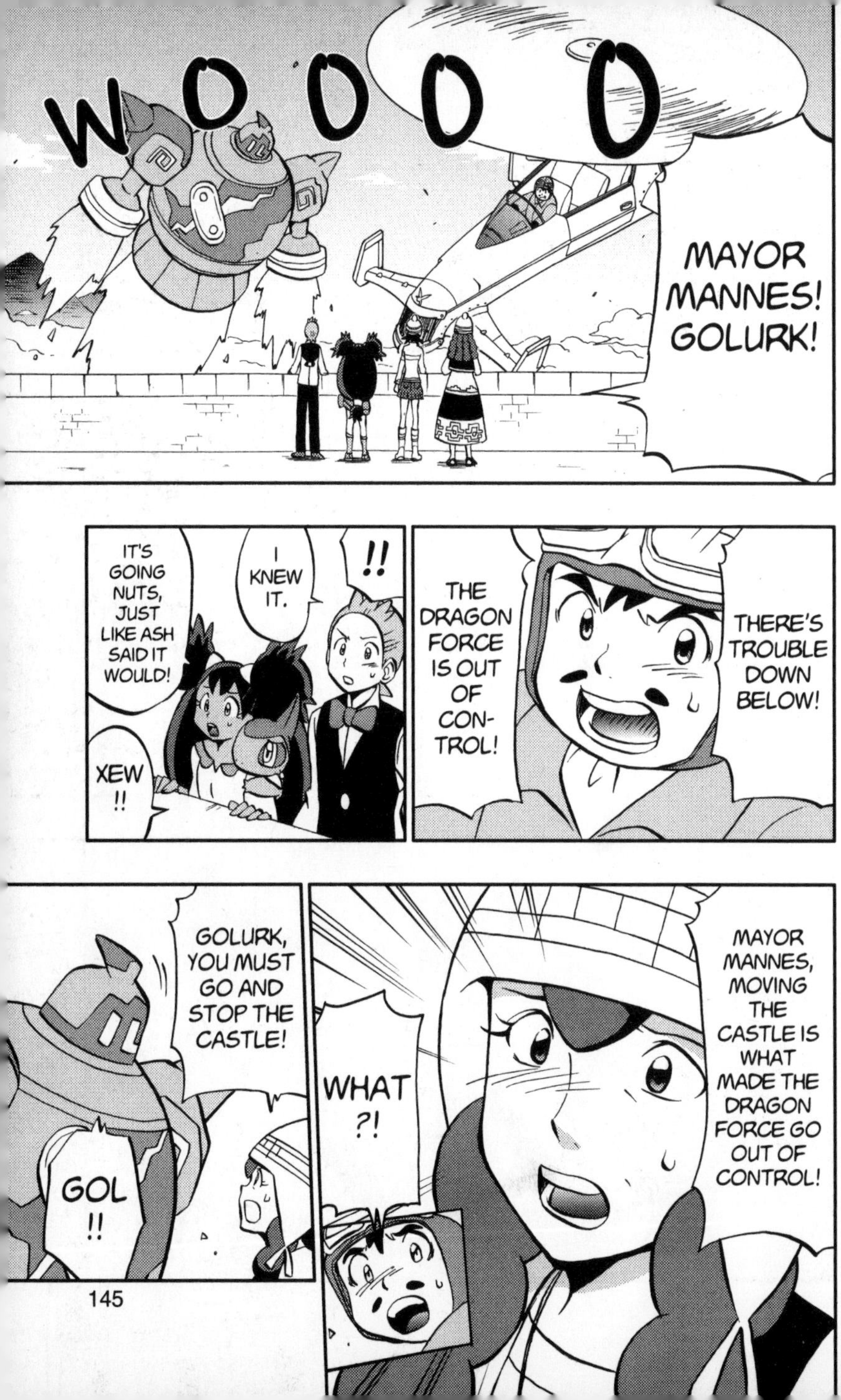
WOOOO
MAYOR MANNES! GOLURK!
THERE'S TROUBLE DOWN BELOW!
THE DRAGON FORCE IS OUT OF CONTROL!
!!
I KNEW IT.
IT'S GOING NUTS, JUST LIKE ASH SAID IT WOULD!
XEW !!
MAYOR MANNES, MOVING THE CASTLE IS WHAT MADE THE DRAGON FORCE GO OUT OF CONTROL!
WHAT ?!
GOLURK, YOU MUST GO AND STOP THE CASTLE!
GOL !!

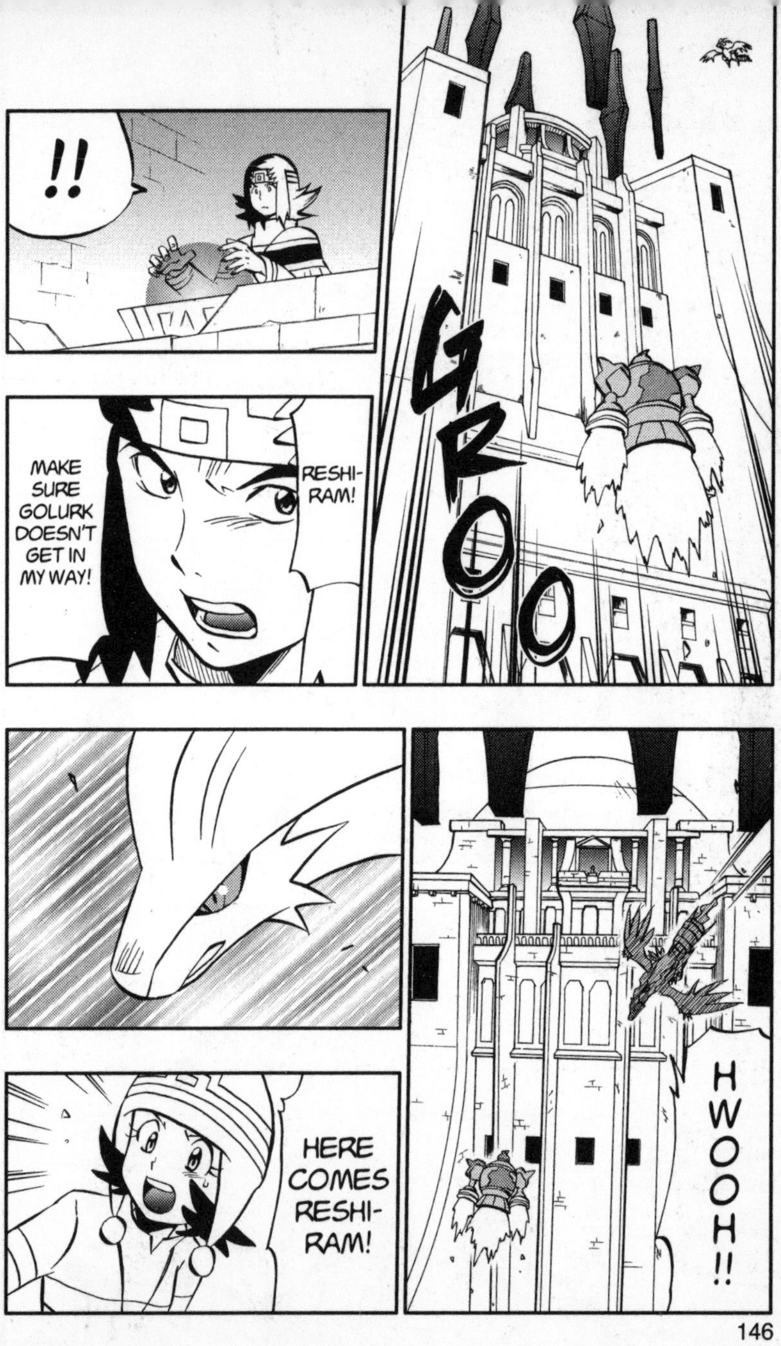
GROOO
!!
RESHI-RAM!
MAKE SURE GOLURK DOESN'T GET IN MY WAY!
HWOOOH!!
HERE COMES RESHI-RAM!

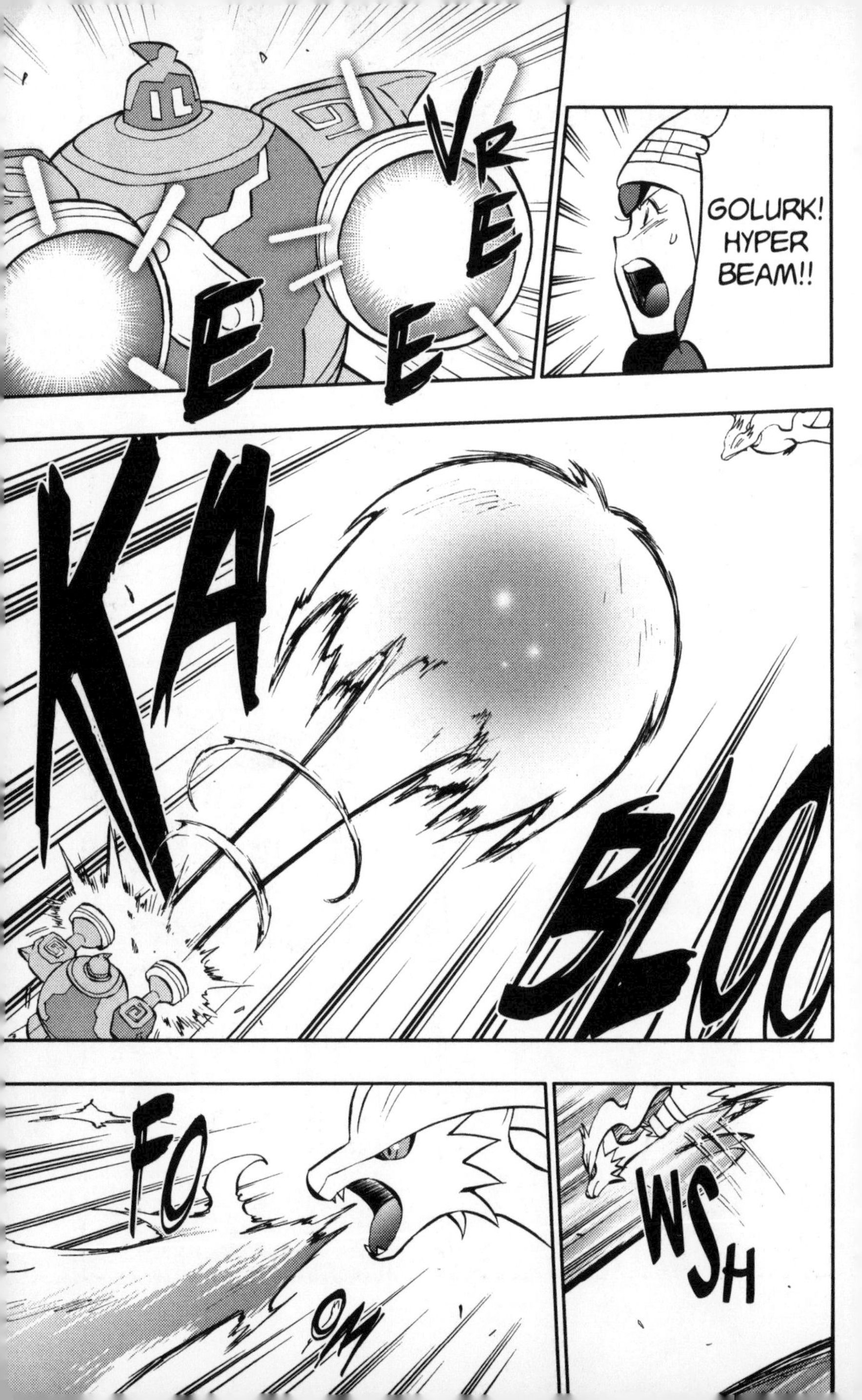
GOLURK! HYPER BEAM!!
VREEE
KA BLOO
WSH
FOOM

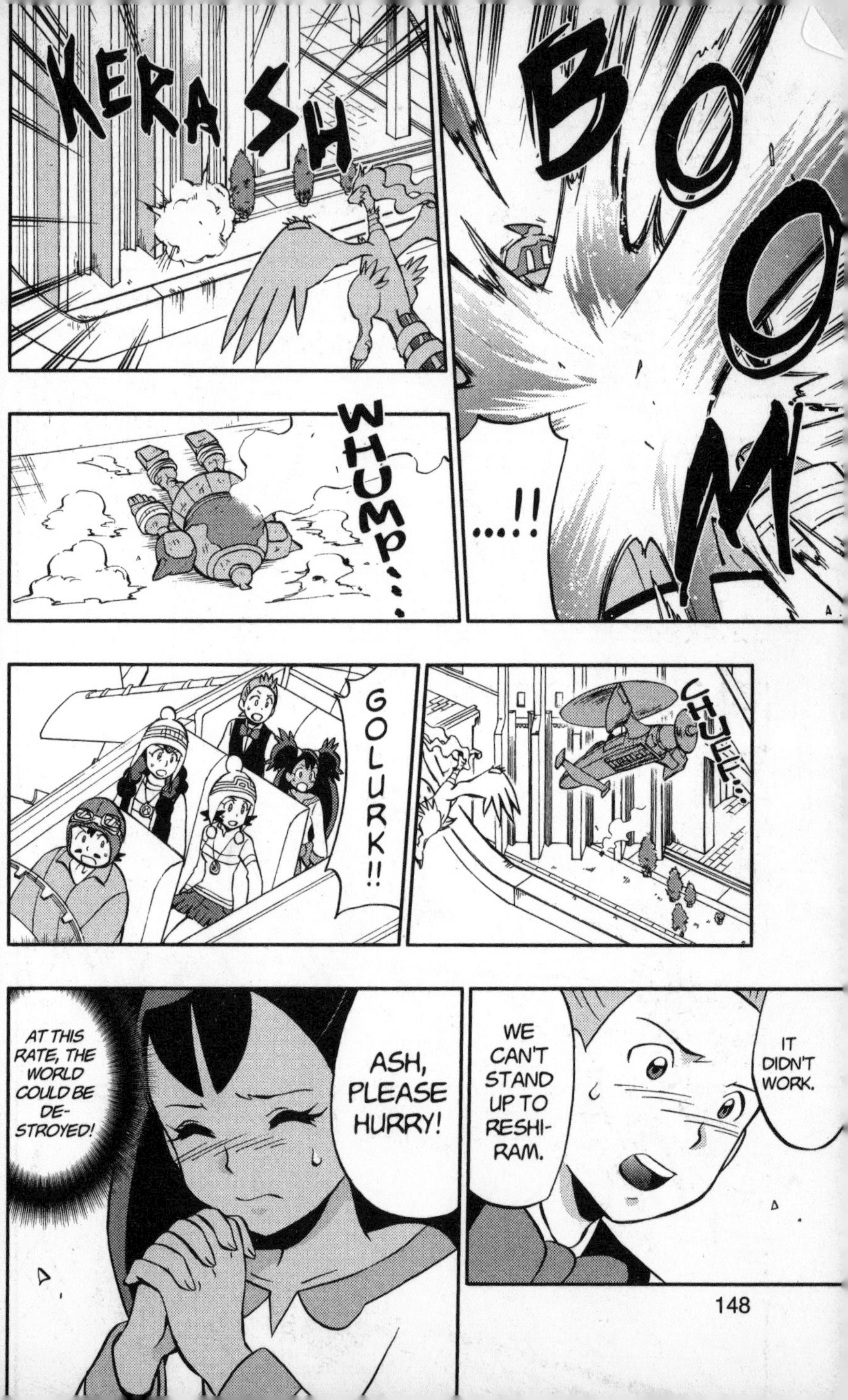
BOOM
...!!
KERASH
WHUMP...
CHUFF...
GOLURK!!
IT DIDN'T WORK.
WE CAN'T STAND UP TO RESHIRAM.
ASH, PLEASE HURRY!
AT THIS RATE, THE WORLD COULD BE DE-STROYED!

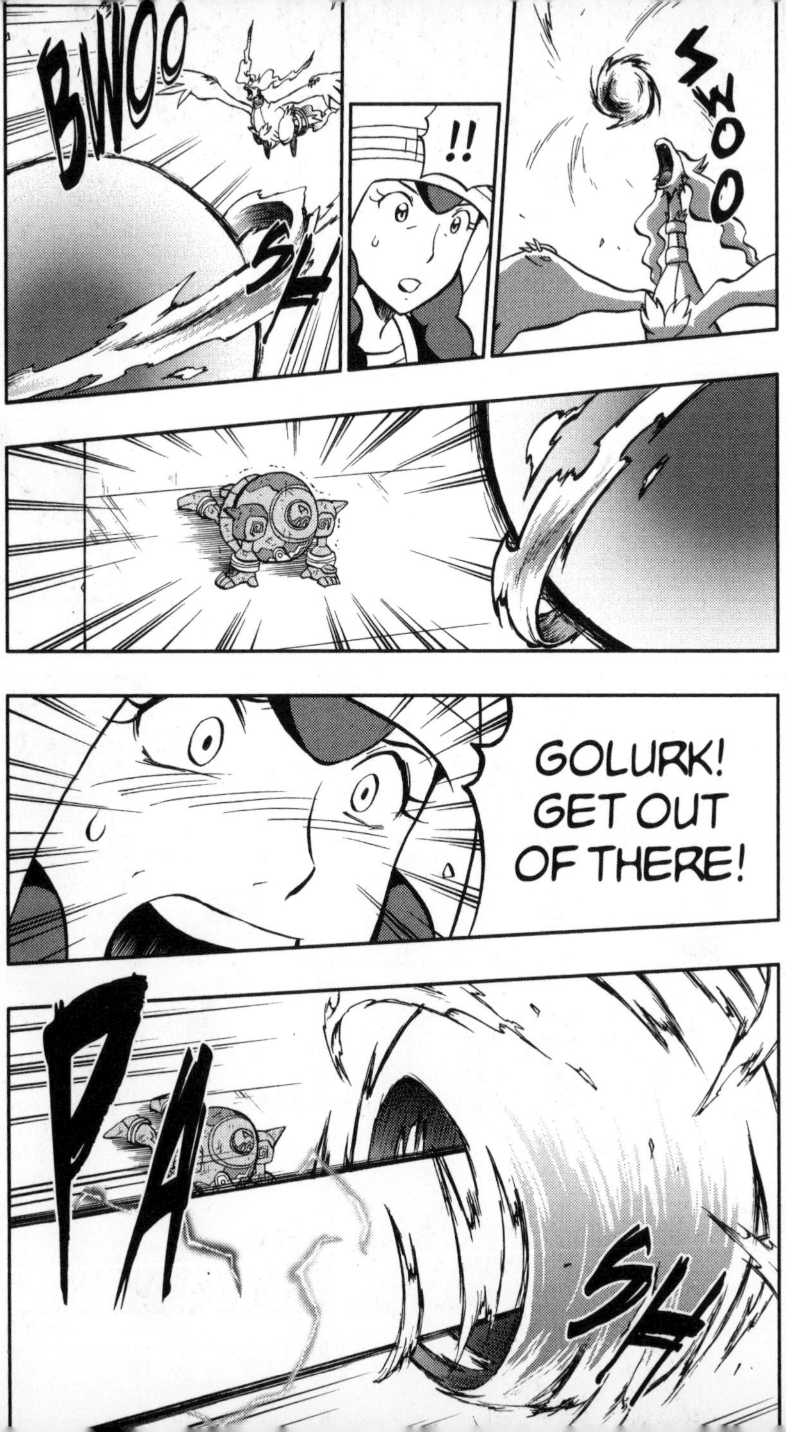
SWOO
!!
BWOO
SH
GOLURK! GET OUT OF THERE!
SH
PA

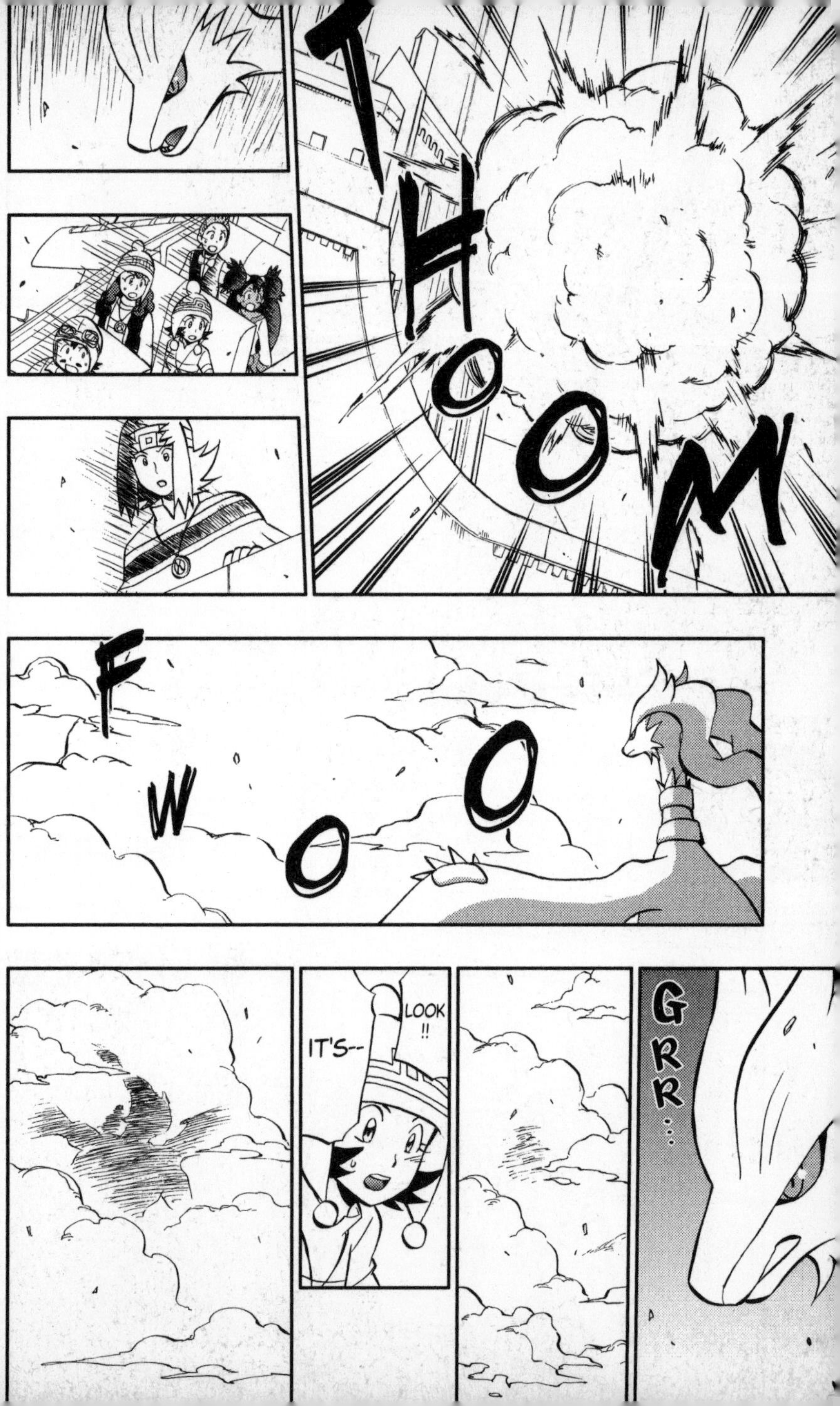
THOOM
FWOOO
GRR...
LOOK!!
IT'S--

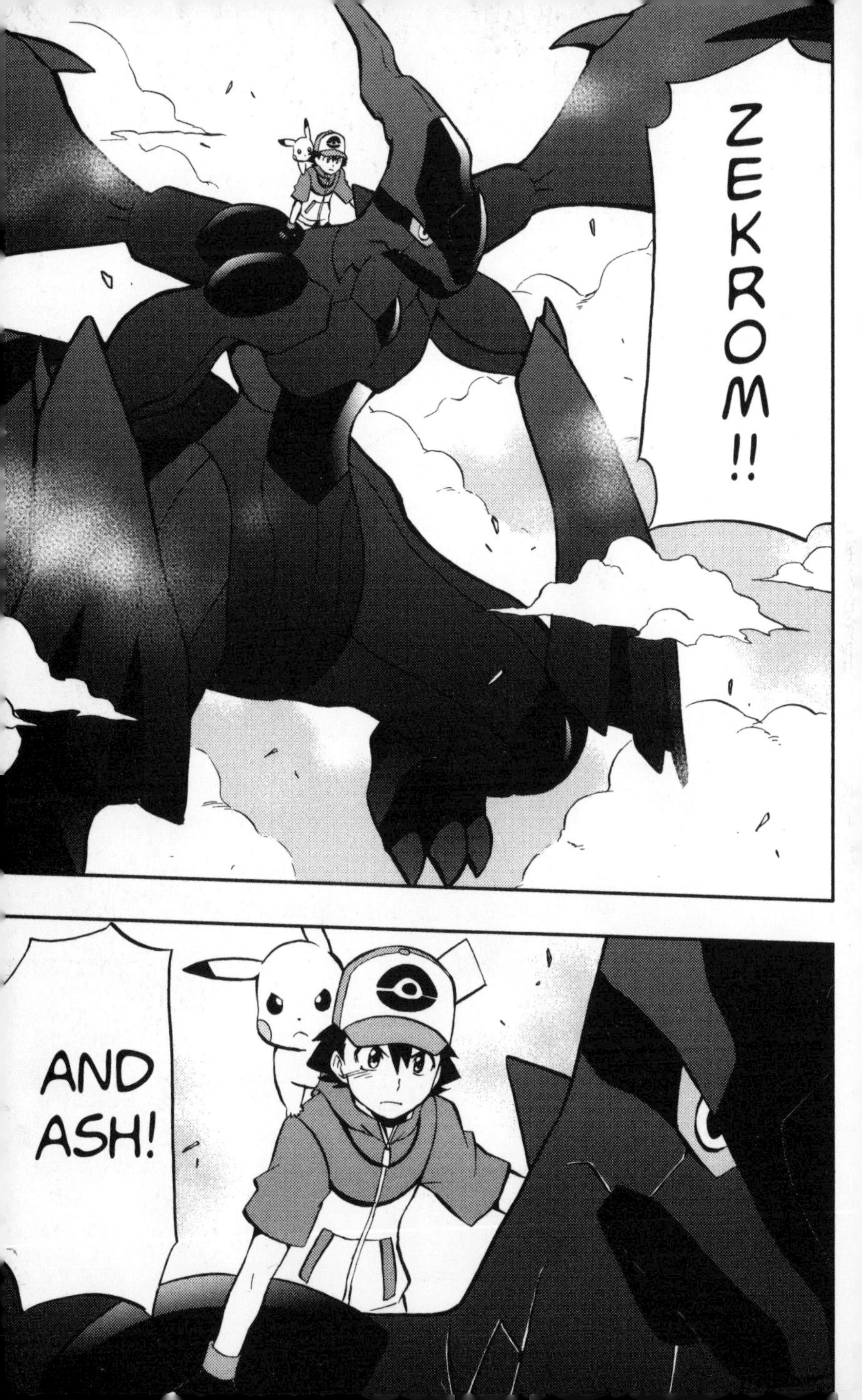
ZEKROM!!
AND ASH!

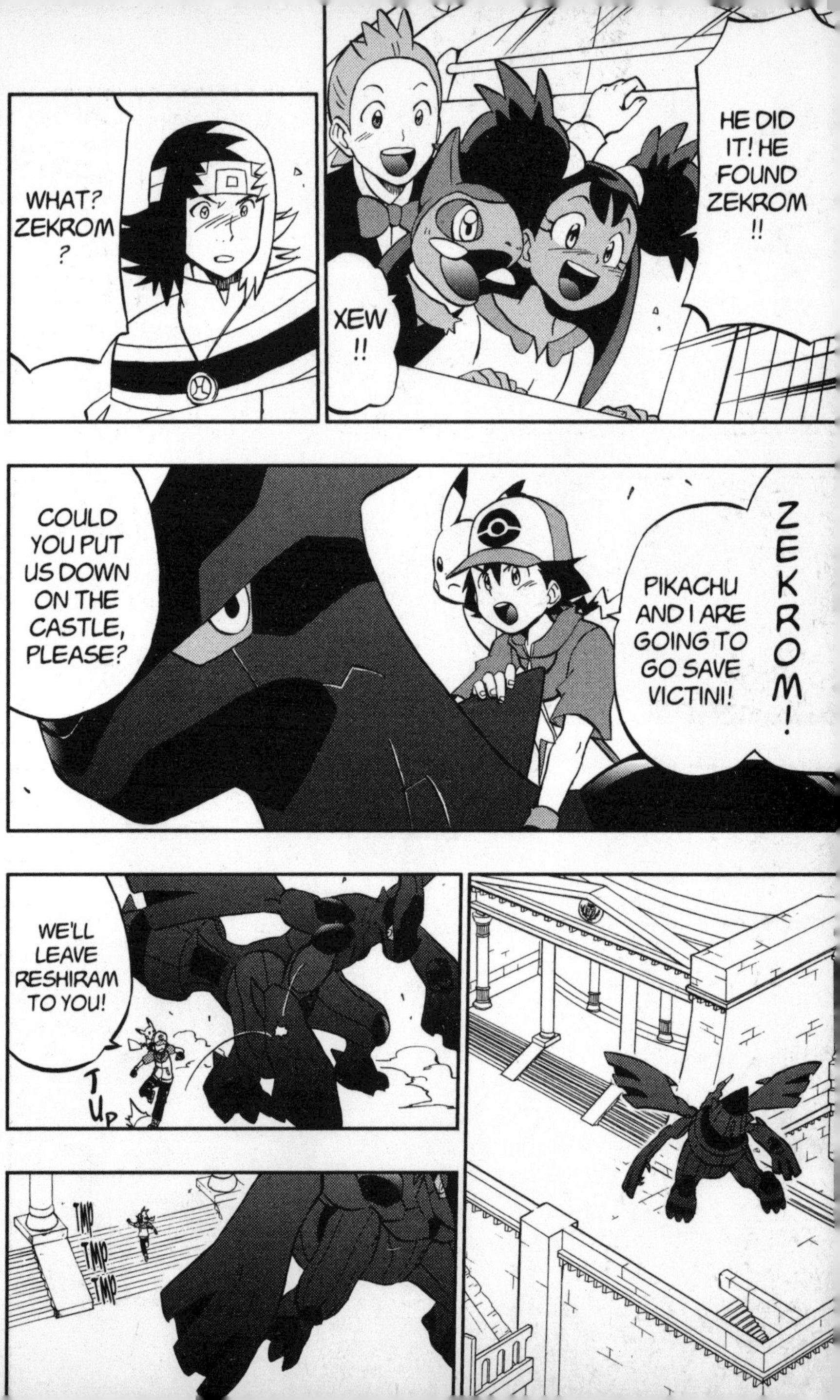
HE DID IT! HE FOUND ZEKROM!!
XEW!!
WHAT? ZEKROM?
ZEKROM!
PIKACHU AND I ARE GOING TO GO SAVE VICTINI!
COULD YOU PUT US DOWN ON THE CASTLE, PLEASE?
WE'LL LEAVE RESHIRAM TO YOU!
TUP
TMP TMP TMP

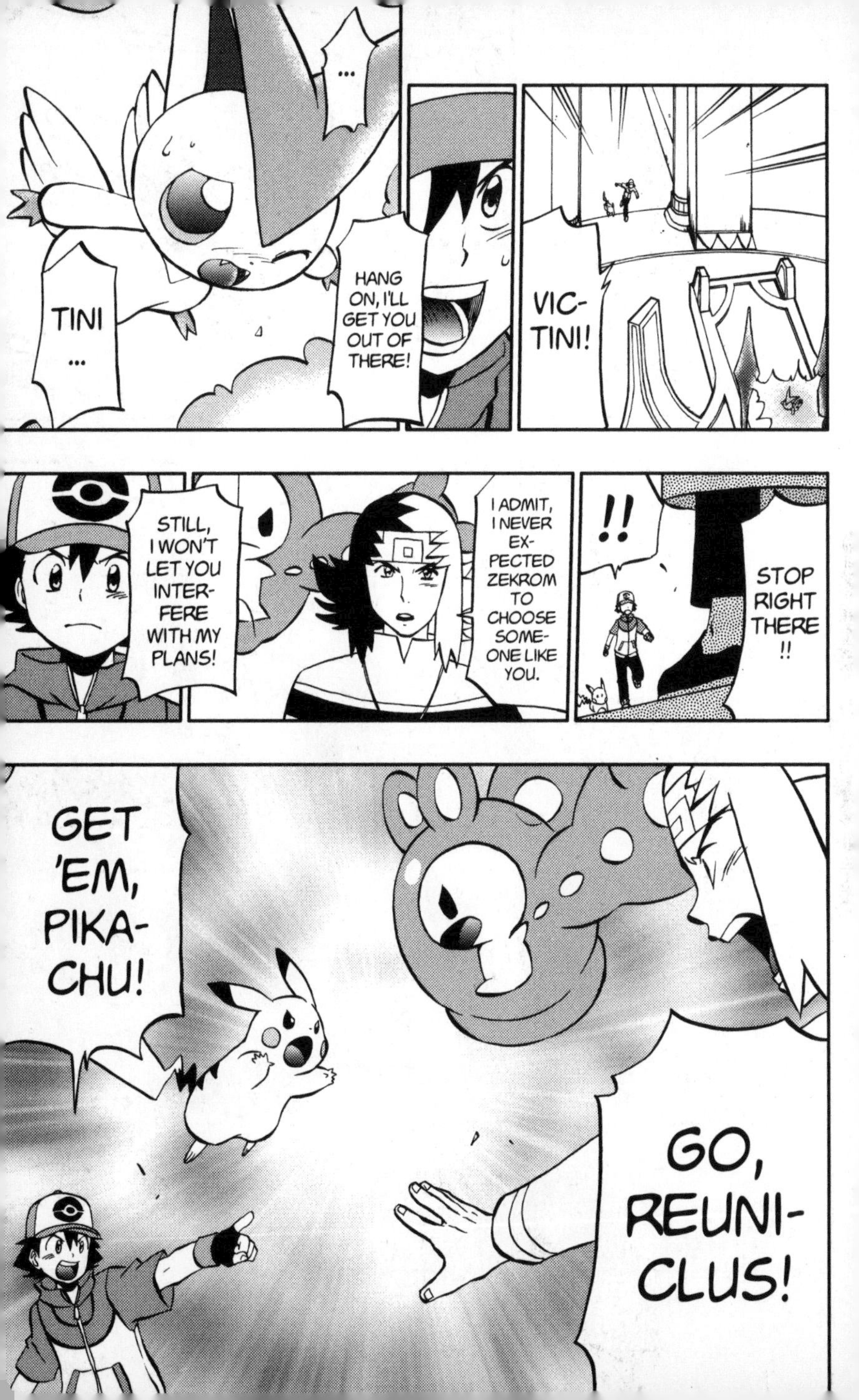

VIC-TINI!
HANG ON, I'LL GET YOU OUT OF THERE!
...
TINI ...
STOP RIGHT THERE !!
!!
I ADMIT, I NEVER EX-PECTED ZEKROM TO CHOOSE SOME-ONE LIKE YOU.
STILL, I WON'T LET YOU INTER-FERE WITH MY PLANS!
GO, REUNI-CLUS!
GET 'EM, PIKA-CHU!

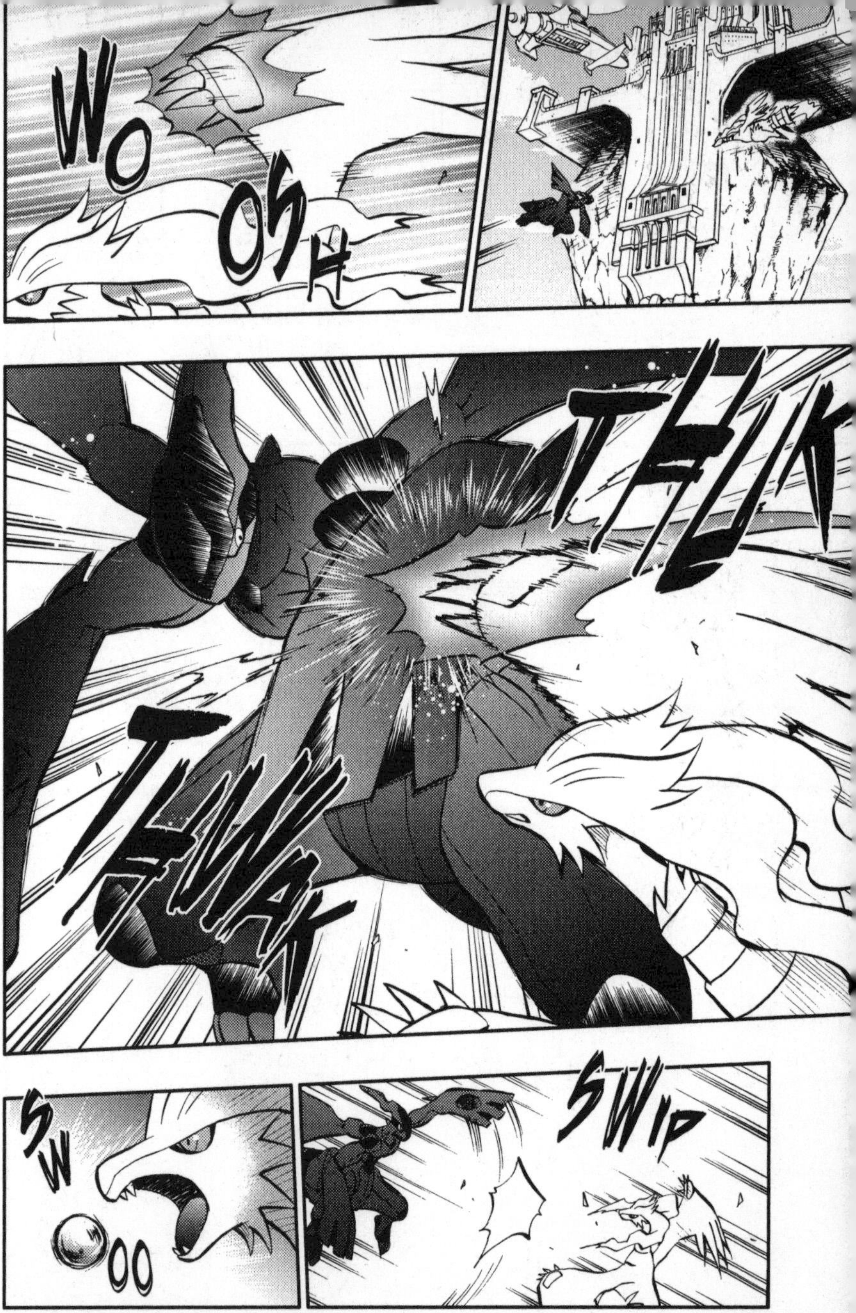
WOOSH
THUK
THWAK
SWIP
SWOOO

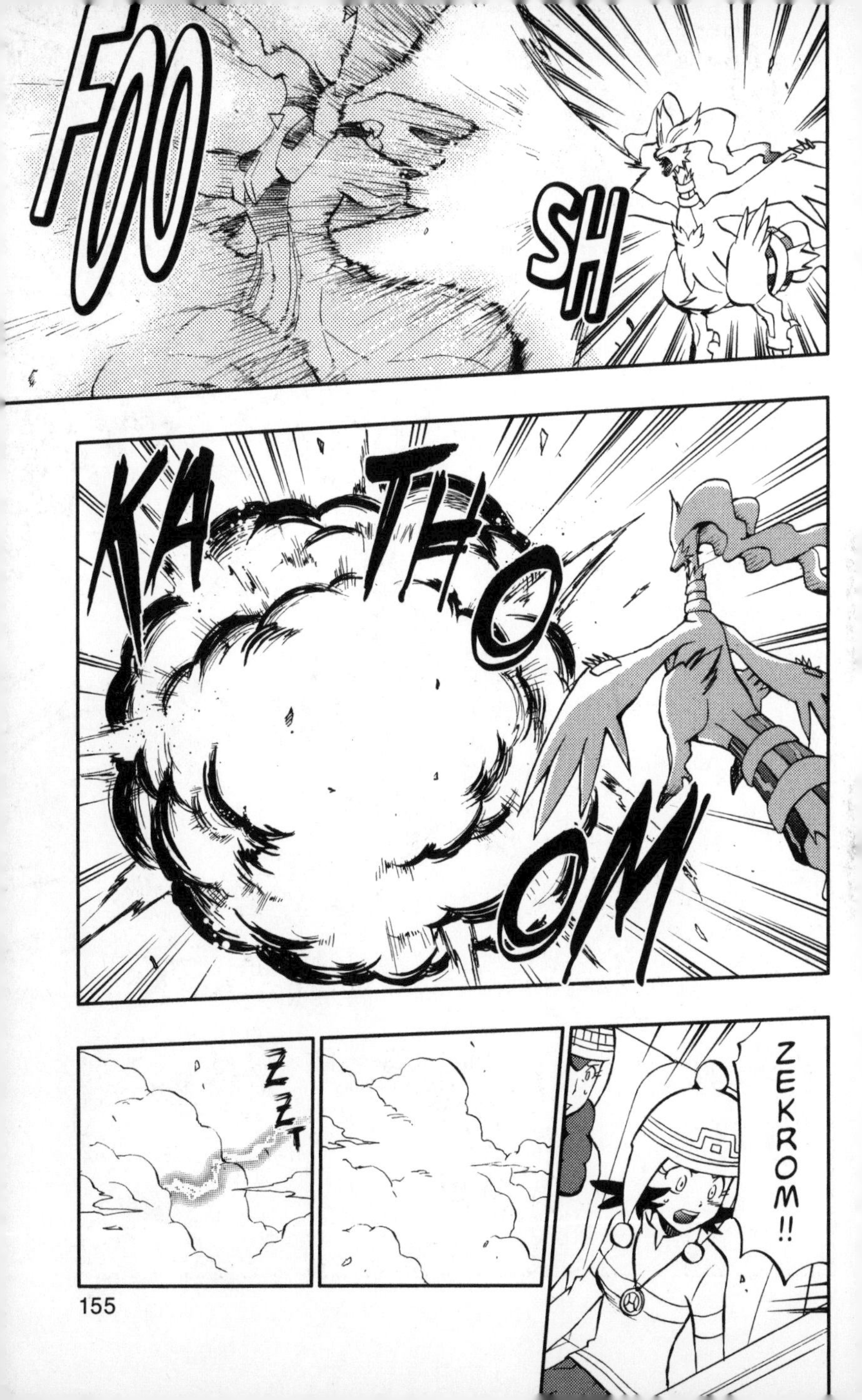
FOOSH
KA-THOOM
ZEKROM!!
ZZZT

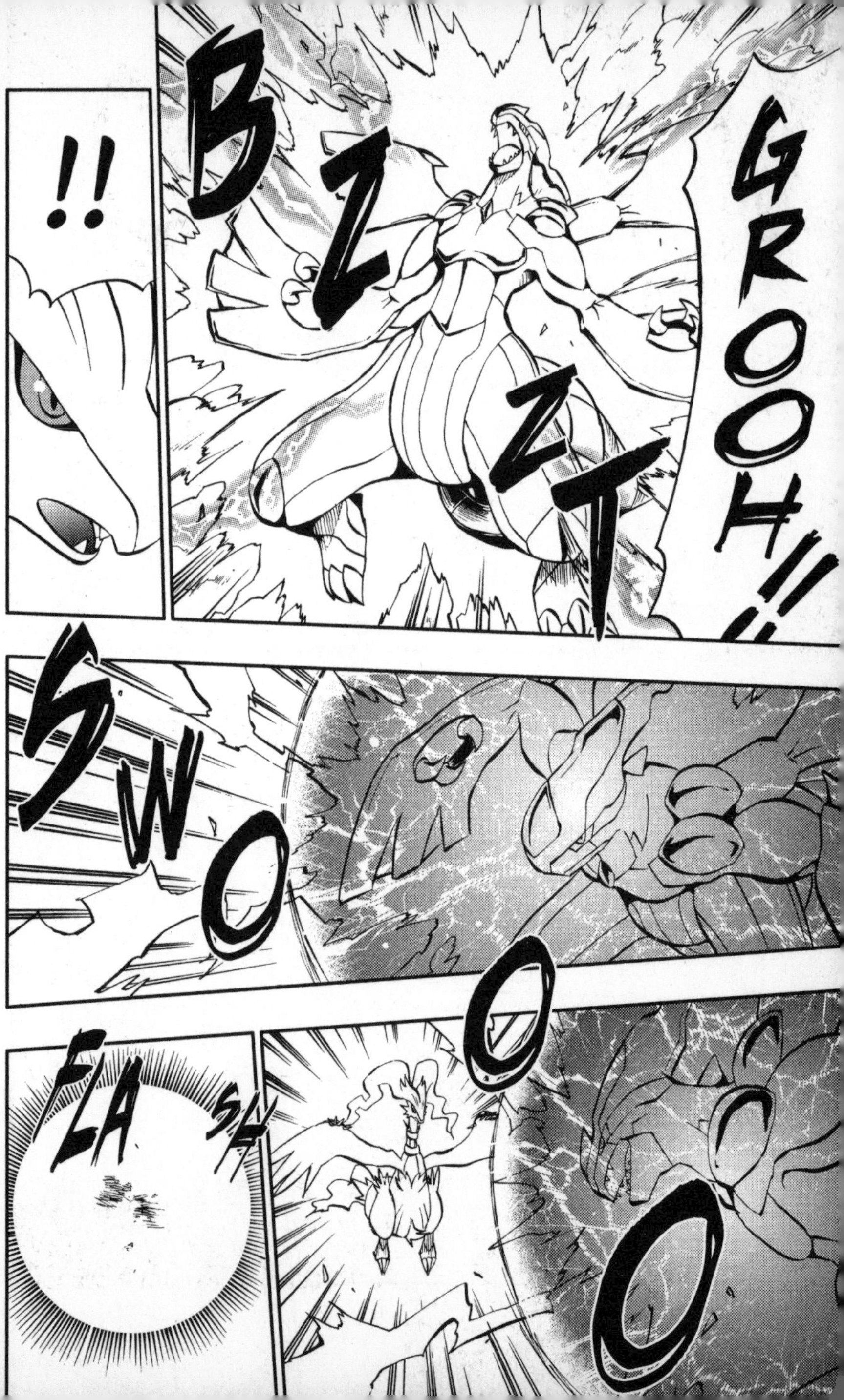
GROOOH!!
BZZZT
!!
SWOOOOO
FLASH

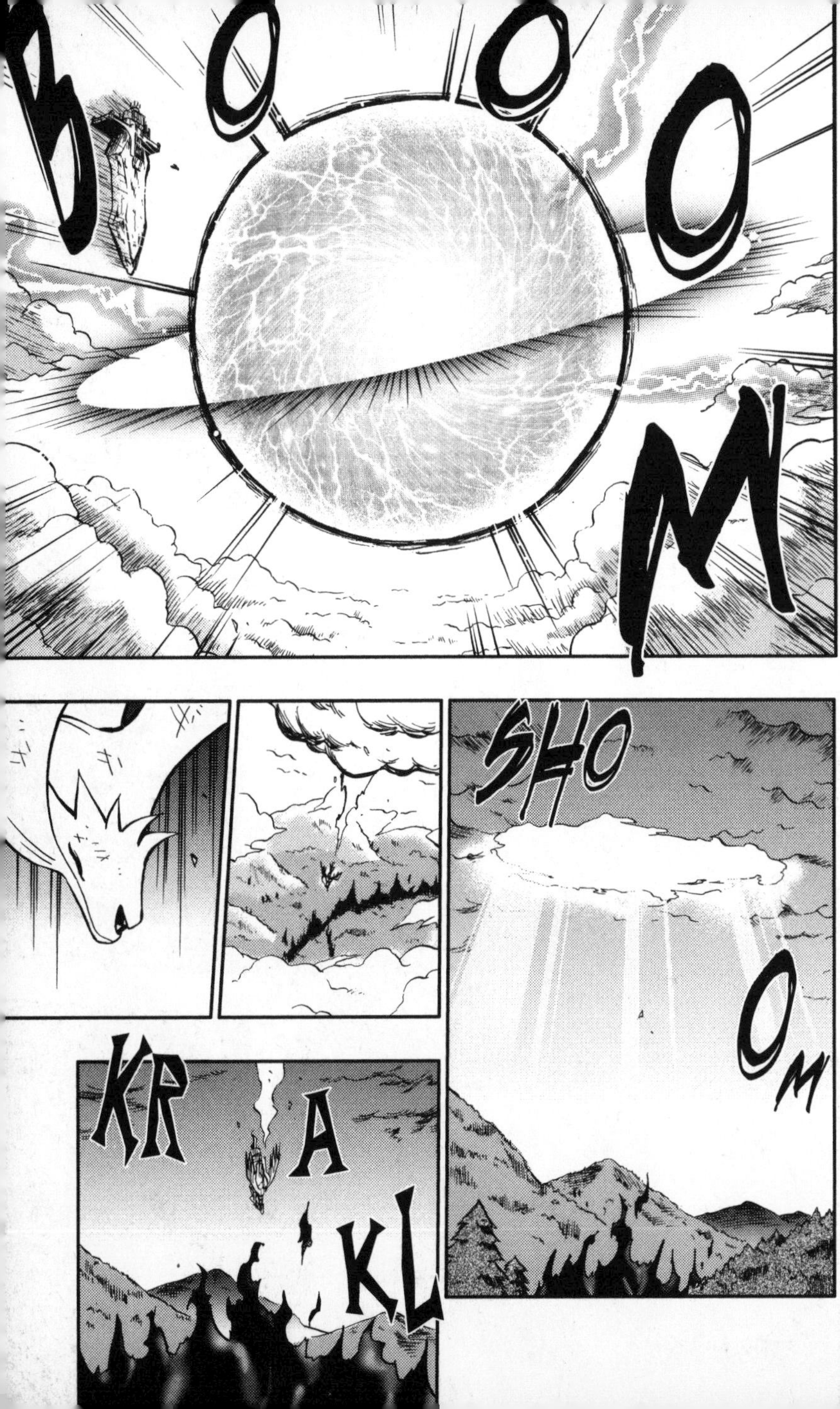
BOOOOM
SHOOM
KRAKL

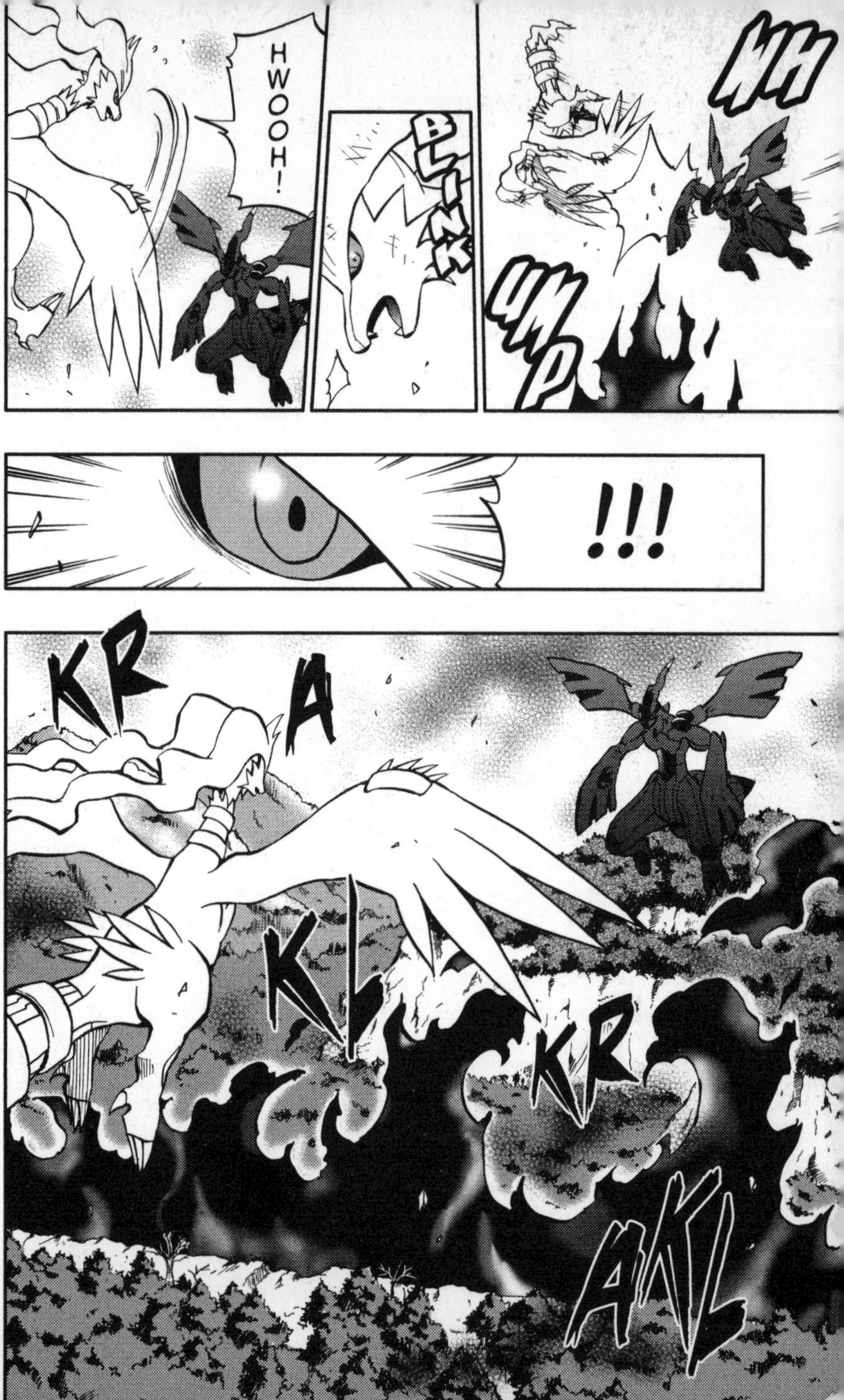
WH
UMP
BLINK
HWOOOH!
!!!
KR A
KL
KR
AKL

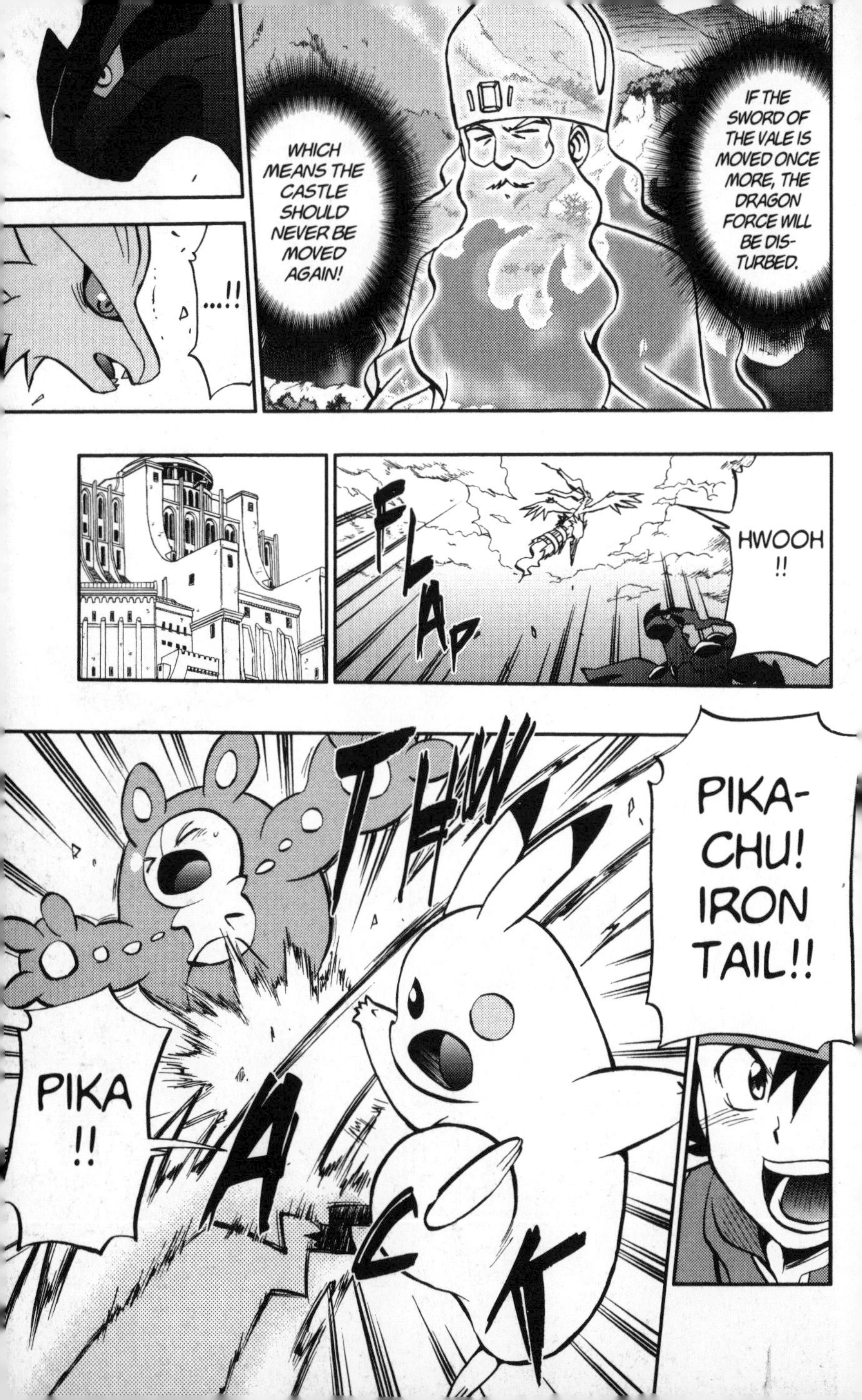
IF THE SWORD OF THE VALE IS MOVED ONCE MORE, THE DRAGON FORCE WILL BE DIS- TURBED.
WHICH MEANS THE CASTLE SHOULD NEVER BE MOVED AGAIN!
...!!
FLAP
HWOOH !!
PIKA- CHU! IRON TAIL!!
THWACK
PIKA !!

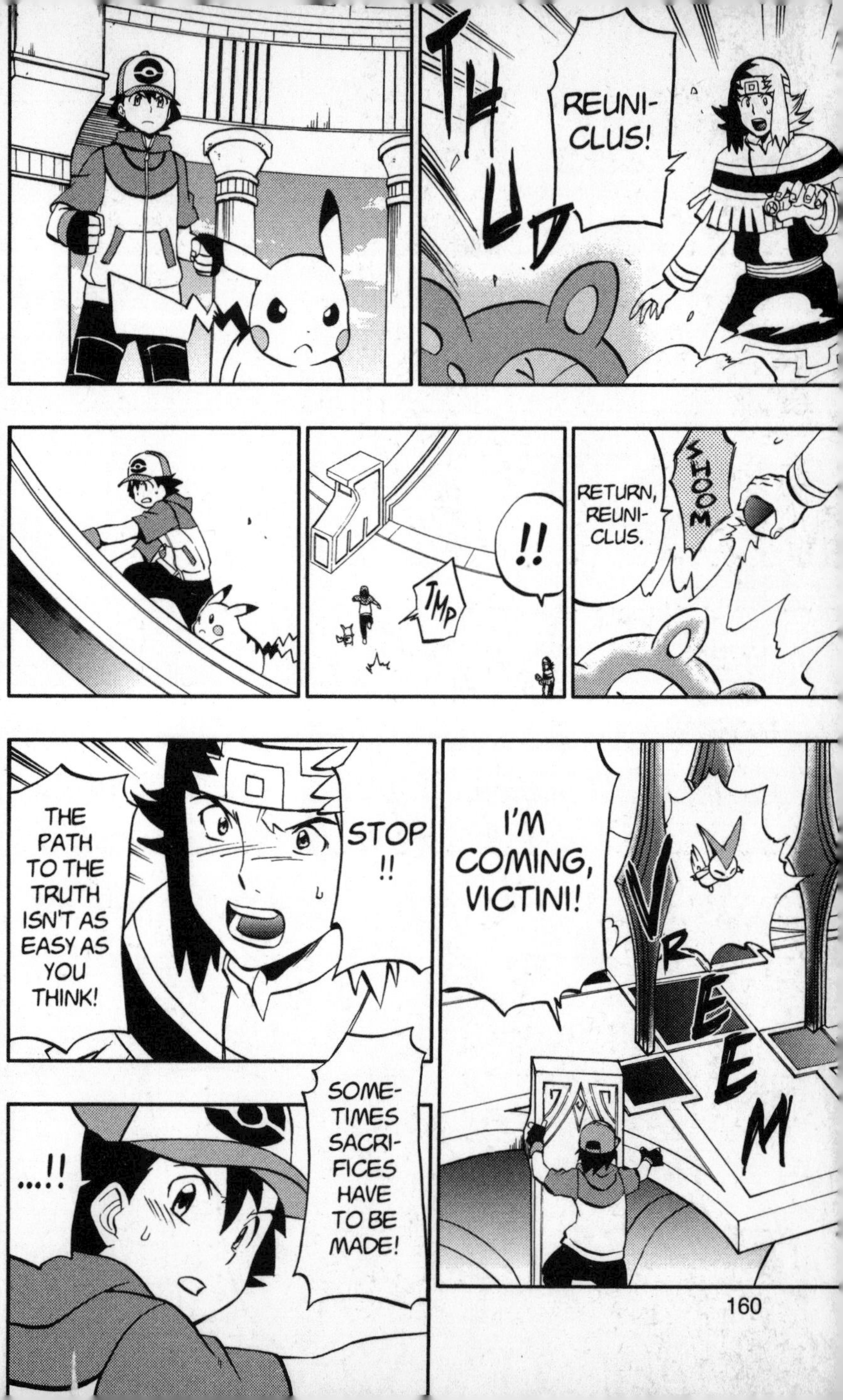
THUD
REUNI-CLUS!
SHOOM
RETURN, REUNI-CLUS.
!!
TMP
I'M COMING, VICTINI!
VREEEM
STOP!!
THE PATH TO THE TRUTH ISN'T AS EASY AS YOU THINK!
SOME-TIMES SACRI-FICES HAVE TO BE MADE!
...!!

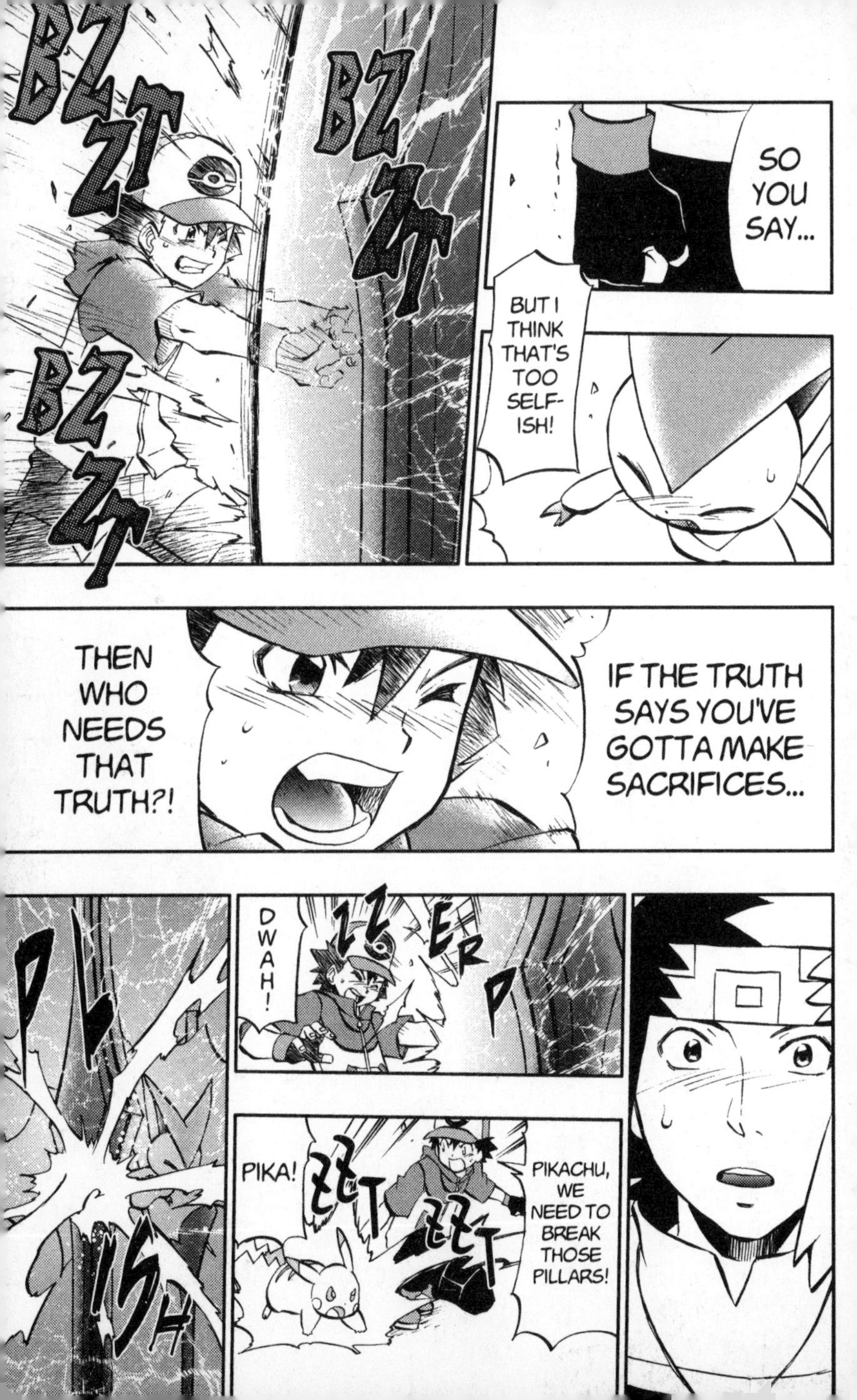
SO YOU SAY...
BUT I THINK THAT'S TOO SELF-ISH!
BZZT
BZZT
BZZT
IF THE TRUTH SAYS YOU'VE GOTTA MAKE SACRIFICES...
THEN WHO NEEDS THAT TRUTH?!
DWAH!
PIKACHU, WE NEED TO BREAK THOSE PILLARS!
PIKA!

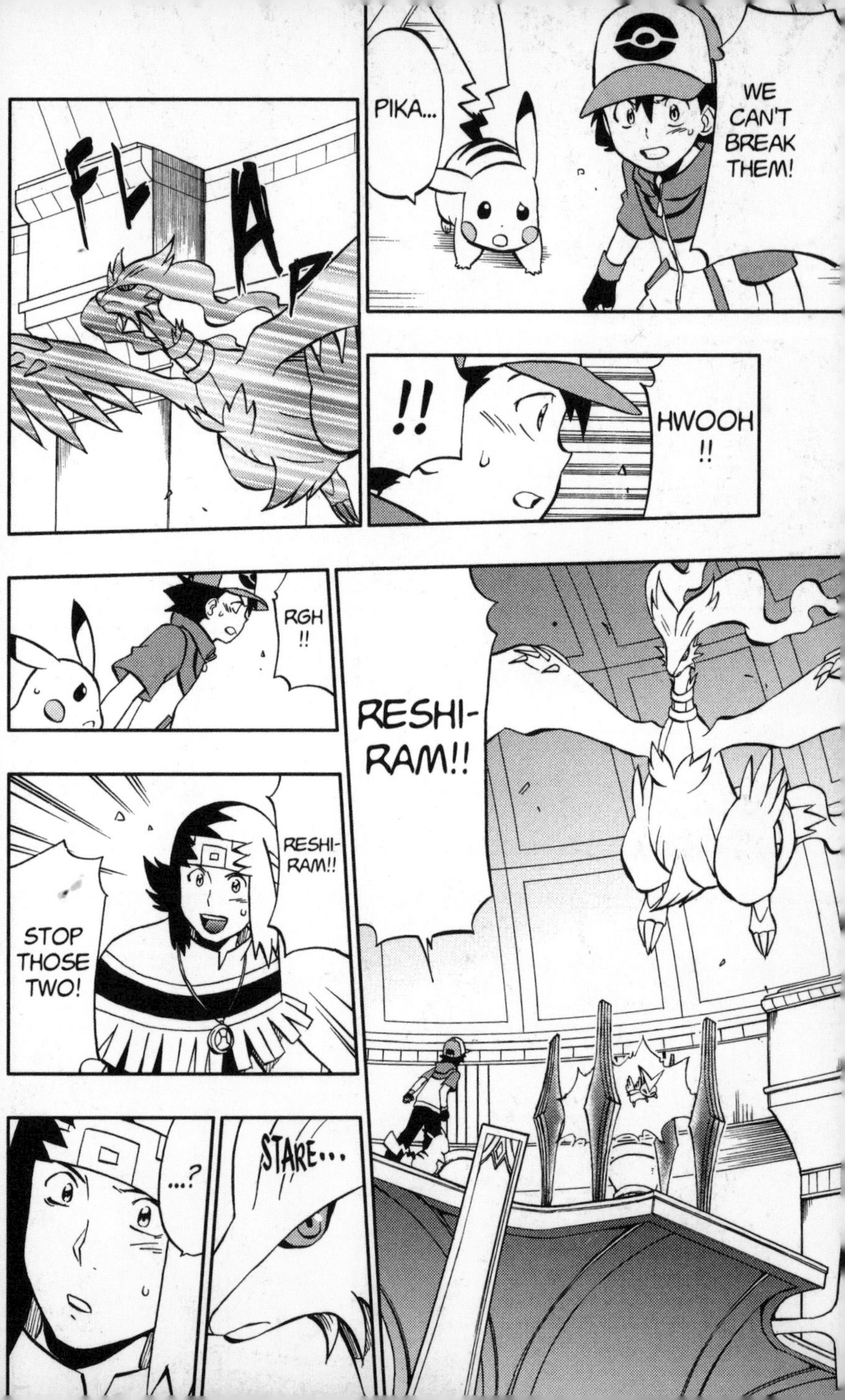
WE CAN'T BREAK THEM!
PIKA...
HWOOH !!
!!
FLAP
RESHI-RAM!!
RGH !!
RESHI-RAM!!
STOP THOSE TWO!
STARE...
...?

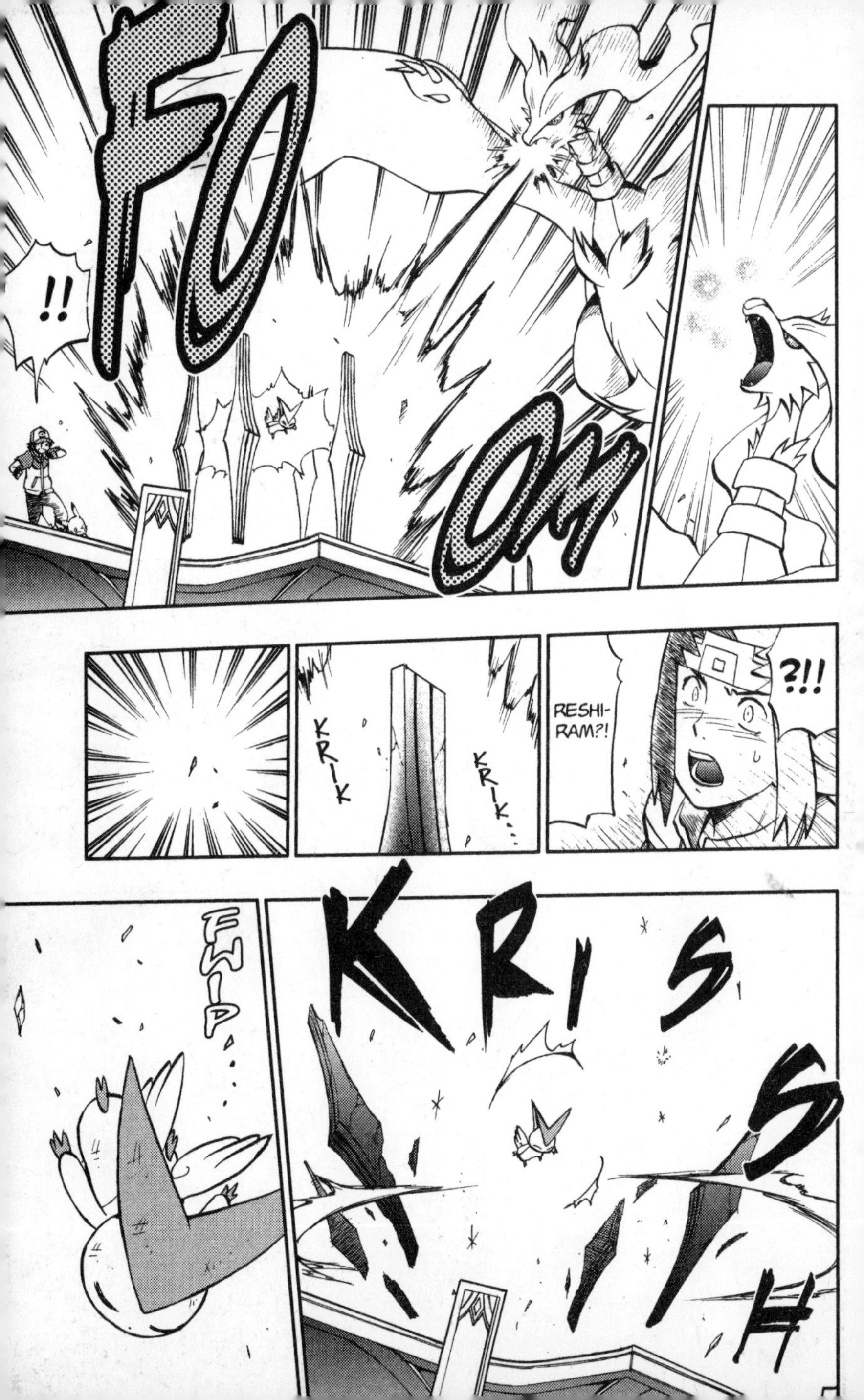

FO
OM
!!
?!!
RESHI-RAM?!
KRIK
KRIK...
KRISSH
FWIP...

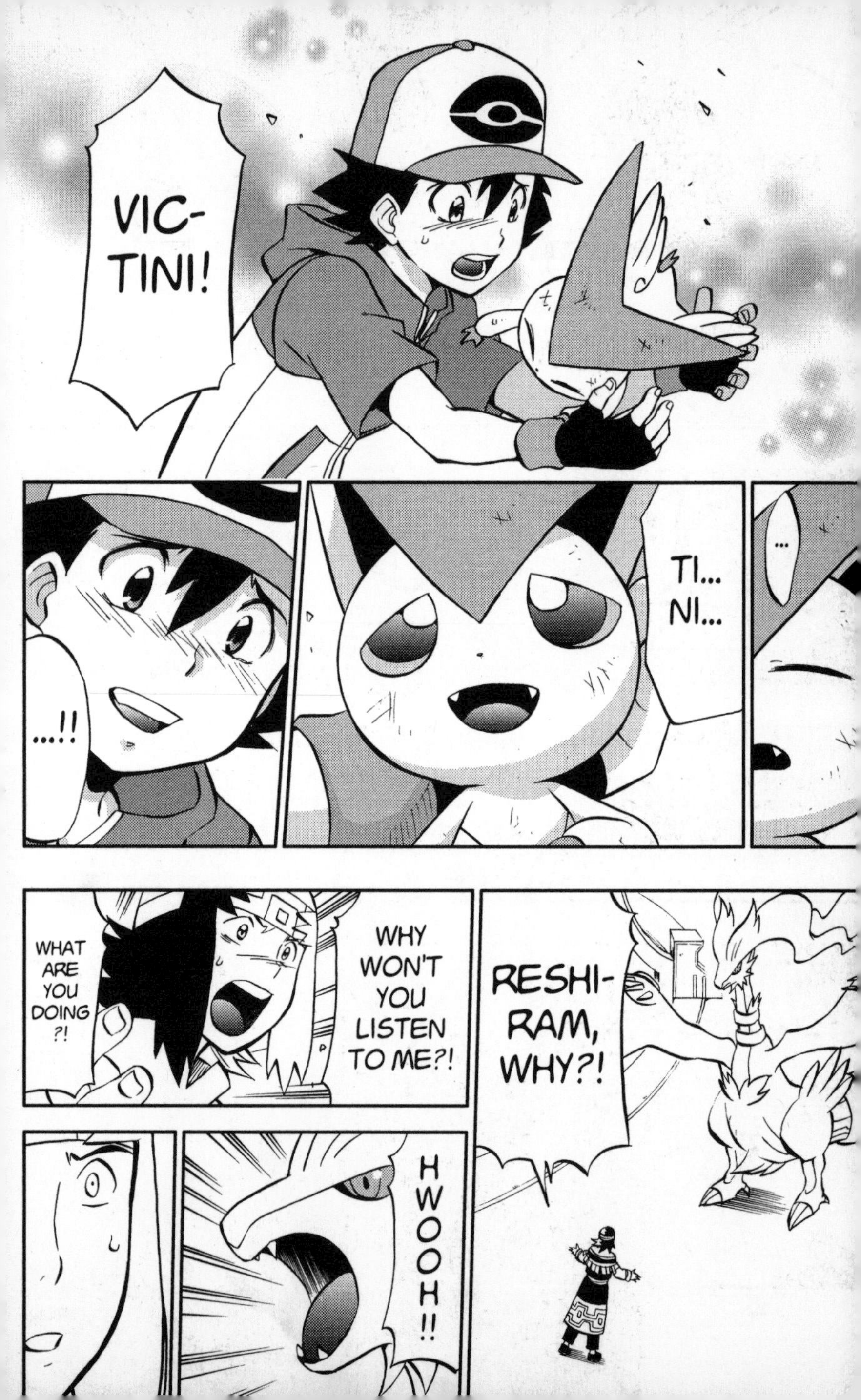
VIC-TINI!
...
TI... NI...
...!!
RESHI-RAM, WHY?!
WHY WON'T YOU LISTEN TO ME?!
WHAT ARE YOU DOING?!
HWOOOH!!

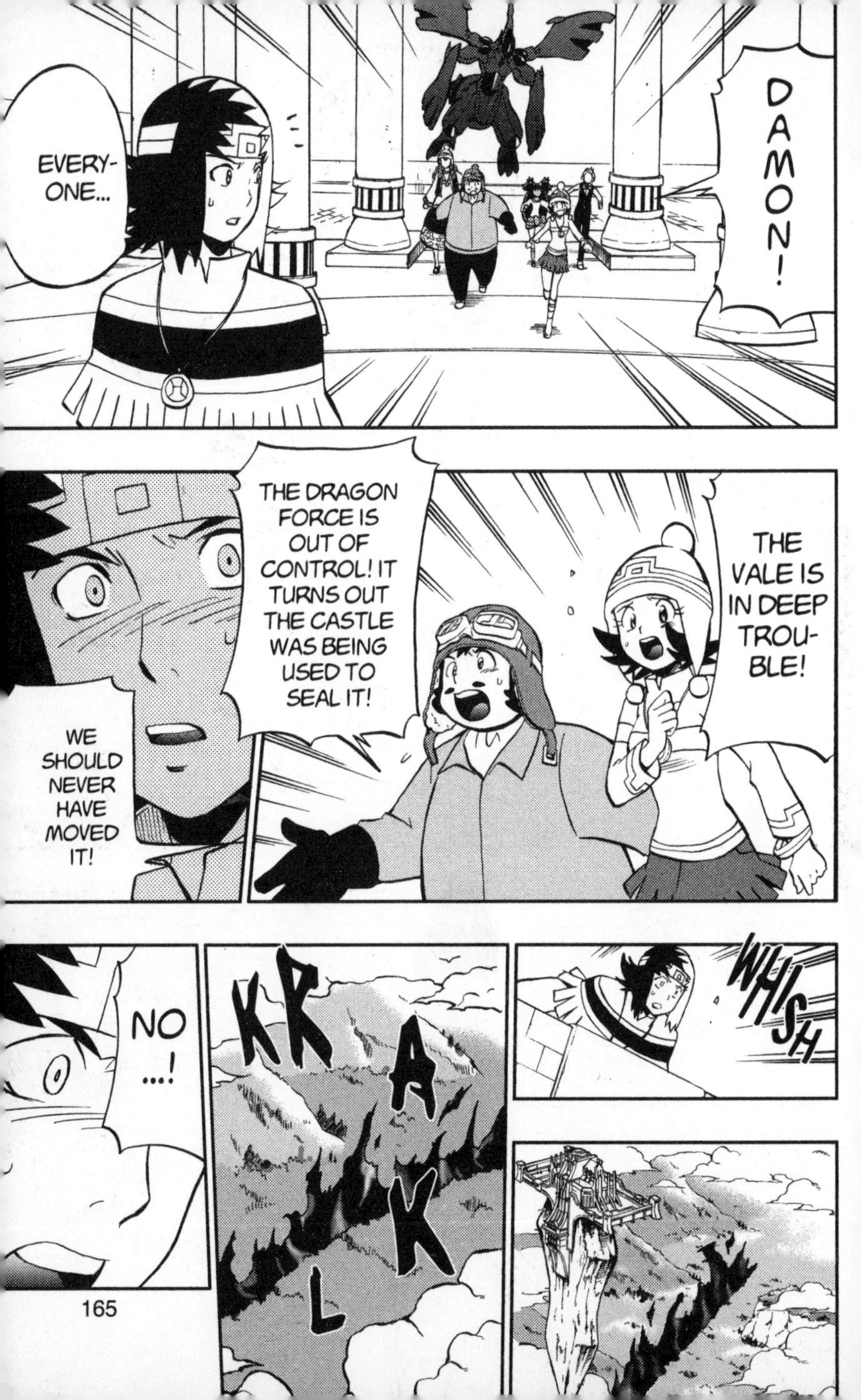
DAMON!
EVERY-ONE...
THE VALE IS IN DEEP TROU-BLE!
THE DRAGON FORCE IS OUT OF CONTROL! IT TURNS OUT THE CASTLE WAS BEING USED TO SEAL IT!
WE SHOULD NEVER HAVE MOVED IT!
WHISH
KRAKL
NO ...!

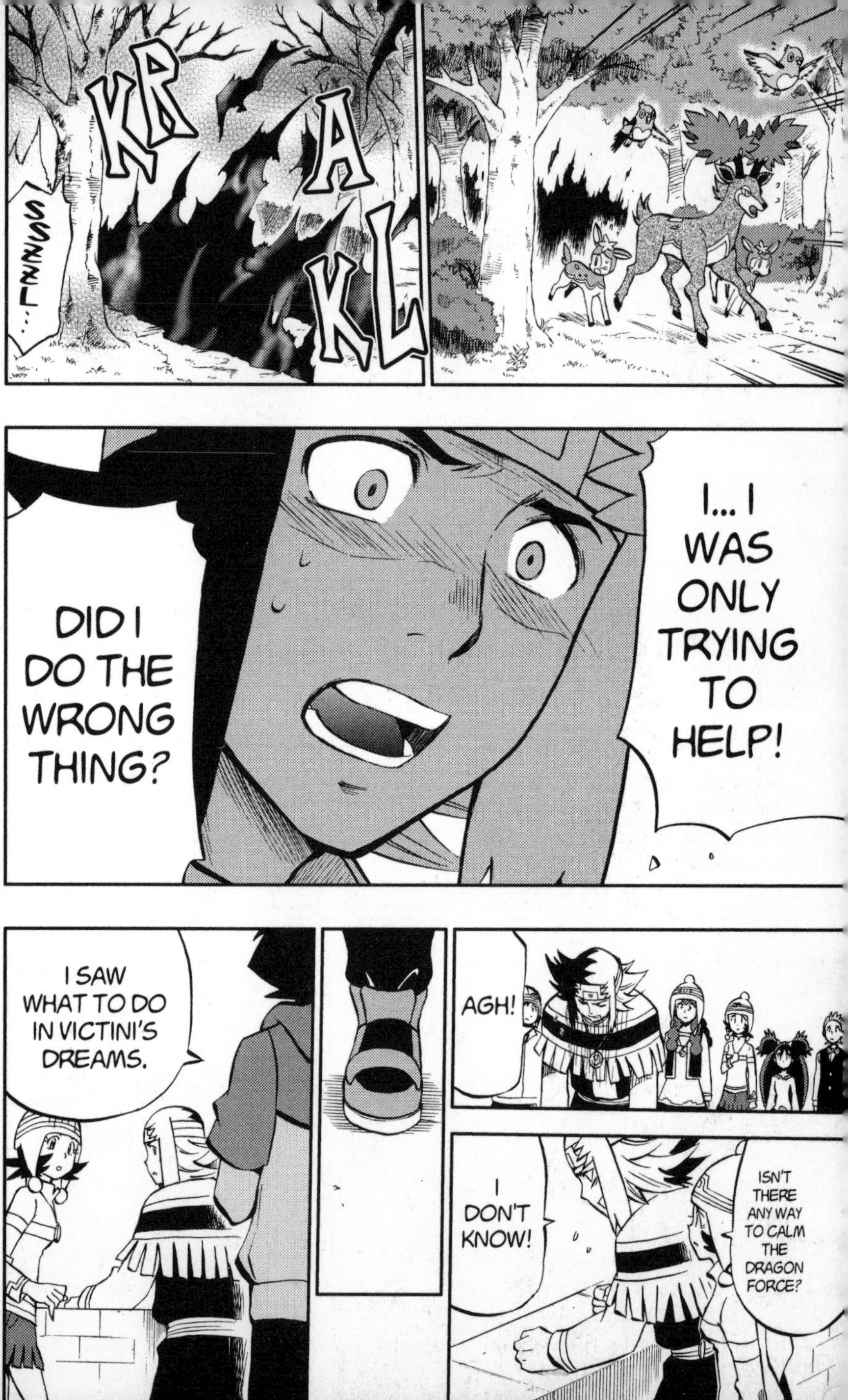
KRAKL
SSZZL...
I... I WAS ONLY TRYING TO HELP!
DID I DO THE WRONG THING?
AGH!
ISN'T THERE ANY WAY TO CALM THE DRAGON FORCE?
I DON'T KNOW!
I SAW WHAT TO DO IN VICTINI'S DREAMS.

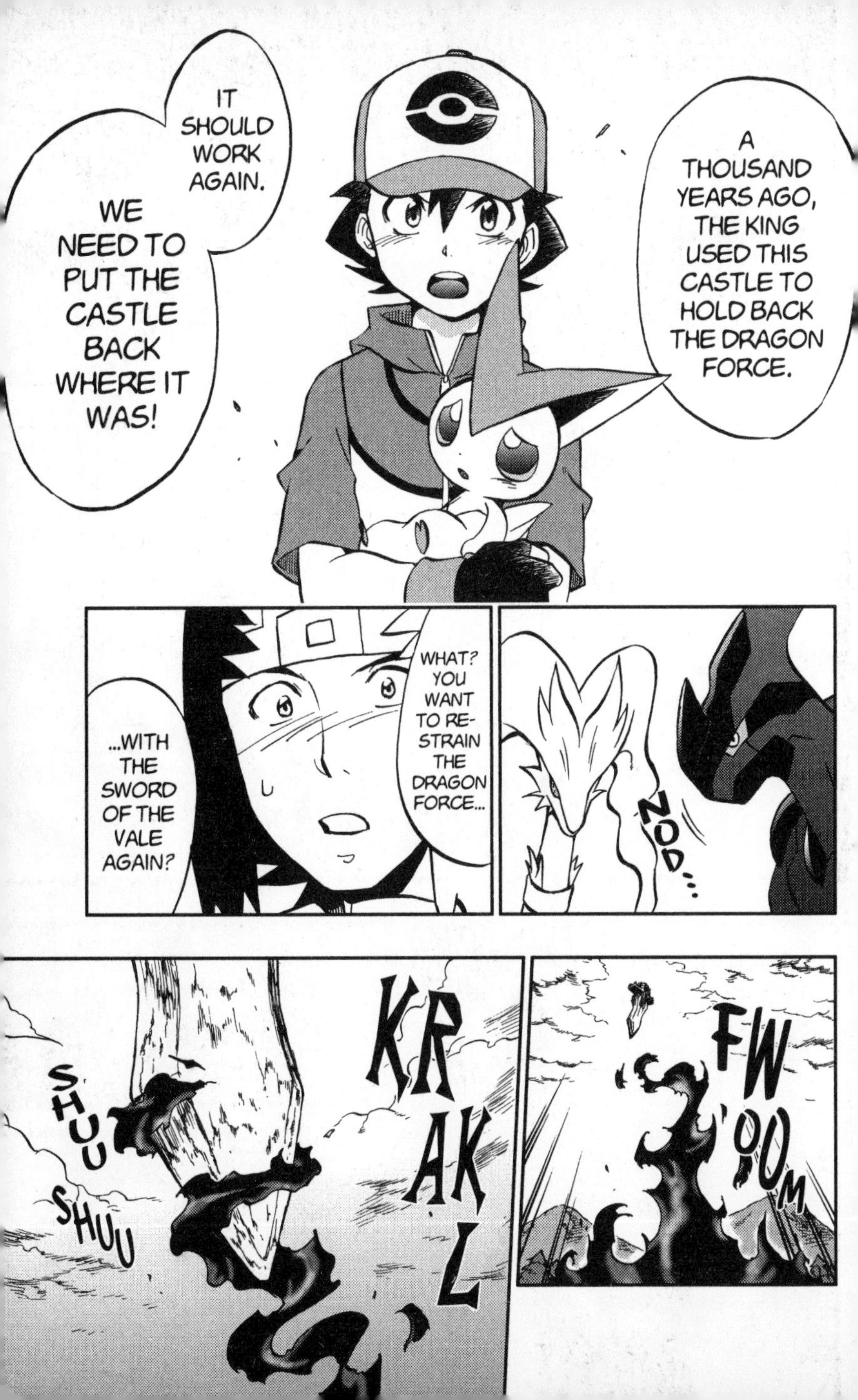
A THOUSAND YEARS AGO, THE KING USED THIS CASTLE TO HOLD BACK THE DRAGON FORCE.
IT SHOULD WORK AGAIN.
WE NEED TO PUT THE CASTLE BACK WHERE IT WAS!
NOD...
WHAT? YOU WANT TO RE-STRAIN THE DRAGON FORCE...
...WITH THE SWORD OF THE VALE AGAIN?
FWOOOM
KRAKL
SHUU SHUU

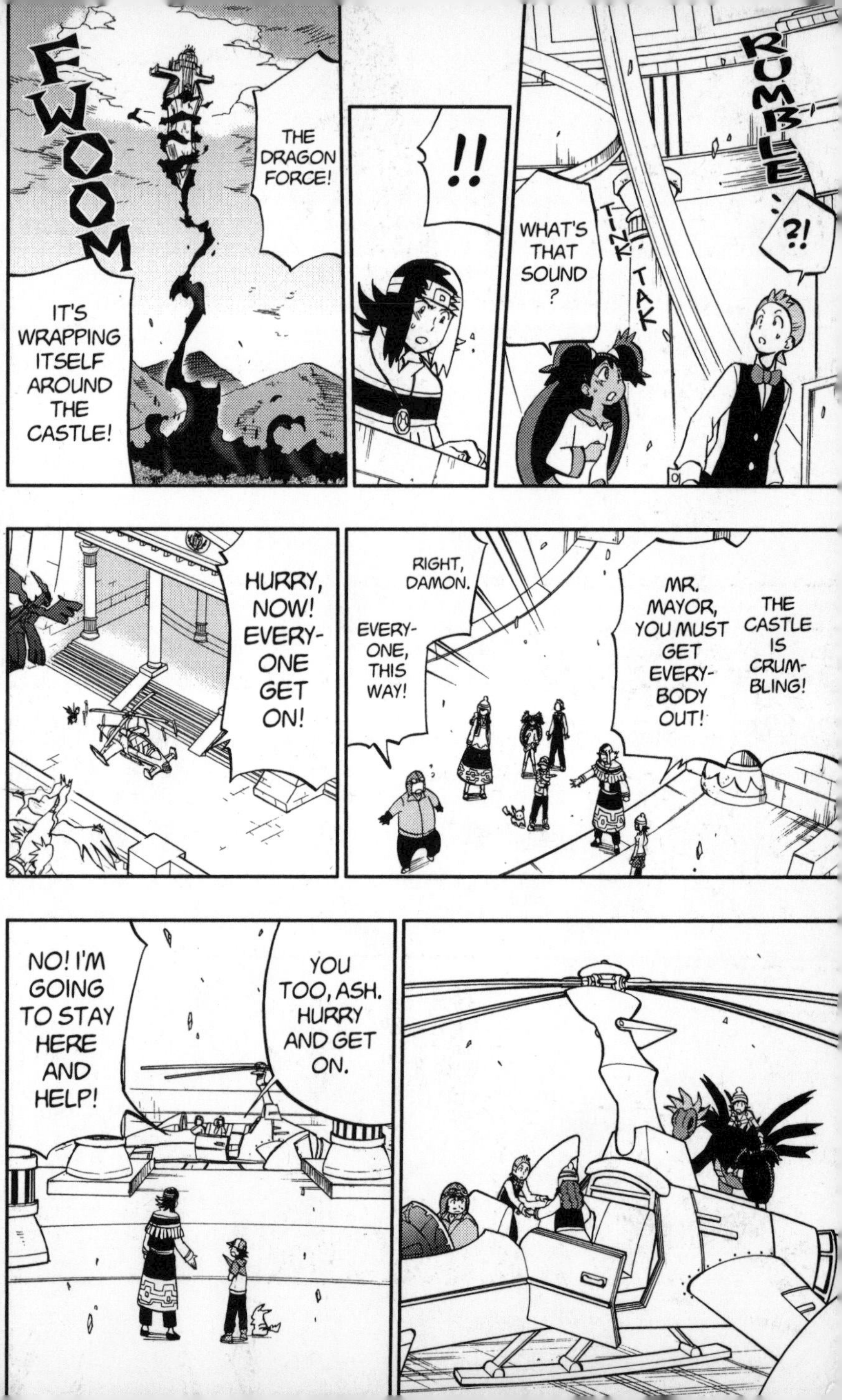
RUMBLE
?!
TINK TAK
WHAT'S THAT SOUND?
!!
FWOOM
THE DRAGON FORCE!
IT'S WRAPPING ITSELF AROUND THE CASTLE!
THE CASTLE IS CRUMBLING!
MR. MAYOR, YOU MUST GET EVERYBODY OUT!
RIGHT, DAMON.
EVERYONE, THIS WAY!
HURRY, NOW! EVERYONE GET ON!
YOU TOO, ASH. HURRY AND GET ON.
NO! I'M GOING TO STAY HERE AND HELP!

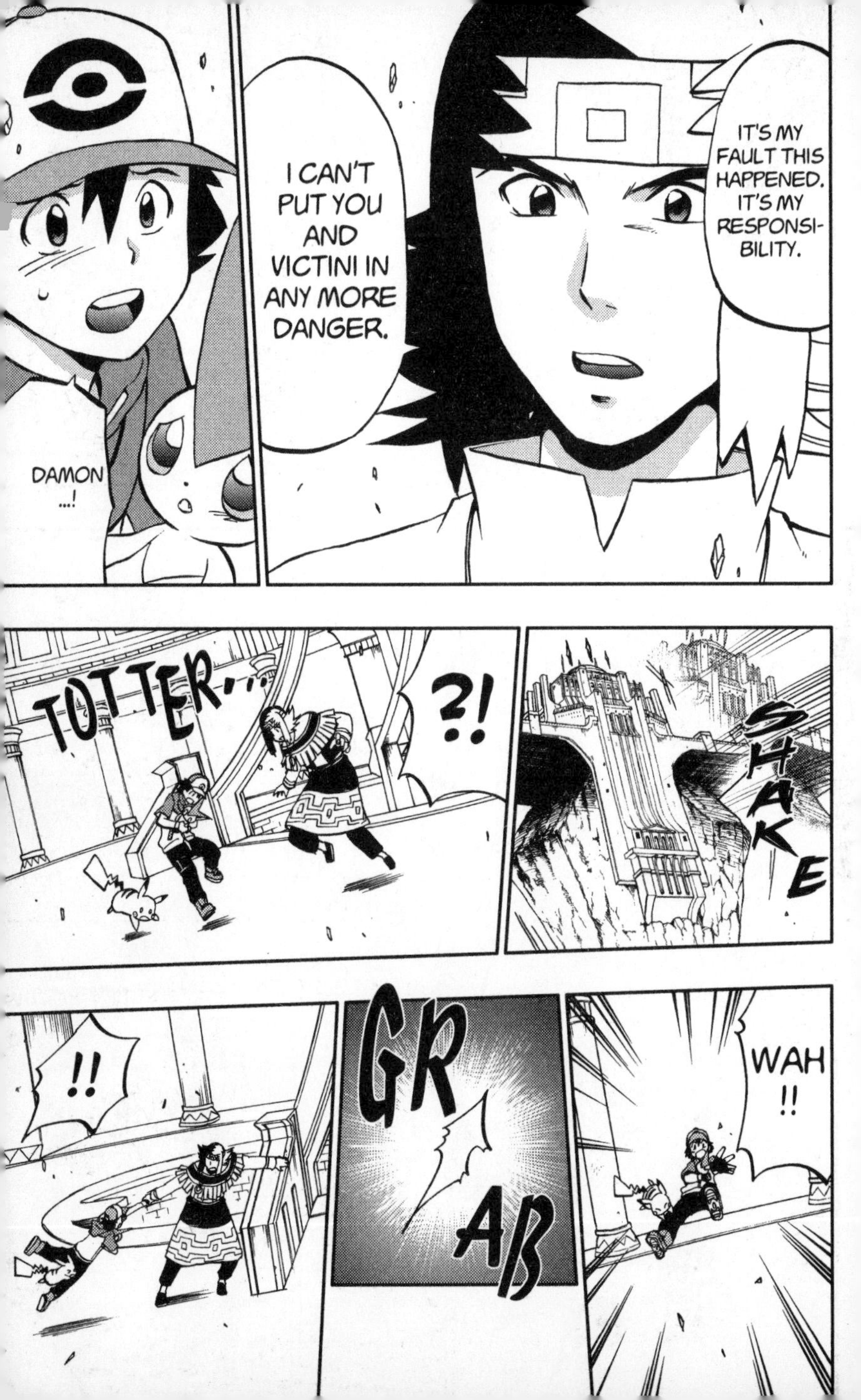

IT'S MY FAULT THIS HAPPENED. IT'S MY RESPONSI-BILITY.
I CAN'T PUT YOU AND VICTINI IN ANY MORE DANGER.
DAMON ...!
SHAKE
?!
TOTTER...
WAH !!
GRAB
!!

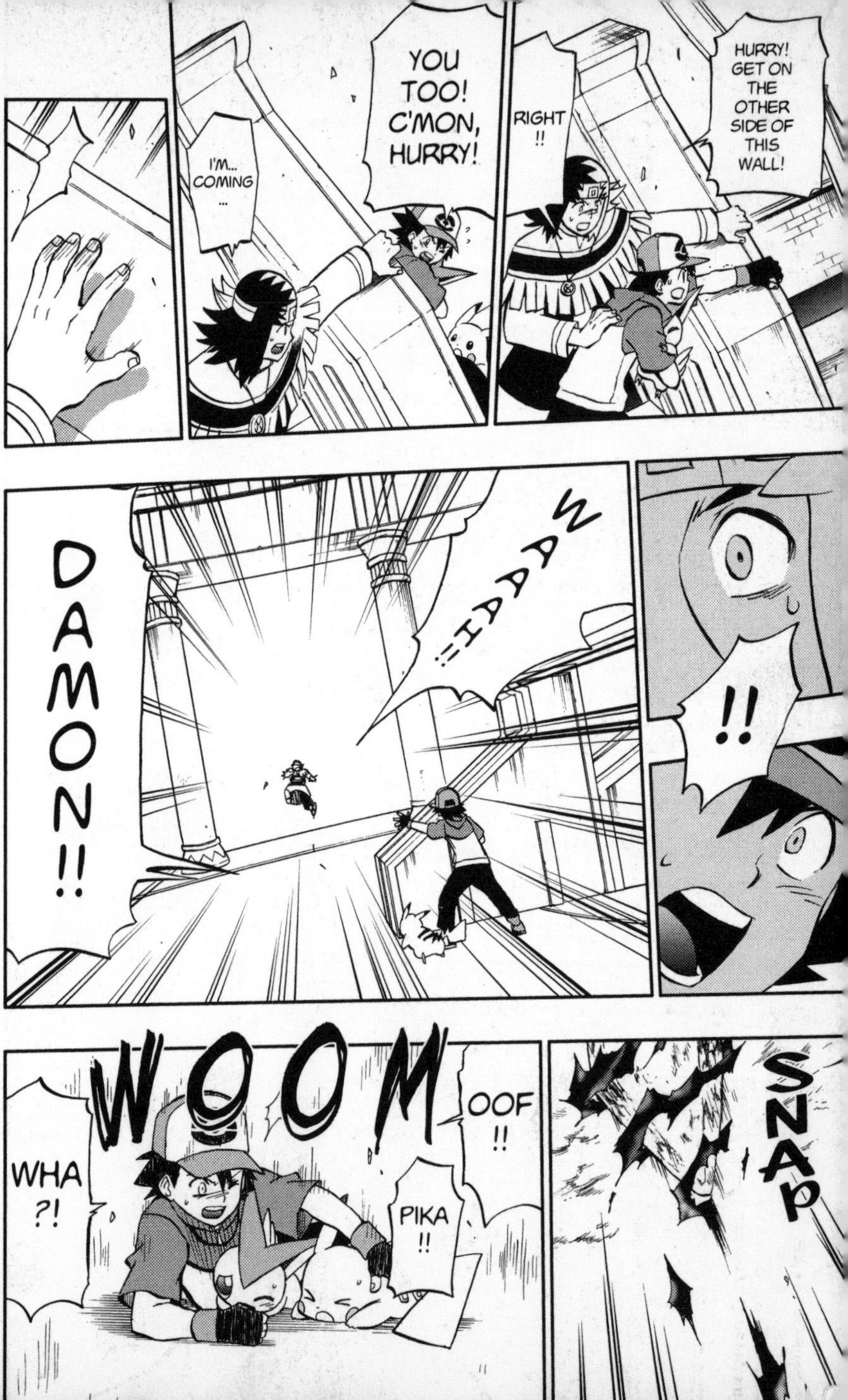
HURRY! GET ON THE OTHER SIDE OF THIS WALL!
RIGHT !!
YOU TOO! C'MON, HURRY!
I'M... COMING ...
!!
WAAAAH!!
DAMON!!
SNAP
WOOOM
OOF !!
PIKA !!
WHA ?!

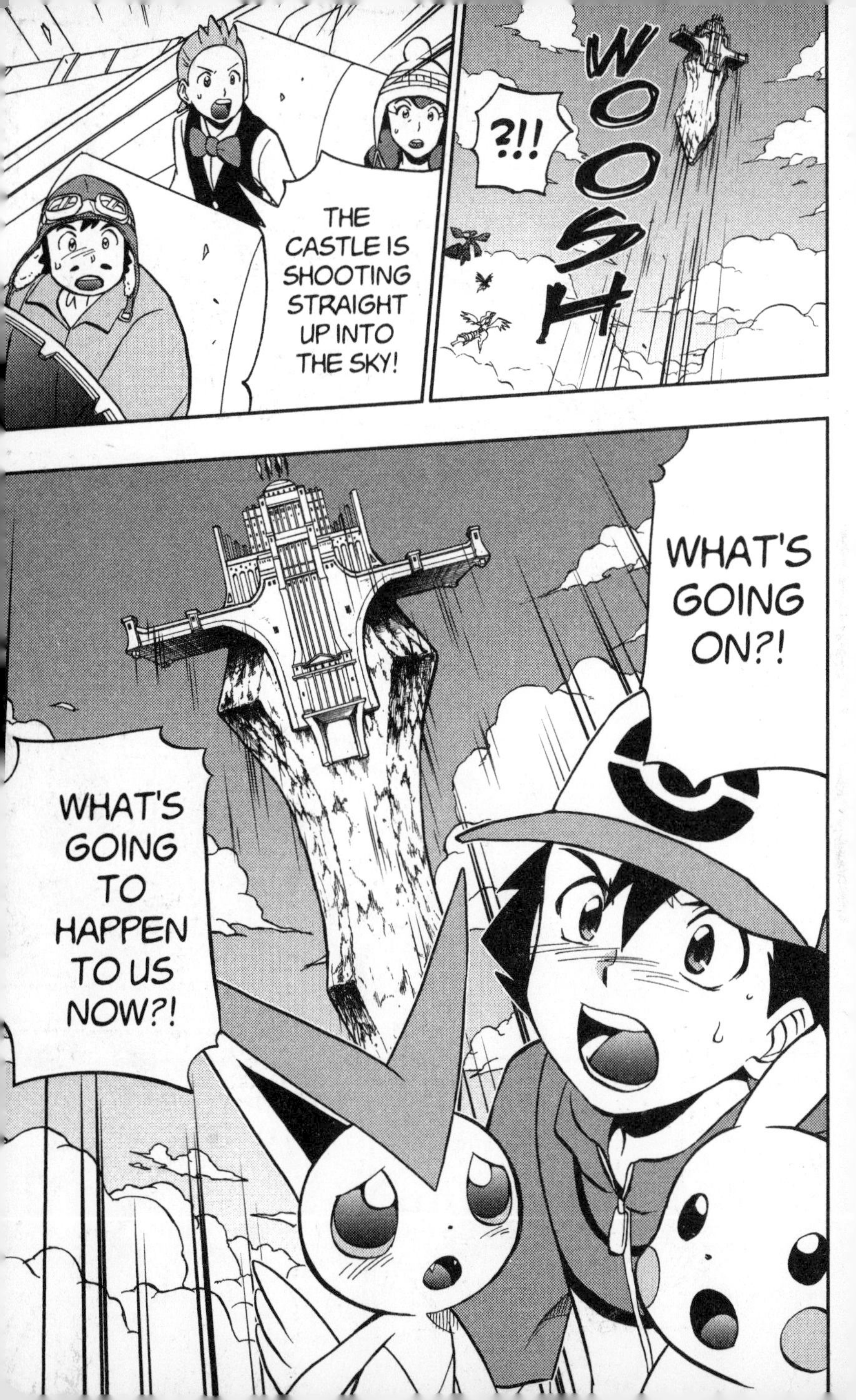
WOOSH
?!!
THE CASTLE IS SHOOTING STRAIGHT UP INTO THE SKY!
WHAT'S GOING ON?!
WHAT'S GOING TO HAPPEN TO US NOW?!

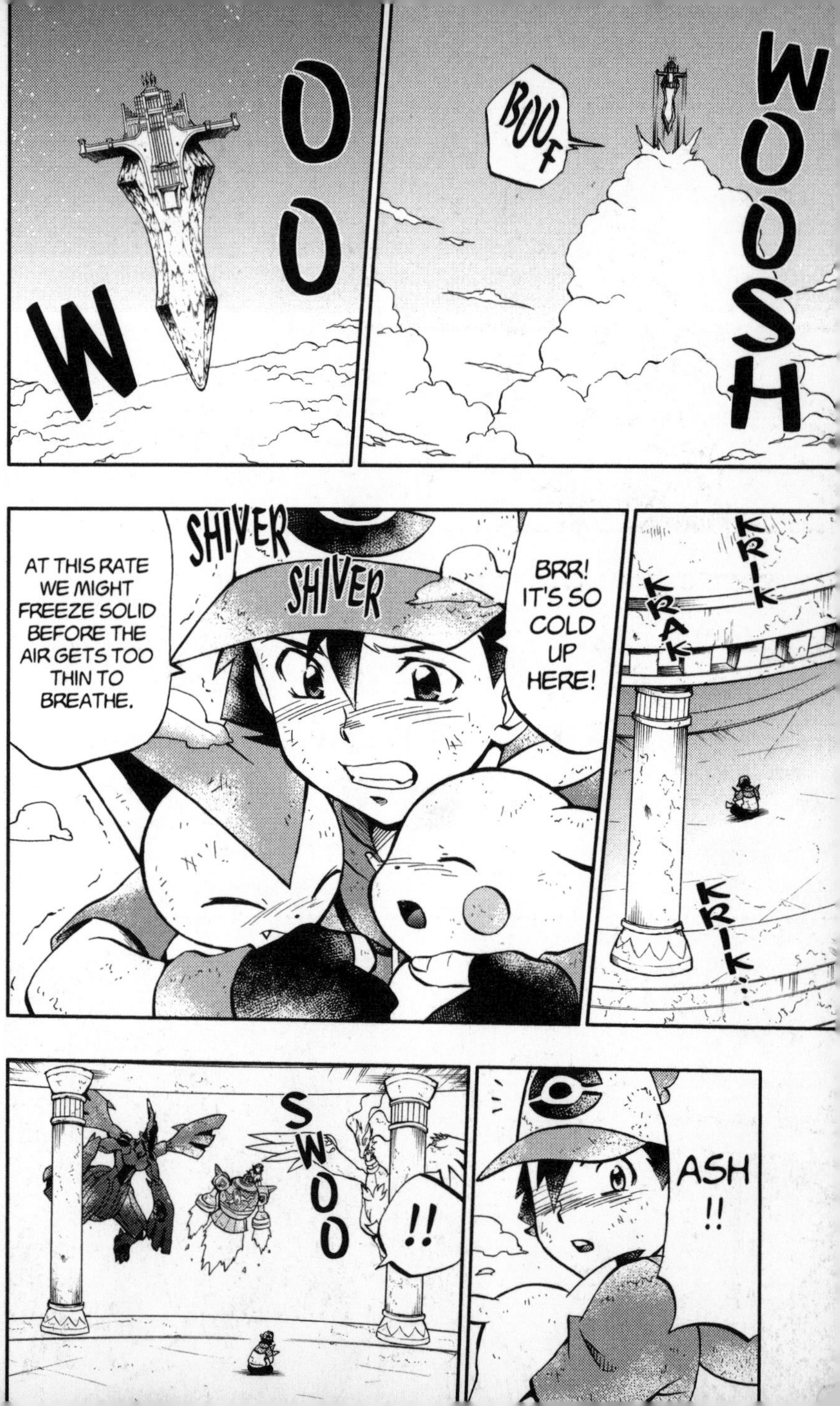
WOOSH
BOOF
WOO
KRIK
KRAK
KRIK...
BRR! IT'S SO COLD UP HERE!
SHIVER
SHIVER
AT THIS RATE WE MIGHT FREEZE SOLID BEFORE THE AIR GETS TOO THIN TO BREATHE.
ASH!!
!!
SWOO

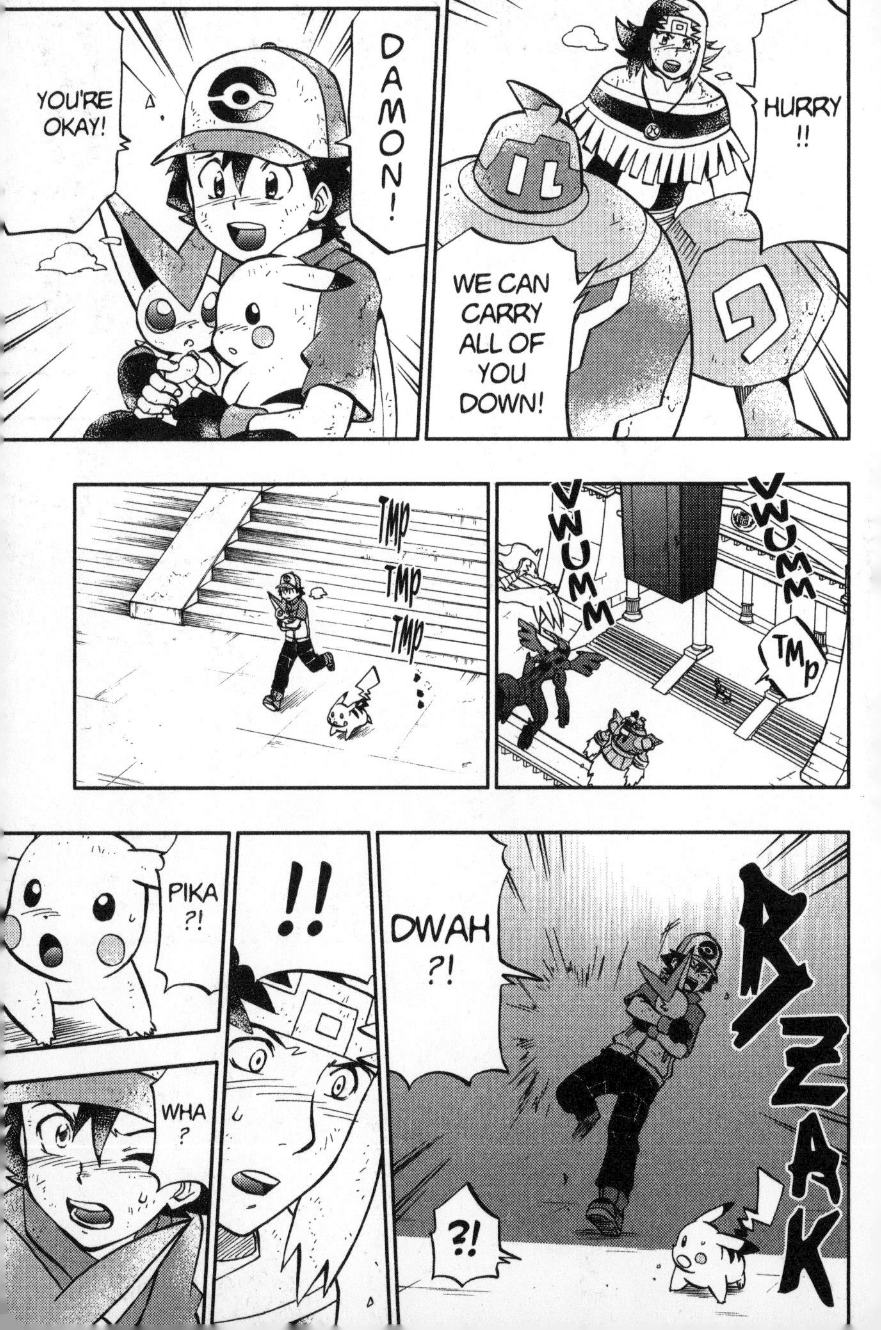
HURRY !!
WE CAN CARRY ALL OF YOU DOWN!
DAMON!
YOU'RE OKAY!
VWUMM
VWUMM
TMP
TMP
TMP
TMP
DWAH ?!
BZAK
?!
!!
PIKA ?!
WHA ?

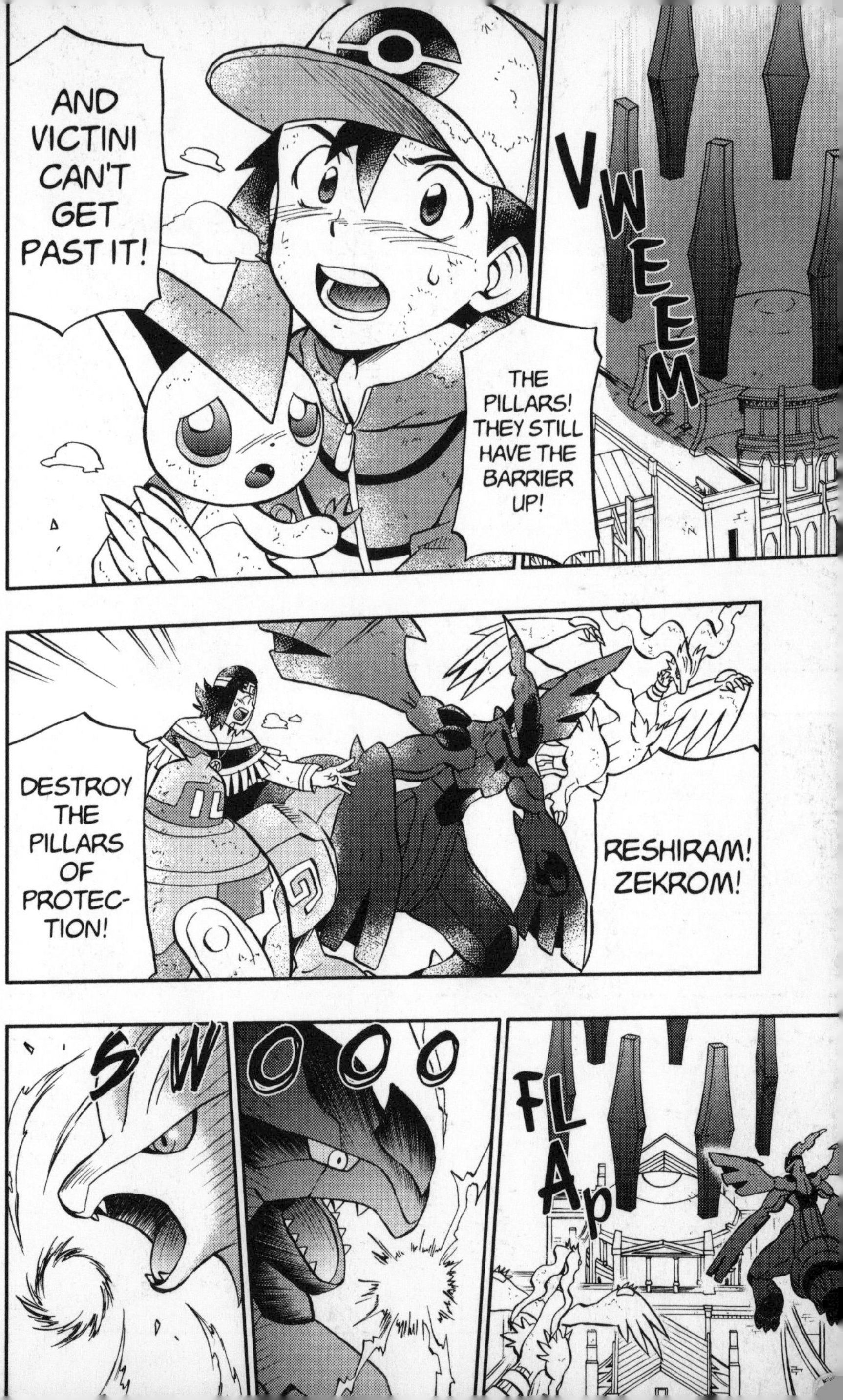
VWEEM
THE PILLARS! THEY STILL HAVE THE BARRIER UP!
AND VICTINI CAN'T GET PAST IT!
RESHIRAM! ZEKROM!
DESTROY THE PILLARS OF PROTECTION!
FLAP
SWOOO

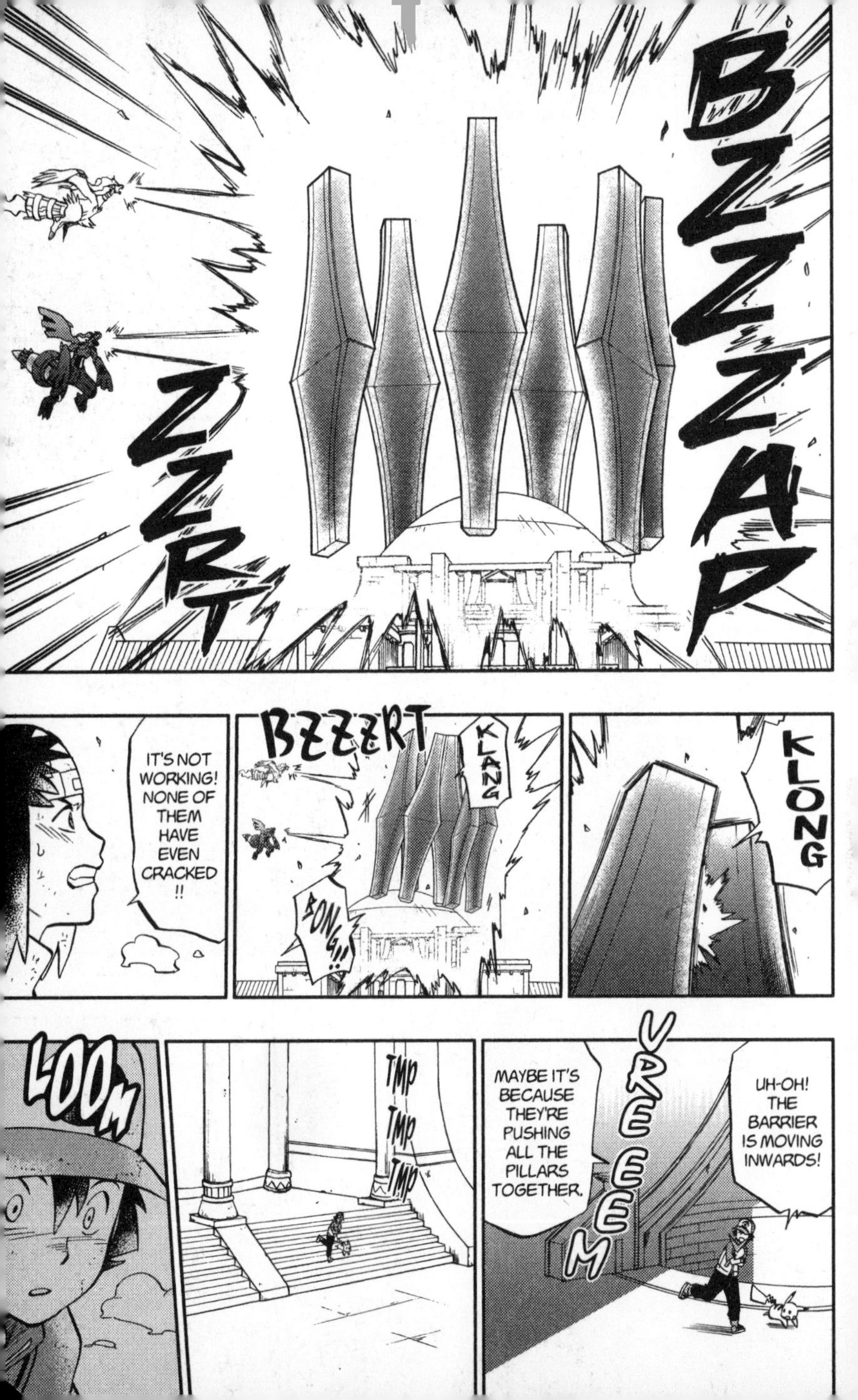
BZZZAP
ZZRT
KLONG
KLANG
BZZZRT
BONG!!
IT'S NOT WORKING! NONE OF THEM HAVE EVEN CRACKED !!
UH-OH! THE BARRIER IS MOVING INWARDS!
VREEEEM
MAYBE IT'S BECAUSE THEY'RE PUSHING ALL THE PILLARS TOGETHER.
TMP TMP TMP
LOOM

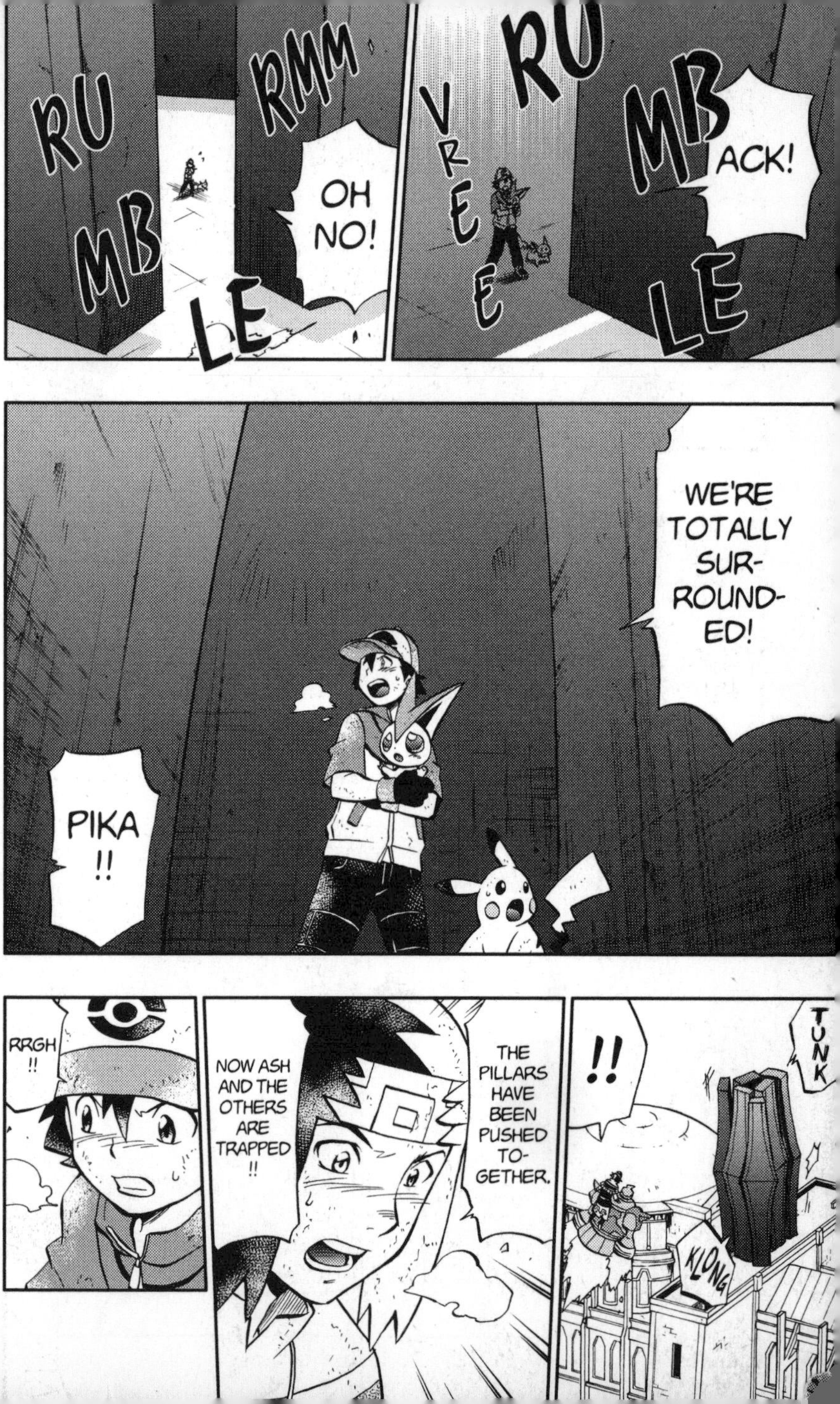
RU MB LE
VREE
ACK!
RU MB LE
RMM
OH NO!
WE'RE TOTALLY SUR-ROUND-ED!
PIKA !!
TUNK
!!
KLONG
THE PILLARS HAVE BEEN PUSHED TO-GETHER.
NOW ASH AND THE OTHERS ARE TRAPPED !!
RRGH !!

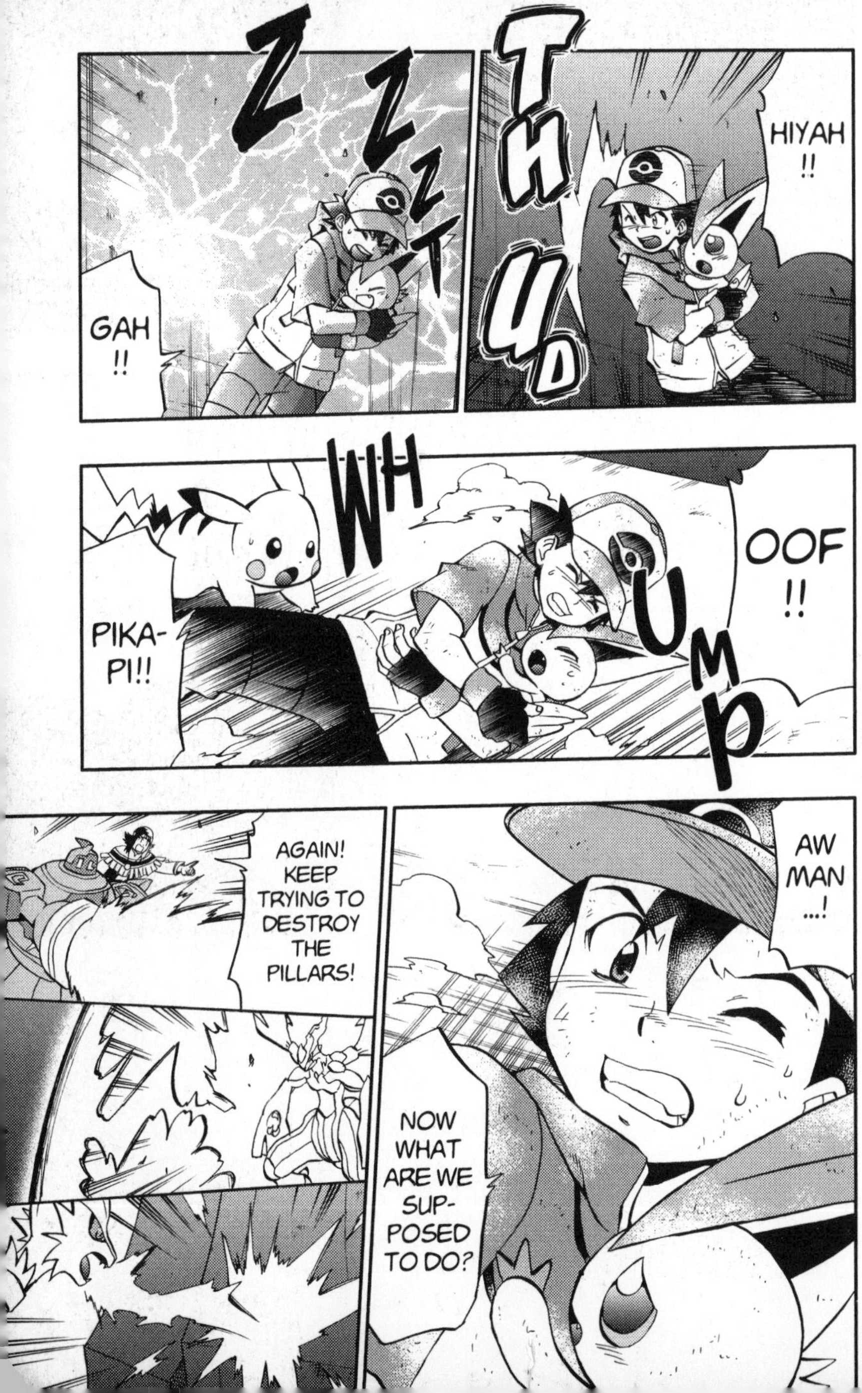
HIYAH!!
THUD
ZZZT
GAH!!
OOF!!
WHUMP
PIKA-PI!!
AW MAN...!
NOW WHAT ARE WE SUP-POSED TO DO?
AGAIN! KEEP TRYING TO DESTROY THE PILLARS!

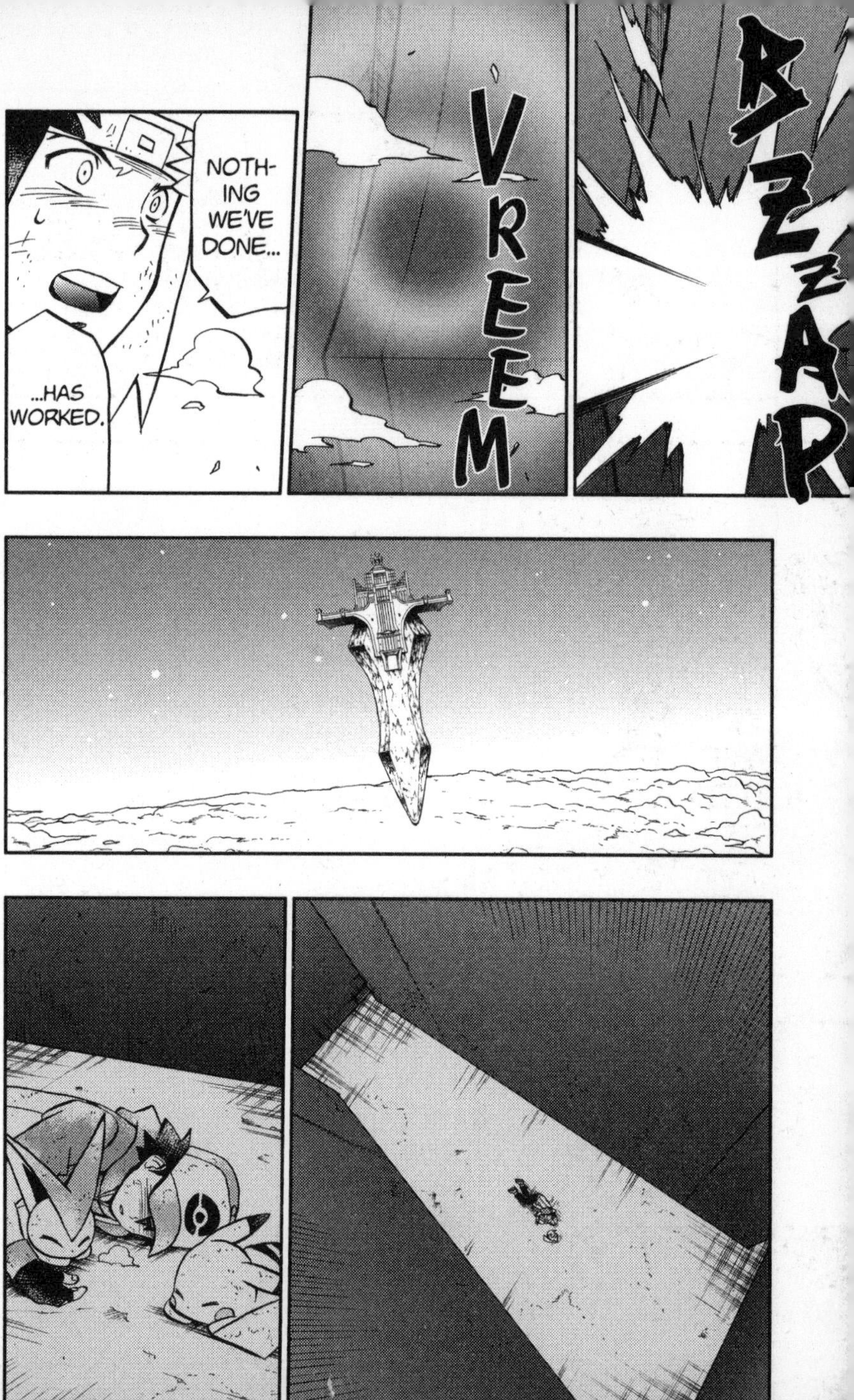
BZZAP
VREEM
NOTH-ING WE'VE DONE...
...HAS WORKED.

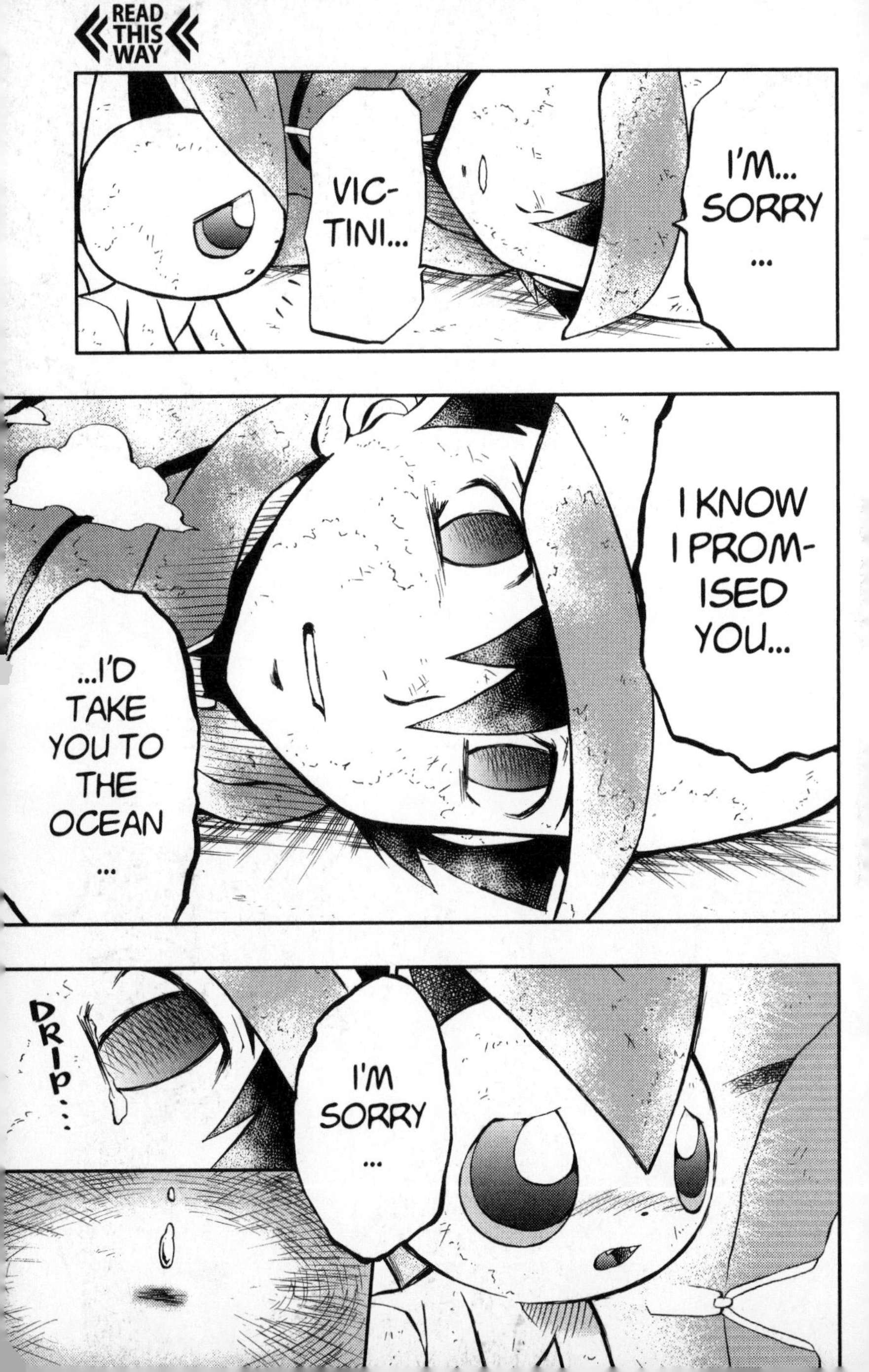
READ THIS WAY
I'M... SORRY ...
VIC-TINI...
I KNOW I PROMISED YOU...
...I'D TAKE YOU TO THE OCEAN ...
I'M SORRY ...
DRIP...

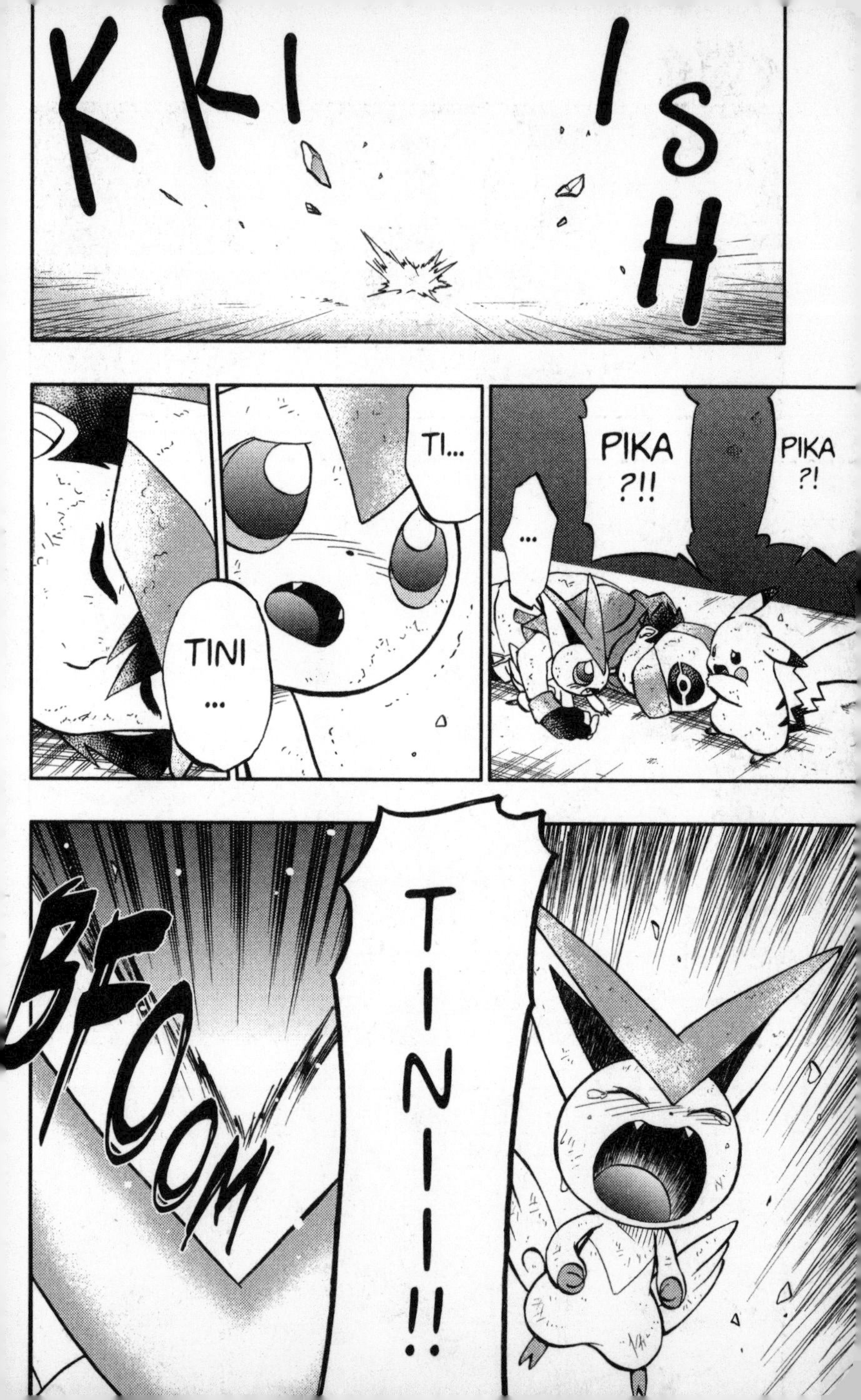
KRISH
PIKA ?!
PIKA ?!!
...
TI...
TINI ...
TINII!!
BFOOM

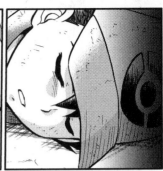

IT... FEELS SO WARM...

WHAT'S THAT...?

VIC-TINI?

WHAT?

BWO O!!

O

WHIRL

TINI!

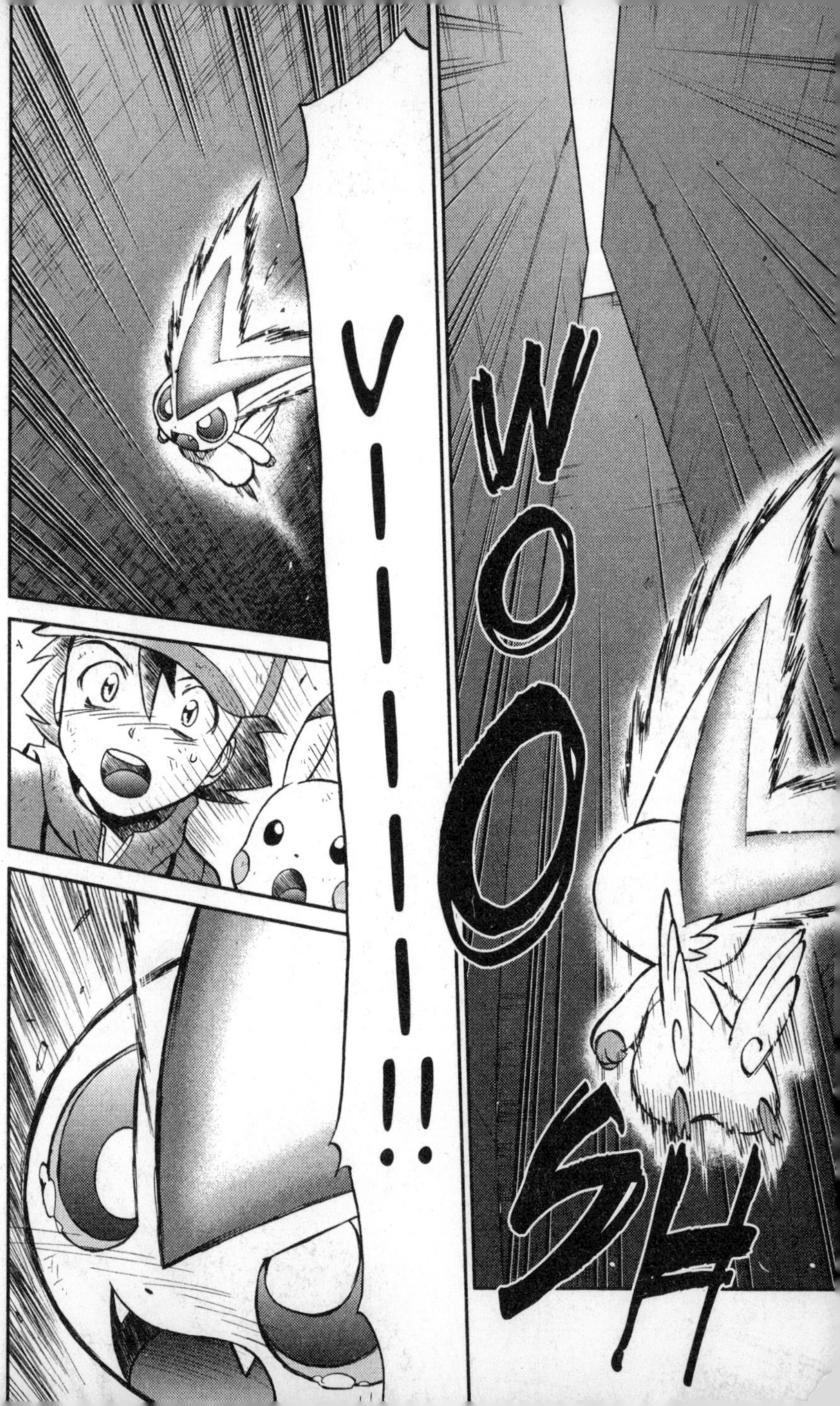
WOOOSH
VIIIII!!

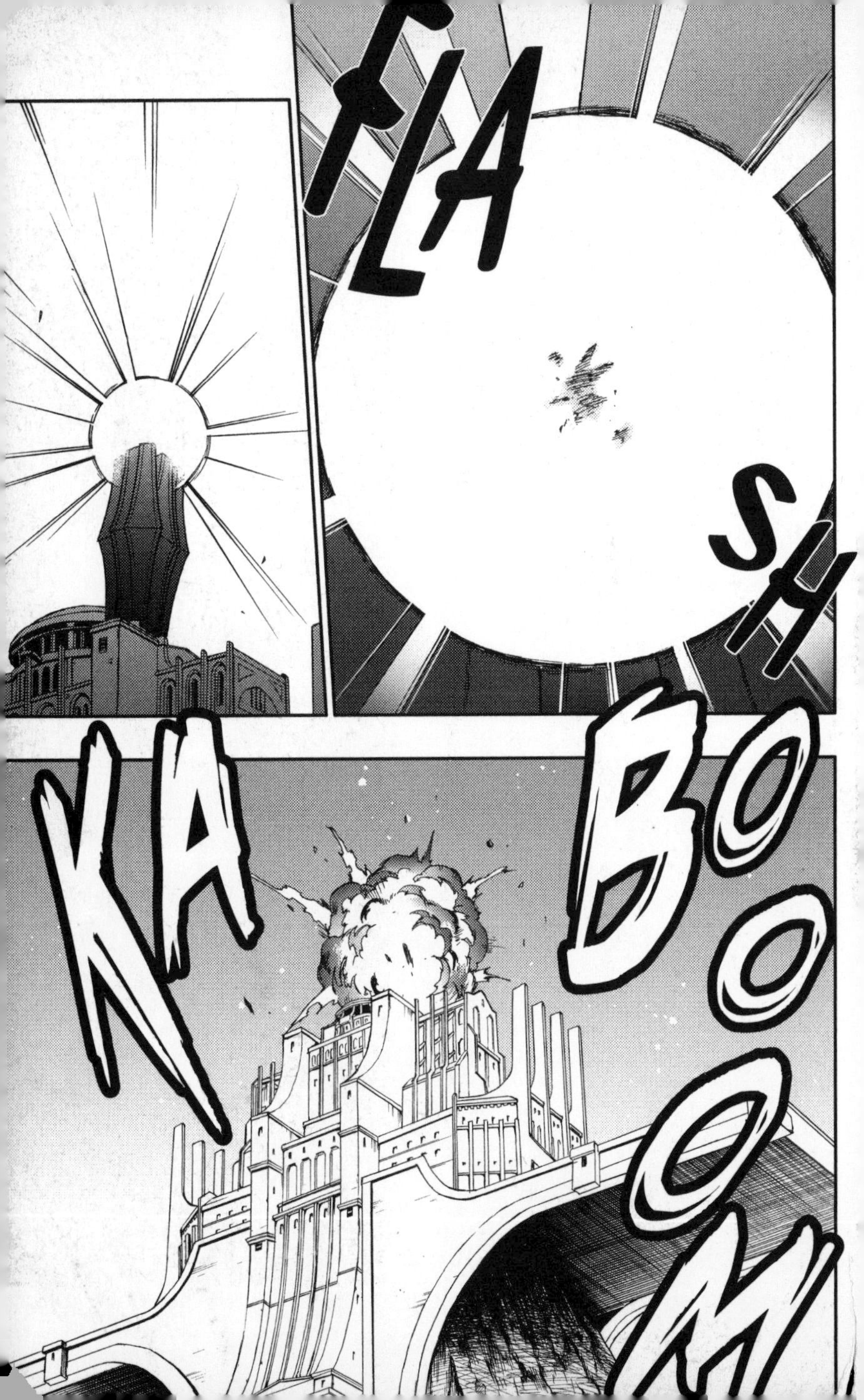
FLASH
KA
BOOOM

...!!

VIC-TINI?!

...

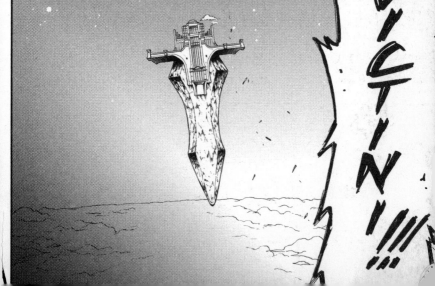

VICTINI!!!!

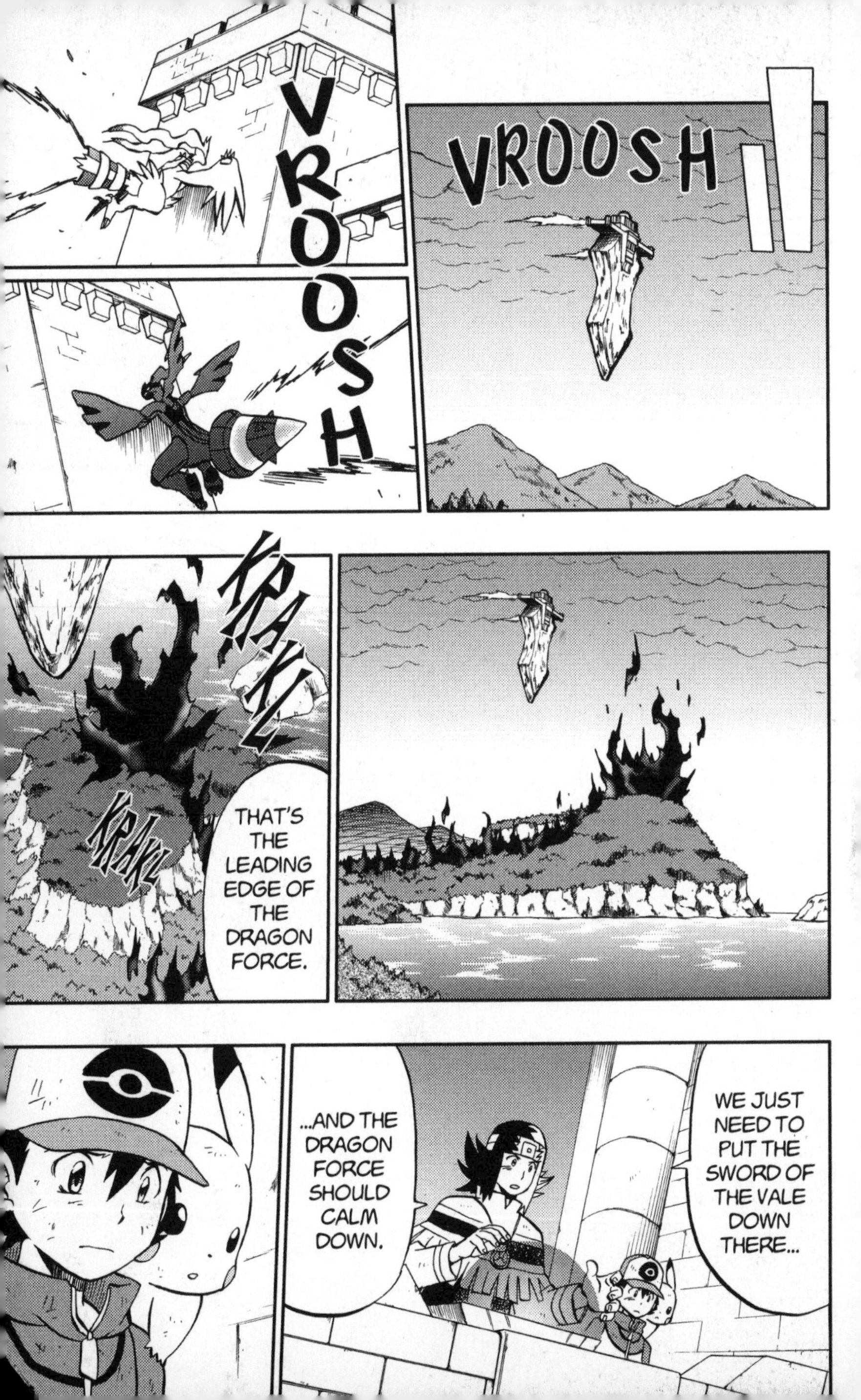
VROOSH
VROOSH
KRAKL
KRAKL
THAT'S THE LEADING EDGE OF THE DRAGON FORCE.
WE JUST NEED TO PUT THE SWORD OF THE VALE DOWN THERE...
...AND THE DRAGON FORCE SHOULD CALM DOWN.

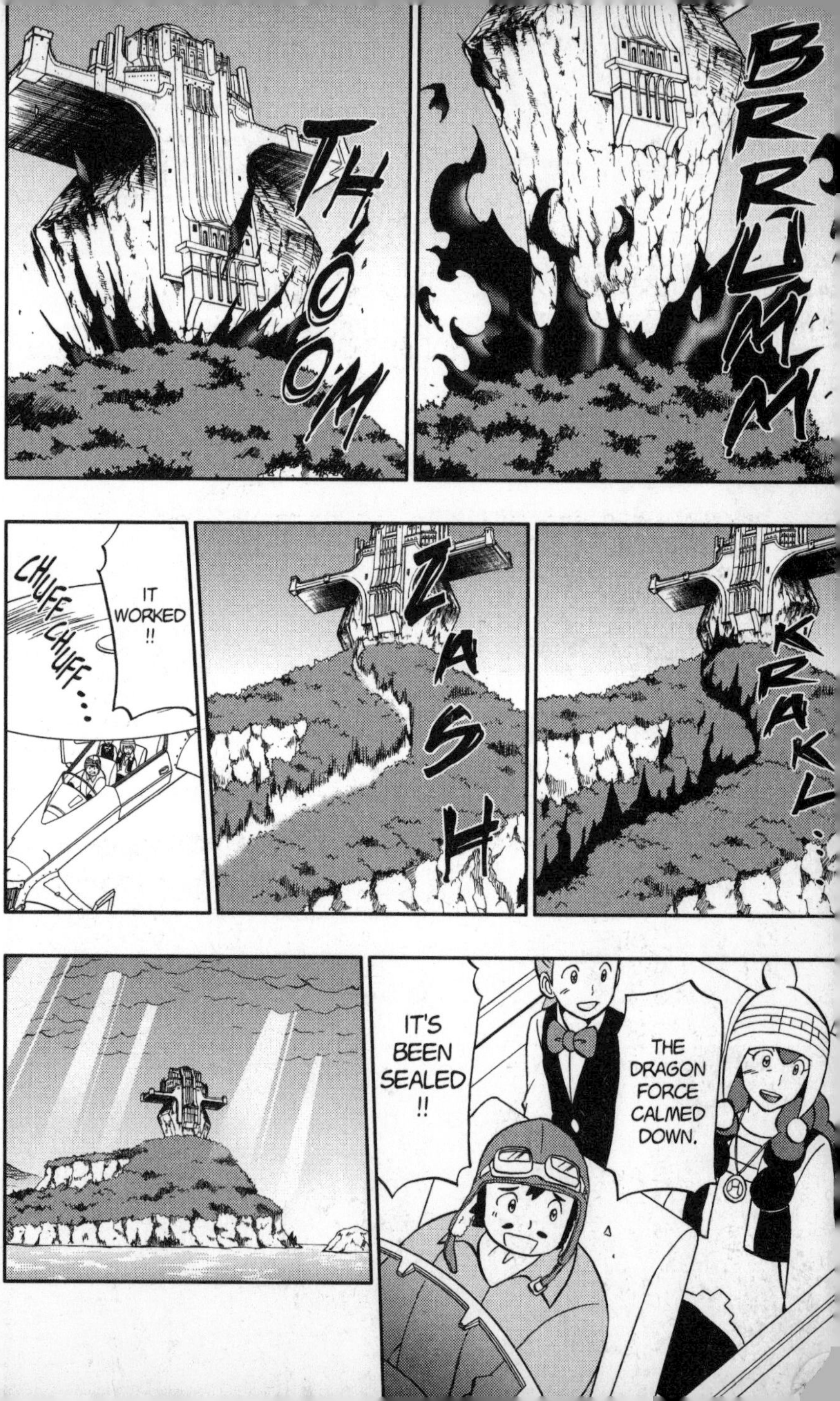
BRRUMMM
THOOOM
KRAK...
ZASH
IT WORKED!!
CHUFF CHUFF...
THE DRAGON FORCE CALMED DOWN.
IT'S BEEN SEALED!!

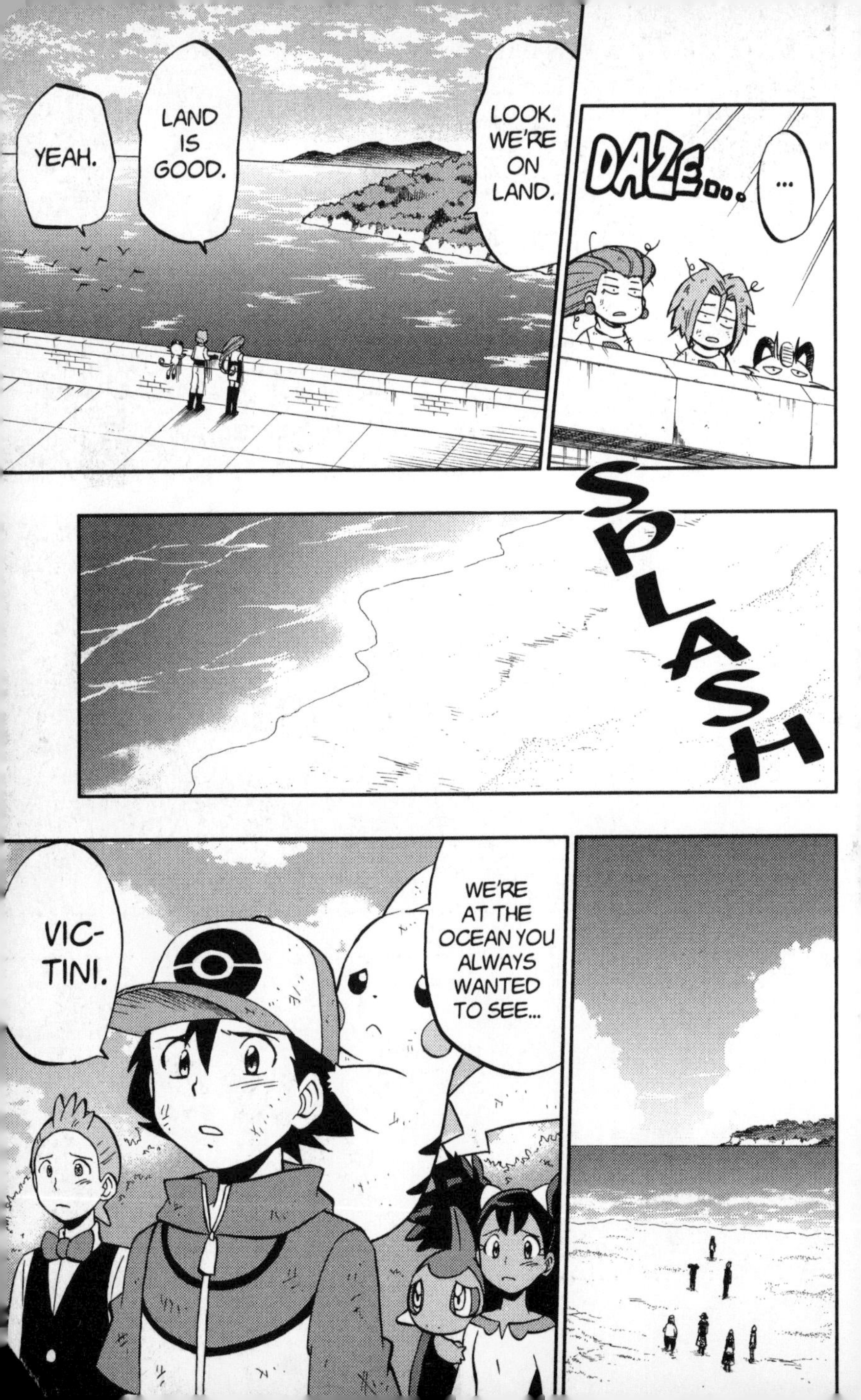
DAZE...
...
LOOK. WE'RE ON LAND.
LAND IS GOOD.
YEAH.
SPLASH
WE'RE AT THE OCEAN YOU ALWAYS WANTED TO SEE...
VIC-TINI.

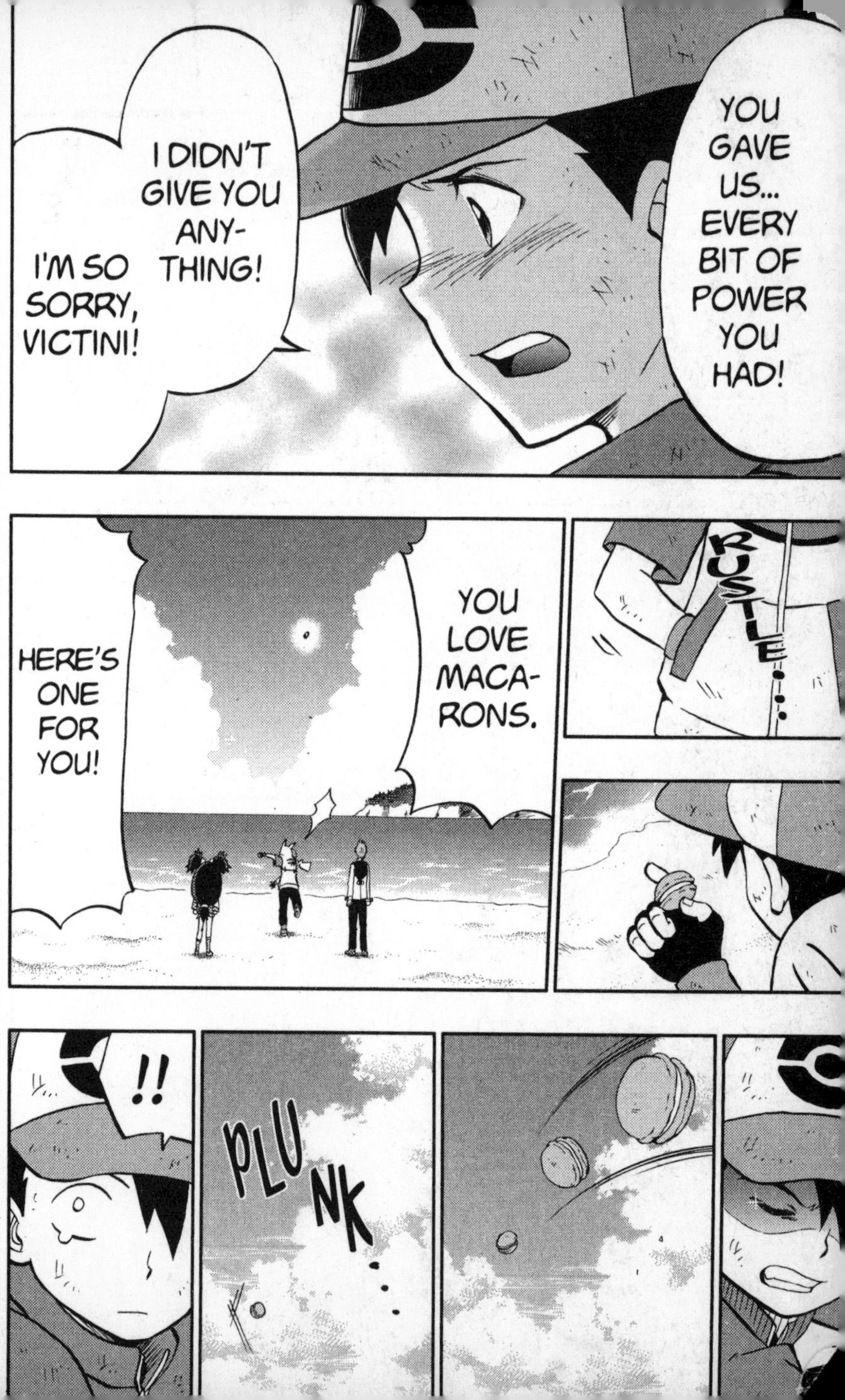
YOU GAVE US... EVERY BIT OF POWER YOU HAD!
I DIDN'T GIVE YOU ANY-THING!
I'M SO SORRY, VICTINI!
RUSTLE...
YOU LOVE MACA-RONS.
HERE'S ONE FOR YOU!
PLUNK...
!!

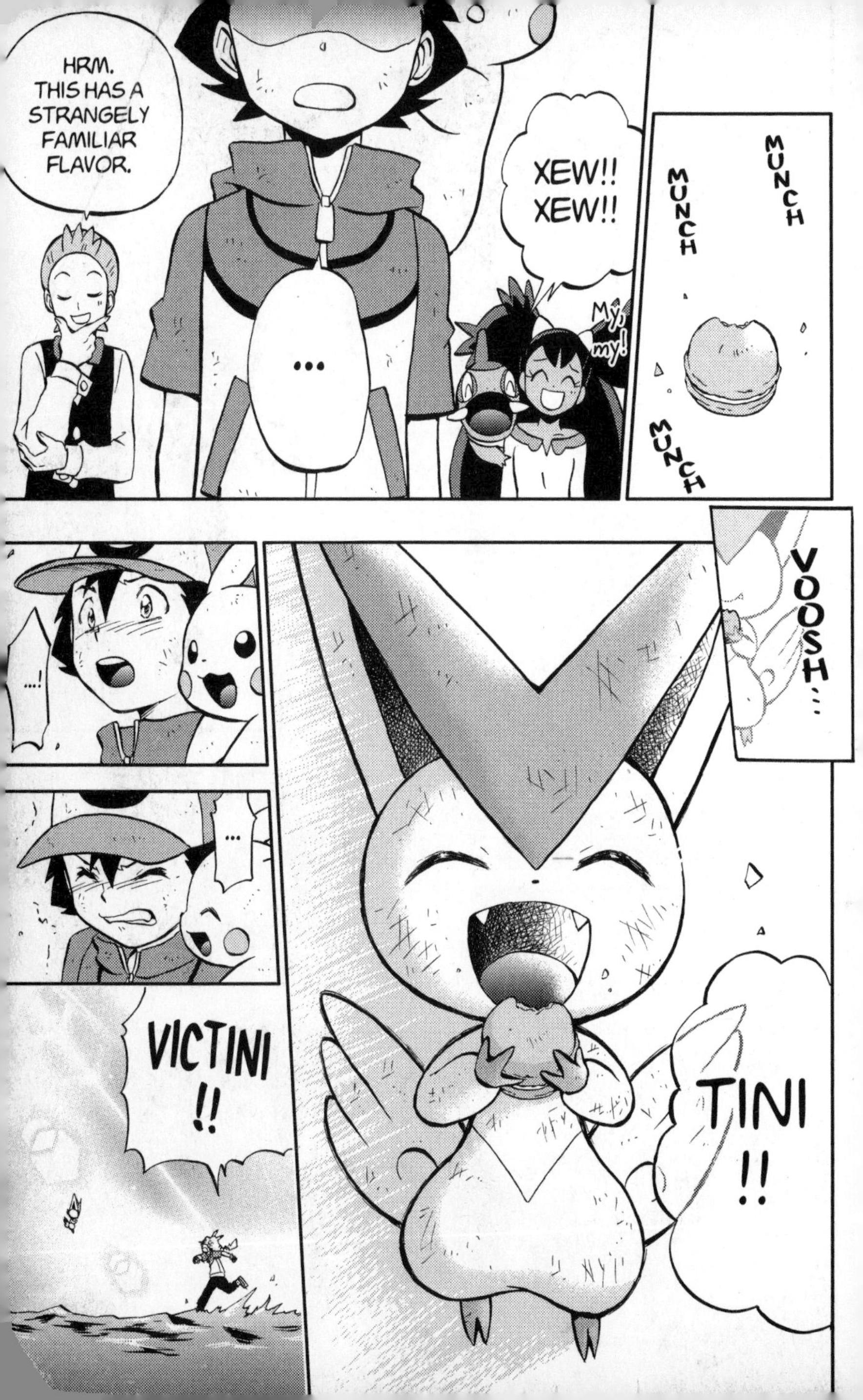
MUNCH
MUNCH
MUNCH
XEW!! XEW!!
My, my!
...
HRM. THIS HAS A STRANGELY FAMILIAR FLAVOR.
VOOSH...
TINI!!
...!
...
VICTINI!!

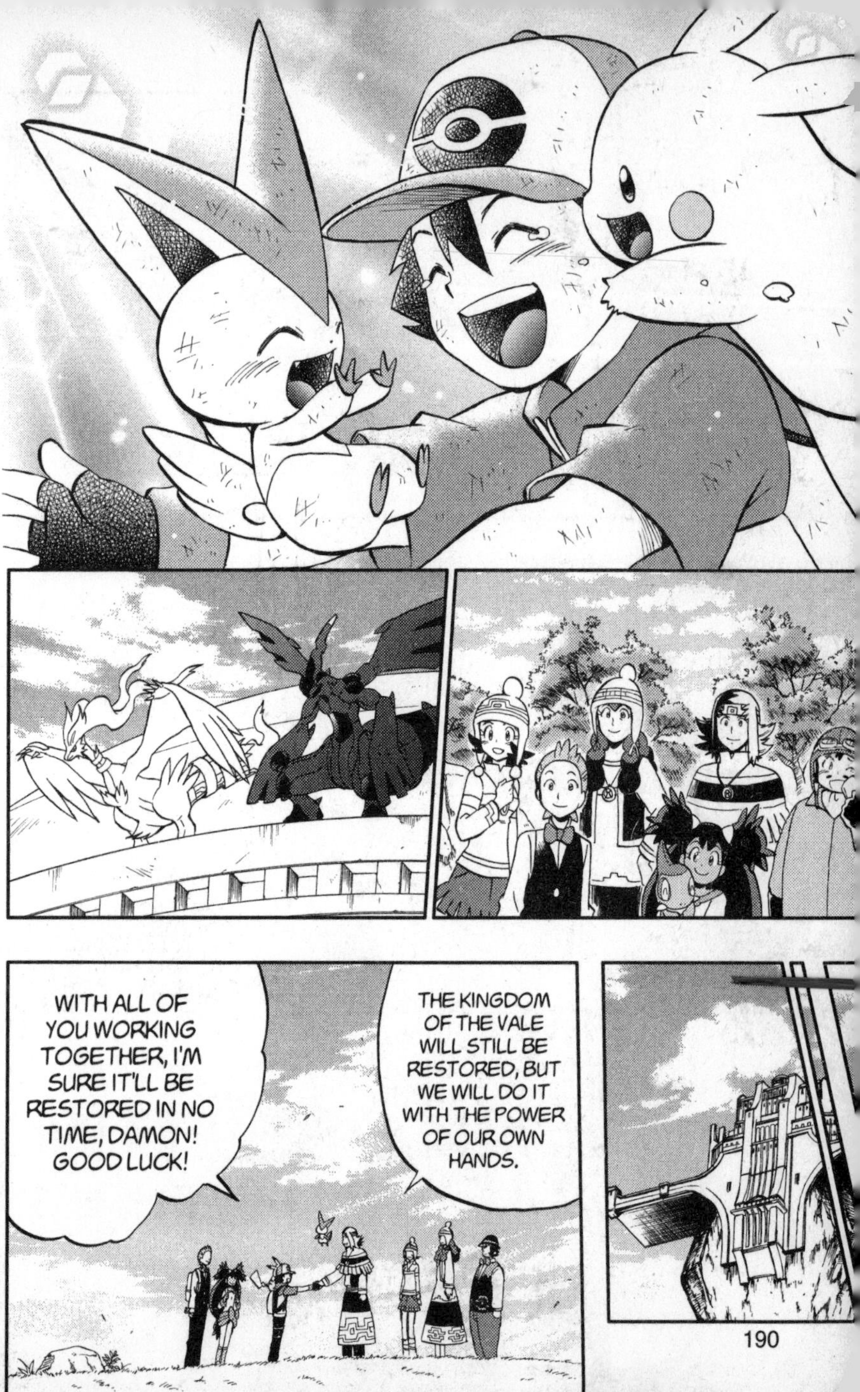
THE KINGDOM OF THE VALE WILL STILL BE RESTORED, BUT WE WILL DO IT WITH THE POWER OF OUR OWN HANDS.
WITH ALL OF YOU WORKING TOGETHER, I'M SURE IT'LL BE RESTORED IN NO TIME, DAMON! GOOD LUCK!

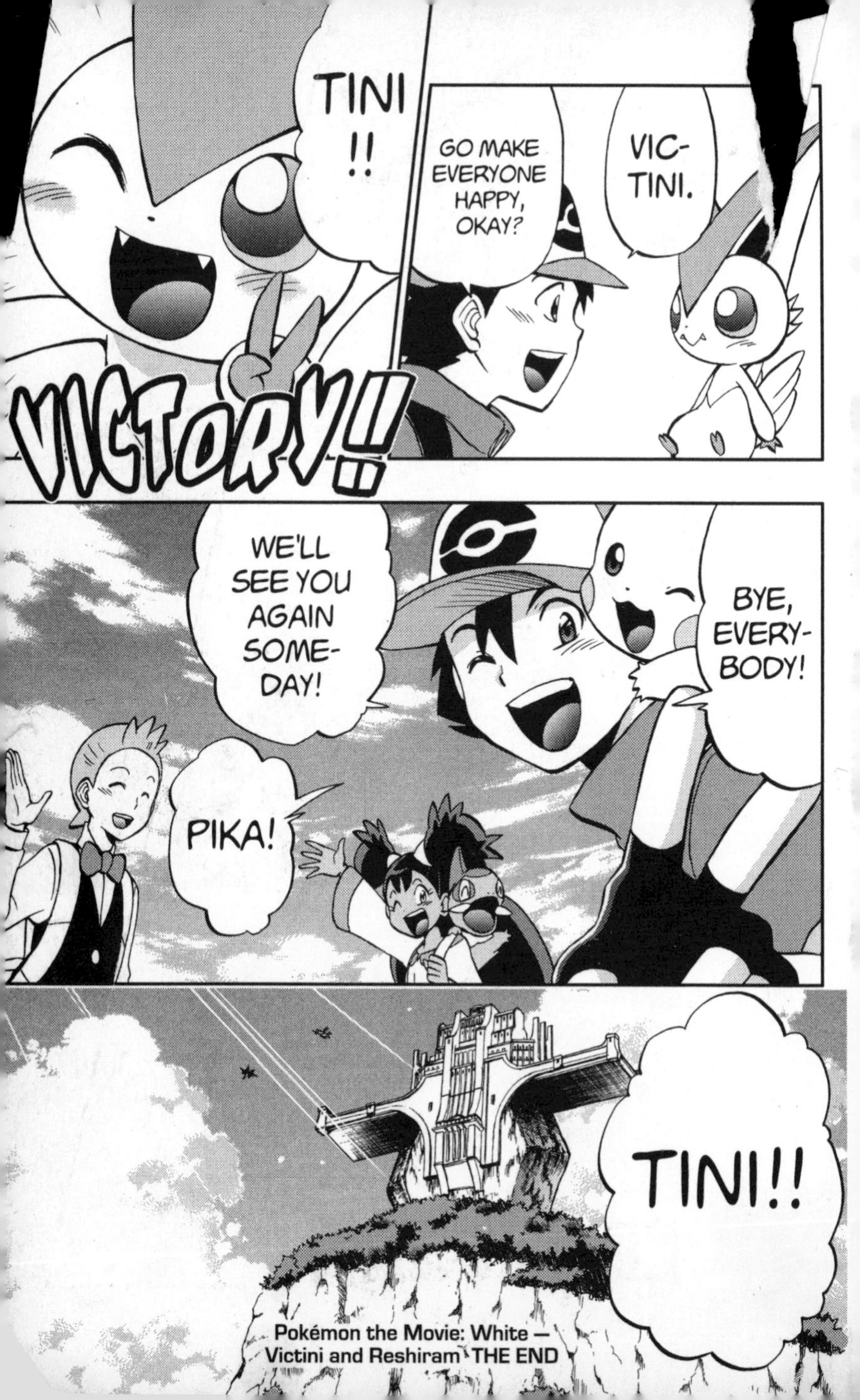
VIC-TINI.
GO MAKE EVERYONE HAPPY, OKAY?
TINI !!
VICTORY!!
BYE, EVERY-BODY!
WE'LL SEE YOU AGAIN SOME-DAY!
PIKA!
TINI!!
Pokémon the Movie: White — Victini and Reshiram THE END

POKÉMON

TM

BLACK AND WHITE

MEET POKÉMON TRAINERS

BLACK AND WHITE

THE WAIT IS FINALLY OVER!
Meet Pokémon Trainer Black! His entire life, Black has dreamed of winning the Pokémon League... Now Black embarks on a journey to explore the Unova region and fill a Pokédex for Professor Juniper. Time for Black's first Pokémon Trainer Battle ever!

Who will Black choose as his next Pokémon? Who would *you* choose?

Plus, meet Pokémon Snivy, Tepig, Oshawott and many more new Pokémon of the unexplored Unova region!

Story by
HIDENORI KUSAKA

Art by
SATOSHI YAMAMOTO

Inspired by the hit video games

Pokémon Black Ve...

$4.99 USA | $6.99 CAN

3 1901 05000 0803

Available Now
at your local bookstore or comic store

vizkids

www.vizkids.com

www.viz.com/25years